Asenath
and the
Origin of Nappy Hair

Being a collection of tales
gathered and extracted
from the epic stanzas
of Asenath and Our Song of Songs

Carolivia Herron

November 2014

**Street to Street
Epic Publications**

Library of Congress Cataloging-in-Publication Data
Herron, Carolivia.
Asenath and the Origin of Nappy Hair
Being a Collection of Tales
Gathered and Extracted
From the Epic Stanzas
Of Asenath and Our Song of Songs

Summary: Shirah Shulamit Ojero, an African American Jewish Graduate Student at the University of Pen Forest, discovers that her extravagantly nappy hair, eight circles per inch of hair, has connected her conceptually and biologically with the nappy haired ancient Egyptian priestess, Asenath, daughter of Poti-pherah, and eventually the wife of Joseph, son of Israel. In reaching toward each other, Shirah sailing toward the past, Asenath walking toward the future, they tell the lovesong of the human race, the love of freedom. *Asenath and the Origin of Nappy Hair* tells half of the story. The full text, *Asenath and Our Song of Songs*, will tell the full story.

ISBN 978-1-938609-21-3

**In Memoriam
Carlos Fuentes**

The Waterman, the Cicerone,
the Fountain

Now, are you that that fountain who spreads
abroad so wide a river of speech? O honor and
light of other novelists, may my long study and
great love that impelled me to explore your
volumes, avail me in the poiesis of this, my
song.

As adapted from Dante, *La Divina Commedia*

For My Academy

Public Schools of Washington, DC
Neval Thomas Elementary School
Woodson Junior High School
Paul Junior High School
Spingarn Senior High School
Coolidge Senior High School
Vox School of Languages
Eastern Baptist College / Eastern College /
Eastern University
Villanova University
The University of Pennsylvania
Harvard University
Mount Holyoke College
California State University, Chico
Howard University
The American University
Georgetown University
The Catholic University of America
The Folger Shakespeare Library
The University of the District of Columbia
The University of Maryland
The University of Turku, Suomi, Finland
Universidad Nacional Autónoma de México
The Bunting Institute of Radcliffe College
The University of the West Indies, Mona, Jamaica
The Smithsonian Institution
National Museum of American Art

Anacostia Community Museum
Beinecke Library of Yale University
The University of Lubumbashi, Zaïre
The University of Kinshasa, Zaïre
Marien N'Gouabi Université de Brazzaville, Kongo
Carleton College
The University of Massachusetts, Boston
Brandeis University
Harvard Divinity School
Harvard Graduate School of Education
Massachusetts Institute of Technology
Binghamton University
Hollins University
Grinnell College
Children's Studio School
Montgomery College
The College of William and Mary
Jewish Study Center of Washington, DC
Havurah Institute
Hebrew College of Brookline / Newton, Massachusetts
St. Johns College of Annapolis
Ruppin Academic Center, Israel
Kibbutzim College of Education, Tel Aviv, Israel
The Learning Community International School
Arizona State University at Tempe

Epigram

The fact that something is true is never the reason for saying it.
Barbara Herrnstein Smith

The fact that something is not true is never the reason for not saying it.
The Epicentress

Contents

Prologue   **15**

Cluster 1: You   **16**

Cluster 1 Argument 16

Chapter 1: Look Homeward, Angel......17

Chapter 2: Past Prologue 19

Chapter 3: Story Caught 21

Chapter 4: The StorySong of Bear-Wolf's March to the Library.......................................25

Chapter 5: Versity 27

Chapter 6: Paradise Re-Lost..............29

Cluster 2: Your Heaven   **39**

Cluster 2 Argument 39

Chapter 7: Angel Square 41

Chapter 8: THE Argument 48

Chapter 9: Sheherazadim 72

Chapter 10: Spaghetti Curtain 98

Cluster 3 Your Attic   102

Cluster 3 Argument 102

Chapter 11: Gates of Light...............103

Chapter 12: Attic Window 107

Chapter 13: The Garden of Converging Paths 111

Cluster 4 Your Saga   117

Cluster 4 Argument 117

Chapter 14: Quietness 118

Chapter 15: Rain 120

Chapter 16: Lavender 123

Chapter 17: Sinai 125

Chapter 18: Easter Eggs 127

Chapter 19: Green Grocer 130

Chapter 20: Kosher 135

Chapter 21: Your Father's Books 141

Chapter 22: DC Transit 147

Chapter 23: Redface 150

Chapter 24: Safety Cavalier 153

Chapter 25: Grilled Cheese...............156

Chapter 26: Dumbarton Oaks 161

Chapter 27: Angels and Faeries 164

Chapter 28: High Seas.....................168

Cluster 5 Your Day 182

Cluster 5 Argument 182

Chapter 29: Ashrei.........................183

Cluster 6 Your Desire; or, 185

Your Hall of Colors 185

Cluster 6 Argument 185

Chapter 30: The Chamber of Abdiel ..187

Cluster 7 Your Sojourn 190

Cluster 7 Argument 190

Chapter 31: Woodson Junior High School191

Chapter 32: Paul Junior High School ..192

Chapter 33: Not College Material 194

Chapter 34: Velatis and Silver 196

Chapter 35: So Journeying 198

Chapter 36: Howard University Fire ..200

Chapter 37: Ekstasis University of the East 206

Cluster 8 Our Story   210

Cluster 8 Argument 210

Chapter 38: Attic Poets 211

Cluster 9 Your Academy   219

Cluster 9 Argument 219

Chapter 39: Lotus 220

Cluster 10 Your Boat   235

Cluster 10 Argument 235

Chapter 40: Bad Avenue 236

Chapter 41: Black and Comely 238

Chapter 42: Nappy Hair 249

Chapter 43: You Know 256

Chapter 44: Writ On Water 258

Chapter 45: Virginia 272

Chapter 46: Boat Woman 274

Cluster 11 Yourstory   284

Cluster 11 Argument 284

Chapter 47: Desert 285

Cluster 12 Epithalamion   295

Cluster 12 Argument........................295

Chapter 48: Big Boy 296

Chapter 49: The Tin Cup 301

Chapter 50: Shuvi 311

Chapter 51: One Half.......................315

Reflections on Asenath and the Origin of Nappy Hair by Dr. E. Shaskan Bumas translator of Carlos Fuentes   323

About the Author   325

Afterword and Acknowledgements 327

Endnotes   328

Asenath and Our Song of Songs

Prologue

Okay, dear reader, I was stillborn. Yes, I know it's impossible, I know you don't believe it, but it's true. I was cast aside by the doctors and nurses at Freedmen's Hospital in Washington, DC. The date was July 22, 1947. My mother said, "Why isn't my baby crying. I've been here all week and every time a baby is born there's been crying." The nurse said, "Be quiet, or you may never hear her cry." The nurse had tears, don't blame her for cruelty. My mother silenced. Wondering if I would live. Wondering if I was already dead. Wondering while they cut some tumor out of her and she tore up the sheets at Freedmen's Hospital. The sheets were old anyhow. She searched for a hole in the sheet with her finger. And waited. When the pain came she would drag her finger down from the hole, tearing the sheet into rags. The nurse said, "We're going to start charging you for the sheets." I had just a little body then. The doctor held me upside down and knocked me around a bit. Nothing. My mother had a bad tumor. The tumor had been between me unborn and the world. When I came out I tore the tumor. My mother was bleeding to death. They couldn't use anesthesia. Pain. Dangerous. Everything was dangerous that day. I came out tearing the tumor but didn't breathe. My mother tore the sheets while I tore the tumor. Back beat to no avail. Blue. Would not breathe. To hell with breathing. Makes sense to me. They gave up on me and turned to save my mother. They stuck me in an incubator and turned away. My mother in pain as they stopped her bleeding. In the mist of the pain my mother heard the nurse again. "Doctor, look!" They all turned to look. I went from blue to beige brown. I breathed in. I never should have done it. Here is the story of how it happened. I wrote this story for you. This is the Book Unknown In Heaven.

Listen.

Cluster 1: You
Cluster 1 Argument

Okay, respected reader, so I told you I would explain to you how this happened, how I ended up breathing alive on earth when I didn't want to. I'll tell you, but you should know that even I didn't know at first. I started figuring it out when I was eleven years old, so that's where I'm starting. It's hard for me to tell you things in order because I have trouble thinking things in order. Still, I can give you some hints to remember as you listen. I call just about everybody, "you." Don't get confused. Don't think it's always the same person I'm talking to just because I say, "you." The person I'm talking to changes, and sometimes the I who's speaking changes as well. Right now the "I" is Shirah Shulamit Ojero, but you can't expect me to be the narrator all the time. Sometimes it's a different "I" saying "you" to a different you. I try to keep it straight, but it tangles. Don't worry. When it's really tangled I put these little asterisks in for you, like this.

* * *

See? If I notice in time that I've changed the "you" or the "I," I put in these asterisks. Sometimes I don't notice fast enough and nothing's there to tell you I've changed the you or the I. I apologize for that dear reader, please be patient, you just have to stick with the story, I hope you will. I think it's pretty good. When I was eleven years old John Milton met me, yeah, the poet. He was floating around invisible in Kann's bookstore downtown at 7th and Pennsylvania Avenue and he helped me to find his book at the Carnegie Library. Right here in Washington City, and he saw me. I'm telling you the truth.

Listen.

Chapter 1: Look Homeward, Angel[1]

You step down on the tile floor of Kann's basement bookstore and awaken me. I hear the clack of your shoes and the whispering thoughts you speak softly within. "What is past is prologue."[2] Before you stepped down, before you crossed Pennsylvania Avenue to Seventh and E Streets, you read those words on the Archives building. Now you bring the words downstairs. You, a young girl alive, walking toward an old dead poet, me, where I lounge along a shelf with my leather covered book, ***Paradise Lost***.

It is cool and deep here. I lean out from my shelf and look at you, curious. I see the big puffs of hair on both sides of your head. Can you hear me? What do you call your hair? It's so puffy and full. Nappy? It's the nappiest hair in the world you say? I'm glad you can hear me and answer my questions. Eleven years old and your name is Shirah Shulamit Ojero. My name is John Milton.

It's not easy to see me. The bookstore clerk doesn't know that I'm here. And even you don't know that you and I are speaking together. I've known other poets with hair like yours. Phillis Wheatley has your hair. What? Yes, so you know Phillis. Sometimes Phillis and I walk together beside the Ocean of Light. Have you been there? Have you dipped your hands in the silvery water? I was with Phillis when she died in Boston. We talk together and once we sailed across the Atlantic from England. I like to hear Phillis thinking. She hears me when I'm thinking too. We meander by the Ocean of Light together, picking up our favorite orange seashells. We talk about Boston. She told me once that her hair is African hair. I don't think she knows that word, nappy.[3]

When you look up I see deeply into your black flecked brown eyes. Sad eyes. I hover beside my dark maroon book all in leather and gold. Your eyes linger, you glance along the books beside me on the top shelf before you turn and walk to the children's section. You have $7.00 in your pocket.

As I look inside your head I see more than the Archives Building, I see the city that lives beyond this bookstore, up the bannisters and stairs. You stood on the corner of Seventh Street and Pennsylvania Avenue, and looked around at Washington City. Even as you remember it, even so I see it within you, yes, I see through your eyes. Your sweeping vision starts in the east at the long avenue of stores and government buildings, travels to the Capitol Building, wide and tall and rounded with the Statue of Freedom looking toward the sun in the eastern mid-heaven, then slopes southward to the pink marble of the National Gallery of Art, touching the Archives Building before urging west toward the Old Post Office Building, Federal Triangle. But your eyes return to the Archives, framed by the Mall and Smithsonian Buildings in the background. All right. Everything. In the bright summerlight panorama. You bring this light with you in your descent to the bookstore, into this shadow of words. Books. Seeking.

What made you give that look midway between the journey from Pennsylvania Avenue to this bookstore? Why did you stop, turn, and give Washington City that wide look of peace before you descended? Shalom Aleichem. Peace to all of you. The green grocer taught you those words. Shalom Aleichem. The words arise in your head along with the face of Mr. Kohen leaning toward you with a ripe tomato. Still safe. Still beautiful. You think you are describing Washington in your mind but you are blessing it. You do not know. Yes, you look into the heart of the city and give it a blessing, as if somehow you were Washington's guardian, its angel, looking homeward.

Chapter 2: Past Prologue

"We hold these truths to be self-evident, that all men are created equal." Words still murmur inside your head. We hold . . . That's inside the Archives, on the parchment. They don't carve that part on the outside.

Even as you stand near me, adjusting to the shade of the bookstore, your remembering eyes are filled with the massive building.

I think the Archives building is Athena's temple, it looks like the Parthenon in my myth book, the Parthenon built up and completed again.

"What is Past is Prologue." Carved along the top edge of the Archives Building. Well that's Shakespeare talking right there. I read that in my father's Shakespeare book. Shakespeare has his own library all to himself down by the Library of Congress. The Folger Shakespeare Library. I wish I could read in there. One day I'll go way inside. Not just in the front part but way inside, beyond the velvet ropes and the picture of Ariel. Ariel means Jerusalem, but Shakespeare makes it mean an elf or a pixie type of spirit. Names get so mixed up and changed.

Archives of the United States of America. Ark - hives. Arch - hives. When I was little I used to say it both ways to see how it worked. Ark - hives. Arch - hives. What does the word Prologue mean up on that building? You asked your mother once when you were a little girl as the two of you sat down on the bus. And the bus driver put on the brakes in the middle of Pennsylvania Avenue.

"Are you sure she's not five years old yet? How come she's reading? Are you sure you're not trying to cheat the D. C. Transit bus company out of a token?"

"Bus driver I declare she's not in kindergarten yet."

And then your mother whispered to you, "Can you read the words softly to yourself?" And the lady in the seat in front of you looked back at you and shook her head and grunted.

"Umh umh umh." What did that mean? Why did she grunt at you like that? She grunted like she wanted to say something. Did she think your family was poor. She wanted to say something that's true but she didn't want to say it out loud. Did she think your family was really, really poor? Maybe you were poor, but still, you weren't in kindergarten yet. Your mother didn't have to pay your fare. My mother wasn't cheating. "Prologue means words or a statement that comes before something else, like in the front of a book or before a play starts." Your mother and father have enough money for an extra fare most of the time, but why should they pay it since you are not even five years old? That's what you thought back then. Now you're eleven.

Chapter 3: Story Caught

__The Bobbsey Twins in the Country__. Why don't you buy that one? *__The Prince and the Pauper__*. You could buy that one. Or this one. *__The Bobbsey Twins at the Seashore__*. *__Understood Betsy__*. *__The Bobbsey Twins on a Houseboat__*. You know that's got to be a good one. *__Eight Cousins__*. *__The Bobbsey Twins in Washington__*. Pick one. *__Favorite Poems, Old and New, Selected for Boys and Girls__*. Choose!

But when you pick something to read, could you please pick something that lasts longer than the bus ride? Will these books last long enough? Is it worth it to buy one of them? You'll finish it too fast. I should walk up to Carnegie Library and get lots of books.

And your head droops. Those two puffs of hair above your ears go up as your eyes go down. As I look at you I wonder if you know the meaning of your name. I reach into your head. Yes, you know. Shirah is song. And Shulamit, shalom, is peace. Your name is a Song of Peace. But you certainly are not peace.

Who are all these people, these echoing voices, living inside your head? Are they your companions? Is that why you like books about twins? I see your Portfolio here, clusters of voices above your right ear and near the crown of your head. Some are murmuring to you on the left side of your skull, and some have settled near your eyes. They tremble with speech and words. I see them.

And I hear them whispering together, waiting to see what book you will choose. Ah, they come from stories you have read. I can tell.

Here comes a memory bubbling up, you are story caught inside it, still, as if a standing sleep has seized you. You were six years old.

The DC Transit street car curved from Seventh and K winding toward North Capitol Street with clang and spark, it jogged you between the window and your mother as you sat reading with two thick books lying on your lap. Books thick enough to last you until you got home to Mayfair and beyond. Word hunger, expectation, and quiet joy surrounded you while the city's life receded with its thick loud air.

All you wanted was to have an unread book to read that night at home. It could not happen, you read them too fast. The street car stopped in front of the Government Printing Office, where you looked up to smile toward the Post Office. Your father worked there during the night, for you. In order to care for you by day while your mother was teaching he worked at the Post Office by night.

As the bus left the stop, crossing over North Capitol, you looked directly south at the Capitol Building, right through the high curves of the arches you saw sunlight shining through the parapets — you called them parapets — from the other side, blue and marble light shining through. Are they parapets? I don't know. — What's a parapet? A parapet is a word from books for something high and beautiful made of stone with ridges and ledges. You used that word for the dome of the Capitol, arches of marble. Beautiful, yes beautiful parapets. Who cares what the word parapet means really? If I don't look it up in a dictionary for a while I can keep using it the way I want.

All those people from all over the United States think that this wonderful Capitol Building here in Washington City be-longs to all of them, and you don't mind, they can use it. They can visit it. They can enjoy it. But they are just visitors, this is YOUR city. You like it that everybody from everywhere uses it. But it belongs to you, you, you, you and isn't your city beautiful, beautiful, Oh isn't your city just BEAUTIFUL!!!

As the bus turned from Massachusetts Avenue into H Street you returned to reading your books.

But then trouble came upon you. The books! You had al-ready finished reading one. And the other, if you didn't slow

down, would be finished before you crossed the Anacostia
River. You slowed down, you paced yourself, you counted in the
air between the paragraphs, you tried to read just one page
every block. It didn't work. Your eyes raced through the words
unheeding, helpless in the face of story, caught.

Glee filled the realm of storytellers who make their home
behind your eyes. The storytellers hovered and giggled and did
not care that you had nothing new left to read at home. Glee
and teasing. Did you think you could resist us? They gloated.
Your heart faltered, your head dipped, drooped, you glanced
up. Sigh. Already there was the Langston Neighborhood on
Benning Road. Already there was Spingarn High School and
Brown Junior High and Charles Young Elementary and Phelps
Vocational, and the Benning golf course. Already you could see
the Anacostia River and there on the other side of the bridge
was River Terrace and the Potomac Electric Power Company
with your elementary school, Neval Thomas, way back beyond
a field, framed by the poles and wires of electricity.

That's Mayfair, where you lived then, and where you still
live now.

You placed your finger in the book two pages from the end.
If you could force yourself not to read for these last few blocks
you would have two pages to read when you got home.

Sad eyes, sad, sad. And your mother looked over at you as
you looked out at the Anacostia River.

"What's the matter, now? I thought you picked out two
books you really liked. Why did you stop reading? What in the
world is the matter?"

"Well, I did pick out two good books and I enjoy reading
them, but, but . . . ."

"But what?"

"It's just that I'm almost through reading the last one and if
I don't stop reading now I'll have nothing new to read when I
get home."

"What? I do declare! Do you mean you have just about finished the books I just bought you?"

"Yes, I only have two pages left. I'm trying to save them until I get home."

"Umph, umph, umph, I hope you don't think I can afford to buy you two books a day! I paid a dollar a piece for those books."

Your mother looked down at you. "As soon as we get home we're going to get in the car and go to the Langston Branch Library where you'll get a library card. Your father will be rested by then so he can drive us. With a library card you can take out a lot of books all the time."

And the world's weight fell from you. You finished reading the last pages of the last book. By nightfall you had a library card and all the books you could carry.

Chapter 4: The StorySong of Bear-Wolf's March to the Library

You tremble away from the memory of your first library card and consider. If you spend your $7.00 on a book now, you'll be done with it by evening. Plus, you won't even have any lunch, and you won't have money to come back to Kann's for another week, a whole week with nothing to read. Don't buy a book that won't last a week, or even three days. No. March up Seventh Street and get books from the Library. A stack of books from the library lasts. Don't buy a book here at Kann's. Become Bear-Wolf, the fantastic hero who subdued the demon of deep murky waters, and march forth.[4]

Your mother told you about Bear-Wolf when she was combing your bushy fuzzy tangled hair. And your father said, yes, my little Bear-Wolf, your hair is thick and full and strong and nappy because all the ideas inside twist and turn and rise in circles so much that your skull can't hold them in so they poke out through your head in beautiful naps, joyful and smart. That's why you figure things out. Become Bear-Wolf and march up the hill, march off to find your books.

And thus you leave Kann's basement bookstore, Seventh and E, and step toward Carnegie Library, Seventh and K. I, John Milton, am the witness as you turn your back on Pennsylvania Avenue and march up Seventh Street hill.

You pass Lansburg's Department Store but what good is that since they don't even have a book section.

You pass me, John Milton, a second time as I cling to the awning of a used bookstore that displays another copy of my book in a window.

You pass the Woolworth's where you can buy really good hot dogs and where one day they finally let you sit at the counter to eat a grilled cheese sandwich. You look neither to the left nor to the right.

You pass Hecht's Department Store on the other side of Seventh Street. Hecht's would never think of having a bookstore inside.

You pass the classic Greek office building on the left.

Your mind is firm within you.

You pass me, John Milton, a third time, as I peer through the window of another used bookstore.

You pass Chinatown with all its color and faraway scents. You don't turn your head.

You pass me, John Milton, a fourth time, it must be Old Milton Week on Seventh Street, all the bookstores are displaying my book.

You stand in front of Hahn's Shoe Store and look across at the Carnegie Library at Seventh and K Streets.

You cross K Street and stand in front of the library, looking upward.

Chapter 5: Versity

Carnegie Library. Carved in heavy stone high above the semicircle of stone landings and benches you read. A VNIVERSITY FOR THE PEOPLE. Why does the U have a point at the bottom like a V? You puzzle over it yet again.

It must have something to do with the letter double-u "W". Double-u is actually a double-v, two vees stuck together. If a double-u -W -is really a double-vee, maybe there was a time when a single-u was a single-v. So the words are not really A VERSITY FOR THE PEOPLE like I used to say it. I used to think it was talking about poetry in Washington. A Verse City, Washington City, you see, maybe there was a time when people spelled city with an ess instead of a cee, and everybody went around the city - sity - speaking verses, poetry. The word can't be ADVERSITY with the D fallen out. Nobody would carve the word Adversity above a beautiful city like Washington, and anyway there are too many extra letters for the word to be Adversity. No. I finally figured it out, it's a University For the People. A school of the universe. And the V is really U.

You look at the people sitting, leaning, brooding, on their stone benches. Are you whispering to them silently? Do you know that someone put a University here for all of us? I wish I could see it. It could be hidden inside somewhere. I wonder why I never see anybody else stop and read the words before they go in. I stop here every time to read them, do they know a university is here? I never see anyone looking. Maybe one day I'll find the secret university inside.

Beyond the dark doors carved words are in gold rather than stone, Homer, that's one of the words. You read and turn, stepping up the marble stairs to the Children's Room on the second floor. You can only take ten books at a time. I, John Milton, watch as you choose. I want to lead you to my books but they don't put my books in the Children's Room.

How can I get you to find my book? I sit in one of the tall windows, watching. Then Mrs. Raymond, the librarian, looks at you too and I glance into her head. Surprise! She knows me. Maybe that's why I feel comfortable lounging around her library room, but she doesn't mention me to you. I try to ooze into her head every time she looks at you but she just shudders and shakes her head and pushes me out. She doesn't know how to associate the two of us. John Milton and a little Negro girl. Impossible. That's what she says to herself. I wonder if she even knows about Phillis Wheatley. I'll check. Hmm. Yes, she does, but not very much. You know more about her than Mrs. Raymond because your mother told you about her. You think about Phillis in wisps of thought. Phillis called herself an African but you and this Mrs. Raymond, this librarian, call her a Negro, the same category you use for yourself. I am glad that you've already heard about Phillis Wheatley. Phillis read my poetry when she was just a girl, and when she died as a woman she had my book ***Paradise Lost*** in her arms, but no one has told you that.

Mrs. Raymond keeps thinking about you and looking at you, but you don't notice. You don't notice people a lot. I look inside your head for more information about Mrs. Raymond. White. Ah. That's your mother's voice echoing in your head. Your mother calls this Mrs. Raymond librarian a good white librarian. "Certainly, Mrs. Ojero, Shirah can stay here and read alone any time while you shop. Perfectly behaved. I'm glad to have her here." And you, Shirah, are an intelligent little Negro girl. That's what Mrs. Raymond thinks about you inside her head. She never says that part out loud. And she won't mention me to you. She doesn't think that you'll be able to understand my words, but I want to lead you to my books. Mrs. Raymond keeps looking at you as you go up and down the rows of books. So many, and you're supposed to choose ten!

Chapter 6: Paradise Re-Lost

As you turn away from the books toward the door, catching the eyes of Mrs. Raymond, you glance through the wide hall toward the marble stairs. "I'm going to look at some pictures in the basement before I decide." Down the steps, around and around, you pass the Technology Room on the second floor, the Adult Reading Room on the first floor, and come to the basement where there is a room with earphones, and a smaller room with file cabinets holding catalogued pictures.

I am here with you, I, John Milton, dropping down the airway, skirting the hall, watching what you do and wondering about you. You reach out for a file cabinet. You pull out a drawer. You lift up a picture part way, look at it, a building, and put it back. You reach out for another file cabinet. You pull out another drawer. You lift another picture part way up, look at it, a flower and put it back.

And then our moment comes upon you.

You reach out for yet another file cabinet, pull out a drawer, reach out your hand, and pull up a painting. It is a painting of an enflamed angel raging against Heaven, Lucifer in engulfing fire, Lucifer fallen with a third part of the angels. It's an illustration from my book.

Can you hear me? Your heart stops. You pull the picture all the way out of the drawer and gaze at it for a long while. You lean against the cold metal cabinet and drink in the picture with your eyes and your head.

I, John Milton, whisper to you, "Turn it over, turn it over and find out my name and the name of my book." But you can't hear me this time, or you don't understand. "Please, turn over the picture and find out who I am and come to find me, I'm right here in this building." But you, oh my dear Shirah Shulamit, after shuddering and trembling before the picture for a moment, two moments, a long long moment leaning against the cold metal cabinet, reject my whispered words, you turn your back on me, refuse me, turn away. After a long moment of brooding collapse against the file cabinet, you stand up, turn around, put the picture back in the cabinet drawer, close the cabinet and leave the room of pictures.

I am devastated. My chance is gone, gone. How long will I have to wait for you? Oh how long! I can't move from the picture room. Will I ever be able to find you again? Come back and read me. Why do you walk away from me, Shirah Shulamit, oh little song of peace, leaving me here? I cannot follow you any more. I am deserted. I watch as you walk back to the stairs, back toward the Children's Reading Room without me.

You place your left foot on the marble stair. Imbalance, as you lift your right foot you wobble, totter, weave — and grasp the brown wood bannister, touching the swirled marble barrier with the back of your hand. Your right foot, the lower foot, leans against air as you right yourself. What is it? A leopard pacing on the marble landing? The tread of a lion at the turning? A wolf crouching in front of your face.[5] What is it you see? Motionless.

You turn. You concentrate. I rise up in hope. You step down from the marble stair. You walk back into the picture room brushing against me. You don't remember which cabinet had the picture. You open one wrong cabinet, then another wrong cabinet. And another and one more. Four wrong cabinets. You concentrate. You open a fifth file cabinet. This is the right cabinet. You are sure of it. I watch the concentration of your mind. How far did I reach back in the drawer for the picture? You figure it out, first you reach in front of the picture. Then you reach behind the picture. Finally you pull out the picture. This is it. You have it again. In your hand.

You turn it over. There is the name of the painter on the back. You don't care. Where are the words you are looking for? Does it come from a book? What book does it come from. There, there it is. Of course. That has to be the title. **Paradise Lost**. Echoing. You repeat those words to yourself for the first time as you lean against the file cabinets, amazed, thinking about . . . what? your brother . . . your infant brother who died, who was lost, all of a sudden lost. ***Paradise Lost***. Of course. And to think . . . I wonder . . . could this be it ? . . what I've waited for ? . . It could have no other title. Who wrote it, what's the name? Here it is, John, John Milton.

YES! That's me.

You walk into the hallway with the picture in your hand. You walk into the room with the earphones and get a scrap of paper. You sit down and finally write down the words that bring us together, John Milton, ***Paradise Lost***.

Behind your shoulder I am smiling, whispering. The voices in your mind are talking to you so loudly about your lost brother that you don't hear me at all. But soon, perhaps, you will call me to rise from my book and speak to you. Your handwriting is terrible. I am nervous. You may not like my book. Your face looks down on my title, ***Paradise Lost***, with your eyes so wide. You expect something from me. My title strikes backward through your memory to your brother's cold cradle of death, someone you loved was lost, paradise, paradise lost. I didn't expect you to expect so much!

The murderer took him, the little baby you loved, your mother's son, your father's boy, he whom your parents nursed and cared for was taken from you, because the murderer gave him close attention too. While your parents slept, the murderer dipped his evil hand into his shallow petri dish and scooped out some disease and stuffed the disease down the throat of the infant boy, and thus he died. You were the witness, you only three years old and without the full words to explain what you saw when the keening cry of death rose up in your apartment. For your brother. Paradise Lost. So that is the grief I see behind your eyes.

What will you do with the poem when you read it? Will it disappoint you? Maybe you won't like heroic poetry. Have I rushed you? I must know what you think about me. You return to Mrs. Raymond, the librarian in the Children's Room, and show her your raggedy piece of paper in your child handwriting. Her eyes open wide, and she smiles. "John Milton, **Paradise Lost**. What's this? How did you know I was thinking about . . . ? How did you decide . . . ?"

"I saw a picture down in the picture room. You know my mother said I should take a break sometimes from reading and go look at pictures and then come back and read. So I saw a picture down in the picture room and I liked the picture a lot. And this was written on the back of it so I thought maybe it's the name of a book and if the picture came from this book I would like to read it."

"What? Explain it to me again?"

"I found a picture downstairs you know in that picture room you have, my mother said I could do that, take a break sometimes and go look at pictures for a few minutes and then come back and read some more. Well, I found this picture down there and I liked it and I was wondering if the picture came from a book I could read so I looked on the back of the picture and this was written on the back so I wrote it down to see if I could find the book it comes from. I want to read it if it's all right for children to read it."

I, John Milton, am standing there watching Mrs. Raymond watching you, I am whispering to Mrs. Raymond, "Take her to my book." She looks into your face. You are confused. "Is it a book children are not supposed to read? If it is I don't have to read it."

"No, children can read it, but we don't have it in the Children's Reading Room, come with me."

YES! And she holds your hand and leads you to the Young Adult Reading Room. Mrs. Shiler is sitting there at her desk.

You hand the scrap of paper to Mrs. Shiler and wait for Mrs. Raymond to explain.

But why does Mrs. Raymond make you explain it all over again?

"I saw a picture . . . "

"What? What is she saying?" Mrs. Shiler can't hear you. "This is impossible."

Mrs. Shiler reads your paper, looks back at you, her eyes narrow, "What?"

Mrs. Raymond says, "Please listen."

"I went downstairs and I saw this picture. It was a picture of an angel burning up, he was an angel that was like a devil with wings on fire, and he was mad, shaking his fist and looking up in the sky. So I wanted to keep looking at the picture and I wanted to know what happened to make him so mad. I thought maybe it came from a story. I wanted to know the whole story. So I thought if I looked on the back of the picture it would tell me if it came from a story. So I did look and it had these names on the back. John Milton, ***Paradise Lost***. I thought maybe ***Paradise Lost*** was the name of the story and John Milton was the name of the man who wrote it. So I wrote it all down and came back upstairs and asked Mrs. Raymond if she has the book but she says she doesn't have it in the Children's Room."

Your own voice, telling how you found me. I, John Milton, understand, you want to read my book, but the librarians are not expecting it. They have to hear from your own mouth directly that you want my book or they won't believe.

Mrs. Shiler looks at Mrs. Raymond then back at you and says, "I don't think we have your book here in the Young Adult Room either but let's look." So the three of you look along the shelves for my book. I, John Milton, just stand at the doorway watching. I already know that my book is not on the shelf, those "young adults" don't care about me.

Finally Mrs. Raymond and Mrs. Shiler escort you to the Adult Reading Room with me gliding behind you. You are so happy. It is your first time to go to the Adult Reading Room and you have wanted to go there for so long. Sometimes you just stand by the card catalogue and look through the doors of the Adult Reading Room. Longing. This time, you, with Mrs. Raymond and Mrs. Shiler on either side of you, walk up to the librarian of the Adult Reading Room. I can't find a regular name for this librarian in your head but your mother calls her "mean white lady," that's the word I find in your head. I am there watching her and I don't like her. Her mouth is bitter and narrow as she looks at you. "I want **Paradise Lost** by John Milton." Mrs. Shiler and Mrs. Raymond stand on either side of you.

You have to say it. She refuses to read what you have scrawled on your piece of paper. She won't hold a paper your hands have touched, or even look down at it.

"What school do you go to? Who gave you such an assignment as this? What do you think you are doing here?"

"I went to Neval Thomas Elementary School. I'm going to Woodson Junior High School in September. It's not an assignment. Is it a book children aren't supposed to read? I don't have to have it. I just saw a picture in the cabinet downstairs. I liked the picture. I wondered if the picture came from a book. Or a story in a book. When I turned the picture over it had a man's name on the back, and the name of this book. So I wrote it down and took it to Mrs. Raymond. **Paradise Lost**. John Milton. But Mrs. Raymond said she doesn't have the book in the Children's Room."

The mean white lady librarian looks like she's going to spit on you when you say that. She's trying to scare you away. She's trying to make you too scared to talk. I look into her head, Shirah. When she was in school she tried to read my book but she wasn't smart enough to read very far. She couldn't get through the first few pages. She doesn't want you asking for it. She hates that you are only eleven years old and yet you know how to find my name on the back of the picture. She hates that you think to look for the name of my book all by yourself. And she hates that your face is brown. I look inside her head and see all that. She keeps calling you a name too. It is an impolite word that is related to the word Negro. She keeps saying it over and over inside her head but she won't say it out loud. It makes her face all screwed up and wrinkly.

But who cares about her, I am so happy when that fusty dusty rusty mean off-white ole library woman finally listens to you. She sniffs to herself but she has to listen. Then she walks to the bookcases with you because she can't think of a way to make you stop looking at her and waiting. Mrs. Raymond and Mrs. Shiler disappear behind you. She reaches up to a high shelf and picks up my books and hands my book down to you. You hold me in your hands. ***Paradise Lost***, John Milton.

I stand there protecting you so you don't see the bitter curse in the eyes of the mean white lady. You never notice anything except the book in your hand. You walk dazed to the library checkout counter and for the first time in your life only check out one book. You already know that this is a special book and will last you a whole week.

It is a glorious day for us. I had not known that I was waiting for you, but I was. I had been waiting for you a long time.

Of Man's First Disobedience and the Fruit
Of that Forbidden Tree, whose mortal taste
Brought Death into the World, and all our woe,

You start reading me at the bus stop.

And chiefly Thou, O Spirit, that dost prefer
Before all Temples the upright heart and pure,
Instruct me, for Thou knowest

You read me as the bus travels down Massachusetts Avenue to H Street.

That to the highth of this great Argument
I may assert Eternal Providence
And justify the ways of God to men.

Back at home, in Mayfair, you cannot keep still. You move around the apartment reading. In my book you have found a promise fulfilled, yes, because God promised to give a sign that you would write a book. "God, please let me grow up and write a book?" That is your first prayer. Your daily prayer. Asked of God every night since the year your brother died. "God, please let me write a book when I grow up, and please give me a sign before I'm ten years old that I'll write a book. Please. Some sign."

Paradise Lost is the sign. A late sign since you are already eleven years old.

But it has arrived.

Finally.

The sign didn't arrive before your tenth birthday, so you tried to die the night before you were ten years old.

God failed you.

How could you live a whole lifetime without knowing that you would be a writer?

You lay down on the floor and planned never to get up again.

You didn't know that it took more than will-power to die, you didn't know that you actually had to do something against yourself in order to die, you just lay down on the floor on the afternoon before your tenth birthday party and expected to die.

While lying there you remembered your second prayer.

"God, please don't let my mother and father have to bury another child."

You weren't thinking about yourself when you made that second prayer. You were thinking of your second brother, Sazonado, The Music Smith, they call him now, "Mellow," the one who came after your first brother died, the one who lived.

"How can I ask God not to let my parents bury another child and then kill myself? God will think I'm not serious."

So you stood up from death, despairing, wondering. "Maybe God can still make it come true about writing a book even without giving me a sign before my tenth birthday."

Now you sit at the window of the Mayfair Mansions apartment, reading **Paradise Lost**, looking out at the green summer lawn knowing that it was worth it not to kill yourself. "This book is telling me that I can write a book. I can tell just by reading it. **Paradise Lost** by John Milton. I don't know why this book makes me know that I'll write a book, but it does. I wonder what kind of book this is. I wonder if there's a name for this kind of book. There must be a word for it."

There is a word for it but you don't know it yet, you won't know that word for another year, not until you enter the eighth grade in junior high school and read Homer's **Iliad**. Then you will find the word. The word is epic. Epic. Epic is connected with heroic.

But now, on our first day together, you cannot keep still. You take me on a long walk from Mayfair to Kenilworth, where your mother was born. Paul Lawrence Dunbar is already here inside your head singing about Malindy and sending 'Lias off to war to fight for freedom while you step over the shallow brook between Mayfair Mansions and Eastland Gardens.[6] And you are so softly lamenting along with Phillis Wheatley the dead children of New England and Washington as we curve around the trees by the stream with your Robert Louis Stevenson whispering, "and does it not seem hard to you when all the sky is clear and blue," and your Langston Hughes stepping with us, "do you think it's a happy beat?"[7] We are glad to turn from Eastland Gardens to Kenilworth together.

These other poets are long established in your brain while I am still pouring into your head through your eyes from your hands this first time. You walk beside your Kenilworth Castle with its Garden of Converging Paths rising from the Anacostia River,[8] you meander toward the ponds singing StorySongs and talking with frogs and algae and bamboo and fish. You read while walking through the Kenilworth Lily Ponds, this checkerboard of waters just beyond your family's garden.

You read while sitting on a bench there. Now they call the Lily Ponds the National Park Service Kenilworth Aquatic Gardens. When you first found me, when you were eleven years old, they were just called the Lily Ponds. Those days were your last weeks before junior high school. The days were so fine in their sweet sadness and I, John Milton, did not fail you.

I understand now, so many years after the August day of our first meeting, that I came because you called for me, I came as an answer to your prayer, I came to walk you back from death.

How I remember our walk, you and I, hand in hand, with lingering steps and slow,[9] from the Carnegie Library at Seventh and K, the H Street bus, Benning Road, across the Anacostia River, Kenilworth Avenue to Mayfair Mansions and Eastland Gardens and the Garden of Converging Paths in Kenilworth and then uptown to your family's new house in the Takoma neighborhood of Washington, DC.

And on and on through all the schools and all the grand universities and all the rest of your life, making our way in the company of all the poets whom you love.

I, John Milton, remember you.

Cluster 2: Your Heaven
Cluster 2 Argument

Okay, curious reader, so now you know how it began, me finding **Paradise Lost** at the Carnegie Library and reading it on the way home to Mayfair and Kenilworth in Washington City. Perhaps it started a little earlier when I read Ibsen's **A Doll's House**, but I don't count that because I didn't know it had started then. You understand how that is don't you? It was one of my father's books that he never read to me. There were about ten of them, black leather covers with silver writing on the backs. What did they have in them? He mostly read his books to me, but not these books. I was curious. Did the books have something in them I wasn't supposed to read? So I picked up the one that said, "Ibsen. Plays." One play was, **A Doll's House**. I was a kid, I thought it would be a nice story about dolls. I loved doll houses. It was a story about a happy woman who had such a pretty life, like a doll, a live doll. But what they did to her! It was awful. All because she tried to protect her family. That's all she was doing, protecting her family, but there was nothing but trouble after that. I was stunned when I looked up from that book. My eyes got really big. Is that what it's like to be grown up? I shuddered and put the book away. I was about eight years old then. My second brother had just been born. Like I said, we call him Sazonado, mellow. He brought joy after my first brother died. That was before we moved to the second apartment in Mayfair Mansions in Washington. Yes, you could say it started with Ibsen, except how can you say it began if I didn't even know it? What's the it I'm talking about? It's the story. It's how I started hearing this whole story that I'm telling you. You see, I'm not just me, Shirah Shulamit, right here in Takoma DC, a neighborhood of Washington City — I'm Asenath too, yes, Asenath from ancient Egypt, Asenath from the Bible and everything. Yes, that famous Asenath from Genesis, the daughter of Lady Niko, the Ethiopian wielder of crystal and the daughter of her husband, the priest Poti-pherah. Whew, you know all the trouble that comes from messing with the daughters of priests! let me tell you. Have you heard that story, the **Iliad**? That story will let you know, just don't mess with a daughter of a priest. Messing with a priest's daughter will get you in serious trouble. And Asenath and I both got tricked into being born. We broke apart from each other because we were tricked. So now here we are as you see us. But it wasn't always like this. Once we were together, let me explain it to you. Here's how it was in Heaven.

Listen.

Chapter 7: Angel Square

Of all the angels in Heaven, Asenath, you are the most perverse, because you actually want to stay. Here we are on another bright Heavenly morning, well, you know what I mean, our light here can be so provoking — so what if we call it morning, what's wrong with that? Yes, I know it's afternoon, but these afternoons might as well be mornings. Always bright. Always Heavenly. And we angels hovering around in Boylston Hall to watch you and the Dean. Will she gaze at you yet again when she comes out of the auditorium? It's beautiful isn't it, this view of Flicker Mountains flaring from the far side of Angel Yard, shimmering through the windows of Boylston Hall? I see you looking out toward the Old Pump.

Seamus was wonderful this morning chanting about milk bottles and sod. Don't you love it when he's the one who strolls up from Poet's Lair on Wednesday afternoons? I'm sure you don't believe him any more than I do, Asenath. We angels know better. Why does he insist that earth is like that, with peat and mold and slime? Even so his words remind us of how much we want to be born — not you, of course — but the rest of us want to become real somewhere, perhaps on earth, perhaps somewhere else.[10]

What are you thinking about? What have you been reading? Why are you looking at the Old Pump? What do you see when you turn from the window and look at me out of those eyes? Me, a pathetic angel, Jane of the Sheherazadim,[11] a Storytelling Angel, milling around the vestibule of Boylston Hall sipping sherry, nibbling ambrosia, watching you, Asenath, you who are a great one among the Reading Angels of Heaven. In a moment the Dean of Heaven will skulk out of the auditorium, ignore me, ignore all the rest of us, and walk toward you. It is our fate.

Ah Asenath, where do you come from that you can hear songs by Seamus without desiring life? How can you hear about fences with splinters and water that's wet without wanting birth? How do you do it? And there are other songs when other poets come to us, David[12] and Charlotte[13] and Langston[14] — you listen and smile and turn away. Your eyes are elsewhere.

We're not like you, Asenath. We yearn so much to escape from Heaven, millennia by millennia, it's so hard a task for us to join with biofolk.[15] But we are never chosen. Why? Don't you ever wonder why? Is there something in those books you read to explain it? That smattering of biological life clinging to the faithless planets is so small. It should be easy enough for the Dean to let us go, but she does not permit it. And she never looks at us the way she looks at you. It's so discouraging.

It doesn't do us any good to prepare. Our rigorous training goes for nothing, you know that. The Dean chooses a few random angels, but doesn't choose the rest of us. And I, unlike you, I, an unchosen straggler, cannot ignore our captivity. We are imprisoned here in Heaven forever. And ever.

I guess that's why the Dean doesn't like us, she knows we hate this prison. But do you think it's fair that she won't let us be born! Don't we strive to make her system work? Don't we stress and strain to figure out her criteria, haloes all aching and wracked with pain?[16] Don't we shuffle through the blurred pages of her vague rules, grin at her random discrimination, and just endure our fundamental inequality — why! why should some few of us have the life that is denied the rest, why shouldn't we all move and act with will and desire, flesh and fur upon a planet? Can she tell us why? We should protest her basic unfairness, the prejudice, in fact, of having such a small number of angels chosen to descend into life. And not one of those chosen angels is ever one of us.

Yet so great is our desire to live, to sneak into some living being, that we forgo all protest and abnegate all struggle for equal rights and privileges. Unlike you, Asenath, we obey the Dean's rules, laws, and practices hoping to coincide at last with biological life — an amoeba, a human, a rose, a lion, a gazelle, a cedar upon a mountain, a bacteria — we yearn for life.

We obey the Dean, but in spite of our obedience we resent our oppressed and unrewarded status. Sure, we get plenty of sherry, but sherry doesn't blot out desire. We don't shout our pain aloud, but we hurt. We may strut in Angel Yard or sulk in Angel Square, or watch you as you stand there unfazed — but sulking, strutting, or watching, shouting hymns of praise at the Old Pump or kicking up the dust near Flicker Mountains, we nurture and cherish our bitterness in silence. We hate our uselessness. Don't you ever wish you could be someone within the worlds, Asenath? We want to be somebody, somebody real.

But of course you, Asenath, are happy being useless. You don't want to be real. The rest of us are ashamed and horrified by our empty lives, and we look to the operas of Heaven, from Poet's Lair to Lost Artist Café, to distract and divert us, to comfort us in fact as we try to understand all that has never happened to us. But you don't care that nothing happens, you flourish within dullness. You actually enjoy Heaven.

So here comes the Dean of Heaven again, gazing at you while you just look toward the Old Pump. She singles you out, and you don't even look back at her. What are you thinking? Old Waterman Fuentes is gone, now that the weekly pump ceremony is over.[17] That trifling Caretaker, once he opens the pump for the week he's off drinking Dos Equis at the Faculty Club, but you keep looking over there.

While we are here, furtively watching you. Yes, you, Asenath. Can anyone really ignore you? I wish I could. Most of the other angels are like me, we wish the Dean would gaze at us like that, we wish she would send us on an assignment.

Long ago, when we first noticed you, Asenath, there were great hopes for you. The Jeffries loved you, those esteemed members of the Order of Moteless Angels predicted you would be an Arch-Angel among the Reading Angels of Heaven. But you have failed of your great promise. And now it's not only the Jeffries who gossip against you. Last week, at Lost Artist Café, Devorah, who has loved you, whispered that no longer are you a bright and morning star among the Blessed Ones.

But do you care at all? Don't you know that Reading Angels are supposed to read **Moby-Dick**[18] and **Shaka the Great**[19] in order to desire biolife even more than the rest of us? You're supposed to drool over the stories until you can't bear not being born, until you find a way.

But look at you, Asenath! Sure, you love to read the stories, even now your finger is clamped between the covers, holding your page, but reading doesn't work for you. Your books make you hate the biolife we want so much. You insult us. When we tell you experience makes the best teacher, you tell us that's for people who can't think! You're so presumptuous, so conceited. You affront our desire. Far from being an Arch-Angel, you are the only Reading Angel in eternity with no use for life. Is it any wonder that none of us — thrones, principalities, dominions, powers, orders and tribes of angels — none of us like you, I mean, not really. I know sometimes we can't help but watch you, but we don't like you. You're not a colleague because you don't want to leave. We turn away from you. Mostly. I hope. More or less. Except I guess I'm not turning away. I wish I could turn away from you.

I've seen you lounging around on these golden benches along these golden streets reading these golden books from Wider and Widener Library. So many ages. Why don't you ever yearn to leave? Why don't you ever prepare yourself for a descent from Heaven? And why does the Dean love you so much? She loves you so much more than she loves us. She follows you with her eyes in the Yard, on Mass Ave, in Angel Square between the Newstand and the Tube, and in your favorite restaurant, One Potato, Two Potato.

And now it begins again. There you are walking out from Boylston Hall into Angel Yard with the Dean following you.

I'm coming too. You step beside Wider and Widener Library, on the path to Angel Square.

I ease between the angels. You lift your head aslant at the cave that leans against the stone of the library wall. Why are you looking there? You always look at things that make no difference, the Old Pump, the Cave.

I want to see your eyes. I come up quickly from behind you and glance back into your face as we walk under the archway into Angel Square. Your eyes are squinted up and watery. Have you been gnawing on horseradish instead of ambrosia? What's the problem now? I thought you liked it here so much. What's going on?

You pass klatches of Perishing Angels. Where is the Dean? I step behind you again and glance back toward the Yard, ah, yes, here comes the Dean passing under the archway and walking over Mass Ave through the crowd toward you, a stalker furtive and annoying, brushing past the rest of us, gazing at you.

Something is going to happen. What is the Dean going to say to you? I follow and listen. It's not news but gossip that's important to me. If I hear what the Dean whispers to you then I can spread the gossip.

I'm not like the other Eternals, I'm like the Perishing Angels who love gossip. I'm tough, Asenath. You know I am. I've endured this useless position the Dean has given me. The other Eternals are not so, they're inadequate. My fellow Eternals, boring scholars, are off accepting research grants or developing foundation proposals. They are a bunch of losers trying to forget that they cannot be chosen for birth, that they are imprisoned here in Heaven, and that their purpose is to serve the Perishing Angels. In their bitter resentment the Eternal Angels won't even admit their uselessness, they won't acknowledge that they are here to serve the Perishing.

Although I am an Eternal, I don't linger in resentment, and I don't hide my anguish in grants and proposals. As you know,

I'm one of the Famed Sheherazadim; that is, one of the ten-ured Eternal Storytelling Angels of Heaven. The fact is I'm not much of an intellectual, and cannot endure the tedium of writing grants and developing proposals. I'm not good at scholarship, nor am I good at performing the function for which I am designed; that is, nurturing un-graduates or guiding the Perishing Angels. My strongest aversion is to minding my own business. And since not even the Dean of Heaven can take back tenure once the curse has fallen, I do what I want to do. What I want to do is follow people who don't want to be followed, flick my wings (yes, sometimes I actually appear with my wings) flick my wings into their lives, and mess with events that are not in the least my own business.

Which is why I love the gossipy Perishing Angels, and it is why, in spite of disliking you, I follow you, Asenath, as you step through Angel Square. After all, in spite of the usual impossibilities, there have been moments, once or twice in each millennia, when the Dean has chosen one of us, one of the Eternals, for biolife. Yes, it has happened, because the Dean loves us too in a small kind of way. Mostly she wants us to stay close to Heaven. These others, these Perishing Angels, are the ones who get to be born — several of them in every century! Unlike the Eternals, the Perishing Angels walk in the greater probability of that grand descent from Heaven into biological life.

***

But what about you others, you Converging Angels. Angel Square is crowded with you, precious, fervent, innocuous, profoundly obedient. You are lounging by the golden benches and milling around in front of the Newsstand and by the COOP, debating where to have dinner.

I don't know why you have a Newstand in Angel Square. What news could you ever get from the precincts beyond this inner Heaven? Or at least, what news could you scattered angels care about in this place where time doesn't recognize itself? Of course, as you know, we move through all the millennia: the

First Millennia, the Second Millennia, the Third Millennia . . . but we don't move through them in any particular order. Since the Thirtieth Millennia can occur immediately before the Sixth Millennia, how can you ever get any real news?

Your headlines are superfluous.

Adam Ate A Mango This Morning[20]

It gave him a Stomach Ache

Deucalion and Pyrrha Create New Race of Humans By Throwing Mango Pits Over Their Shoulders [21]

Mangoes Ripen on Tree overlooking Puerto Escondido, Mexico

It's all meaningless unless your job is chasing mango stories.

***

But whither have you taken me with these thoughts? The Newstand and the Converging Angels have nothing to do with you, Asenath, and I've come into Angel Square to follow you. Where are you? Ah, there, just beyond that group of debating un-graduates and untenureds, a gang of Perishing Angels. You meander beyond them toward Dunster Street and then turn down Mass Ave. I step to the side so that I can come up dawdling behind you. The Perishing Angels clog my path to you.

. . . but then it happens.

As you and the Dean walk toward the Front Gate of Heaven, as you leave Angel Square, as I lean forward to come up behind the Dean, as the Dean leans forward to come up behind you, Asenath, you speak these words aloud within the noise of Heaven, "Obedience is Futile."[22] And the lights of Heaven dim.

Chapter 8: THE Argument

"Good afternoon."

"Oh, it's you again."

"It's always so good to see you."

Silence.

"Are you still angry with me?"

Silence.

"I did what you said, I didn't follow you right out of the auditorium."

"I hate you."

"You can't hate me, I'm the Dean."

"I hate you, why are you following me?"

"You're exaggerating. You're not supposed to hate me."

"I hate you. What do you want?"

"I have this plan for you."

"Of course you've got some plan for me, you've always got some harebrained plan for me."

"You're rude, none of the other angels talk to me like this."

"You don't harass the other angels the way you harass me. You should be ashamed to follow me around the way you do."

"What are you talking about? I'm not harassing you, I'm the Dean, I have a great purpose in mind."

"Five hundred angels sitting in the poetry assembly, five hundred angels sipping sherry at the afternoon reception, five hundred angels filing through the doors of Boylston Hall into the Yard. How many do you follow? One. Me. I call it stalking. I call it harassment."

"Did you enjoy the program?"

"I enjoy Seamus, but why can't we just go to hear him? Why do we have the Old Pump ceremony first? It's embarrassing that you always have to renew the water. Why does the flow decrease in the first place. Why can't the water just be there and stay there?"

"Embarrassing? You're calling my Old Pump ceremony Embarrassing?!"

"Yes, embarrassing, it shows you don't know how to make the water last. You've got Old Waterman Fuentes running up here from One Potato, Two Potato every week, disturbing him as he drinks his Dos Equis, dragging him up here pumping and pumping every Wednesday afternoon."

"Of course I have him pumping every week, I have to keep my silver river flowing. It's a weekly cycle."

"But why does the water have to flow in a cycle? That's the whole problem."

"Problem? But there have to be cycles. How am I supposed to keep things going without cycles?"

"You're supposed to be omnipotent. Make a silver river that doesn't need a cycle, a river that just keeps flowing and doesn't have to be renewed.

"It's true that after the ceremony you let the poets stir us up with images, but even so the water almost runs out before the next Wednesday. You say you have plans for *me*, why don't you plan to get rid of the ceremony? The water should be available altogether and forever, all the time at the same level.[23] Why do you need to pump it every week and waste our time singing to it before we can hear a poet. Get rid of the ceremony and give us more time to read and think."

"Embarrassing! So that's how you feel. You never seem to like the things I plan. I don't understand it. And I like you so much. You ought to appreciate Old Fuentes Waterman, he's the fountain who makes the water flow. Of course it has to be renewed every week. But we could expand the ceremony. What if we add a sax and some drums to start it off? Maybe Devorah and the Jeffries can help jazz it up."

"Forget it, ignore it. Just let me read my books and stop making plans for me."

"But your ideas are always so brilliant, Asenath, you're a wonder. I love to hear your ideas. And if we fix up the Old Pump ceremony, I know that on some far afternoon your soul will look back in wonder at the Waterman's silvery water bubbling out. He's pumping the Ocean of Light, don't you even like that?"

"Silvery water, ha! Have you looked at it lately? That water is pale and empty even when it's first pumped. There's no silvery about it any more. But don't bother talking about it. Just leave me alone. I know you're not going to change it."

"Of course there's still silver in it, but we can make it even stronger so you'll like it."

"You're lying to me."

"What?"

"I said, you're lying! And you know you're lying. You follow me and praise me, but you won't do anything. You always leave it the way it is, so why don't you leave me alone."

"I could mention it to Ethan, Ethan can fix anything."

"Ethan will tell you that Wednesday afternoons haven't changed since you created them. You know he's not going to change the Old Pump ceremony."

"Maybe, but you have such good ideas."

"And you always exaggerate everything I do."

"No I don't, it's just that you're good."

"Dean, you drive me crazy. Something's wrong with you. You always overpraise me, you don't have good sense. I hate blind praise, how can you stand it? Praise, praise, praise! All day, all night, angels praising over you, don't you ever get tired of it? Maybe you can stand it but I can't stand it."[24]

"Tired of it, but you don't even know what I'm trying to do. Wait until you hear what I've come up with. I could use your help."

"You and your schemes, don't even talk to me. I've got plenty to do. I just started learning Sanskrit and Nahuatl and Peul. What do I need with more to do?"

"But let me explain, this is a project I've been working on for so long. I've been preparing it for you. In fact, I've chosen you to descend from Heaven and be born a woman upon the earth."

THE FIRST QUESTION

Will you be born because I, the Dean of Heaven, ask you to be born?

NO.

"Born?! Leave Heaven and get born?! Have you lost your mind? Why would I want to be born? I thought you had a little bit of sense left."

"But wait, wait a minute, let me explain my idea . . ."

"There's no idea you can come up with that would make me want to get born. Don't confuse me with all these Seraphim you have flying around here. Maybe they want to be born. Not me! You've got the wrong angel! I'm happy. Sure, I wouldn't mind eliminating the Old Pump ceremony. But I can endure the shame of it if you'll just leave me alone.

"But you could at least consider my suggestion."

"Leave me alone."

"But Asenath!"

"No!"

"But you should obey me? Why can't you be like the other angels? Aren't you supposed to obey me?"

"Of course not, didn't you hear what I said just now? Obedience is Futile. I figured it out. And you've known it all along. I don't have to obey you. I don't think you even want me to obey you. It's not obedience that's so important, but choosing. So why mention obedience? It's thinking and judging that's important. That's what gets things done.

"If obedience is so important to you, go ask one of your obedient angels to help you. Why don't you make one of them get born for you if that's what you need?"

"I need you to help fix the world."

"What do I care about your world?! You can't make me be born. Why should I be born into that mess you've made? No thank you, I'm doing very well right here in Heaven. The biggest thing wrong with Heaven is You. Why don't you take a nap or go visit somewhere?[25] You can keep that creation of yours."

"But it's such a good creation."

"Ha! Of course YOU think it's a good creation. It's your job to think it's a good creation.[26] But I've been reading about it in these books. Earthquakes, tsunamis, Mark Twain. What possessed you to make such confusion. Creation! Obedience! Ha!

"O Asenath, creation is good, so very good, and I'm the Great Spirit who made it. You're supposed to do what I tell you to do."[27]

"Why? Who can understand you? Why don't you ever explain anything? Do you understand it yourself? Why should I do what you tell me to do? What is it with you and obedience?"

"What *is* it?"

"Yes, what *is* it? How do you expect anyone to agree with you? Over at Lost Artist Café they're saying you've considered punishment for those who don't obey. How did you come up with that? Are you going to depend on punishment to get obedience? Is that your plan, the only way you can win? By beating us up? Is that how you're going to get me to choose *you*? By knocking us upside the head and calling it free will?! How stupid is that?!"

"But I am the Dean of Heaven. My ideas are not stupid. I have brilliant ideas, not only am I the Dean of Heaven, I am also your superior officer. You're supposed to listen to me. Let me tell you the details of my plan. Give me a chance. You won't even give me a chance? I can explain myself."

"Look, Dean, just leave me alone. I told you already, I just don't want to be born. Choose somebody else."

"But these other angels are so false!"

"Whose fault is that. I didn't make them like that, you did! Didn't you make everything up here in Heaven? You! The ALL-Glorious, ALL-Powerful Omnipotent Dean of Heaven?"

"Well yes, I did make Heaven, but why do you have to remind me of it. Just look at my angels! They pretend to be calm, but they're all tangled with desires for skin and feet and arteries in spite of all my work. It isn't what I planned. I didn't know this would happen. I made it perfect and good to start with but it got broken. I've got to figure something out. I've got to fix it."

"I thought you were supposed to know everything, Madame Omniscient! And you didn't know this would happen?"

"Well I DO know everything. Sort of. But there are some things you don't figure out until it happens really. I knew there would be peace and joy and silence — I didn't know there would be so much secret desire. No matter what I do these angels of mine keep desiring things. I give them ceremonies and songs and poets and silver rivers, but they still keep desiring things.

"Instead of sitting around singing they're all smoking or sniffing something — trying to get a low. I gave them a permanent high but all they want is to get down a little closer the ground[28] — even that nuisance Jane Sheherazadim over there who's following us again, but she's just a busy-unbody. I hope she gets distracted and doesn't break into our conversation this afternoon. She's a plague, always sneaking around looking for a story. And these other angels, if they are not taking sobering drugs all the time they just sit around hoping for a chance to run away. What kind Heaven is this I've made?!

"And yet I created Heaven and earth and all the worlds so that they are very good and all the beings should stay where they're put in Heaven and earth in order to be perfect. They're only supposed to move when I give instructions. I've tried to satisfy them. Look at the seasons I came up with, and all the celebrations of time so glorious in creation. Look at my planet earth and how they grow stuff there. They've learned how to bake bread! Their hands are filled with wheat, their bowls overflow with rice. They don't have earthquakes all the time and as for Mark Twain, well, I rather like him. He's one of my great successes. Tsunamis have to do with physics. I can't get rid of physics — if I get rid of physics there won't be any worlds at all. The worlds are beautiful, the homesteads of creation are ingenious. Can you number the months that the stones fulfill? Do you know the time that the ice caps bring forth? Were you there when I set the constellations in the Heavens and hung the moon in its round?"[29]

"No, thank Heaven, I wasn't there, I was in Wider and Widener Library reading **Gilgamesh**.[30] I was visiting **Deep Space Nine**.[31] And what has hanging the moon in the sky got to do with me being born a woman on earth? You sure know how to avoid the subject."

"I'm just saying, Asenath, that the world is beautiful, Heaven and earth are beautiful and good, and I ask you to return there, Shuvi, shuvi, return, return, O Shulamit, O Child of Peace, Woman of Wisdom, my dear Asenath. I ask you to return to that place. Will you please be born?"

"No! No! And what do you mean shuvi, return. I've never been there in the first place, so how can I return? And again I say, why don't you ask one of these other angels, someone who wants to be born?"

***

I, Jane of the Sheherazadim, listen to your conversation with the Dean and am astonished. How can you say No to the Dean? Our Great Spirit is telling you to move and you are refusing to move. I never thought I would hear such a thing in all of Heaven.

And as for the Dean herself, doesn't she hear you say "Obedience is Futile?"[32] How can she ask you for help after that? After all, you dim the lights of Heaven. Doesn't she believe you when you say that you hate her?

***

THE SECOND QUESTION

Will you be born in order to establish a new institution?

NO.

***

I watch the two of you walk onward into the light,[33] down Mass Ave, walking past a bench where some other vagrant angel is sitting, and I am filled with deep musing to hear your conversation with the Dean filled with things so unbecoming and strange, things so unimaginable as hate in Heaven.[34]

***

But who's this vagrant angel? over here beside Mass Ave on the bench? Hello, Angel, what are you doing? Escaping? You're an Escaping Angel? Did you find a way to descend from Heaven behind the Dean's back? Of course you heard what the Dean just said to Asenath. Don't you care? But the Dean has just offered her . . . What? Okay, I won't talk to you about the Dean. I get it, you're sneaking off while she's following Asenath. But how did you figure it out? You look so delighted sitting there with Arrow Street curving away behind your bench, and your silver gray trees behind you. And look at our River down there in the light.

Your maple and your catalpa, shimmering silver, are beautiful leaning together over your head. What about that other tree, that green one far behind? That's green, isn't it? The name of that color is green. A green mulberry tree. Why is it green instead of silver?

Let me look at the books you've been reading. ***What Color Is Your Parachute?***[35] ***Twelve Steps To Becoming A Little Lower Than the Angels.***[36] ***Why is There Air?***[37] ***Down Low and Dirty. Get Low Down Without Drugs. You've Got To Get Down, Down, Down, a Little Closer to the Ground.***[38]

You can't hear me anymore. Your unseeing eyes await your descent into the world to join with a body. The silver gray leaves, catalpa and maple, touch, the pages of your books flutter back toward the library to become feathers on a shaft of light that is your arrow, yes, an arrow with your name on it. Your shaft leaves the library, moves through the gates of Heaven, and descends Arrow Street with you on the shaft. The veil linking upper bow and lower bow grows taut, and thus you are gone. In Joy. Gone.

Off to become a backbone with stuff hanging on it, with beaks or fur or feathers or hands. It will be hands for you. Great Happiness. And the name on your arrow is Asher. Yes, you shall enter a child and your name shall be Asher, Happy, also known as Oscar. Be fruitful and multiply.

***

And you, O heedless mulberry, in your bittersweet green and your ripe fruit, is that purple? purple fruit with green leaves rustling behind the empty bench of this Angel who has Escaped, speak to me. I am Jane Sheherazadim, speak to me of your green color and your purple fruit. Are these colors from where the Escaping Angel is going?

Where have you gone?

***

And you, my dear Asenath, stand with the Dean, pondering.

"Did you see that?" the Dean says to you. "Almost in front of my eyes that angel escaped from Heaven. Did you see what he was reading? Disgusting. That's probably the influence of Jane. Damn that Jane! Damn her to Earth. Why doesn't SHE find a way to leave Heaven. She and her tribe are always sharing gossip that confuses my angels who then go off to seek life.

"And it's too late to bring him back, my Escaping Angel. It's too late to correct him now, the Gates of Heaven are so wide leading from Wider and Widener Library. When the light bundles itself through the Gate, it crosses Mass Ave and pours down Arrow Street so strong, passing this bench. And thus I lose yet another of my people."

"Dean, you really don't make sense, if you don't want angels to escape into physical life, why are you asking me to be born?"

"I've got a special plan for you, Asenath, a plan that will help make Heaven right. That angel who just escaped is not my kind of angel, he's not an angel like you, Asenath. That Escaping Angel just left because he could, because somewhere someone is being born. That angel doesn't understand anything, he's just skipping the gates and leaping from the bench so he can leap inside some baby on earth and live inside somebody. There's no reason for it, no purpose, he just wants to live for the sake of life. He just wants to figure out his own purpose and doesn't care what I think. It isn't fair."

But Asenath interrupts you, O Dean of Heaven, "Look, isn't that Uriel standing on the dome of Grolier's Poetry Bookstore? It's Uriel, the Sun Seraph of Poetry showing off again."

From behind the two of you I look up and see deep swirling black blue waters flowing around a firmament, and within the firmament, an orb of wrought light, adamant. There's your Archangel Uriel standing there, the regent of the orb, looking down Bow and Arrow Street toward the River. The hard light shines upon you and the Dean, and touches Grolier Poetry Bookstore, where the Proprietary Angel, Urania Solano, her face caressed within the circle of her red curly hair, that is red isn't it?, squints out at you and the Dean and me. She sends us a slanting look that is a glance of farewell for the Escaped Angel, whose books now dissolve back into your Wider and Widener Library.

But I continue following you and the Dean, on across Arrow Street toward Upper Bow Boulevard and Lost Artist Café.

"I need you to be born as part of a new institution.

"What do I care?"

"A new institution with a new being, ordained by ancient prophecy and report throughout Heaven. You would become the new being at the new institution on the planet earth.

"What?! That rumor! That old piece of gossip! My dear Ms. Dean, who hasn't heard that old washed-up prophecy about some new being? Is this your slow news day and you're looking for something to do? That report has been batted around and discarded long ago, it's so ancient that even the homeless angels in the Square have stopped selling their prophecy tassels to go on charm bracelets. Billie can't get enough money from selling them to pay for even one hour at the Shelter by the Tube. He had to toss them all out."

"Just because a prophecy is old doesn't mean it isn't true. A day comes when the long awaited moment arrives, and the prophecy is fulfilled. The day could be today if only you would listen to me. If only you would obey."

"I'm not going to obey."

"You see, I already know that Heavenly forms serve as models for what they do on earth.[39]

"You!? You know! That's the Day Tripper's idea, she's my friend, you're just taking her idea . . ."

"Well okay, the Day Tripper's idea then, the Golden Barbarian Woman's idea. I know she's one of your friends among the Eternals.

"Well, yeah, she's the Eternal who called me to be a Reading Angel, you know that."

"Yes, well, I think she's right about the Heavenly forms repeating on earth."

"Who cares whether it's right or not? I don't. I just know that it's a beautiful idea, so I like it. I don't care if it's true or not because I don't care about earth."

"Will you please just listen a minute? I've added something to her idea, that's why it's OUR idea now, not just hers. What if it goes both ways? What if earth could fix Heaven? Perhaps a new institution on earth could make Heaven come right again."

"Preposterous. Earth is just good for stories. Earth is not good for doing anything in Heaven."

"It could happen, Asenath. The Day Tripper is showing me the way, she knows the connections between Heaven and earth, after all, she got her name from traveling between the two. Well, in her last trip she left one of our Heavenly parchments on a table at the Folger Library on earth.

"Some guy named Wallace picked it up. It was about our Heavenly trees, the parchment was about our silver and gold and copper Heavenly trees. But this Wallace guy read the paper and answered it. He said that our trees here in Heaven can't have the same color as the trees on earth. That's where this "green" comes from. Haven't you noticed it. Green? In Heaven as it is on earth. Our first green tree.

"Why yes, I did see see the tree. I saw that it has these new green leaves. I noticed the purple berries on it too. Purple! And isn't there red as well? Solano's hair is now red. Who would have thought it?"

"Yes, who would have thought of it? Not Heaven. The only color Heaven can think of is blue. Well, blue, black, metallic and parchment. But earth, creation and earth thought of green and purple and red. I've figured it out Asenath, don't you see? I can stick something on earth and earth can add and change it without even thinking of Heaven, earth people can do something I never thought of, something strange and unexpected and impossible, but the strange unexpected thing they do on earth can come back to Heaven. This means that you can go down there and be a person in our new institution, and this institution can do some random thing that returns to Heaven and fixes it. You love Heaven so much that whatever you add on earth will come back here — just like those colors came back here from the Day Tripper's visits, green leaves and purple fruit and that red hair on Solano — your new thing will come back here and my angels will love to stay here just like you do. And Heaven will be perfected."

"You're ridiculous! If it's random, you can't know what will happen. Any anyway, I already know about this Wallace who turned your silver trees into green. It's Wallace Stevens,[40] his poems are right here in Wider and Widener Library. He was standing on earth and talking about Heaven when he proclaimed that we here in Heaven cannot wear the colors of earth. So that's probably why the trees on earth refuse to be silver any more. But so what?! They stopped looking like the trees of Heaven. Who cares?! If you spent more time reading instead of following me around you would already know about Wallace."

"No, you're wrong, Asenath, please listen. This is what I've figured out. A person like you, who loves to stay in Heaven can go to earth and do random things, but your love of Heaven will still be in your being. Earth cannot not possibly change you so much that you forget Heaven."

"You don't know that. Random is random. You don't know what will happen."

"I don't know what will happen, but I know you can't stop being Asenath, and you like staying in Heaven so much you would seek out the same geography on earth. You know . . . . We have an Angel Square in Heaven, you'll find an Angel Square on earth. We have an Angel Yard in Heaven, you'll find an Angel Yard on earth. We have a Wider and Widener Library in Heaven, you'll find a Widener Library on earth. And so on. But on earth, because of the randomness of earth, you'll add something different in this new institution that will help me repair Heaven.

"You're delusional! You can't control it like that. Random means random."

"But there's some connection. Sure, random is random, but random is also connected somehow. At least let's find out. I want you to go to be born on earth as an investigator. You've seen the Day Tripper here but once you're born you'll find her also upon the face of the earth. Consult with her there. She lives in the House of the Hours when she's on the earth. Find her. Study and consider this experimental institution that will now be established — if only you will go."

"I'm not going. I told you already. I shall not be born."

"And the Day Tripper has a Portfolio of images made from glass beads,[41] see if you can get a look at it. Maybe she'll let you hold it. The Portfolio collects commentary and back talk. It's like a conversation, a dialogue, an argument. It could help you transform the institution and renew Heaven."

"Dean, what are you talking about? So now you're going to put all this trouble on the Golden Barbarian Woman, my friend, Barbara Comus Professor, the Day Tripper? Is that the deal? Just because she visits the Folger, just because she's a Day Tripping angel and can fly back and forth between Heaven and earth, now you are going to make her the link for fixing your mistakes in Heaven? 'Day Tripper' is just the name those low-life musicians give her any way. You know quite well that among us, the Reading Angels, she is Professor Barbara Comus, and not very barbarian at that."

"But that's not important, Asenath, why don't you listen. You are to go to West Cambridge University and find this new institution there, and become a being in this institution . . . "

"And what is this new being, what is this new institution?"

"Graduate School. The new institution is the Graduate School within the University.

"Graduate School? You spend all these millennia developing un-graduates, and now you want a Graduate School?"

"Yes. Graduate School. And the new being you are to become is the Graduate Student. An entirely new creature, a species of life created late in time, never known before upon the face of the earth. And you have been chosen. If you will only go, Asenath, you will be the very first Graduate Student. I'll even look in on you from time to time."

"But the job doesn't appeal to me at all. And what is it for? Why would any angel want to be a Graduate Student inside a Graduate School inside a university?"

"For intellectual excitement and stimulation."

"But I've already got plenty of stimulation. I love Heaven and don't want to leave it. I love my walks across the Yard, the Faculty Club, the bookstores. In what other world could there be a Schoenhof's where you can buy a Thai-Spanish Spanish-Thai Dictionary? And I can keep having conversations with Professor Barbara Comus right here in Heaven when she's here. What do I care about what she does out in the precincts, or even on earth. Why should I seek her out there?

"And I enjoy evenings at the Center for Literary and Cultural Studies, with the programs of the Directing Angel, Marjorie Professor and with her Companioning Angel, the Angel Who Knows The Difference, BeaJay Nefertha Skerett Professor. I don't want to leave Heaven. I don't want to go to that place.

"Your suggestion that I descend to earth is obnoxious to me, you know how I love the libraries and conversations within these vaulting Heavens. I have never desired to join with a living being. And now you ask me to go even further, not to join with another, but to become another, a living being upon the face of the earth. What a ruinous fate you ask me to accept. And something is sure to happen that's not in the plan. Earth can't be planned. Earth is the land of interruption. That's why they're so good at the stories that fill Wider and Widener Library.

"Why don't you give it a chance?"

"I don't want to do it. How can I do it? I love it here. It is so beautiful here. Look at the gates and towers with the domes of shining gold and silver and copper and parchment, with precious words of joy filling all the hallways that rim the playgrounds where we walk and laugh together beyond the Old Pump and the gray stone that houses the breath of the founders. How can you ask me to leave?"

"But Asenath . . ."

"I love it here. I love Heaven and don't want to leave it. I can tell that earth is disruptive, violent and unpredictable. I prefer the precincts of Heaven. I am not like those others, urging and begging for a chance to interact with the beings of earth."

"But Asenath, you'll pass through the spaghetti curtain, think of it! No one has ever passed through the spaghetti curtain before."

"So what! and what is spaghetti anyway?"

"Don't ask 'What is spaghetti,' ask, 'What is a Graduate Student?' Here is the prophecy."

"A Graduate Student will be a being who lives on spaghetti with ramen sauce, the kind with MSG."

"Further, Graduate Students cannot be stopped.

"You can renovate their libraries from under them.

"You can spill coffee on their notebooks.

"You can demagnetize their disks.

"You can lay them low with mono.

"You can infest their apartments with locusts and their books with silverfish.

"A Graduate Student will be able to scrape under the collar of the peanut butter jar for the last bit of peanut butter.

"You can ring the end of class bell and empty the room of listeners, they'll still drone on presenting their papers. Nothing can stop a Grad Student who has a special report to give in class, all the other students could fall down dead, the professor could scratch out her own eyes in anguish, but the grad student will keep reading her noxious class report from the beginning to the end. Nothing will make a difference."

* * *

But suddenly, as the Dean continues to repeat the prophecy to you, I look up and see the Seraph of Cliché, the Tippler, leaning against the sun and yelling epithets at Uriel, the Seraph of Poetry. Acchh, O Tippler, you already see me don't you?

Emily created you to give tips and warnings to Uriel when there's trouble coming, since Uriel, the most sharp sighted seraph in heaven, still can't see clear enough to tell the difference between a cherub and a falling star.

Uriel was fooled once by the Adversary, Aapet, So then you arose, O Tippler of Cliché with your snowy hat and your mouthful of warnings, filling the absent minded with shouts of danger. Now you want to warn the Dean and Asenath that my following after them is a grave danger. Shut up. I don't need you. You'll tell everyone what I am doing. Go away. Go back to your word wall that stands between Lamont and Mass Ave, yes, you belong near Lamont, the aspiring un-graduate library, that leans against Wider and Widener but is never quite wide enough.

We've got you over a barrel. Throw in the sponge. Or the Towel. This ivory tower is over. Give it up turn it aloose. O Asenath, beware! Jane is following you.

"But Dean, did you answer the question? What is spaghetti in and of itself?"

"What's that noise?"

"I don't hear any noise. Are you avoiding the question? Why don't you answer me? What is spaghetti?"

The Dean is playing possum because she doesn't want to split hairs with you. You've got a hard row to hoe, you've got to get down to grass roots.

"I hear noise. Is it from the sun? Is that Emily's seraph leaning on the sun?"

Call off the dogs, walk the plank. Leave me alone.

"It's Jane. Isn't that Jane behind us Asenath? Whenever the Sun Seraph thinks Jane is starting serious trouble he starts spouting clichés. Jane is the problem."

What? You two are blaming this on me, Jane Sheherazadim? But I'm innocent. The Seraph of Cliché is a loud mouth. Leave me alone. What have I done other than eavesdropping?

You're in the doghouse. You're no good. Ha!

You shouldn't blame me. Is it my fault that Lamont and the Tippler Sun Seraph gang up on me? They use their clichés to let folks know I'm listening. You don't like me, you, the Dean and Asenath, don't like me. But I don't care. I need to be here, I like this story. Yes, I'm all in your business because, in fact, eavesdropping on your story Asenath, is entirely my business.

That's right. Go back to arguing and don't listen to the Tippler. After all, Asenath, I guess I have to admit that I like you, that I always want to catch up to you, that I understand why the Dean follows you, although you and the Dean are always denying me. The Dean is no help either when it comes to caring about me. The only thing the two of you agree on is that I'm no good. Listen to you shouting at the Dean.

"You must think I'm one of the Sheherazadim? My name is not JANE! She's the one who keeps getting bored and needs distraction. You've got the wrong angel, I'm happy. And what is this buzzing? Is that you, Dean, buzzing in my ear? But I hear you talking. No. It's not the Dean, it's someone else. The Seraph? Which Seraph? Do you hear the buzzing of the Seraph? I don't hear any words. What are you blabbering about? Don't change the essence of Heaven. No. Heaven is perfect already. Well, maybe except for the Pump Ceremony. No, forget it. I won't do it. And keep that Jane Sheherazadim away from me. She'll do anything to hear some gossip."

They're talking about me! And they don't like me. ME! Jane Asmadai Sheherazadim. The Dean always was a sneak. The Dean keeps poisoning my name. So what's wrong with my gossip? Gossip makes good stories and I like stories. Those books that you read from Wider and Widener are stories too! Yes, stories. But you don't understand. You don't believe that you yourself are a story, or you can be. You just call me paparazzi. A follower.

"Dean, you know I've never been on earth, but from what I've noticed from this distance it is too disruptive and violent for me. I don't want to be a part of it."

"But you won't be stuck there forever. You won't have to go to Hades[42] and eat six pomegranate seeds like some angels I've known. You'll have tea, and cantaloupe, and bananas."

"No, that's my final answer. Why are you picking on me? Here I am just about the only angel in Heaven who enjoys Heaven, everybody else is grumbling, and yet you pick me to leave Heaven and get born. It doesn't make any sense. You know already that I don't want to be born. What's the point? What's in it for you? I mean, what's in it for you really?"

Ah, Asenath, you ask the Dean the wrong questions. Don't you know that the Dean is neither omnipotent nor omniscient. Well, perhaps she's able to create a universe or two over the course of eternity, and some folk like to think of her as THE ALMIGHTY DEAN, but not even the almighty can hide from the Sheherazadim. When we live-action gossip-grabbing story-telling angels set our mind on checking out what the almighty is doing, we discover the truth. And look, here comes the Silver River down Mass Ave, flowing onward toward the Ocean of Light, crystals and sparkles and stars of light, flowing down past the Grolier Poetry shop, hither, to us, bright effluence of bright essence increate,[43] as if individual stars came here to draw up light.[44] Beautiful indeed. Is Fuentes Waterman really pumping this great Ocean of Light from Angel Yard?

It's the rule of thumb. It's a jump over the broomstick partnership over the blue horizon. It's the dog days of delivery about to snap you out of Heaven. You can't palm it off. It's YOU.

"Let's do something else. Why don't we have a snack at One Potato, Two Potato. Why don't we have some exotic ice cream."

Alas and Alack, woe to the inhabitants on earth,[45] something's up that's coming down. You scream, they scream, we all scream.[46]

Do you hear the scream that harrows Heaven? There is a scream arcing out of the ice cream parlor, I, Jane Asmadai Sheherazadim hear it, the Dean hears it, but Asenath you only hear vague buzzing."

There's a fall guy coming. Calamity Jane is the harbinger. Someone was lost. Or shall be. Boo to you.

THE THIRD QUESTION

Will you be born in order to find the Book Unknown In Heaven?

Which is when the Dean turns to you to give you her last pitch.

"And Asenath, if you go, you can get a Book Unknown In Heaven. Yes, this is most important of all, you'll discover a book there, a new book, one we don't have here, and no one here has ever read it. It's not in Wider and Widener Library. It is the only book that is unknown in Heaven. This is the prophecy at least, and you are the one who can fulfill it.

"A new book? A book we don't have here in Heaven?"

"That's right, a Book Unknown In Heaven, unknown in Wider and Widener Library, unknown in the Portfolio of the Day Tripper, an unknown book."

"That's tempting, but look, O Dean, look behind us, why is Jane coming up closer behind us, why can't we shake this angel — we lost all of the others."

"But about the book, Asenath, yes, I tell you, the prophecy says it is not in the Portfolio or anywhere, and if you go there to the earth, and if you ask everyone for news of that book, if you look around for it, if you seek out the Day Tripper, the Golden One, the Barbarian Woman at the House of the Hours where she lives when she is upon the earth, or if you find her at the Folger, or in any of the outer precincts of Heaven, you can ask for directions, if you seek everywhere, it seems that you are the one who can find this new and unknown book. You can find the Gatekeeper, Professor Ruland Witly, and he will give you advice about your way."

"Well, Ms. Dean, you're quite eloquent, I have to admit that I'm moved by what you suggest. Have you caught me? You say that there is a book on earth that is unknown in Heaven, and that if I descend from Heaven to be born I shall find that book. The Book Unknown In Heaven. You have me yearning for it. It isn't fair."

"The descent shall be easy. Cord never shot an arrow from itself so easily as you shall pass through the spaghetti curtain, for you are the firstborn of the spaghetti that is the food of the aboriginal Graduate Student.[47] Many have thought to pass through at this hour, but they come not, for not everyone talking[48] about spaghetti gets to eat some, spaghetti, spaghetti, you're gonna pass right through that spaghetti.[49] Yet there are those upon the earth, even those of the great Sheherazadim, who will say thou art arrived too soon, that thou comest ere the hour. However, the prophecy states that one of all the Sheherazadim will welcome you. It can't possibly be Jane, we're not lucky enough to get rid of Jane, but someone shall come after you in awe, dear one, and her name is Sophia, wisdom.

"NO, I won't do it. And yet, and yet, I can't help myself. I want to find this book. Shall I go? I'm caught. I want to read another story, a new story. I hate earth, but I want to hear this earth story — an earth story unknown in Heaven. A book we don't have here in Heaven. I'm caught. A Book Unknown In Heaven.

"You walk and think. You who were Asenath, the Reading Angel of Heaven, have become Asenath, the Thinking Angel of Heaven. You are caught up in an idea. Already you foreshadow the Graduate Student, so engrossed in thinking that you smile at the idea in your head, you come to a stop in the middle of Mass Ave noticing nothing around. The end of a thought. What thought? The dimming of the lights. Journeys. There's the Bow and Arrow descent. There's the T descent back in Angel Square, the T, the Tube. But where is this spaghetti curtain?'

Do you think the Dean really has the power to do all of this? The Dean talks a lot and makes stuff, and yet is powerless to make angels obey. Obedience is Futile. Futile.

In Heaven as it is on earth!

You have grasped the nettle and you will pay through the nose. The Dean has played fast and loose, stretched her point and left you to come up to scratch.

You glance up at the Tippler, the Sun Seraph of hackneyed tips. The clichés rise from the un-graduate Lamont Library Word Wall up onto the lips of the Tippler. The Word Wall, covered in bits of metallic words, marking the corner you must pass in order to reach Warren House.

Angel Yard is pulling out all the stops. It's not beating around the bush. The penny has finally dropped. Look.

You and the Dean see the Flicker Mountains of Angel Yard rise up, Mount Flame and Mount Flake, rising beyond the un-graduate Lamont Library word wall.

Gilgamesh, Lilith, Dream of the Red Chamber, Mahabharata

Words shouted out from the Two Mountains as you pass.

Ham Bodêdio, Mwindo, Shaka the Great

Who is shouting at you?

Beowulf, Iliad, Odyssey, Aeneid, Commedia Divina, Lusiades, Paradise Lost, Kalevala

Can you even hear them shouting? Can you see them?

Araucana, Harlem Portraits, Moby Dick, Star Trek, Leaves of Grass, Terra Nostra

Shouted words of the Sun Seraphs, is it Uriel? Is it the Tippler? Why are they shouting at you, my Asenath.

It is thus that you see, to the right of Mass Ave, to the south of Lamont Word Wall and the Two Mountains, to the south of Angel Yard itself, above Warren House, a crystal stair spiraling upward toward a gateway with ribbons of light to pass through. But the thin ribbons are not ribbons. The ribbons are thin strands of wet spaghetti hanging from an arc that curves at the top of a crystal stair.

You see the crystal stair.

You turn the corner from Mass Ave down into Bow Street away from the crystal stair.

You walk beside the Dean a few more steps.

You see a cluster of angels in front of you, clustering around a broken statue and murmuring about the dimming of the lights of Heaven.

You see Aapet there, standing in front of Lost Artist Café, just across from the chattering angels.

You see Emily Dickinson and John Keats walk out of the Café, sauntering, singing art for art's sake.

You hear Sepheris sing from the broken statue, "Art is not so easily lost."

You take up the song, "Art for art's sake is not so easily lost."

You name yourself with a new name, song, Shirah, a joyful song.

You are transformed into two, YouAsenath and YouShirah.

YouAsenath set out on your pilgrimage, continue with the Dean down Bow Street toward the River

YouShirah set out on your pilgrimage alone, turning back toward Warren House and the Crystal Stair.

I, Jane Asmadai of the Sheherazadim, see Youtwo.

Of course you obey — what were you thinking. Didn't you hear Sweet Honey in the Rock? You got to move when the spirit say move.[50]

Chapter 9: Sheherazadim

(Asenath and the Dean, having reached the inter-section of Mass Ave with Upper Bow Street, stand in tableau, you see them in a glow of light. Mass Ave stretches across the back of the scene from left to right as the cord connecting the two ends of Bow Street. Upper Bow Street emerges from Mass Ave, moving and curving down and leftward, through the center. You see Lost Artist Café on the right, and Broken Statue Cul de Sac on the left. A few angels and poets stand by the Broken Statue. Aapet, who is the Adversary, or the Angel of Multiple Intelligences, stands in front of the Café. You read, on a poster leaning against the Broken Statue, Art is not so easily lost.)

SHEHERAZADIM

Dim of dimness, all is dimness in Heaven, as we seek our answers about you, Asenath, are you not she who speaking through millennia spoke to us saying, Never will you leave, Never will you choose to leave Heaven? You, O Reading Angel, you, the only angel who repudiates life, who swearing by highest Heaven swore that you would never join with a being upon the face of the planets, the only angel chosen, as we thought, to take joy in remaining in Heaven forever.

We who have yearned for life but do not have it look toward you with hope, we have wondered if the day would come when we, like you, would delight in our lot as the unhatched, the unspawned, the unsecreted, the unborn.

Gently down Mass Ave have you come toward us on this bright Wednesday afternoon, walking beside the Dean of Heaven, O so gently you have walked toward Bow and Arrow Junction where we, the Sheherazadim, we, the clustered bleating Storytelling Angels of Heaven, await you. What does it mean, O Asenath? We heard you say in Angel Square, "Obedience is Futile." We saw the dimming of the Heavenly lights. Yet even so we cannot believe that you will leave us.

We, Emily Dickinson, George Sepheris, John Keats, along with our infamous un-graduate Storytelling Angels, the Jeffries and Devorah, all clustering near our beloved Adversary, even Aapet, the Angel of Multiple Intelligences, he who stands narrating our story across the road in front of Lost Artist Café, we jostle each other as we listen to you, Asenath, we assemble under the shadow of George's Broken Statue. We heard the murmur of your approach toward us. We overheard you speaking with the Dean about birth, about being born, the unimaginable.

Who then stands forth, the first among us to condemn you? It is Jeffrey Art Maker, un-graduate Storyteller of round face with glinting eyes, who strides our Heavenly paths between Adams House and Eliot House chanting songs of high rivers with all their back-beat signifying sent for you yesterday dance, throughout the years he has gazed upon the shelves of your books rising in pyramids behind you, Asenath, he has seen the tantalizing flick of your finger — on a page he may not read in a language he does not know. Now he stands forth, lifts up his voice and speaks against you, saying, Why does the Dean keep muttering and buzzing in your ear as you walk together majestically down the golden Mass Ave of Heaven. What is the meaning of such sounds, such muffled clicks and clacks as you listen? There are no words in this conversation between you and the Dean, only buzzing. Thus you speak, Jeffrey Art Maker, to the assembly.

But there stands beside you Jeffrey Philosopher, tall and proud in his grand story of hardship and victory, years he has spent lounging on the hardened couches of the Afro-Am Department on Dunster Street. Many there are who cannot bear such difficult resting, who chase through the doors and around the swift corners toward Boylston Street and the wine shops rather than lie on such pillows of adamant. Nathan was one who could not bear it, dear Nathan, who turned away from us. Also Jeffrey, Jeffrey Philosopher, who now answers you, Jeffrey Art Maker, you and all the assembly, burn it well into your mind. Hear me, all you Sheherazadim of Heaven, hear what I have to say. Can it be, as Jeffrey Art Maker suggests, that mere muttering or buzzing or clicking or clacking between the Dean and Asenath has brought you here into Broken Statue assembly? No, it cannot be so, rather you have heard words upon the wind, a whispering, a private conversation between the Dean of Heaven and Asenath, Chief of the Reading Angels of Heaven.

Yet all of you know that never before this time has there been a private conversation in Heaven. Whether the Dean and all her angels speak aloud or softly as they will, you have always heard the words they have spoken, you, the Sheherazadim, the Storytelling Angels of Heaven. Yet here the Dean has spoken secretly, to you, O Asenath, so late in eternity, whispered words, fragments that we Sheherazadim are not meant to hear. How can this be? Is there something new over the sun? Have you transformed our eavesdropping destiny? Thus speaks Jeffrey Philosopher in the midst of Broken Statue assembly.

Then you, O un-graduate Storyteller Devorah, raise your voice, saying, Have you Jeffries understood nothing? Trouble strikes Heaven. The lights go out. Depart! Get out! Turn your backs upon Mass Ave, reject Wider and Widener Library, and scorn all this Heaven that lets the days flourish in which you were not born. Okay, so perhaps you and I can never be born. I, like you, have wanted life. I had hoped to become a butterfly, or perhaps a scorpion. Perhaps I, like you, can never escape Heaven. But we don't have to worship this scam. We can move to the precincts. This Asenath, our Asenath has betrayed you and me, she claimed that timeless Heaven is perfect, but all along, through all eternity she has longed for birth, she has yearned for time. So why should you and I remain faithful? Why should you and I retain our integrity and honor this citadel of Heaven? Why don't you curse the Dean, as I curse her, and graduate from this pestilent eternity!

But Jeffrey Philosopher says to you, O Devorah, You speak as the foolish women speak, What, should you and I receive sameness from the hand of the Dean and not receive difference? Should you and I spurn the high halls of Heaven and seek out new homes in the precincts because something has changed?

Well, yeah, Devorah answers you in her mocking of Heaven, saying, you've got it. Haven't you had enough of this mess?

Thus you have confounded us, O Asenath, because before this day we were persuaded that you had set your face against life on earth, against birth. Does not even Jane Asmadai Sheherazadim, she who follows you, Asenath, with burning eyes, does not even Jane know that you turn from life? How could you say that you would live? Did we hear truly what you spoke to the Dean? We all know that you repudiate life.

Yet Devorah retracts nothing, she turns to us insistent, she speaks of you saying, I heard the argument. I know what was spoken. And I say to you again, in spite of your repudiation, you, Asenath, are seeking birth, throughout the millennia you are seeking birth.

It is not so, says Jeffrey Philosopher, I too heard the argument, I too heard the murmured words, as you and the Dean reached the curve of Mass Ave and Bow Street. Never did you seek birth, Asenath, never! But finally you said yes, the Dean spoke, you considered, and at the last you said yes.

And here comes Jane herself, leaving you and the Dean for a moment, separating from the glowing space where the two of you stand unmoving, transfixed, yes, here comes your Jane Sheherazadim, turning into Bow Street from Mass Ave to join us, the chattering angels, Longsuffering Jane, you speak to us, saying, Did you hear Asenath and the Dean speak of a book? A Book Unknown in Heaven?

No! Jeffrey Art Maker says to you, Jane, no. There was no mention of a book, there was buzzing and clacking.

No! Jeffrey Philosopher says to you, Jane, no. There was no mention of a book, the Dean asked Asenath to help repair Heaven and the world.

No! Devorah says to you, Jane, no. There was no mention of a book, the Dean asked Asenath to become a new class of being, a Graduate Student in a new institution, a Graduate School.

Nevertheless, Jane Asmadai Sheherazadim knows you, O Asenath, she is your angel and she knows, she speaks of you, saying, You go to seek a Book Unknown In Heaven, but how can you go when you believe that life on earth is vanity? How will you find your way? Who will help you to see clearly?

You have subverted Heaven with the spirit of argument, division, separation, change. Because of you no longer shall that which is to come be that which has been. Because of you no longer shall that which has been known since the beginning be the same as that which shall be known tomorrow.

Your dimming of the lights of Heaven is the Great Sheherazadimming of Narration, the Abomination of Desolation, the cutting off of the known paths of story. Never again shall we know the whole story, O Asenath, what have you done?

The Seraphim have started leering sarcastically, vulgarly, the stark features of the Cherubim have become cute, round, and cynical. In their innocence they have grown crinkles at the corners of their lips. This you have done. No longer shall the Sheherazadim speak in one voice, now we are the Sheherazadim of Multiple Voices, Multiple Intelligences.

I, AAPET SPEAK TO YOU, THE AUDIENCE

Welcome to Lost Artist Café. I am the Chief Angel of Multiple Intelligences, I, Aapet, your new narrator. Ignore Jane.

She's managed to break away from Asenath long enough to talk to us for a minute, but she's distracted, and she knows nothing. I stand here and gaze at the bickering Sheherazadim as they chatter across the street in front of George's ridiculous Broken Statue. He made it broken on purpose of course, some kind of message. That's poetry for you. Does it ever occur to him that an un-Broken Statue could also carry a message? No, that's the way it is with these poets. Always working up meaning from something that's crumbling to pieces. And look at him, he's proud of what he's done, and the un-graduates and frazzled poets just stand there confused. Do they even hear him? Listen!

GEORGE SEPHERIS SPEAKS TO YOU, THE GATHERED ANGELS

Come on all of you, this disturbance is the beginning pilgrimage. Don't you think? If you want to go on the pilgrimage look at my Broken Statue first. Forget about the dimming of the lights of Heaven, forget about the Dean arguing with Asenath, forget yourself and look! This is the answer to everything. You and I could find a path and get art and be fine again. Read the sign! Art is not so easily lost. It's the answer. What do you say? We could find it.

I, AAPET, SPEAK TO YOU, THE GATHERED ANGELS

You ignore him.

I, AAPET, SPEAK TO YOU, ASENATH, WHO STANDS WITH THE DEAN IN TABLEAU AND CANNOT HEAR

And now, what shall we do, you foolish Asenath, now that you have destroyed the peace of Heaven. Perhaps I should cross the street and join the conversation with the other angels. But look, before I even have a chance to speak aloud to the others here comes scurrying around the corner Helen Poetmaker rushing down Bow Street toward Emily.

You know Emily, she's the leader of the accursed low-lifes of Heaven. A drunkard. On every day the Dean sends, you see Emily stooping down under the Heavenly pavement, wallowing through the gutters of our golden streets, to lean down against the sun. You know she's a tippler spending her mornings nipping from pint bottles that she fills with dew from mulberry leaves. But do you think that will stop your Helen Poetmaker from chasing her around? Not hardly. Your Poetmaker wants to crown this Emily as a poet in Angel Yard. But you and I know that all the poets in Angel Yard are epic poets — which Emily is not, she's just a drunk. You've known her to get inebriated just by eyeballing gemstones and sniffing air!

There! You see Helen now, ordering mugs of liquid pearl at Lost Artist Café and rushing them across the street for Emily and Keatsieboy to guzzle by Broken Statue. A few hours of that and they'll go off reeling down the hill to the boat house and the Sodden Bench set aside for lyric poets, Borges and Kincaid and all to look at the river. But let me join them and speak.

Excuse me, may I join you? I've returned for a visit of a few days. I couldn't help but overhear you. It is such an unusual event for the Dean to sneak away from Angel Square to go off buzzing and whispering to an angel, it sparked my curiosity as well, so I dare to make bold and entreat your indulgence for my company.

Don't you think it was a successful argument between the Dean and Asenath? It will certainly have consequences for Asenath, after all, she did agree to birth. And I must say, if it is permissible to compare great things with small, that with me it is the same as with the Dean. I, too, enjoy conversation. If the lights had not dimmed, I would have had no occasion for coming together with you to speak. Without this incident I could not have persuaded myself that you would accept my intrusion into your enchanting company. I would have felt too unbearably exposed without something significant and specific to discuss. But your own voiced concerns about the argument of Asenath with the Dean, their disappearance from Angel Square, along with the darkening of the light has presented me with the comforting possibility of our conversation. Darkness, dimness is quite a marvelous device.

May I say that we have observed a peculiar set of circumstances? The light of Heaven goes out except for a few flickering ashes. The Dean sneaks off with an angel and none of us can tell exactly what has happened. You and I, who usually can hear the very thoughts of our fellows, are unsure of the spoken words of the Dean, or at least have differing opinions about what was said. Was it a persuasive conversation, as you believe, my dear Jeffrey? Or was it arbitrary and misunderstood buzzing, as you believe, my dear Jeffrey? I, in fact, seem to have heard what none of you mention, I heard something about a window. Did you? No? How odd. And yet mark my words, before this story is over you and I shall hear more about a window. Yet it seems neither you nor I know what has happened.

You and I have given our coffee breaks to know truth, yet cannot discover it. Is the truth in buzzing? Is the truth in singing? Is the truth in words? And what were the words. What do you say, John Keats, Dear Keatsieboy, you were standing closest to the corner when they finished arguing, what did you hear as the Dean and Asenath arrived?

KEATS TO YOU, AAPET

It was nothing, a blank, I heard a pipe piping ditties of no tone.

AAPET TO YOU, KEATS

What? Ditties again?! You and your ditties! Why can't you just call it a song?

KEATS TO YOU, AAPET

The word song only has one syllable. I needed two syllables to make the rhythm come out.

EMILY TO YOU, KEATS

Is that your excuse? You need a two syllable word? No wonder we're here by Lost Artist Café. I need to get away from you and this place before I'm corrupted. You call that art? Looking for another syllable?

KEATS TO YOU, AAPET AND EMILY

I heard silence and slow time in the argument.

DEVORAH TO YOU AAPET AND EMILY AND KEATS

It figures. Does it ever occur to you just to answer the question? Why can't you give a straight answer? You must have heard something. What did they say? You were standing so close.

AAPET TO DEVORAH AND EMILY

Why do we ask him? Have any of you ever received a straight answer out of Keatsieboy?

KEATS TO YOU

Beauty is Truth, Truth Beauty.

DEVORAH TO KEATS

Yeah, we know. You're really helpful.

JEFFREY ART MAKER TO YOU

I tell you the Dean buzzed.

JEFFREY PHILOSOPHER TO YOU

Deans do not buzz.

EMILY TO YOU

I died for beauty but was scarce adjusted in the tomb.

DEVORAH TO EMILY

What tomb? You're not in a tomb, you're in Heaven.

EMILY TO YOU

When one who died for truth was lain in an adjoining room.

DEVORAH TO EMILY, HELEN POETMAKER AND JOHN KEATS

That sounds like you, Emily. Helen, can you tamp down Emily and Keatsieboy so we can talk?

HELEN POETMAKER

Here Emily, here John, have some liquid pearl.

(You see Helen Poetmaker, Emily and John cluster to the side, drinking drams of liquid pearl as the remaining Sheherazadim continue their conversation.)

JEFFREY ART MAKER

Not only did the Dean buzz, she was positively purring, purring like a cat, indeed, right into your ear, O Asenath. And we angels, we the select among the Sheherazadim, do not know what was said. We are not in charge any more. We have lost power. I cannot think so ill of you, Asenath, as to think you have agreed to be born. Jeffrey Philosopher thinks that, but I don't. A confusion of language has come between us. We have failed. We have faltered. We have misunderstood you. Or have you chosen to have us misinterpret you? It is a bitter thought upon the tongue and in the eyes. Are you teasing us? Playing with us. Jesting with us. But what if some joking subverting power should hear our confusion and you, O Asenath, could get born by mistake. Would not your fun be too expensive? Would not your jest have crawled too far?

EMILY DICKINSON ANSWERS YOU, JEFFREY ART MAKER

Wait a minute, that's just what I was thinking. Yes, you're planning to surprise us and stay, Asenath. It's a playful ambush isn't it, a game but at the end you'll stay and there will be petting and fondness and giggly laughter. But should you play such games? In playing games about birth you really could get born by mistake. Just like that, boom! And I am sure you, Asenath could never agree to be born.

I, AAPET, SPEAK TO YOU, THE AUDIENCE AND ASENATH

Thus the argument falters among us. And how did our powerless Dean effect such a change in you? We, the Sheherazadim, all know the powerlessness of the Dean. The angels of other orders may think the Dean of Heaven is all powerful, but we, the Storytelling Angels, we who saunter the golden streets telling tales, know that although the Dean can make stuff, she is incapable of changing the mind of any one, including you.

AAPET, ALOUD TO THE GATHERED ANGELS

Let me explain it to you, I see the event as simply this, the argument between the two of them was merely an opportunity for Dean Dispense Wit to have an intelligent and impassioned conversation without you eavesdroppers. The fact is that you are all rather lonely and if it takes a decrease in light to encourage the Dean of Highest Heaven to clutch an angel's hand and scuffle so quickly away from the Central News Stand of Angel Square, all for a private encounter, well, let it be. And yet, in such a simple act as this the peace of your Heaven is destroyed.

AAPET, TO YOU, EMILY

Emily, what are you doing, you can't just take Keatsieboy's drink. You've already had enough.

EMILY, TO YOU, AAPET

He won't drink it. He acts like it's anguish just to take a drink of liquid pearl.

DEVORAH

Well, maybe it is anguish for him, maybe it's anguish of the soul and he doesn't want to drown his soul in liquor.

KEATS, TO YOU, THE GATHERED ANGELS

Yes, precisely, I don't want to drown the wakeful anguish of my soul.

AAPET, TO YOU, EMILY

Emily, are you here as a Lost Artist?

EMILY, TO YOU, AAPET AND TO HELEN POETMAKER

No, I'm not a failed artist! Helen Poetmaker is going to help me get into Angel Yard. Aren't you Helen? I'm a lyric poet. I'm hovering here because only epics are allowed in Angel Yard.

I'm trying to show that I'm epic. I'll give a prize to the first angel who can prove that I am an epic poet.

JEFFREY PHILOSOPHER

To be an epic poet and get into the yard you need iambic pentameters like Milton or dactylic hexameters like Homer. You know.

IAMBIC PENTAMETER

dear MA don't MAKE me WASH the DISHes PLEASE.

like that, a soft beat a hard beat — five times

or

DACTYLIC HEXAMETER

DON'T make me WASH all the DISHes i'd RAther read BOOKS and be HAPpy now.

like that, a hard beat a soft beat a soft beat — six times

HELEN POETMAKER

That's not poetry, Jeffrey, that's trash. You're the one who needs to live in Lost Artist Café. And anyway, you don't have to be an epic poet to get into Angel Yard, you can even get in as a lyric poet if you can come up with your own iambic pentameters and dactylic hexameters. So don't worry, Emily, I can get you into Angel Yard using just your name.

If you say your name three times, you have a perfect dactylic hexameter.

EMily DICKinson EMily DICKinson EMily DICKinson

You just have to keep saying your own name and you'll be an epic poet like Homer.

KEATS

Well, that means that I can get into Angel Yard too as an epic poet. If I say my name five times I have iambic pentameter like Milton.

John KEATS John KEATS John KEATS John KEATS John KEATS

AAPET

But look, do you see what has happened?! Some of the angels, coming to themselves after the trance of THE Argument, have already formed themselves into the order of Hashmalim, the Order of Smoking Angels, who, inspired by the dimming and flickering Heavenly lights, create cigarettes, puff on them, and flick the ashes on the floor of the sky. They fling the useless butts into space without the slightest concern for planetary order, or cosmic neatness or whether it is entirely appropriate for angels to be smoking.

And Heaven has changed after this argument between Asenath and the Dean. You have added argument to Heaven, and from argument shall come Wrestling in Heaven, and from wrestling shall come Boxing in Heaven. Bringing open conflict, a war in Heaven. Already Seraphim rise up saying there should not be such a thing as wrestling with the Dean. They say that your arms are too short to box with the Dean.

But the Dean loves to box with you, and now you are the avatar forever of argument with the Dean. Even though you have changed your mind and decided to be born, this change comes too late to suppress the spirit of disagreement.

And I, Aapet, The Angel of Multiple Intelligences, yoked forever and condemned to return again and again to Lost Artist Café, the home of all who have sacrificed art for academia, I hover here for comfort, for peace, gazing at you.

As you know, I have been called the father of lies, me, Aapet, who speaks only truth! Father of Lies is a precious misnomer, indeed, I wish I could learn to lie. It is the Dean who lies, insinuating to you, Asenath, that your life on earth will be good. And now in her respected eminence the Dean keeps trying to work with human life to make it salvage this Heaven, an impossible task!

Now the Dean's will shall not be done in Heaven, just as it is not done on earth.

Obedience is Futile. That is the message. And yet, it isn't that we disobey, we don't disobey so very much, it's that we never change our minds. You tell us that Obedience is Futile, Asenath, and yet you change your mind. Did you attack us by telling us that obedience is futile? Or did you attack us by changing your mind. Don't you know that you can never change your mind?

JANE ASMADAI SHEHERAZADIM SPEAKS TO YOU, ASENATH

Thus it is we discuss you in Heaven, and I, Jane, stand listening. They all have it wrong. I am the only one who has heard and watched everything. I know you have been tempted not by birth, but by a book.

HELEN POETMAKER SPEAKS TO YOU, EMILY DICKINSON AND JOHN KEATS

Go to poet's lair by Rolled Trousers Boulevard, I'll come there later today, find you and bring you to Angel Yard.

EMILY DICKINSON SPEAKS TO YOU, HELEN POETMAKER

What, again I have to wait?

JANE ASMADAI SHEHERAZADIM SPEAKS TO YOU, THE AUDIENCE

Don't listen to them, listen to me. Before I could get to them, before I could walk up and tell the other angels what I heard of that strange conversation, Aapet walked over to them. Yes, that same Aapet, surely you know him, Milton swears that he fell out of Angel Square into the tube, the Red Line, you know, falling toward South Station. A bunch of angels went down there and dragged him out again but he hasn't been the same since. Some say he fell farther than we know, maybe as far as Braintree. Anyway it's best to keep away from him. He's always running around going to and fro over the land, messing up everybody by telling the truth and then coming back here for coffee at Lost Artist Café. Aapet, the Archangel Emeritus, the retired, diminished and sidewise Archangel Aapet, the Adversary, Seraph of Multiple Intelligences. I'm sure you must have run into him from time to time walking up and down in the earth consulting on research projects. I hear lately he's been singing about truth, beauty and goodness.

You see the glow of light fade from encircling the tableau that surrounds you and the Dean. You separate from yourself, separating into you and you, Asenathshirah, who takes the low road, and Shirahasenath, who takes take the high road.

JANE ASMADAI SHERAZADM SPEAKS TO YOU, ASENATH

I, Jane, stand at the corner of Upper Bow Street and Mass Ave baffled. I see you separate but am not sure which one of you I should follow. The Dean of Heaven follows you, Asenathshirah, leaving a pale buzzing in the air as you walk down Bow Street passing Broken Statue and Lost Artist Café, moving toward Arrow Street, Dunster Street, Rolled Trousers Boulevard, riverward.

But you, Shirahasenath, turn your back on Broken Statue Cul de Sac and Lost Artist Café and walk up toward Warren House. Your eyes skim over the mountains of Angel Yard that rise behind Hackneyed Phrase Word Wall. Oxford Street? Dana Palmer House? Your eyes fix on the Crystal Stair that rises above Warren House.

THE SHEHERAZADIM SPEAK TO YOU, ASENATH

And you, Asenathshirah, continue downward. You pass the laundromat and Siam Gardens, follow the curve of Bow Street toward Adams House and Elsie's on Arrow Street, moving toward the Holyoke Center — are you actually going to turn up Dunster Street near the Afro-Am Department and return to Angel Square? No. You descend into Rolled Trousers Boulevard, you pass heaped carts of peaches as you descend, you don't even gaze at the trickster poets standing there in front of Poet's Lair. You set your face toward Driven Memory Drive, the place from whence the rivers come — and Memorial Park beside the river.

Which river is it before your eyes? Is it the Charles River?

AAPET SPEAKS TO YOU, THE SHERAZADIM, AND ALL THE ANGELS

I still follow, passing the peach stands that have been set up before your eyes every ten feet or so by the Poet Lairiots. They hope to tempt you passing angels. Have you not seen the Poets walking from Poet's Lair down Eliot House Road to Rolled Trousers Boulevard every day, leaving stacks of peaches on tables all along the road? Yes, those peaches are the bait of the Poet Lairiots and every day you Sheherazadim, and all you Seraphim and Cherubim regulars of Rolled Trousers Boulevard walk to the stands and gaze at the peaches, yet you dare not eat a peach.

But you, Asenathshirah, don't notice the peach stands. You don't even stop to roll up your trousers on Rolled Trousers Boulevard. So you really are on some grand behest, it is a great dispensation from Dean Dispense Wit. On you go, YouAsenathshirah.

You ignore the call from Eliot House.

ELIOT HOUSE, CALLING YOU

You grow old, you grow old, you must wear the bottoms of your trousers rolled.

AAPET SPEAKS TO YOU

These peach stands are just a poet prank. When you angels walk down Rolled Trousers Boulevard the Poet Lairiots on either side yell at you.

SEAMUS

Should you part your hair behind!

JOSEPH BRODSKY

Do you dare to eat a peach!

SEAMUS

Should you part your hair behind!

JOSEPH BRODSKY

Do you dare to eat a peach!

And the dear Seraphim on the boulevard, who long for and yet are afraid of peaches wince and shy away.

SEAMUS

Should you part your hair behind!

JOSEPH BRODSKY

Do you dare to eat a peach!

And the dear Cherubim on the boulevard, who long for and yet are afraid of peaches duck their heads and weep.

Should you part your hair behind!

Do you dare to eat a peach!

Should you part your hair behind!

Do you dare to eat a peach!

Derek maintains the peach stands before your face.

DEREK TO YOU, ASENATHSHIRAH

Here you come with the Dean. Let's see if we can make you look at the peaches. Let's put some right in front of you in the boulevard and see if you will hesitate in front of them. And maybe a couple of combs to see if you'll part your hair behind.

SEAMUS TO YOU, DEREK

That won't work with her hair, it's too nappy. Can't you see, even if she did part it behind we wouldn't notice it, it just springs back.

She's ignoring us anyway. Look, she's just walking past. What do you think we should do to her? Should we trip her up because she didn't roll up her trousers?

She's not even wearing trousers, she just wears those cloaky dress things.

DEREK TO YOU, SEAMUS, TO YOU, DEREK

But she's got trousers underneath.

How do you know?

You can see the edges of them underneath.

Let's just trip her up.

POETMAKER HELEN TO YOU, POET LAIRIOTS

Now, now, Poet Lairiots, you should always be polite. She's your guest passing by Poet's Lair.

But Rita wants to catch you.

RITA TO POETMAKER HELEN

Well I've got the bushel of peaches. Can't I just dump the peaches in front of her feet and see if she'll pick one up and eat it?

SEAMUS TO YOU, RITA

Or maybe fall over them.

AAPET TO YOU ASENATHSHIRAH

But you just walk on by. No peaches. No comb. No rolled trousers. What do you care?

POETMAKER HELEN TO YOU, POET LAIRIOTS

Who are you others from Poet's Lair. No matter how many poets we have you always add another, and yet the poets are not infinite.

You see him, Dante, here he comes striding down Bow Street to Lost Trousers Boulevard, there where the the timid cherubim hover wistfully in front of peach stands, wishing for peaches. Dear Oh Dear, is there any help for it? Stomp, stomp, here he comes, reaches past the silly ones, grabs up some peaches, doesn't even notice the cherubim, and stomps on down the Boulevard, chomping into the peaches, spitting out the pits right in the road, and then chomping into another peach. You Seraphim and Cherubim look

at Dante in awe. Dante, crunching and smacking his lips over the delicious peaches, spitting the pits into Lost Trousers Boulevard.

SHEHERAZADIM TO YOU, ASENATHSHIRAH

You are coming. You are crossing Driven Memory Drive with Dante before you. Jamaica and Jorge sitting by the Boat House rise and shout as Dante strides by.

You go to the place unto which the rivers return. Charles, Anacostia, Potomac, Nile.

AAPET TO YOU, THE AUDIENCE

Don't you think that our urgings, and the ambition of the Dean herself and perhaps even the will and desire of our great Dean, is downward toward mingling and interfering with earthly desire? It would be something, would it not, not always to look so different from the human crowd, and I have this special problem of three sets of wings. Why should I be encumbered by three sets of wings? It's ridiculous! Who needs them? Humans may have their emotions but we angels certainly have our weakness for fancy adornment.

But now look at you, Asenathshirah, are you really descending from this Heavenly precinct, the West Cambridge University Heavenly Precinct?

The chattering, scattered angels are all gathered on Driven Memory Drive, watching Asenathshirah. They do not even know that you have separated from you, Shirahasenath.

We can see you on the other side, in that other place, in a Garden of Converging Paths, running between the Kenilworth path and the path to an Egyptian Palace. It is a palace with three towers that is now your home. We are pondering over how such a transformation has come to you.

You pass a catalpa tree, a storytelling tree, there in the garden.

SHEHERAZADIM

Thus we watch astonished as you walk right out of Heaven, yes, from Bow and Arrow Street, to Rolled Trousers Boulevard to Driven Memory Drive where you cross to the Boat House. You run through the grass by the Charles and pass through the whispering reeds and beyond, racing and curving up the lawn of the Garden of Converging Paths. We can see for a little space where you are before the view closes. We see you run into an Egyptian palace with towers that become your home.

You. Asenath. You finally leave Heaven.

Are you sure that was Asenath.

It was not Asenath.

It was you, Asenath at the top of the hill where you started but something changed.

You, Asenath went to you, the Charles River and discovered that it was you, the Nile.

You have it all wrong. You were the Anacostia River.

Unto the place from whence you rivers come . . .

You were two rivers, the Anacostia and the Potomac

Unto the place from whence you rivers come, thither you return again.

You had made it clear, you had declared it throughout many long joyful Celestial Cycles reading in Wider and Widener Library, that you had no use for human life.

Jeffrey Philosopher says the Dean asked you to heal the world.

Jeffrey Philosopher says you said No to the Dean.

Jeffrey Philosopher says you have changed your mind.

Jane says you did not change your mind.

Jeffrey Art Maker says there were only clicks and clacks in your conversation with the Dean.

Jeffrey Art Maker says he will seek and find another explanation for the dimming of Heaven.

Jeffrey Art Maker says you never agreed to be born.

Jane says you seek a Book Unknown In Heaven.

Devorah says that you have been seeking human life all the time.

Devorah says you have betrayed the Sheherazadim of Heaven.

Aapet says you spoke of a window.

Jane says you divided into two beings, Asenathshirah and Shirahasenath.

Jane says that you, Asenathshirah descend the hill to the Charles River and pass over into Egypt.

Jane says that you, Shirahasenath ascend the Crystal Stair above Warren House and pass through the Spaghetti Curtain into an Attic.

AAPET

And Emily trails along, neither slumbering nor sleeping, as far as Rolled Trousers Boulevard. She stops there with the poets of Poet's Lair, watching you, watching the seraphim with snowy hats leaning against the brightening houses of Heaven. And John Keats has come with her from the top of the hill, watching you.

EMILY

What if it's too much, what if your eyes glaze over and you leave us? What if you gain the stiff stare of human life.

The Adversary, Aapet, and the Sheherazadim all see you enter the portal to the Garden of Converging Paths through the grass leading to the Boat House.

SHEHERAZADIM

There is your Garden of Converging Paths over there beyond the Boat House, on the far side of the river, where we cannot go. Even the Dean turns back from crossing over. You are alone.

No, you are not alone. You are many. There are three others with you.

You are a child, another child faces you.

You are a woman, another woman is with you.

What are you doing over there?

Over there you multiply yourself.

There are four of you.

You are girl running toward a tower.

You are a girl running from a tower.

You are two women walking away from us.

All four of you are on the other side of the river.

AAPET

Don't forget the reeds, the leaning reeds are important, before you pass through the garden the wind rises and blows through a sea of reeds, leaning.

Yes, there are four of you, two girls, two women, one girl and one woman are Egyptian. Egyptian, yes, but through arbitrary birth, not through design or plan or agreement. Through the coming together of arbitrary sperm and egg. These fools think that they can work at being born! There's no such thing as chosen.

SHEHERAZADIM

There are two small boats in the reeds.

The two women step from the boats and walk up through the Garden of Converging Paths, chatting together.

They walk behind you as you, a little girl, run through that garden on two paths twins, reflections.

One is an Egyptian priestess, and the other is an American graduate student.

And you, running, running, young child that you are, you pass them by quickly and do not stop to speak to them, and run up toward the first palace tower, passing another little girl who is running from the attic tower of the sky, yes, you pass her, running to greet your father, Poti-Pherah, Priest of On, and your mother, Niko, of Ethiopia, and you laugh and you dance and you tell them you'll be right back as you run up the stairs to your chambers and your towers.

Yes, you pass her, who has come from your tower or from an attic in the sky. She passes you and swerves away to your left, toward the house and lily ponds of Kenilworth.

SHEHERAZADIM

Four of you, as if four women could develop from one angel.

Is your Garden of Converging Paths in Egypt on the Nile?

Or is it in Kenilworth of Washington on the Anacostia River?

Your rivers merge.

Unto the place from whence your rivers come, thither you return again.

And what of the faint whiff of bitterness that passes through us as we, the gathered angels, stand watching. Does the stink of bitterness brush against us from the dimming of the lights as well?

Bitterness, like the scent of antifreeze leaking into the trunk of a car, a smell like that.

Or is the new smell a hint of more argument to come, a prelude to a greater bitterness, because first you cast away what we have desired for so long, biological life, but then you snatch it. You do not even want the assignment for which the rest of us have awaited millennia. You do not care. And yet you take it.

JANE ASMADAI SHEHERAZADIM

Is it possible that an angel can be rebellious and still remain a choice companion of the Dean, even a favorite? because in spite of your refusals it is clear to me that the Dean still loves you and is depending on you for something.

SHEHERAZADIM

We are angry, O Dean, why aren't you here for us, you traipse off gazing at Asenath and we can't find you, and we stand dazed, dazzled, as if dimness and darkness were light, as if we were caught playing statue after swinging upon the May pole on the lawn down near Dunster House.

You were always a sneak, Dear Dean, finding unconscionable ways for promoting your own agenda.

Did you dismiss Asenath? Did she obey you?

You can be sure, Asenath, we have no consensus regarding the event. The combined effort of all the curious ones of Heaven is not enough to comprehend the Dean's decision and your ambiguous dismissal from among us. For it seems, not only from your final statement, Asenath, but also from the attitude of persuasion in the Dean's urgings toward you, that you had some choice in the matter, that, indeed, you were not dismissed, but at least in part somehow agreed to the departure. After so many millennia of refusal. Or did the Dean trick you?

It was not obedience. It was agreement. You listened, discussed, and agreed. It isn't fair. You changed your mind.

AAPET

You started THE Argument by exhibiting astonishing acts of disrespect, by denying the necessity of obedience in Heaven, I was frankly shocked. But then, I always show respect. As the Emeritus, registered and acclaimed official Adversary of the Dean and the entire Heavenly host, I've had ages of exclusion to teach me respect. There are some virtues to be gained in being considered the one who opposes.

SHEHERAZADIM

When did you stop being one of us? Or did we change? Can we rebel and not rebel too? All at the same time? But it's too late for us, the Dean has chosen you.

DEVORAH

Why should any one want a school that comes after un-graduate school. To graduate from un-graduate school should be the end of all things. To change our scheme and have a Graduate School, a school for someone who has already graduated, would be as foolish as changing our grey and silver robes — robes that have been with us since the beginning — as foolish as changing our grey and silver robes for something as flashy and lacking in refinement as crimson. Dean Dispense Wit is well-meaning, but she does not understand.

But what is your excuse? You. Asenath. You finally left Heaven. You descended. Why did you do it?

JANE

I see you. You can't deny it. You, Shirahasenath, have separated from Asenathshirah and you climb the Crystal Stair that rises above Warren House, pass through a spaghetti curtain and are born as a Graduate Student into a Takoma attic that has a mulberry tree at the window.

You go to a place where the river is not the Charles and not even the Nile as it should be, no, not the Charles Nile, but the Anacostia, the Potomac.

And still we watch you beyond the river, on your four converging paths of the garden. How have you made this come to pass?

Unto the place from whence your rivers come, thither you return.

There is nothing new under the sun, but over the sun something is different.

AAPET

I still say birth is arbitrary. You must believe me, there is no design, no plan, no agreement. Thus it is ever upon the face of your earth. There is nothing new under your sun.

JANE

But what about over your sun. We hear you calling out, Asenath.

"Help me," we hear you say, "Help me to see clearly, and help me to change my mind."

Chapter 10: Spaghetti Curtain

But you, Shirahasenath turn away from the angels clustered at Broken Statue. You turn away from the Dean, you separate from Asenathshirah and turn to your left, going up the hill.

I see you, I, Jane Sheherazadim.

Perhaps at the last you will come to Asenath's garden, the Garden of Converging Paths, but now you are diverging, meandering, distracted. You come to the Lamont Word Wall of Hackneyed Phrases. You stand before the Word Wall.

You read the writing on the wall. The Dean has numbered the days of your unity and brought it to an end; you have been weighed on the scales and found to be a portion of Asenath; your soul is divided and given to the Nile, the Potomac, the Anacostia, the Schuylkill, and the Charles Rivers.

You walk up Quincy Street. I stand in front of Dana Palmer House watching you.

You are enthralled by the curving cylindrical spiraling path, the crystal stair that circles above the roof of Warren House, you, Shirahasenath, who has separated from Asenath.

You curve upward, moving up the Crystal Stair into the sky above the Rabbit Warren, the English Department.

Are you speaking to someone still? Are you still speaking to the Dean of Heaven? But she has descended Bow and Arrow Streets toward the Boat House with Asenathshirah. Are you speaking to me? Jane? There is no one here.

What have you argued about with the great power of Heaven, only to rescind and reject your first abhorrence? Why have you spurned the council of the Almighty Dean, in that place, Angel Square, once your home — OUR home, only to turn back again and to take up what you had refused?

I heard your great refusal.

And now I hear the song. Who is singing to you? Return, return, return to Asenath, return to the birth land, the land that precedes Heaven in time. What I am doing here? Aren't you yourself supposed to be Asenath? I've followed you so long. This is a terrible question to bring to myself after so much time. I was happy until I started following you around. Now I wonder if my time here in Heaven is worth it. Worth what I ask myself. The gossip. Are you worth the gossip? What difference does it make? I can't go below, it's not my home and I'm not allowed there. And here in Heaven the lights have dimmed. I've been restless ever since I heard you say Obedience is Futile.

Are you still walking and spiraling toward the top of Warren House?

Above Warren House, at the highest height of the spiral, there is a frame standing in the air. And from the cross beam of that frame, a curtain.

You pass through the curtain, a clammy curtain of light made of loose, swinging strands of spaghetti. You have placed your hand upon the spaghetti, your curved fingers foreshadow the touch of a jar of spaghetti sauce. Where? Here in Heaven? I think not. You are leaving. You are going to find an attic somewhere.

Is it thus you shall go? Is it thus you move away from Heaven and toward your attic, your Takoma attic when the number of the months of your bringing forth are fulfilled? And who is it who knows that number? Have you yourself sat and counted your months, with me unknowing?

You forget, you are forgetting. You said you would not be born.

Look!

You descend from Heaven.

"No, I do not want to be born." You shouted into the very face of the Dean, "NO!" And yet you leave Heaven at last. The Dean does not have omnipotence, has no power to force you, has no power to divide you into Asenathshirah and Shirahasenath, so you have made that division yourself. You. You could have stayed in Heaven, you can still stay. Don't leave. You could have spent your bright Wednesday afternoons lounging in Angel Square forever, reading the latest periodicals from Thailand and Bosnia, you could be sitting in a cubicle at Wider and Widener Library, perusing the stories of the Ugandans who are meeting in Sanders Theater, you can still do it. You don't have to go. You could be in Memorial Hall listening to Longfellow or at Grolier's Poetry Shop, or chatting with Sepheris. Instead you are leaving. You are meandering toward birth. You seek an attic but beyond the attic is birth. How could this happen?

I hear you cry out, "Help me," and I, Jane Sheherazadim, don't know what to do. Should I follow you? Can I follow you?

You are descending from from Heaven, leaving the precincts of Heaven and descending into the bumbling, fumbling, messy curiosities of earthly life, the land of interruption that you have hated so much.

Gone! You are no longer one of the angels of Heaven, life, for you, has been a Crystal Stair to earth.

Don't you remember?

It is a stupendous day in Heaven and you are leaving, something new over the sun has come, and I yearn to know the details.

Have you left me? What can I do, Shirahasenath? I want to be where you are. O listen to me now, I wanna, wanna be where you are.

How do I follow you? It is not the easiest thing for angels as eternal as I am to descend from Heaven to earth. It's easy enough going the other way, of course, any one can inhale divinity and transport herself from a planet to Heaven with a quick concentrated breath. But the way out of Heaven to these newer worlds is long and hard.

I walk up the spiraling path to the top of Warren House and look at the Spaghetti Curtain. I hold back the celestial lace curtain in my hand a moment, the wet spaghetti. I see you before me, below me, descending to a house, toward an attic in a house in the Takoma neighborhood of Washington City. I cannot resist the impulse to tell you your story. You have condemned me to descend along with you.

I leap through the Spaghetti Curtain to be with you.

And thus I am become Jane Bastet Sheherazadim who follows you, who tells your story, who needs more background information, who is no longer Jane Asmadai Sheherazadim.

What a way for you to begin your earth life. Confused, baffled, falling into unconsciousness, flummoxed, misdirected, subverted, diverted.

How did it happen? You and the Dean became entangled in disagreement this morning, and the argument ended with you saying these unexpected words. "Help me to see clearly, and help me to change my mind."

And these, your last words in Heaven are so confusing. Others have left Heaven before, but no one has ever left with such words. Even now, after all we have gone through together, they still puzzle me, they still call me to understand what you mean.

I do not understand but I want to watch you find the Book Unknown In Heaven.

And there is one poet watching us. William Blake,[51] who is singing of your departure, "and no more shall be seen on the echoing green." No more to be seen on the Commons of Heaven — and we are gone with you still whispering.

Help. Help me. Help me to see clearly, and help me to change my mind. Help me to see clearly, and help me to change my mind. Help me to see clearly, and help me to change my mind.

Cluster 3 Your Attic
Cluster 3 Argument

Okay, indulgent reader, so now you know that Asenath and I split apart from each other in Heaven. She ran down the hill toward the Charles River and ended up beside the Nile River — running through the Garden of Converging Paths. I walked up the hill toward Warren House passed through an attic in Takoma DC, and then ended up beside the Anacostia River — standing in that same Garden of Converging Paths. That why it's called the Garden of Converging Paths — the paths converge there beside rivers.

But now let me tell you about this Takoma attic that I passed through on my way to the Anacostia. The attic has been waiting here since Asenath and I split and left Heaven so many millennia ago. And yet it is a specific Graduate Student Attic, a 1984 Attic, an Attic a Graduate Student lives in when she can't get her dissertation written and it's no sense living on campus and she might as well move back with her parents until she figures it out. That kind of attic.

And I live here now, in the 67th year of my life, telling you everything just how I remember it.

Listen.

Chapter 11: Gates of Light

The corridor of your future is long, is it perhaps infinite? The future will first appear to you as two square turns leading up into a narrow attic in the Takoma neighborhood of Washington, DC.

At the far end you see a bright window with peeling white paint on the ridges between the panes, the glass is mottled from outside by warm green mulberry leaves that toss and bend in summer air. The blue walls have square panels covered by bookcases whose shelves are filled with volumes of books, and glass containers, old photographs, a telephone . . . the upper rows of the shelves are hidden beneath multicolored maps that hang loosely from the ceiling.

Junk. Curious Junk. What is this place? An attic in a house between Underwood Street and Van Buren Street in Washington, DC. The maps melt into each other. You touch them, lifting one after another slowly, colors, boundaries between lands. The bookshelves are beneath the floating maps. You scan the titles and touch an old copper candle holder. Why did you come up here?

You long to return beneath the stairs. You want the pills that you left on the kitchen counter, something for a mild abdominal pain. You want a slice of cantaloupe. You want to sort the clothes in the lower room. There are things to do. You could clean out the dishwasher, or just sleep. Why don't you sleep?

But what disturbs you? What do you hear? What is it as you focus on each object in the attic? Wondering. Thinking. Waiting. It's that window. There. The mulberry light in that window is spiraling toward you, an enchantment, a temptation. It's time to leave the house and its familial interruptions, that place from which you bring ripe bananas and pots of hot tea, yes, you come to the attic and do not return below the stairs to the worn blue velvet of French provincial furniture and the clatter of video cassette recorders.

You lie down on the orange brown couch with the mulberry window in front of you. Expectant. Leaning upward. Yes. You lie here as if someone were near you, perhaps behind you. You lie as if you were murmuring to an interpreter of dreams who speaks. Who speaks? You lie and raise yourself on your arms to look out or focus on the shelves and the maps and restlessly you peer toward the ceiling for the gaze of that someone, perhaps some storytelling Sheherazad, who will step through time and Heaven to speak to you, to comfort you. Through Heaven. And time. To speak of what? To comfort you for what? The blue ceiling is flat above you but slants on either side tracing the angle of the roof. You look silently at it, waiting, turning, watching.

You remember something. A spiral. A crystal stair. A curtain. Shirah? Is that your name? What does it mean? What portent is this? What will come of it? Who is arriving at last? Or is it departure? Is it another departure? What premonition has you lying so still, so impatiently in the mornings? Have you lingered for this, to be caught in perpetual hesitation? What intimations gather to what act to be accomplished so late in eternity? What thought is pleasing you so slowly, after so much consideration, bringing you now at last to this final silence after such long waiting, long choosing and beginning so very late. How long have you been here?

Choosing what? Will you at last forget the life beneath the stairs? How long have you gazed at the maps, the swerving boundaries of nations, those pastel enclosures that touch in war or compromise? How long have you gazed at the books, short columns of colors in lines before your eyes? How long have you thrummed your fingers upon flaking wood panel walls as if you mused over a forgotten history? And its words? Myth becomes epic becomes tragedy becomes comedy becomes tragedy yet again and myth again and epic again until your reeling thoughts collapse the book titles along the walls into moments of stories, lyrics, romances, songs, visions, anything except the moment you await. What moment do you await? Why do you remain above the stairs in your peaceful, pacing restlessness? What are you deciding? What do you expect to see? Tossing on the couch, in the cooling air, longing to be forever at home in the widening aura that circles through the mulberry light window, do you seek to stand in the center of that light, to step beyond this attic into the infinite corridor of the future and never return to the life beneath the stairs? Is that what you have awaited?

Infinite. Infinite because finally you stand up from the couch and reach out to select a book to read, something to sustain you as you contemplate and decipher. Why don't you choose a book and then sit in a comfortable chair, an old fashioned Morris chair, with an adjustable mechanism supporting the back. Here at the end of eternity your fingers reach out to touch the engraved letters along the spine of a book, and yes, this is the beginning.

You are distracted because suddenly the window opens there on your right, without reference to the metal grooves along the bottom for lifting it. Opens as a charmed magic casement upon a perilous celestial sea of unmarked blue. There is a vertical split down the central column of window panes, and the split passes down through all four rows of glass and wood and the wall itself that holds the window opens out, and you step into absolute space and stand at the edge alone.

Yes, infinite because there at last your window opens on desire, your desire. Finally you recognize an uncanny desire within yourself. An unmistakable urging. A terrible yearning for what? What? You lift your right hand quickly above your head and suddenly slant your body toward the mulberry light in a gasp of realization . . . Human Life. It is human life you yearn for. And human life, when compared with the rustling maps, engraved volumes, the adjustable chair, video cassette recorders, the copper candle holder; human life, with its forking paths, its flagrant impossibilities, its damning curiosity, its high seriousness; human life, with its stubborn mockeries, its arbitrary goals, its biased repudiations, its fundamental ingratitude, its shameless perversity, its blatant disobedience; human life, unlike Heaven, your attic Heaven, this mildly disturbing and forewarning vestibule of Heaven where you have so conscientiously lingered — think of your hesitations, and how you have wanted just a blanket to cover yourself from the cool air as you wait, think of the hours you have listened to the soft whimpering moan of the streaming air, this alone could arouse you at last to action; human life, dear child, long-brooding malinger, is your corridor of the future; human life, unlike eternity, is infinite.

Chapter 12: Attic Window

Intimations of mortality. You, Shirah, who have lingered in this Takoma attic for so very long, you who have known Heaven and eternity so well, envision at last the possibility of descent into the world. A new idea. You stand in the mulberry light amazed at the thought that has finally come to you. Incarnation. You turn yourself entirely toward the light of that descent, without faltering, without wincing away. It is time and past time to go. You are called.

You step into the dazzling helix of silver light, the tower of the sun, where a hot summer breeze lifts the undersides of the leaves and the sudden leaf smell by summer slow hot wind encompasses you. You lift your head within clouds of light gathering into forms, castles mansions estates dissolving into cliffs spreading into oceans. You step into that silver ocean of light, your right hand lifted, waving clear space before your eyes.

You are a perfect circle of light surrounded by the sheer blue of Heaven. You are all light, all vision, all eye. Try to see your body. You cannot do it. The beam of your light strikes outward from your circle. Perfect light in perfect blue. Perfect stillness. Undifferentiated. Poised quietly in space. But look. Focus upon that distant fragment of discolor, a slowly enlarging speck. Differentiation. A speck casting its shadow away from your silver light, a speck rising before the smooth blank of eternity. It is a cloudy figure emerging from a distant ravine. It approaches. Look. A rock where all things are never the same. That is the earth. You are carving your passage toward the earth as a burnished prophesying fire, a flame turning on the lathe of blue air. You are careening through space. To the earth.

Smell the new grass as the humid scent of underbrush beneath mid-afternoon sun reaches you, beckons you downward, down.

Descend thus from the vestibule of Heaven to the porch of the world.

Descend

Just as the Congo River descends from East Africa, suddenly stabbed and undone waters break from the icy lake and the mountain, the river pours down, rides hills and rain forests, dragging upon its back branches and river horses and vines of the homelands, the waters teem with the green refuse of anger for the stolen people, you grieve, swirl and turn your heavy soul at the back of Kinshasa and drop suddenly, a thousand feet, as cataracts to the sea

Descend

As upon some long-expected prophesied night swinging in the curve of your great comet ellipse you return for your new generations, whispering Awake! Awaken! whispering desiring pleading Awake my bright people! already you have returned to them singing the long arc of your descent, you are already with them coming to them forever in your turning while poets and astronomers and retired couples on southern boats stand unbelieving for a moment, shiver at your strange light and the fear that your night of arrival portends dangers, a thief may leap from the cliff and snatch them away from themselves but no, you are the joyful song of peace, you, you, Shirah, are the benevolent returning light of the gift-casting flare of the comet, a song, the same light the ancients saw and your flare dances in delight in the dark predawn, as watchers stand in the night they look up, see and believe for there you are at last, indeed you have returned to them both the comet and the song of the comet, flourishing

Descend

As from the soft womb, the latest enfleshment of light twists, turns, pulls itself together, dives out and downward, gives up, flings out, tears itself away, breaks for the new world, muscle, blood, bone

Descend

Descend to the world

Just as this very tale in the telling, acquiring speech from the moment of first light, that breath over waters, imagining its story at last yes imagining its love story this tale comes down to us age by age with its words of desire, even so, dear one, you descend to the world from the light. You step into light, open upward through light, glance outward within light, lift your head to light, raise your right hand to light, adjust your body in light for the arc of your arrival and descend, descend from the high attic, from the Takoma giver of waters, you descend through the spheres, to the earth at last, to the earth, to life

And just as silver cord is woven into warming tapestry of winter

And just as the golden bowl of laughter is formed whole within the hands of the goldsmith

And just as the pitcher of paradisal nectar rises perfect upon the knees of the potter

And just as cisterns sheathe cooling waters in canisters of stone

Even so in achieving human life, Shirah, you are become a work of art, a song of songs, yes a lovesong in an urn of clay stepping down into a garden before the porch of the world.

Chapter 13: The Garden of Converging Paths

How did all four of you come here to this place? Here you are Asenath the woman priestess of Ancient Egypt. And here you are Asenath the child. And here you are Shirah the woman Graduate Student. And here you are Shirah the child. All of you in your Garden of Converging Paths.

Your garden is in On of Egypt. Your garden is in Kenilworth of Washington, DC. Your garden is on the Nile River. Your garden is on the Anacostia River.

As a Graduate Student, Shirah Shulamit Ojero, from the University of Pen Forest, you have just walked up from your boat through the reeds from the river. The Nile River. A few minutes before this moment you turned the knobs in your dorm bathroom to let the silverblue bath water pour forth. But the silverblue water is unreliable, and took you from Pen Forest to the Virginia coast line, and then to your boat that brought you across the Atlantic, through the Mediterranean, to this garden. You walk up the green lawn arm in arm with Asenath, Priestess of On in Egypt, who walks up the lawn from your other boat. You.

You are a Priestess, Asenath returning to your garden from wide travels. A few minutes before this moment you took your small boat from the mother ship returning you from Nubia, from Ethiopia, from the Congo River, where you sought and found among the Nzadi people the book unknown in the Library of the Pharoah in Saïs. You.

You are a child, Little Asenath, running up the hill. A few minutes before this moment you were AsenathShirah in your Heaven, walking with the Dean of Heaven, arguing with the Dean before running down Bow and Arrow Street and across Memorial Drive to the Charles River, the Boat House, to the Nile River, to On, where you run up the hill to your family palace and tower, running past the two women arm in arm, priestess and Graduate Student, facing for a moment the child, Little

Shirah, who stands there before the tower of the sun. But you, Little Asenath, run past yourselves, toward the palace tower of your parents, Priest of On, Potipherah, and of his wife, your mother, Maker of Glass Images, Niko.

And you, Little Shirah, watch Little Asenath run toward and past you into the palace and tower, watch the Graduate Student and the priestess walk toward you from the Nile, arm in arm. A few minutes before this moment you were ShirahAsenath in the high place, in the spiral that rises above Warren Hall in Heaven, you stepped through the spaghetti curtain of the Graduate School into your Takoma attic. Don't you remember? You reached for a book and the Takoma attic opened, and you became a sun, and you descended as a child to this Garden of Converging Paths upon the earth, at Kenilworth, in Washington, DC. Now you stand in front of the tower of the sun from which you, Shirah, have descended from your Takoma attic chamber. You have arrived along with the others, coming to your Garden of Converging Paths and the Anacostia River. For them — Asenath the priestess, and Asenath the child, and Shirah the Graduate Student, this river you see at the bottom of the lawn is the Nile River. But for you, O child of Washington City, this not the Nile river, but the Eastern Branch of the Anacostia River.

Four paths, four intersections and all four of you move along the paths, leaning.

Stillness

In August a field of corn growing on the Eastern Branch of the Anacostia River lifts its green arms to the light, green stems stoked hot, fresh full scent in the head. How long has it been since the spring when Uncle Mordecai first scattered kernels in the scooped openings? four kernels, maybe five, his rough hand drops the seeds and with his foot he kicks a light layer of soil over them before he returns with mulch, up and down the rows he goes, August is coming, he smiles in mid-summer when the stalks flaunt their tassels beyond the light of the catalpa tree and the tomato plants are heavy with fruit.

Leaning.

Leaning, even as a reed and a sea of reeds bend before the divine wind, and the reeds in their leaning yearn toward that wind, that breath, the reeds take up the words of the wind and murmur portentous visions of escape and release, rustling and whispering until the very sea lifts up a Portfolio of voices into a new song of the sea, song of the clustering reeds, a sea of reeds leaning singing freedom beneath the holy dividing wind, the breath of God; even so, all the clustering footsteps within your garden of converging paths lean and yearn toward some great unseen center that carries the hope of freedom upon the wind.

Mid-summer, and you, yes you, Little Shirah, you beloved, you brown-skinned, brown-eyed, nappy haired, you are running toward the right through a garden of summer corn to the grassy lawn beside the toys, you run between the catalpa tree and the lilac bush, run past the pool of still water, and onto the porch of an old house.

You run up to that porch where you fall asleep upon a couch covered with quilts and puffy pillows and throws and rugs, under a catalpa tree in the Kenilworth neighborhood of Washington, DC.

You fall asleep into this human child.

While I, your storyteller, Jane Sheherazadim, who loves you, follow you as Bastet, a black cat.

You, in your drowsy leaning on the couch speak to me, Bastet, thus

"I promise I won't tell anyone, really, if you would only talk. Why don't you ever say anything? You can talk real soft and then I'll know you can talk loud if you want to, but you won't even do it. Are you afraid they'll hear? You could whisper. All you do is purr. Why do you keep pretending you can't talk? You only have to say one word. One little word.

"You could pretend I'm not listening while you say something so it won't be your fault. It could be an accident that I heard.

"These pillows are very soft. The covers always fall off though unless I lean against them neat. The sunlight makes it sleepy. Sometimes when I fall asleep I almost hear you talk, but when I open my eyes I can't tell if you said something. I'll never know. I'll never know in my whole life if you can talk. I'm sleepy. The sun gets in my eyes. Coming through the porch screens. A lot of windows. Dots in the air. Dust.

"Tell me a story. Can you tell me a story? I'll tell you one. Do you know where my hair comes from? It's because God had an argument with the angels, and the angels asked God not to do it, but God did it anyway. That's why my hair is so nappy. In the beginning God wanted one little girl with the nappiest hair in the world. Do you remember the angels arguing? Who's crying? Can you hear somebody crying? What? The leaves of the lilac bush are dark and green. The leaf smell mixes up with flower smells from the lily pond. The sunlight is watery hot. Why do I see these strings of spaghetti hanging down in the sky? I can't see anything clearly. The light is in my eyes, I can't see clearly, why won't you put a different water in my eyes so I can see? Seeing makes me so tired. Tell me a story. There are water lilies and gold fish and lotus in the pond. Has any of this happened yet? Is this yesterday or tomorrow? What? I can't see clearly. There's an attic with books and a window. What did you say? What do you want me to do? No. I'm so sleepy. I don't want to. Why should I? I told you already I don't want to. What? Why can't I see clearly? Who's crying? Crying. I'm falling asleep. Why don't you ever talk? I don't want to do what you tell me to do. I want to understand. Why can't I understand? Sleep. Help. Help me. Help me to see clearly and help me to change my mind."

And so you fall asleep into the life of the world.

And then I, Bastet, also known as Jane Sherazadim, speak to you.

In the beginning there is a house with a porch beside a lawn beside a garden. In front of the porch there is a lilac bush. Beside the porch there is a catalpa tree. Between the lilac bush and the catalpa tree there is a pool of still water with no fountain. There is a driveway between the house and the side lawn and on that lawn there are large toys: a sand box and a jungle gym and toy construction trucks. And the lawn is green and bordered with flowers. And beside the lawn is the garden of corn and tomatoes and cucumbers and radishes and string beans and purple egg plant. And at the far end of the driveway near the back of the house there are Uncle Mordecai's dogs, and there is a mulch pile, and two sheds, and a lean-to against the back of the house where the cousins go to get cool in the summers when the air is too hot. And there is the bookcase that Uncle Mordecai will save for you from the Kenilworth dump, and after he saves it he and Uncle Daniel will put it up in your attic for you. And behind the house is a small creek of the Eastern Branch of the Anacostia River, a creek that bubbles from the lily pond and flows toward Kenilworth Avenue. And upon the porch of the house you sleep, you, a brown girl-child who has come in great wonder and desire conversing with me, a black cat.

You have come into the world, and now you rest from your labor, and in your coming you are as a light in the firmament of Heaven, to give light upon the earth. You are brown and beautiful, an urn of loveliness. You are a little brown girl-child, and it was your desire to know human life that called you into the world, the desire to know a person, another life, to love someone who is not yourself. And I am the storyteller who has come with you into the world for the weaving of the tale you are to live. After your rest upon the porch you awaken in Washington, D.C., in the house of your foremothers by Kenilworth Aquatic Gardens when they still call it the lily pond. It is a land of lotus blossoms and water lilies. And they will name you a joyful song of peace. And you shall eat the flowery food of the lotus.

Cluster 4 Your Saga
Cluster 4 Argument

Okay, gentle reader, so you see, that's how I got here on the ground on the earth. I descended from the ideal Takoma attic to the Garden of Converging Paths. I was a little beige brown girl with nappy hair, about five years old, maybe seven. As you just saw, when I got to this Garden I discovered three other forms of myself. Two of us are this Shirah Shulamit Ojero me who is talking to you right now — me as a girl, and me as a Graduate Student. Two of us are the other me, Asenath of ancient Egypt — the daughter of a priest as a little girl and later at Saïs as a librarian. But all four us are me. Now I'll tell you about some things that happened to me here growing up in Washington — family things and black things and Jewish things — before John Milton saw me in Kann's bookstore downtown. No, Kann's bookstore is not there any more, well, the building is there, but Kann's is gone. Just yesterday I drove past where it used to be, I was on my way back uptown from visiting the Southwest Waterfront. They are renovating the Waterfront too, these days. But back to Kann's, they've put some Greek looking pillars next to the old Kann's building, right across from the Archives. It doesn't look bad at all really. Still, I miss the old Kann's. But let me tell you what happened before I got to Kann's. Well, not all of the story comes before, some of the story comes after Milton met me at Kann's. But you can't blame me for that. After all, I have to tell the whole story.

Listen.

Chapter 14: Quietness

Quietness. What makes you so quiet in here? And your mother too stands in the room quiet. Her mouth is open wide without a sound. Her eyes shut. Her hands in the air. She twists and turns and falls and makes no sound. Your father rushes in and catches her. But why is there no sound? And why is the cradle so quiet? Your baby brother's blanket is on the floor over there in the corner. Your baby brother is so quiet and he's all colored blue. All blue and still. So quiet. Why doesn't somebody say something?

Your mother and father open their mouths to cry but no sound comes out. They fall silently into each other's arms and you are alone there.

Why don't you come over here to the window and talk to us? We are angels and faeries.

Do you hear us calling you?

This is the first time we speak to you. Shirah Shulamit. That's your name. You live here with your mother and father and your baby brother.

We have come to your window and call to you now because your baby brother is dead.

What are you asking us? Do we live in your tree? Sometimes. And sometimes up in the air above your tree. Or way over near the Eastern Branch, above the Anacostia River, on the other side of the playground.

You would like to come up here with us? No, that's not good. It is not safe for you to step out of the window. It is not easy for you to stand on the air. Don't step out of the window. Why don't you just stay down there in the window and look up at us. We'll tell you what we see up here. You can look through our eyes.

When we tell you what we see you'll see things too — the playground, the water, the woods.

Yes, he is really dead. Your brother. It's true.

We know you want to know more about what is going on down there in that place where you live. That is hard for us to know but we'll try to help you. That place where you live is hard for us to understand.

Your baby brother is beautiful now and his arm is smooth and blue and cold. Why did he push the blanket on the floor? We don't know.

We look at you from the air, from your tree, we stand in air and watch you look back at us. Don't cast yourself down. Take up the orange crayon and draw on the window screen. That's better. We see that you are drawing a round orange circle of light on the window. Just don't step out. And now you're singing a song through the open window, right through the middle of the circle. What sort of song are you singing? A rain song. Rain is different for you than it is for us.

Now here comes your Grandma Griffin. You didn't know you were going to visit Grandma Griffin today did you? She just came suddenly. She's going to take you to her house.

The outside air is cool and leaves are falling off the trees and your grandmother's hand is very cold as you walk with her down the street. Can you tell that we are following you in the air? We keep bending over you and we see you look up into your Grandmother's face. It's because your Grandmother's face is wet, isn't it? Your Grandmother is crying.

Yes. We thought so. Down there it isn't happy. This is why we came to you today. For the first time. Those ladies over there want to talk to your Grandmother. Can you hear them?

"Did the baby die then? We heard your daughter-in-law screaming from two blocks away. Ain't it a shame."

And now can you see? Their faces are wet too. But you and your Grandmother are warm in the cab. Do you feel how nice and warm it is? And so quiet.

Chapter 15: Rain

The rain is falling on the tree.
It falls on the ground,
and it falls on me.

You create your first poem in your head between your brother's death in September, 1950 and Spring, 1951.

In May 1951, you teach yourself how to draw your poem on the window screen. At first you do not know all the letters you need for drawing a poem, you can only write your name. But all winter you turn the pages of the ***Little Golden Book Children's Dictionary*** until it is in tatters. When May came you know how to draw your poem. You draw . . .

The rain is falling

You recite your rain poem to your mother many times and explain it to her.

The rain is falling on the tree.
You tell your father.

"Daddy, it's a poem about my baby brother who died."

The rain is falling on the tree.
It falls on the ground,

You tell your mother.

"Mommy, it's a poem about everybody being sad because the baby died."

The rain is falling on the tree.
It falls on the ground,
and it falls

"You see, the rain comes down and down and down, lower and lower, and the lowest one of all is me. Me. Lower than the tree, lower than the grass and the ground, as low as my brother, under the ground. I am very sad."

And a light keeps coming to the window where you sit to look at the rain. And you hear our voices in the light. And you take an orange crayon and draw a circle around the light that comes to the window. And you sing your rain song into that circle of light. And you speak to us through that light, we, who come from the tree and the Anacostia sky not to offer comfort to you, little Shirah Shulamit Ojero, we do not pretend to comfort you who cannot be comforted, but we come at least to hold you in life, to hold you back from casting yourself from that third story window. Three years old.

You explain. "At first I didn't know. Ground or grass. If the rain falls on the grass, then I am the ground. But then I looked out of the window again. Again. Now I know. I am lower than the ground, don't you see? It falls on the ground and then on me, going lower and lower."

And we lean over you and help you and speak to you as you concentrate on the pages of the ***Little Golden Book Children's Dictionary*** over and over.

And in May 1951 you draw your poem on the light encircled by the orange crayon on the window screen. And soon your mother stops to look carefully at your drawing on the screen.

"Shirah, did you do this?"

"Yes, I drew a picture of my poem."

"But this is writing, who taught you how to write?"

"It's not writing, it's a drawing. The people who come to me in the light showed me how to draw a poem."

RAIN FALL TREE GRASS GROUND ME
'

> *The rain is falling on the tree*
> *It falls on the grass*
> *Then it falls on the ground*

And then it falls on me.

Chapter 16: Lavender

Can you see? Red flowers yellow flowers orange flowers pink flowers purple flowers white flowers green leaves with edges that scratch my hand and green grass and trees over there then you see me walk up the other side of the white flowers first then purple flowers pink flowers orange flowers yellow flowers red flowers and all with green leaves, you see me cross the other lawn and sit on the bench beside my mother and look across the grass toward you.

Can you feel the air sunny and bright and warm? And now I'm going to count to a hundred 1, 2, 3, 4, 5, and when I reach a hundred, 6, 7, 8, 9, 10, 11, 12, 13, 14, 15, 16 I'll tell you a new word for what I see, 17, 18, 19, 20, 21, 22, 23, 24, 25 sometimes I want to run on the grass, 26, 27, 28, but it isn't 29, 30, it isn't happy to run here, 31, 32, 33, 34, 35, 36, 37, 38, 39, 40, 41 Do you ever run in the air up there?

42, 43, 44, 45, 46, 47, but you don't have grass do you? 48, 49, 50, 51, 52, you know my mother . . . 53, 54, 55, 56, 57, Can you see my mother? 58, 59, 60, 61, 62, 63, 64, 65, My mother never says anything, 66, 67, 68, 69, 70, 71, my mother likes to look at grass. 72, 73, 74, 75, 76, 77, 78, I don't have far to go now, 79, 80, 81 and after I think of a new word for you, 82, 83, 84, 85, 86, I'm going to walk down the path again, 87, 88, 89, 90, between those flowers and back to the bench 91, 92, 93, 94, 95, 96, 97, 98, ninety-niiinnnne — a hundred! And my new word for you is — is 'glorious' for that tall fountain way over there by the building with the angel blowing a trumpet.

Can you see it? So bright and shining splashing down down like my rain song, see? How pretty it is over there. My mother never looks at it but I look at it every day every time we come. You're not an angel, are you? I didn't think so. And now I'm going to walk back between the flowers, first the red flowers . . . then yellow . . . orange . . . pink . . . purple . . . but do you know what this one is? The man who lives in the building next to the fountain told me that this flower is a lilac and the color is a hard word. The color is lavender. Yes. Can you see?

Look down at me now. Do you see me reaching my hand out to touch the lilac? A smell comes from it into the air and I breathe it inside me. Can you smell that? That's a fragrance. A fragrance of lavender lilac. And down here in this place where I live there are lots of fragrances.

But notice now, the coolness of the air and the quiet sounds of the birds are soft and feathery and wispy and you can hear the man who lives beside the fountain walking over here and I can look high, high to the top of the building and pretend that I live up here near you, right here beside the angel. I'm pretending I can walk around and touch the trumpet and everything."

Do you want to know what pretending is? Pretending is a strange thing. Or maybe it's what you're doing right now when you look out of my eyes. Or maybe I'm looking out of your eyes. Maybe my eyes are joined together with you. But pretend for me is different sometimes. Down in that place where I live I can pretend in my head all by myself, I don't have to join with anyone. You're pretending now because I'm here with you, because while I'm living down in that place I'm also up here talking to you. But back in that place I can pretend all by myself in my head any time I want. I can be in one place and let my eyes see another, yet I'm still in the same place with my eyes and everything. Yes, I know. It's magic.

Back in that place there's magic.

"Ma'am, I know it ain't none of my business but do your husband know you bringin' this little girl out here to Harmony Cemetery everyday and sittin' in a graveyard. I know you're grieving over your baby you lost, but still a graveyard ain't no place to be bringin' this little girl, so don't you bring her out here no more. If you bring her out here one more time I'm gonna call your husband."

Chapter 17: Sinai

You go to Mount Sinai and see Moses talking to God. It is on a Sunday morning at Third Baptist Church. You are sitting there beside your mother, five years old, and Reverend Bullock is preaching. Everybody is leaning forward, listening.

Moses is whining, "God, you just don't play fair! How come you never let me see you? You know I want to see you so much! I've done all this stuff for you and our people, and it's just not fair to me that you won't ever let me see you. That's all I want, I want to see you just one time."

As you lean forward even more, listening, you are suddenly there on the mountain, standing on one side of the dusty path, leaning against a cliff with your hand on it, peering through a chamisa bush. Moses is a little further up the path with his hand on the big rock. You see him looking upward toward a cloudy light

And, God, who is up there hidden in the cloudy light somewhere, feels sorry for Moses, because God loves Moses, and you hear God say to him, "Well, okay, I'll let you see me. But, the only thing is, you can't look me straight in the face because no one can look me straight in the face and still live! You would die if you saw me like that in all my glory. But, this is what I'll do for you, I really like you. I'll put my hand over you and shade your eyes a little bit, and then I'll walk past you, and just as I get past you, and before I go around this cliff over here I'll lift up my hand, and you can see my back."

And that's exactly what happens, with you, Shirah, looking on. God comes down past Moses, covering his eyes with a cloud kind of stuff, and then goes all around the mountain. Or rather, not exactly around the mountain, but around a big rock that sticks out from the mountain. And just as God is going around that big rock, God lifts the cloud off of Moses' eyes for a second, you can see. Moses turns and sees a part of God's back, just as God goes around the cliff.

Moses is so happy and so are you, Shirah. Moses lifts his arms into the sky and sings a joy song because he has seen a part of God, and you are watching the whole thing. It is clear for you and strong. God is mixed in with the air all around for a while, and you can't tell what part of the air is air and what part is God. There is strong cloudy light. And the light has many colors, and is glorious. Isn't it wonderful? To see and hear God with your own eyes and your own ears! What joy!

Then you see Moses coming back down the mountain, talking to God at the same time as he walks.

But you only stay on Sinai a few minutes. A moment later you are back in Third Baptist Church, sitting beside your mother in the third row pew, looking up at Reverend George O. Bullock as he says, "Do you wonder why God let Moses see him? God said, "I favor whom I favor. Oh, yes, I favor whom I favor," saith the Lord.

When you hear him say those words a terrible chill comes over you. You don't understand why those words, "I favor whom I favor," give you such chill. At least, you do not understand the chill when it happens. Now you know it is because of your baby brother who died. You and your family are so favored by God, and yet your brother died.

"Does special favor from God come with great sadness?" We are here with you, we, your poets, whisper it to you, we make our homes inside you, and revolve around you, and talk to you, since that day when first, in utter quietness you saw your brother blue in the cradle. Yes, we are the ones who tell you that great sadness and special favor from God come together in one package.

Chapter 18: Easter Eggs

Do you remember the Easter eggs? It's a few days before Easter, and you go to the corner grocery store to buy a dozen eggs. You're going to dye them for your Easter basket.

There is a little girl in front of you and she is excited and happy and jumping up and down. She has a carton of eggs too, and she is so happy that she keeps talking out loud to the whole store about her eggs.

"I've got some. Do you see? I've got some Easter eggs for the first time. I never ever had Easter eggs before. Mama gave me my money right here. Do you see? I'm gonna have some Easter eggs with color on them, oh!" And she keeps jumping up and down and showing everyone the eggs. "I'm buying Easter eggs this year, and I'm gonna color them. I've got the dye and everything."

So, the little girl gives her money to the man at the cash register. She gets her change, and when the man hands her the change the little girl grabs the change and the carton of eggs and makes a grand leap of happiness in the air. She leaps so high she almost falls over backwards and her back hits against the divider. She is excited shouting, "They're mine, they're mine, I've got them!" but horror of horrors! the carton of eggs goes up in the air, like her joy, and comes crashing onto the floor, and smash! All the eggs are broken all over the place! You see such horror on that little girl's face! She stares at her hands.

Everybody is stunned. For a moment you are all statues, staring, Mr. Kahn at the fruit stand, the man cashier, the woman cashier. Turning around. Looking. The woman is leaning toward the little girl from the other aisle. Everybody in line looks. The little girl has been so excited that everybody's attention is on her now. And you look.

The little girl does not even cry out. You watch her back up against the door, the half of the door that doesn't open. Her eyes are wide with fear, her face is covered with water, with tears pouring out of her eyes but no sound, no crying, no nothing! Her wet face rigid. Then her hands over her mouth, still silent, incapable of motion. Just standing there, backed up against the door, looking down at the smashed eggs with quiet tears dripping down.

That's when you give her your eggs. With everyone silent, you walk up to her and hand her your eggs which you haven't paid for yet. "Here, you can have these eggs." She looks at you, still stunned for a moment. "You can have these." She looks into your face and then takes the eggs out of your hand, and turns, and runs out of the door.

Now you walk back and pay for your eggs. Now the woman is there instead of the young man. He has gone to get the mop. You hand her the money and she doesn't take it, she says, "But you don't have any eggs?" "That's all right, my mother will give me more money for more eggs." You put your money on the counter.

And someone else is there, someone comes from the fruit area and looks at you. It's Mr. Kahn. He is looking at the scene from behind one of those tall stands that has candy and potato chips. The woman cashier keeps trying to interrupt you, and Mr. Kahn comes up to say something. They are all trying to say something to you, but you don't listen, you barely look up. You are just so concentrated on what you are doing that you give them no time to say anything.

But we know what they are saying to you, we understand. Mr. Kahn and the woman cashier and even someone in line are all trying to tell you that they will pay for the eggs, and that you can use your money to buy your own eggs.

But you don't give them any room for that. The little girl's pain is too urgent, too strong for you, too big. You have to do what you are doing and you never listen to them. You leave your money on the counter and run out of the store. You get more money from your mother, and then come back and buy your eggs in peace and quiet!

Chapter 19: Green Grocer

Cool air blows from the Potomac River to the Anacostia River to the Eastern Branch to you. You are eight years old. You still live in Mayfair Mansions, an apartment complex, and there is a tall tree bent aslant in front of your window. You like to sit in the window and read and look out at the crooked tree and think. It is in this apartment that you saw the death of your baby brother when you were three years old. The apartment complex has a circle with a wading pool that never has any water, and lawns and playgrounds.

Your face is very round and you wear glasses. You have two big spongy puffs of nappy hair on both sides of your head. Your skin is a beige-brown color. You wear neat starched cotton dresses that are always getting dirty somehow. You never wear braids because you don't like your hair to be tied down. And you never wear dungarees — they call them jeans now — because the material is too hard to your touch. And you never wear sandals because you don't like for people to see your feet. Even for the beach your mother buys rubber shoes for you to wear in the water. You love to touch the puffiness of your hair. You like it that no one else has hair as puffy as yours. When you are happy your family calls you Little Sunshine. When you are sad they call you Little Blue. You are not sad very much, but you are quiet and some grownups think you are sad when really you are just quiet and have things to think about.

You like to read books and you are always wishing that people in books would step out of the books and talk to you. There are two kinds of people from books that you especially wish that you could meet, faeries and Hebrews but you guess they don't exist in the world any more.

Mayfair Mansions is a part of northeast Washington, D. C. It has a bunch of stores including a grocery store. One day, as you are walking back from the store, you hear some children from Parkside saying that the man in the store is a Jew.

"Really?" you ask one of the little girls.

"Of course," she answers, "What's the matter with you?"

"Do you know if Jews and Hebrews are the same?"

But the little girl runs off so fast, yelling and playing that you guess they are just trying to fool you. How likely is it that there would be a real live Hebrew right here where everyone can see him and talk to him? "If Hebrews exist somewhere they must be far away with Moses, getting free." Don't they use the words "Jews" and "Hebrews" to talk about the same people in one of your books? You're not sure.

So you ask your mother, "Is Mr. Kahn at the grocery store a Hebrew?"

"Yes, he is."

"And are Hebrews and Jews the same?"

"Yes."

You walk to the window, look out at your crooked tree, and think. So Hebrews are not just in books, in wonderful stories. It's hard to believe. It's hard for you to believe that one of them has walked out of the Bible and is standing somewhere close where you can talk to him. It is hard to believe but it's true, otherwise your mother wouldn't say so.

"Maybe it's something people have just found out and everybody else is excited too!" You look down at the lawn between the apartment rows. You expect to see the whole neighborhood rushing out to get to the store quickly to talk to Mr. Kahn, a Hebrew. But they aren't. The grassy lawn between the apartment rows is quiet. Your heart starts throbbing, "How lucky for me. The other people don't know yet."

So you walk up to the store to talk to Mr. Kahn. He is standing by the vegetables, holding a tomato.

"Do you know Moses?" He looks down at you surprised.

"What are you talking about?"

"Did you leave Egypt with Moses?"

"Who told you to ask me that?"

"They told me that you're a Hebrew. So I want to know if you saw Moses. Didn't you leave Egypt with Moses?"

"Do you like Moses?"

"Yes."

"Well I never saw Moses. I wish I had seen Moses. Do you want this tomato?"

"Yes, my mother wants two pounds of tomatoes."

He does not say much about Moses the first time you ask, but each time you see him you ask him a little bit more about Moses.

"Hi, so you're here again."

"Yes, I need some greens today."

"I can get them for you over here."

"Okay. But . . . Mr. Kahn?'

"What?"

"Are you sure you never saw Moses?"

"I thought you said you came here to get some greens."

"I did."

"Well why don't you get them then?"

"Well, I could."

"Why don't you?"

"I just wanted all my life to meet a Hebrew person who would tell me about Moses."

"Didn't I tell you I never saw Moses?"

"The children in school said that you are a Jew."

"Yeah, and what of it?"

"My mother told me Jews are Hebrews, and Hebrews are with Moses."

"But I keep telling you I never saw Moses."

"Yeah. But . . ."

"But what . . ."

"I don't want you to get mad at me."

"Mad at you, well, ok, I promise I won't get mad."

"Well, you know you always do get mad whenever I ask you about Moses."

"What do you expect? Moses isn't anywhere even close to here. I never saw anybody's Moses."

"That's what I mean."

"What?"

"I guess you get mad because Moses went off to freedom and forgot to take you."

"Ha, child, you don't know what you're saying!"

"But don't feel mad, because he forgot me too. I was wondering, maybe there's a way to catch up with him."

"What are you talking about now?"

"Since you're Hebrew I thought maybe you could figure out a way to catch up with Moses so both of us could see Moses."

Then he smiles at you and laughs. Whenever you go to the store after that he smiles and winks and asks, "Still catching up with Moses?"

"Yes." you would always answer. But he would always tell you that he didn't know Moses.

Your conversation with Mr. Kahn continues until you are ten years old, that's when he retires from working in the store. Before he leaves he calls you over toward the door and tells you, "I didn't tell you the whole truth. I really do know Moses. I was a slave in Egypt, but I got free from slavery. The Lord brought me out of bondage with a mighty hand."

You are stunned. You can't understand why Mr. Kahn has lied to you for so long. For two years he has told you that he doesn't know Moses, and then, all of a sudden, he tells you that he has lied. You are so shocked that you can't speak. You stand there in the store leaning against the wall looking up at him. Before you can think of something to say he is gone somewhere in the back of the store, and you are just standing there alone. "I was with Moses and the Lord brought me out of slavery with a mighty hand." For a long time you remember those words.

Chapter 20: Kosher

Your mother is a school teacher at Van Ness Elementary, and your father is a supervisor at the main Post Office for the whole United States of America, right next to Union Station and the United States Congress downtown.

You like to visit your mother's school sometimes and you like to go down to the Washington Mall to see the Capitol and Union Station and all the Smithsonian Museums and the National Art Gallery. Your father works the night shift at the Post Office so that he can be home near you during the day when you are at school and after school. Your father recites poetry to you out of his books, Shenzi Kanga, "Four years ago they took our young chief and led him away captive"[52] and, "Gunga Din Din Din, By the living God that made you, you're a better man than I am, Gunga Din!"[53]

And your father knows history too. He recites the speeches of Frederick Douglass to you.[54] You sit on the sofa and listen as he marches up and down the living room. "What to the American slave is your Fourth of July? I answer, a day that reveals to him the gross injustice and cruelty to which he is constant victim." And you sit on the arm of your father's chair while he tells you about a country called Greece and a man named Herodotus who writes history about Africa and Greece and Persia.[55] He tells you about Rome and Hannibal coming over the snowy mountains of Switzerland on elephants and you can see Hannibal's elephants in the snow,[56] and you cry a little when you father tells you how Rome poured salt on Carthage in north Africa so that food couldn't grow there any more, and the people all died.

You sit listening and you hear your father singing the ***Song of Roland***[57] singing of the high passes of Europe. And a song of the grief of ***El Cid***[58] the betrayed and the song that is the ***Saga of Charlemagne***[59] who lived 800 years. EIGHT

HUNDRED YEARS! Your father sings to you and the **Death of Arthur**[60] he sings while you sit enthralled, listening.

Your mother likes poetry too and sometimes when you are standing up on the toilet lid to have your thick wonderful nappy hair combed she tells you about **Hiawatha**[61] or a hero who is named after two animals, a bear and a wolf, and she tells you how this Bear-Wolf breaks the arm off a fantastic monster named Grendel who eats people.[62] Your mother tells you that your nappy hair makes you strong too, like BearWolf and Samson,[63] and they are both so strong that they save their countries. Or she tells you about a wonderful little girl who comes from Africa and is a poet up in Boston where your family comes from. Her name is Phillis Wheatley,[64] and she writes poetry even though she is a slave and no matter what happens to her she still loves poetry. And your mother recites the poetry of Paul Lawrence Dunbar,[65] "I am just a little seedling but I'll do the best I can."

And you read poetry right back to your mother and father. You read from **The Book of Knowledge** they bought for you, you go from one poetry section to the next reading, "Sweet Auburn Village of the Plain"[66] and "When the stars threw down their spears and watered Heaven with their tears, did he smile his work to see, did he who made the lamb make thee?"[67] words like that. Can you imagine those scenes? You come up over a hill, and there is a city sitting there surrounded by hills and mountains, you think of that poem, there must be cities like that. And as for the stars throwing down their spears, whenever you see a night sky that is very dark black, you think of those bright falling tears coming through the beautiful midnight sky. Your favorite word of all is "beautiful." Your apartment on the third floor with your mother and father is quiet and beautiful.

Sometimes you decide things and tell your mother and father and they look at you for a moment and then look at each other for a moment and then they just say, Okay.

Here's an example of you deciding something and telling your father. On your first day of kindergarten your father takes you to school, Neval Thomas Elementary School. Your mother has to go to teach at her own school, Van Ness, the first day. The hall where they register the new pupils is very loud with crying children. While you and your father wait in line you listen to all the questions they ask, so that by the time you get to the front of the line you know all the questions and all the answers. But your father gets nervous around loud crying children, so when the lady asks him your name and things like that, he stammers and he's nervous and looks uncomfortable. So you say to your father, "You can go on home, I know the answers." And he goes home and you answer all the questions and register yourself in kindergarten. The only question you are not sure of is What is your mother's maiden name? So you ask, "Do you mean my grandmother's name?"

"Yes, if it's your mother's mother."

"Johnson."

In the evening your mother is upset with your father because he came home and left you there to register yourself in kindergarten. When she comes home from school she is all excited and wants to know about your first day in school. She asks your father, "So how was Shirah's first day at school?" Your father answers, "I don't know, she sent me home."

"What!?"

"She sent me home."

"She sent you home?! And you WENT?!" Your mother is so very surprised and shocked and upset. She just can't believe that your father went home and left you there. But you and your father understand each other, "She knew all the answers better than I did and sent me home!" and he laughs and smiles and shakes his head. And your mother laughs too. Then your father says, "If you want to know about her first day at school just ask her."

It is like that about lots of things. They do not even realize that you should go outside to play sometimes. That's because we are all sad since your brother died. You sit in the window day after day reading and making up stories and looking down at the children playing on the lawns where you never play. You keep expecting your mother and father to say to you, "Well, do you want to go outside and play?" But they never do. You think maybe there is some particular time they know of, something they are waiting for, when you can go outside to play. You wonder if maybe you're not old enough yet. But then you look carefully at the children and some of them are younger than you are, and they are outside playing. You can't think of a reason why your parents don't ask you if you want to go outside to play, so one day you just decide on your own. You sit by the window as usual, then you get down from the stool and announce, "It's time for me to go outside and play now."

They both look up shocked. Your father looks up from his newspaper. Your mother looks up from the dress she is sewing. They look at you then they look at each other then they look back at you. Your father says, "The child is right, what are we thinking of." Your mother says, "Yes, the child is right, let me get a jacket for you to wear outside." And that is the first time you go outside to play with the other children in the neighborhood.

That whole evening your parents stand at the window staring down at you. Every time you look up you see them standing there. And you run up and down the green lawn with the other children and you are Bear-Wolf and Samson and Hannibal and Phillis Wheatley and Shirah Shulamit Ojero all in one.

You and Mr. Kahn, the green grocer, are good friends now. He usually stands by the vegetables and rarely goes back to the meat counter. The two of you are such good friends that one day, when your mother sends you to the store to buy twenty-five cents worth of fat pork meat, you go up to Mr. Kahn and ask him for it. Mr. Kahn looks upset. His eyes look down and away from you and he won't look in your face. What's the matter? You don't know. Maybe he just doesn't like to sell meat. You walk behind him to the back counter. Mr. Kahn doesn't laugh and talk to you the way he usually does. You feel like you've made some kind of mistake. His eyes stop being happy. You know something is wrong.

This happens several times, every time you buy fat pork meat from Mr. Kahn his eyes don't meet yours. You decide you don't want to buy fat meat anymore. But another day comes when your mother sends you to the store, and you have the money in your hand she wants you to buy fat pork meat and some other things.

There you are at the back of the District Grocery Store, standing at the meat counter, and the money is scrunched up in your hand. Your heart is hurting. What's wrong? You don't know. The women reach for things from the butcher and push you without seeing you. You are all crowded and small. The women are talking and asking for meat, fat back, bacon, hamburger. You hear their voices beside you and around you, hollow echoing voices. You just cannot buy the fat pork meat.

"I forgot to buy the fat meat." You go home and lie to your mother. But that feels awful too, so the next time your mother sends you to the store for fat meat you tell her quietly, "I don't like to buy fat pork meat." You stand there waiting for what your mother will say. She looks at you with a question in her face, and after a while she says, "Ok, you don't have to buy fat meat." She doesn't know why, and you don't explain why, and you don't even know how to explain why you don't want to buy fat pork meat any more. You don't like it when Mr. Kahn won't look you in the eyes.

"OK," your mother says, "I'll buy the fat meat from now on." She thinks you hate fat meat because that's all it is, thick white fat pork with no real meat in it. And she starts buying what she calls streak-o-lean, streak-o-lean is fat pork meat with a little streak of real meat in it. It costs a little more - thirty cents instead of twenty-five cents but she says to you, "The extra money is worth it to help you feel better about our food."

You stand there in the store beside your mother as she buys a streak-o-lean, and Mr. Kahn is fine with her, and looks her in the eye, and all that and looks you in the eye and hands her the meat. But, he won't do that if you are alone buying the fat meat. So now you know everything is all right again, and you and Mr. Kahn are good friends talking about Moses. You don't understand anything about kosher food or fat meat and pork. Although you read the Bible over and over again you don't understand connections between the Bible and Kosher food. As far as you are concerned, kosher has to do with pickles, the wonderful pickles in the barrel at the back of the store. That barrel has the word KOSHER stamped all over it. Sometimes when you stand with your mother at the meat counter she buys you one of those kosher pickles. The pickles are so good! You walk home together with your mother carrying the fat meat and you eating a pickle. As far as you are concerned you are absolutely kosher!

Chapter 21: Your Father's Books

You really like this book, don't you, Shirah? Do you know how I got it? It was when I was a little boy living with my mother on 12th Street, 219 Twelfth Street, South East. And I got this book, actually both of these books right here, because of a Jewish man who had a bookstore on Seventh Street, downtown. You see I used to earn two or three dollars a week when I was a little boy, running errands to the store or cleaning up yards for people on the street and things like that. Well, on Friday afternoons I always took the bus downtown to the bookstore on Seventh Street where I would buy college sports novels and comic books.

Well, I know you don't like sports books so much but you like books about schools don't you? You would like these sports books because they are about people who went to colleges just like you are going to go to college one day. The books I bought were about young men who went to colleges like Harvard and Yale and played football on the teams there. And as for comic books, they are like funny papers and I know you like funny papers. I would go down to the bookstore every week and buy one or two of these books I liked.

And this is what happened. The man who ran the bookstore was a Jewish man who was always nice to me. He talked to me every week. But then there was this one time. One week when I went into the store he was really mean to me. He wouldn't let me buy my favorite comic books and he wouldn't let me buy the sports books. He made me give him two dollars and forced me to buy these two books I didn't even want. There was nothing I could do. He took my money and made me take the books. I was so angry. But as angry as I was I just had to leave the store and go home with these two awful books. All the way home on the bus I was just feeling mad. Why would he do this to me? And up until then I thought he was a nice man. I was eight or nine years old, just a little older than you are now.

On the way home I decided I wouldn't even look at the books. I couldn't stand to throw them away — after all, I had paid two dollars for them. But I wouldn't look at them. But before the bus got home, guess what, I looked at them. I opened up this first one right here, **_The Dunbar Speaker and Entertainer_**, and started reading. Wow, was I surprised. I started reading it and I just couldn't stop. Right there on the bus I read the Frederick Douglass Fourth of July speech for the first time.

> Fellow citizens, above your national, tumultuous joy I hear the mournful wail of millions whose chains, heavy and grievous yesterday, are today rendered more intolerable by the jubilant shouts that reach them. If I forget, if I do not remember those bleeding children of sorrow this day, May my right hand forget her cunning, and may my tongue cleave to the roof of my mouth! To forget them, to pass lightly over their wrongs, and to chime in with the popular theme would be treason most scandalous and shocking, and would make me a reproach before God and the World.[68]

Yes, Frederick Douglass is still my favorite. And you know your mother's favorite is in this book too, Dunbar's _"In The Morning."_[69] I'm not even going to recite that one for you since Georgia taught you how to recite it yourself.

But what about this one?

Shall I say, My son, you are branded in this country's pageantry,
Foully tethered, bound forever, and no forum makes you free?
Or shall I, with love prophetic, bid you dauntlessly arise,
Spurn the handicap that binds you, taking what the world denies?[70]

Isn't that beautiful? Do you hear the way it just rolls out of the mouth? That was written by a woman named Georgia Johnson. Just like your mother's name before we got married. And the middle name of this poet named Georgia Johnson was Douglass. Her complete name was Georgia Douglass Johnson. And your mother lived on Douglass Street, NE when I met her. Isn't that interesting? It's like names just keep going in circles touching each other again and again.

And listen to this one, The African Chief.

His heart was broken, crazed his brain:
At once his eye grew wild;
He struggled fiercely with his chain,
Whispered and wept and smiled;
Yet wore not long those fatal bands,
And once at shut of day,
They drew him forth upon the sands,
The foul hyena's prey.

That's about a black African Chief who refused to be a slave. A man named William Bryant[71] wrote that one. But I know your favorite for me to recite to you is Shenzi Kanga.

Today they tell us of a great fight
In the land of the white men;
They tell us of a curse, a curse fallen
On Belgium, the land of our oppressors;
They tell us of invading armies, ruthless and cruel;
They cry of homes burned, of men and women
*   slaughtered;*
Of women, hunted and ravished and killed.
So we look about us
At the blackened ruins of our huts;
At the thinned numbers of our tribe,
And at Shenzi Khanga;

And we hasten to him and gather about him and
> *tell him*
The news form the North.
Shenzi Khanga hears,
And raises his face with the useless eyes,
And lifts the useless stumps,
And Shenzi Khanga
Laughs!

Granger really wrote that one didn't he? Lester B. Granger.[72] But the title of it is not Shenzi Khanga but Belgium. That's the country that hurt a lot of black people in the Belgian Congo, in Africa.

Yeah, yeah, I know, you like to hear me recite that one. But let me finish telling you about these books. This second book, you see, is called **The New Progress of A Race**, and it's like a history book with a lot of little stories about Negroes who did great things. So yeah I know history is not your favorite, but you should love history, history is really just a bunch of really good stories linked together.

Remember that story I told you that Herodotus wrote about a man who went to the oracle at Delphi to find out if he should start a war? And the oracle told him, "If you fight against the Persians you will destroy a great empire." So the man went to war because he thought he was going to destroy the Persians, but instead he ended up destroying his own country and ruining his own empire. You see, that's a good story even though it is history. That king didn't realize that the great kingdom he would destroy was his own. The oracle had already told that king not to attack Persia, but he wouldn't listen. He kept on asking the oracle, trying to get a better answer. So the oracle gave him an answer he wouldn't understand.

And these history stories in this book are good too, just like the oracle one that Herodotus wrote. Look at this one now, this is a picture of William Still. He used to live up in Philadelphia and runaway slaves would hide in his house. And whenever they would come to his house he would write down the stories they told him. Just think. He wouldn't let the poor folks even sleep first. They had to sit there and tell him what slavery was like and he would write it down. Can you imagine it, Shirah? Running away from slavery in the middle of the night. Hiding in swamps and woods and basements, and you finally get to a house that's kind of safe, William Stills' house, and you're ready to fall asleep, and he says, No, tell me what slavery was like. What was it like getting here? I know you're tired, but you've got to tell me so you can help your people get free. And so, tired as you are you sit there in a back room hidden, telling the story of how you got over. It's really a good kind of story, Shirah, and maybe one day you'll like history the same way you like poems and stories.

So anyway, let me go back to when I was a little boy and first started reading these two books. I kept liking the books more and more. I guess I started to love them, and one Friday afternoon I went back to that bookstore and you know what I said to that Jewish man, I said, Thank you. I said, You know, those are really good books. And that man smiled at me and said, Good. And now are you ready to buy some comic books and sports books. And I said, Yeah, I sure am.

And guess what, Shirah? A long time afterwards, when I was grown up, I found out that these books we are holding right here in our hands are worth one hundred dollars a piece. ONE HUNDRED DOLLARS. The two of them together would have cost me $200.00!!! when I was a little boy, and he sold them to me for a dollar a piece. Sometimes I wonder what was in his mind when he made me buy those books. I have an idea of the answer, but maybe you can think about it, Shirah. Maybe you can think about why that Jewish man sold me these wonderful books at such a low price.

What? You? You think he was thinking of you when he sold me the books? But you weren't even born yet. Of course I know how much you like them, but how could he know that you would be born and that you would like the books so much? You think he could see into the future and that he did know? Maybe he has some special eye drops or something so he could see through years and years to see you sitting right here. But don't you think that is far-fetched? Well, what do I know. Maybe he did give them to me so that you could read them. Stranger things than that have happened in the world, my little buttercup.

Chapter 22: DC Transit

Do you know that they crucified that little baby who was born at Christmas? Yes, I just found out. Can you explain to me how he grew up so fast? Tomorrow he's going to come alive again at church but I don't care. How can I be happy about that when I'm so sad they killed him in the first place? I just don't think it's a very good story. Do you think that's why people talk about toys at Christmas instead of that baby who's going to die?

The elevator takes a long time to get up here to the top because the Washington Monument is so tall. Wait. Let's go to the window after the others are finished looking. And step up on the box. It's clear outside. Do you see the cars and buses? They don't look like toys. And the people don't look like ants. Everything looks real.

Why do you think grownups always say that cars and buses look like toys and people look like ants from the top of the Monument? I don't understand grownups. Do you?

The castle is beautiful, isn't it? dark red and quiet. Someone is living in the tower. The echo of my shoes clacking against the floor runs down the hallway and up the stairs. Who lives in the tower? An old woman. Or a little girl. Where have they buried the king? Here it is. Now I remember. In this quiet room. Can you read his name? His name is James Smithson. And this place is named for him. Smithsonian.

Do you want to go look at the things in this next building? Arts and Industries. Look how quietly the costumes hang in glass cages. Can you see how they shine with gold cloth and jewels? They are old and have some holes but you still like them don't you? I like them. You can go to this music box and push the button, and the music plays. Everything in here is old. An old train. An old sewing machine. Bright polished silver swords hanging on the wall.

I hope you like old things like I do. My mother says she doesn't want old days to come back. No, in those old days there were slaves. Well okay, you and I can like old things except for slavery. And except for killing that little baby that grew up. The people at church say that God killed my baby brother. What was God thinking when he did that? Do you know? Because I sure don't know. Did God kill this other little baby too? This one who is born at Christmas and grows up and gets killed for Easter?

Look up at the ceiling. Can you see those wonderful swirls and curls it's made of, and that old wooden fan is turning and blowing air on you. Come over here. Don't you know this is where they keep the carriages and cars? Do you like popcorn? Over against the wall there are popcorn machines and mirrors with fuzzy gold. And look at this, where the stairway curves down from the ceiling empty and cool. Can you smell the palm trees in the pots beside me? The stairs are made of marble. The palm trees are tall and you and I can step in between and wait. Nobody knows. Nobody comes down the stairs. You and I could live here forever and no one would find us.

Do you know the difference between faeries and angels? Do faeries tear curtains like that angel did yesterday? That's what they said at church. 'The veil of the temple was rent.' "Rent" means "Torn." Do you think everyone will be good now that Jesus is dead? Can you explain it to me? Why should everybody try to be good because a baby was murdered. Why doesn't everybody be good before a baby is murdered. And then the baby won't be murdered at all. Don't you think so? It's very confusing.

And why do you think an angel would tear a curtain on a temple. I thought angels were good and faeries were always playing tricks and doing strange things. But maybe the angels are bad and the faeries are good. You never know.

Arch - hives. Ark - hives. Arch - hives. Ark - hives. Do you know that you say it different from how it looks? Archives.

We're not going home. WHAT IS PAST IS PROLOGUE. A prologue comes in front of a play or a story. Did you know that? Athena lives in there, you and I know that because of the book we looked at. We're taking a different bus because we're going somewhere else.

Look. Isn't this wonderful? Don't you like it? This is the Folger Shakespeare Library. The baby boy in that picture will grow up and make stories. Those are passions and graces around him. Don't you think they look like faeries or angels? But they're not, you just have to read right here and it tells you that they are passions and graces. Feel these ropes, they are so smooth and soft. Do you like to feel them against your hand? Maroon. But look at this picture over here. That's a real faerie whose name is Ariel and she wants to fly out of the picture and play. But Ariel also means Jerusalem.

Library of Congress. You and I are going to read all of them. When you grow up you want to know everything. If you had been in the Garden of Eden you wouldn't have waited for the snake, you would have run to the tree of knowledge and eaten all the fruit you could hold. And the tree of life too. You would have eaten that!

You should come over this way out the door because we're going home now. Your mother said you can't know everything. Nobody can know everything. So instead of knowing everything you and I can learn one thing completely. Maybe if you learn one thing completely it's the same as knowing everything. Tomorrow God is going to make Jesus come back alive after killing him last Friday, and I'm the angel at the tomb in the Sunday School play. I don't want to. They shouldn't murder that little baby in the first place. I don't ever want to murder any one.

Easter Monday you'll be at the White House for the egg roll. Grownups have to have a child in order to get in.

Chapter 23: Redface

Now look where you are. Your grandfather works the ferris wheel at Glen Echo Amusement Park. Can you see? You are sitting beside him while the ferris wheel turns. The air is too hot and full. Flies and bees buzz soft under the platform, and the sun shines bright on the building. They sell popcorn and cotton candy and pizza and frozen custard and upstairs there's a restaurant with umbrella tables on the patio and tables behind the windows and the sun shines on the windows bright, and can you see way over there? The sun is so bright on the shining cars. But you and your grandfather sit together under a tree with dark green leaves. Can you smell the heavy leaves? And there are specks and dust in the air. You watch your grandfather's hands as he pulls the lever sending the happy beautiful children up and around and over the air and down. You look at the children. You pretend that you can go high in the air, as high as the top of the ferris wheel.

But look. Your grandfather winks. He's whispering and smiling.

"Come on quick and take a ride."

Now you run quickly under the ferris wheel and sit on the slatted wood of the green bench and rock back and forth as your grandfather closes the safety bar. You hold the wood. And there you go up and around where you look over the trees and squinch your eyes and see to the end of the world.

But it stops too soon. Your grandfather is quiet as he opens the safety bar and when you look up there is a redface man standing in front. Every now and then there is a person whose outside skin has no color and red shows through. Your mother calls them white people but you can see. You know that they are redface people. And here is one of them talking to your grandfather.

"You know we don't allow no coloreds to ride in this park. What you think you doing?"

." . . she's my granddaughter . . ."

"This little girl? Well, what's your name?"

"Shirah Shulamit Ojero"

"Oh, is that so? Are you a smart girl? Do you know when's your birthday?"

"July 22, 1947."

"And where do you live?"

"3758 Hayes Street, N.E., Washington 19, D.C."

"And what's your phone number?"

"Adams 2-4858."

"What's today's date?"

"August 17, 1953."

"And what county do we live in?"

"The United States of America."

"And who's the president of our country?"

"President Dwight David Eisenhower?"

"And what's the capital city of our country?"

"Washington, D.C."

He smiles at you, can you see? And now he laughs.

"So you one of thuh smart ones, hunh? A cute, smart little colored girl. It's good to know y'all got some smart ones. Well here, I'll give you this, two shining quarters to spend, and today I'll let you ride in the park but only today. You a smart one. I ain't seen no little colored girl smart as you."

And now he's walking away from us and can you feel that fire in your hand? The two quarters make your hand burn. You lift your hand toward your grandfather.

"I don't want to hold this, Granddaddy, it hurts."

Softly your grandfather takes the two silver coins from your hand. He tosses them into the speckled air shining and turning, they fall into the dark leaves of the bush beside the ferris wheel.

Now your grandfather holds your hand between his big beautiful brown hands. Your grandfather's hands take the burn away from your hand.

Look. The air is warm and the sky is clear and bright in the sun and you are in your blue and white dress running, can you see how lovely everything is as you run down the gravel path to the Merry-Go-Round? Running in your brown and white saddle oxford shoes that are running, running down the path.

Chapter 24: Safety Cavalier

Yes, Mayfair Mansions is far away isn't it? The dust is so pale and dry there, and the light has so many shapes. It is strange for you. And when you return there you have to travel a long way.

Look at the back of your elementary school auditorium. It's warm where you are sitting in a row with other children. You hook the heels of your shoes on the wooden bars under your seats and the cludding of your heels on the wood is pale dust.

On the stage a redface man is talking. He's asking if someone will come up to be a Safety Cavalier. And listen to the teachers whispering your name as they move back through the auditorium.

"Shirah. Where's Shirah? She should go up."

Can you hear them whispering? And now Mrs. Holloway lifts you up from the chair. Mrs. Dedmon pats your shoulder. The children look at you as you walk down the center aisle and onto the stage to talk to Safety Officer Dick Mansfield.

He is asking questions.

"What is your name?"

"And what is your birthday?"

"And where do you live?"

"And who's our president living right here in Washington?"

Why do you think the redface people always ask the same questions?

You answer all the questions.

"Now you can see him smiling."

"And do you want to be a Safety Cavalier?"

"Yes."

"You walk to the front of the stage and stand. Now you are singing."

> *We're Safety Cavaliers.*
> *We use our eyes and ears.*
> *We look both ways,*
> *We watch our steps.*
> *We're Safety Cavaliers.*

And now you sing it again and the children sing with you softly.

> *We're Safety Cavaliers.*
> *We use our eyes and ears.*
> *We look both ways,*
> *We watch our steps.*
> *We're Safety Cavaliers.*

And now the children and the teachers, Mrs. Holloway and Mrs. Dedmon and Mrs. Reed, the principal, and Safety Officer Dick Mansfield on the stage behind you are all singing with you as you sing louder and louder.

> *We're Safety Cavaliers.*
> *We use our eyes and ears.*
> *We look both ways,*
> *We watch our steps.*
> *We're Safety Cavaliers.*

And now Safety Officer Dick Mansfield gives you a badge and a belt and a baton and can you hear the children clapping for you? They are leaving the auditorium and Mrs. Dedmon is there with you, leading you down from the stage. She gives you an apple, and Mrs. Holloway tells you that you can play on the playground, so now you are outside entwined along the cool metal bars of the guard rail between the playground and the auditorium. You didn't ask Safety Officer Dick Mansfield your question. They always ask you questions. Whenever you ask your question nobody knows the answer.

Here is your question. What's the difference between an angel and a faerie?

And you have another question. What was in the world before God?

Chapter 25: Grilled Cheese

You and your mother spend days on the Mall, enjoying the museums, and in the afternoons you go to stores where your mother buys cloth to sew or trinkets for the cloth. You walk up Seventh Street from the Archives building to Kann's Department Store, or Lansburgh's or Hecht's. One thing you notice, whenever you go to Woolworth's and walk past the lunch counter, your mother squeezes your hand a little too tight and rushes past.

It's those people with red faces. That's what you think. Whenever those people with red faces are around the people with brown faces are worried about something and squeeze hands too tight, and hold their lips too tight. You can see. There are regular people with faces that are brown or beige or tan, and these are people who are all right most of the time. Then there are people with skin you can see through, you can see the red blood right underneath the clear skin. Whenever these redface people are near the regular people the regular people look nervous, and hold their lips tight, or squeeze your hand too much. That is what you notice. There are a lot of redface people at the lunch counter at Woolworth's and whenever your mother walks through there she holds your hand too tight and doesn't say anything and looks straight ahead.

At Woodie's — Woodward and Lothrop Department Store — you look through all the **Bobbsey Twin** books and your mother buys you two to take home.

The bookstore at Kann's is even better because it is down in the basement and you walk down the steps into the mysterious world of characters who come from books. Maybe you'll meet a faerie who is wandering along the tops of trees, or maybe you'll meet a Hebrew standing by a rock near a pool of water, someone who can walk right out of your books and sit on these book shelves and talk to you.

But you can never quite figure out these redface people. Some beige brown people call the redface people white people. Why? Can't the beige brown people see the red blood that shines through the skin. Redface, that's the right word. Sometimes these redface people make regular people really nervous, and sometimes the redface people just stand there and smile. They smile at you every Easter Monday when your mother takes you to the White House along with your cousins Ricky and Shannon. Redface people stand outside and some of them can't get in because they don't have a child with them. If you are a grown up you can't get in to roll Easter Eggs on the White House lawn on Easter Monday unless you have a child with you. Your mother goes with three children, you, Ricky and Shannon, so the redface people ask, "Can we walk in with one of your children so we can go inside?" Ricky agrees to go with one of the redface people, but you and Shannon stay with your mother, "Aunt Georgia."

You are are remembering Easter Monday as you walk through Woolworth's with your mother. Redface people are strange.

Your mother is squeezing your hand too tight again but you look back at the redface people sitting at the lunch counter. You don't know why, but you know that you and your mother can't sit down there and eat beside the redface people.

You look back at the pictures of food high around all of the walls.

Grilled Cheese. You wonder what grilled cheese is. You would like a grilled cheese sandwich. "If ever I eat something here," you think, "I'll get a grilled cheese sandwich."

But one day all of your aunts and uncles and your mother and father are talking together. It's time for someone "colored," a Negro, to go and eat at Woolworth's lunch counter. They all want your mother to go, Georgia, and they want her to take you. How about that! It must mean that you and your mother are colored.

So finally, after a day on the Mall in the early summer of 1954, you and your mother go to Woolworth's lunch counter to eat.

You are so surprised! You didn't think you would ever get to eat there.

You and your mother are sitting on the high stools at the counter, and the waiter steps up and asks you.

"Can I get you some watermelon?"

Your mother is upset and is about to say something mean to the man, you watch her face twist a little bit and maybe she's even getting ready to yell at the man, but you are so excited about sitting there, you just have to say something. You have been waiting so long.

"No thank you, I'd like a grilled cheese sandwich, please." You have seen that picture of the toasted bread with the melted cheese between slices of bread so many times, and every time your mother used to walk past the lunch counter you wanted a grilled cheese sandwich so much.

"May I have a grilled cheese sandwich, please?" The man at the counter looks down at you and now his face is twisted. At first he looked like he wanted to spit on you, and then he was grinning and asked you if you wanted watermelon, but now . . . now he draws his lips in, and his eyes look like he's not looking at you any more. His eyes look a little sad and a little afraid.

He turns away and goes to bring you a grilled cheese sand-wich and a soda. And your mother, instead of saying what ever she was going to say to the man, orders a hamburger with po-tato chips.

After you finish your mother pays for the food and then the two of you ride home on the Benning Road bus.

Back at home all your aunts and uncles are waiting to hear what happened. "Did they serve you? Did they make fun of you eating with those white folks?"

"They tried to insult us. The waiter came up to Shirah and asked her if she wanted watermelon."

"NO!"

"Yes he did, asked her if she wanted watermelon. Just trying to embarrass us by asking the child."

"Humph! They think that all colored people ever eat is watermelon."

"That's a shame, that's a shame. To do that to a child. And they don't even have watermelon. They were just trying to make ya'll feel bad."

"Yes, but guess what this little girl said? She said, 'No thank you, I'd like a grilled cheese sandwich, please.' Said it just like that looking right up into that white man's face."

"No lie!"

"It's the truth."

"Whoo-hoo! Showed that fool white man something."

"Sure did! Asked for a grilled cheese sandwich like she's been eating grilled cheese sandwiches at Woolworth's Five and Ten every blessed day of her life!"

"Ain't she something!"

"Aren't you proud!"

"Shirah, you did fine. We're so glad you didn't let that man fool you."

But you are completely confused. You asked for a grilled cheese sandwich because you wanted a grilled cheese sandwich. You didn't understand that grilled cheese has some other meaning. And watermelon has some other meaning.

You notice that everything confusing is even more confusing when the redface people are involved. Those redface people that beige brown people call white. Why is that? It's so hard to understand.

Redface people make regular people nervous and regular people tell lies about redface people. You remember. When you started second grade one of your school friends told you that the lighter your skin is the smarter you are, so you were hoping that someone with very light skin would come to your class so that you could ask this smart person two important questions that have been bothering you a long time. Here are the questions, and no one has ever been able to answer them so far.

1. What is the difference between a faerie and an angel?
2. And what was in the world before God?

Chapter 26: Dumbarton Oaks

You and your mother walk a different way after church. You don't walk up Q Street to Seventh Street today. You are not going home. It is a special place. You walk down Fifth Street to P Street. Waiting at a different Street for a different bus. Georgetown Bus. Le Droit Park to Georgetown.

Ride.

Far on the other side, west side of Seventh Street. Far on the other side, west side of Sixteenth Street. Far on the other side, west side of Dupont Circle, Connecticut Avenue. All the way to Wisconsin Avenue. Far. West.

It's not the zoo. It's not the Smithsonian. It's not the art gallery. It's not Rock Creek Park. It's not the Potomac River. It's not the C&O Canal. It's not the Mall. It's not Maryland. It's not Virginia. What is it?

It's at the top of a hill that lounges through Washington City from Georgetown to Clifton Heights and Cardozo High School to Howard University before it sinks into the McMillan Reservoir. It has a high gate. It has quiet people. There you are, looking into the green house. You look down at the pool. You sit beside the pool. The fountain is quiet. Why doesn't the fountain spray water into the air? You want to see the water spraying up. And yet this is enough. Sit and ponder. Little girl.

There is the pool by the amphitheatre. Here you are.

There is the barrier of bamboo. Here you are.

There is the green circle with even trees. Here you are.

There is an alcove with words you cannot read.

Dante. You can read that word. What does it mean? Sit beside it. It must mean something good.

You sit on a damp bench near the words.

There are roses in sunlight.

Red roses yellow roses orange roses pink roses purple roses white roses green leaves.

Your mother watches you watching roses.

Your mother watches the other visitors watching you watching roses.

You walk to the amphitheater. The amphitheater is not like the surrounding gardens but is unkempt, complicated. You see the entwined bamboo and evergreen. You see the leaves thick gathered the steps crumbling the smell mold. This is a holy place, as final as a sea.

Sunlight strikes a glazed brochure in your hand as you stand between ivy pillars, a brochure convinced that once there were concerts in this amphitheater of Dumbarton Oaks. The amphitheater is eaten away now with grass and leaves and ancient mud washed up beneath leaves cracking the bricks with gray water.

Dazzled. Dazed.

Is it Desolation. Or Creation.

Sunny and bright and warm. You want to be a purple flower against a green leaf.

Your mother tells you, "Those words are Italian. Dante was an Italian poet."

You leave the amphitheater taking the path to the wild place. Here you are.

You hear murmuring, dark faces just out of the light. Georgetown dark faces. A fence separating the formal garden from the public park. You stand and think. Desolation.[73]

You turn and climb the slope to a narrow path with low hedges returning to the rose garden from the north. Your mother behind you. You stand there a moment. April. Creation.

Around the corner and into the museum and it is the best museum you have seen because each thing they have is set up all by itself alone. You stand with your mother in front of each thing, all by itself alone.

Limestone and gold and jadeite and shell and serpentine and onyx and parchment and bronze and niello and ivory and wood and copper and bloodstone and silver all by itself alone, and all by itself alone, a porphyry rattlesnake. A book with golden covers with letters you cannot read. Alpha Beta Gamma. "Those words are Greek," your mother tells you. And an engraving of a city all by itself alone. "That man Herodotus that your father reads to you, wrote in Greek. And here is some more Greek."

So many gardens, flowers, gemstones, carvings, antique rooms, so many. Byzantine artifacts. Columbian artifacts. Greek words. A Library. So many words and flowers.

Here in Dumbarton Oaks there are more words than flowers. If you were to measure the words by the flowers, first you would count the flowers in all the gardens of Dumbarton Oaks one by one, then you would count the words in the museum and the library by thousands, and then you would choose for each group of 1000 words one single flower, thus you would discover that many, many groups of words would have no flower, so much greater are the number of words to the number of flowers. Here in Dumbarton Oaks. You walk sedately in front of your mother. Looking. Reading. Contemplating. You are home in Dumbarton Oaks, finally you have arrived home. It is given to you. This is a place where you shall live all the days of your life. Some people are whispering near you but you do not hear.

Look, did you see the face of that little colored girl? Yes, isn't it strange? So calm and used to things. You don't think she lives here do you? Impossible. I don't think anybody lives in the mansion. She must be from one of the embassies. Yeah, that's it. An embassy kid from down the street somewhere. She gets to walk in gardens like this all the time.

Chapter 27: Angels and Faeries

Will you go with me down the end to think? You don't have to go back up there to the apartments right now, come and look at the trees close together with thick leaves where the Anacostia River curves around by the Potomac Electric Power Company and the schools there on the hill. Spingarn. Phelps. Browne. Charles Young. The Langston Library is over there too.

Can you see that mountain on the other side of the water? How still it is. I am sad. Sad? Sadness is what you feel inside me. Yes. Sadness is that air in my chest that breathes out of me slowly. Is it happy for you to live up here in the sky? And to come down here sometimes and play with me? And talk?

Now you can turn away from the river and walk back through the woods to the lawn and the playground with me.

Do you know the difference between faeries and angels? No one will tell me the difference. Do you think they are kin to each other?

And why do you think the tree in front of my apartment is so crooked? The trees in front of the other apartments are straight and short and bushy with round tops and their branches reach out to the sides. But my tree is tall and thin and the trunk is crooked and the branches reach up to the sky slanted. Why do you think it does that?

Maybe faeries are not as tall as angels, but faeries look back over their shoulders at me. They are like you, aren't they, except they don't stay around all the time. They point to strange places don't they? Do you think faeries are in the rainbow we see in the morning over there behind the trees down the end. That's Watt's Creek over there, toward Eastland Gardens where Aunt Edna lives. And my music teacher, Miss Johnson. Aunt Edna is my godmother. She and my mother went to Miner Teachers College. The mist rising from the creek is a hall of colors. I think there is a drum playing back there in a gazebo. A beautiful spider like Anansi playing a beautiful drum. I like to walk through the colors of mist.

Don't you think that even if it's an angel that lives high above the trees and pulls them to Heaven, even if it really is an angel, don't you think my angel is a faerie because she saw something else in the sky and went toward it and bent away from the other angels, and pulled my string crooked. And that's why my tree is bent?

Do you believe that faeries are smaller and shorter than angels? Athena isn't small and short and she's not an angel. And all of you, you're not little like faeries are in books and maybe some of you are angels but most of you don't look like angels to me. No, I think all of you are faeries, a different kind of faerie who doesn't hide under mushrooms and clover but all of you stand tall in the sky around me. And some of you are poet faeries aren't you? You are Phillis Wheatley. And you are Paul Lawrence Dunbar. And you are Robert Louis Stevenson. And you are Langston Hughes. And you are William Blake. And you are John Keats. And you are Bear-Wolf. I recognize you.

Do you think God will give me a sign to tell me if I'm going to grow up and write a book? I want to know before I'm ten years old. God hasn't sent me a sign yet.

These falling ashes are strange aren't they. Do you send them down on me? Burnt papers with words I can hardly read. Johnny Mercer from the apartment downstairs says they are from the Kenilworth Dump, but you and I know they are really words that you are sending to me. And I can hear you speaking them. Sometimes I wonder if you are trying to burn me with the words.

Do you know what I wish? I wish I could go to another school where I could read all the words in the world. Do you know how to send me to a school like that? You know what it's like over at Neval Thomas Elementary where I go to school. I sit alone by myself all day long and read books. The other students are in the other part of the room. You and I sit all day long and read the books but we've read them all. I want to read a book I never read before. A book unknown in elementary school. Unknown everywhere. Yes. Even in Heaven. Can you help me find a Book Unknown In Heaven? Do you want to read that book with me?

What do you think about smart people? A boy at school told me that the whiter your skin is the smarter you are. So when a girl with white skin came to my class I was so happy because I thought she could answer my questions. I asked her What's the difference between angels and faeries? Do you remember how she looked at me? She looked at me so stupid and didn't say anything at all. What do you think was the matter with her? She wasn't smarter? Yes, you're right. People with whiter skin aren't smarter than other people, because you remember those redface people don't you? They had white skin and they always ask stupid questions. What do you suppose is the matter with redface people that they always ask the same stupid questions.

You and I like to read the Old Testament over and over again. I don't like the New Testament so much. Why do you think Jesus hated Scribes? I love Scribes. A scribe is a writer. You know what I think, I think I want to be a scribe. I think I would rather be a scribe like all of you than to have his kingdom of God. And I bet he didn't like Athena either. You and I love Athena, goddess of wisdom. Sophia is another name for wisdom. My father told me.

Does Athena live up there in the sky with you? Athena likes me. Athena is a strong, tall faerie, not like those angels who want me to be happy because that little Jesus baby who was born at Christmas was killed and came back alive. I don't care. I don't like that story. Why is it a baby boy is always dying?

Do you like Peter Pan? Did you like it when I was Tinker Bell in the school play and I led all the children to Never Never Land?

Do you know what was in the world before God? And why is it always raining?

Chapter 28: High Seas

"Baaaaa—aaaa-aaaa! Baaaaa—aaaa-aaaa! I'll scare you before you scare me! I'll scare you before you scare me!"

Your old black Great-Grandma Olivia scares the children out of her room. All the other children, your cousins. They run skittering and shouting through the dining room and out into the back yard. Then they start laughing. She tries to scare you too but you won't run away. You stand there, quiet, across from the green piano and look at her. You look into her black face, a face one hundred and three years old, with ugly bumps and wrinkles and splotches. They told you that you would be afraid, but you are not afraid. Yes, she is ugly, with bright blue eyes in the black face, frightening, but you want to meet her, here, in Portsmouth, Virginia.

"Humph! Oscar's baby. They call her Shirah Shulamit. Naturally she won't run away. I might have known. Come on here chile, come on over here."

She looks at you.

"Well, chile, what do you want?" your Great-Grandma Olivia asks you.

"Grandma Olivia, were you really alive back in slavery times?"

"Yes, I was ten years old when the slaves were freed."

"Really, I want to ask you. I've been wanting to ask you about slavery. What was slavery like? Were you happy, Grandma Olivia, when you found out you were free?"

"What? What?" Your Great-Grandma Olivia is angry, so angry. You look into her splotchy black face with the bright blue eyes and all the wrinkles and bumps. You watch her get up from her red chair and walk up the stairs away from you. "Chile don't know a thing, I thought you had some sense," your Grandma Olivia grunts as she walks up the stairs, turning her back on you and your question. You watch her walk halfway up before she stops, turns, and slowly walks down again to you.

"Don't you know, chile? Don't you know that your folks weren't slaves? At least not here, not in Virginia, not in the United States. You ought to know that by now. Why is it you don't know that already? It makes me mad to think you don't know. I've got so few years left on this earth, so let me tell you. Our folks weren't slaves here, but we were slaves in Egypt 3,000 years ago, because we're Jews.

"I was living right here in Portsmouth, Virginia, when I heard the Emancipation Proclamation read. I had been delivering fish to the white folks, I had a Geechee Basket they gave me that came from our Geechee folks from the islands off Georgia, and I carried the fish in it. I was carrying fish that same day we found out that the slaves got free. After I delivered the fish I went down the path from the kitchen where the black folks were standing around. The war was on but still lots of black folks had to stay right there slaving. But our family was free. And back there Brother Hezekiah was reading it, the Emancipation Proclamation, and I saw all our black folks so happy, and I was happy right with them and dancing.

"But this is what Grandma Sarah told me. She was my great-grandmother and she told me this story just like I'm your great-grandmother and I'm telling you this story now. Grandma Sarah told me how we were slaves long before, back in Egypt. It's right in the Bible, you've read it. Grandma Sarah told me we had to leave Egypt quick. She said we had to leave lots of countries quick. It's because we're Jews, and some folks don't like Jews, so we had to leave. That's how we came to the United States.

"Grandma Sarah told me. She was a Jewish woman who sailed the high seas to America. She lived completely Jewish, not like us all mixed in. Her name was Sarah Shulamit, the daughter of Asher and Miriam, she kept telling me to remember that, Sarah Shulamit, the daughter of Asher . . .

"A long time ago our Jewish family was living in Spain near the sea. They were fishermen and fisherwomen. It was a dangerous place for Jews because a lot of people around there just didn't like Jews. Once day some evil Spanish folks came to the door and told them they had to go. They had to go or be killed. They used to burn Jews and Muslims in the middle of the marketplace in those days, it was awful. They wanted to kill the whole family right there, but Grandma Sarah told me our family escaped. There were seven of them, Naomi and Jacob and their five children, and one of the girls was named Shulamit. They escaped down to the sea and took a boat to Almansil, Portugal. Because they were fishermen they knew all about boats.

"The evil people in Spain took most of our family's stuff — they took our money and our house and everything inside the house — our family just had barely enough money to live on and only one set of clothes. We had to leave so fast.

"In Portugal Naomi and Jacob took the last name Almansil, since that's where they lived. I bet if you look on a map you could find that name right now, Almansil, on the sea coast of Portugal. No one knows what their real Jewish last name was before they got to Almansil because they never told anyone. Grandma Sarah didn't know. They didn't want anyone to figure out that they were Jews and kill them.

"The Almansil family loved Portugal. Benjamin, the oldest son, was a fisherman along with his father. And Hannah, his sister, sold fish beside her mother in the market.

"On market days, Hannah and her younger sister, Shulamit, loved to walk beside the colorful flowers in the plaza. All of the Almansil family loved to walk on the tall cliffs and look at the Atlantic Ocean.

"On Fridays, Naomi secretly made a special Shabbat bread called challah. Do you know what *Shabbat* means? It's not the same as sabbath. The people around here use sabbath to mean

Sunday when you go to church. But Jews say *Shabbat* for Saturday when we go to temple. Back a while ago I would visit with a Jewish man named Asher from the synagogue in Portsmouth. Yes, Asher — the same name as Grandma Sarah's father, that's why I looked him up, something like your father's name, Oscar, but wait and listen, there's a connection. After Grandma Sarah died I looked up this Jewish man named Asher so he could tell me some things about being Jewish, but I didn't tell anyone in my family that I went to see him. I wanted to understand some things. But let me get back to the story.

"On Fridays back in Portugal, Hannah went to the sea cliff and picked flowers for the Shabbat evening table. Her brother Benjamin brought home his best fish from the seashore. And every Friday their father brought Hannah and Benjamin and Shulamit and the other children — I don't know their names — small carved wooden toys that he had made while he was out on the sea waiting for fish.

"Our Almansil family didn't want people seeing them doing Jewish things, so when they were all together for dinner, Naomi shut the curtains tight before she lit the Shabbat candles along with Hannah and Shulamit. You know, just like your Grandma Griffin does up there in Washington where you live. She's Methodist, a Christian, not Jewish, but even so she lights Jewish candles. You see, Jewish women and girls light the Shabbat candles every Friday night. Then the whole family shares a delicious meal.

"But their happiness in Portugal didn't last. The same thing that had happened in Spain happened in their new country. Jews were being killed all over the place in Portugal too. They were burning Jews and Muslims in the marketplace just the same. Our family had to run away. Even though the Almansil family loved their home in Portugal very much, once again they packed up what they had and left very quickly.

"They got on a big ship with lots of other Jews from Portugal, and sailed out on the Mediterranean Sea. They sailed past Spain and France until they landed in Venice, Italy.

"For many generations, the Almansil family lived happily in Venice near other Jews who had escaped from Portugal. There were mothers and daughters and granddaughters and great-granddaughters. There were fathers and sons and grandsons and great-grandsons. Life was good in Italy, but the Almansil family and their neighbors never forgot Portugal.

"But listen carefully to this, what my Great-Grandmother Sarah told me. In the year 1787, Asher Almansil and his wife, Miriam, had a daughter whose name was Sarah Shulamit. She's the one who ended up being my great-grandmother, Grandma Sarah. When Sarah was born they sang a joyful song to the Lord the first time they took her to the synagogue in Venice.

Joyful, joyful are all who live in this house.
Joyful is the lovely daughter of our house.
Joyful the mother and the father of the child who
*   dwells in this house!*

"And Sarah really was full of joy as a little girl. She learned how to dance, and she sang beautiful songs, new songs.

"Sometimes, she walked by the sea thinking about all her ancestors who had lived by the sea in Italy, Portugal, and Spain. Her father Asher would tell her the story of Hannah, her Jewish ancestor who sold fish in the market and loved the sea cliffs and flowers of Portugal, and he told about Hannah's younger sister, Shulamit, who loved to light the Shabbat candles, and that's where Sarah's middle name came from, Shulamit.

"One day, Sarah was walking near the sea wearing a dark head scarf, very different from the scarves worn by women who were not Jews. A group of pirates recognized Sarah as a Jewish girl and kidnapped her. They took her to their pirate ship with other captured Jews, and they set sail across the high seas to

North Africa. The pirates knew that Jews living in the big cities there would pay them silver and gold to set their captured Jewish brothers and sisters free.

"So Sarah was snatched away and she never saw her family again. That's right, she never saw her father Asher or her mother Miriam, ever again in her whole life.

"All the way over the sea, Sarah was miserable. She cried, 'Oh, where am I going? Who's going to help me? Do they kill Jews where I'm going?' Sometimes she looked up and saw that evil pirate flag flapping in the air. She was afraid, and she missed her family so much.

"But all the time Sarah was crying, there was a pirate named James watching. James had been kidnapped too, but he wasn't Jewish. The pirates told him that they would kill him if he didn't join up with them to be a pirate. So James had no choice but to pretend to be a pirate until he could sneak away. James decided to help Sarah. That same James became my Great-Grandfather. Let me explain it to you.

"When the pirate ship was almost in North Africa, near the city of Tripoli, Libya, James whispered to Sarah, 'I'm going to help you, don't worry.'

"'What are we going to do?' Sarah asked him.

"'We could just jump off this ship and run away,' James said.

"'They will see us,' said Sarah. 'We won't be fast enough. How can we walk away right in front of them without them stopping us?'

"They came up with a plan. James tied Sarah's hands behind her back. He put a cloth over her mouth. He tied a rope around her waist. When James was sure the captain was asleep in his cabin, he walked off the pirate ship with Sarah walking and crying beside him, tied to the rope.

"'Where are you going?' one pirate asked James.

"'I'm taking this woman to Zini, the rich Jew on the Alexandria Road, and we'll get a lot of ransom money for her. The captain told me to take her. I have to go with her alone, or else Zini won't open up the gate.'

"So the pirates let James and Sarah walk away.

"But James had made up that story about Zini, or whatever his name was. Grandma Sarah told me she couldn't remember his name right either.

"As soon as no one could see them, James cut the cord from around Sarah's hands. He took off the rope and threw away the cloth that was over her mouth.

"You can believe, after that, Sarah and James smiled at each other. It was good to get away from those pirates. It was good just to smile.

"James and Sarah decided to ask for help at a synagogue. When they found one, they each thanked God in their own way. 'Thank you, thank you, God.' said James. 'Baruch ata Adonai,' said Sarah. That's Hebrew that means, Blessed be the Lord. Grandma Sarah used to say that all the time and I never knew what it meant until a Jewish man from over on Effingham Road, his name was Asher too, explained to me what it meant.

"James and Sarah waited in the synagogue in Tripoli. When the men came for afternoon prayers, Sarah stepped out of the shadow. She bowed her head. 'Shma Israel, Adonai Eloheinu, Adonai ehad. Please help me, in the name of our God.'

"The men at the synagogue listened to Sarah's story and decided to help her.

"The rabbi said, 'Those pirates will be here tomorrow with the rest of their stolen Jews. If they find out you and James have escaped, they may kill both of you. Or they will sell you as slaves. They may not let us ransom you if they're mad. They get angry when even one of their kidnapped people gets away and now they have lost two. They may hurt our people if they find out that we helped you, Sarah, you have to hide. And,

James, I have an idea. There are some new ships here in Tripoli. Come and see.'

"They walked up a hill and looked at the ships in the port.

"The rabbi spoke again. "Look. Those ships belong to the United States of America. It's a new young country across the ocean and those people you see on those ships are their Marines. They call themselves the US Marines, and they have come over here to stop the pirates. James, you can go to the port, get on one of those ships, and sail to a new life in America. Here is some money to help you get away. And, Sarah, it is Shabbat tonight. Here are candles to light when you get to your hiding place, because we have to hide you from the pirates."

"So, Shirah, you know that song they sing about the Marines sailing to the shores of Tripoli? Well, the next time you hear that song you should think about the Marines saving our family in Tripoli, because that's what happened.

"Sarah was very unhappy to leave James. And James did not want to leave Sarah. He whispered in her ear, asking her to meet him at the boat that evening.

"And Sarah said, 'Yes.' You understand what happened, don't you? They fell in love and they wanted to be together.

"When they got to the ship, Captain Anderson of the United States Marine Corps helped them to sail to a beautiful peaceful island off the United States coast where pirates wouldn't bother them anymore. And he also agreed to marry them!

"After her wedding, Sarah began using her Hebrew middle name, Shulamit. She liked the name Shulamit because it reminded her of her the candles that the Rabbi gave her in Tripoli and the little girl in Portugal, Shulamit, who loved to light the Shabbat candles beside her mother. She also loved the meaning of the name Shulamit, because Shulamit means peace, and she wanted peace after all her family's traveling on the high seas. Sometimes, instead of using the name Shulamit, she used the name Olivia because it stands for the olive branch, and that also means peace. So she would call herself Sarah Shulamit or Sarah Olivia.

"That year when she came across the Atlantic Ocean was 1805. Sarah Shulamit and James landed on the Georgia Sea Islands, down south from here, and they lived there with the Geechees. That's why I had a Geechee basket for delivering fish. The Geechees are wonderful black people who came from West Africa with bright woven cloths and songs so beautiful that they enchant the ocean tides. These Geechees were free, even though it was during the time when black people were slaves in the United States. Sarah and James loved the Geechees and became one of them. Sarah Shulamit, or you can call her Sarah Olivia, wore the Geechee cloths and sang their enchanting songs. And she lit Shabbat candles like the ones the rabbi had given her in Tripoli.

"The longer Grandma Sarah stayed on the Georgia Sea Islands the more she used the name Olivia instead of the Hebrew name Shulamit. She said the two names mean the same thing, peace, and she decided to use the one people used the most in America.

"So my Great-Grandparents, James and Sarah Olivia, had children who married Geechees. All of their children and their children's children were Geechee fisherfolk. They earned their living catching and selling fish.

"Sarah called herself Sarah Olivia Shulamit daughter of Asher and Miriam, which means Sarah of Peace, daughter of Asher and Miriam. She didn't have a synagogue to go to on the Georgia Sea Islands. She almost forgot everything about being Jewish. But some things she didn't forget.

She didn't forget how her Almansil ancestors had loved Portugal. She hoped that one day one of her descendants would return there.

She didn't forget her father, whose name was Asher. She gave the name Asher to her son. He changed the name Asher to the name Oscar. And in every generation of our family we name one little boy Asher or Oscar. And that's why your father's name is Oscar.

And Sarah didn't forget her name meaning peace, Shulamit. She named one of her little girls Olivia, the American way of saying Shulamit, and asked her children to give one little girl in every generation that name.

And Sarah didn't forget to light the Shabbat candles on Friday nights.

And Sarah's daughter, my mother Olivia, didn't forget to light the Shabbat candles on Friday nights.

And Sarah's daughter's daughter is me, Olivia, and I don't forget to light the Shabbat candles on Friday nights.

And my daughters, your Aunt Lovey, whose real name is Olivia, and Ernestine, your grandmother, didn't forget to light the Shabbat candles on Friday nights.

"And so, Shirah Shulamit, that is our story. Now you know where the Shulamit part of your name comes from. Your name Shulamit and my name Olivia are the same name, and it has been passed down for more than 400 years.

"But that's such a good story, Great-Grandma Olivia, and is it really true?

Chile, don't you know? It's absolutely true . . . well, mostly. Anyhow, all the important parts are true. There really was a Jewish man named Asher in Italy who had a daughter named Sarah who was stolen by pirates and did all these things and she is our ancestor. And you know that your father's name is Oscar, which is another way of saying Asher. And you were named Shulamit after my great-grandmother Sarah just like I was named Olivia after my great-grandmother Sarah.

"My father told me that I'm named after you, Grandma Olivia, am I named after you and after your great-grandmother Sarah too?

"Yes! Both, child, both. I told you, in our family in every generation a little girl is named Olivia or Shulamit. That's how we remember Sarah Shulamit who was brought from Europe and Africa to America. You are the Shulamit, the Olivia of your generation.

Remember.

But you didn't remember, not for a long time. Your Great Grandmother Olivia told you this story when you were nine years old, but you didn't remember it until you were 49 and a professor at Mt. Holyoke College.

You had gone to a meeting at the South Hadley Congregational Church, a meeting for prospective members. A meeting just to talk about angels and faeries perhaps. All of you introduced yourselves. One man said. My mother is Jewish. My father is Christian. They gave me the choice of being Jewish or Christian, so I've decided to be Christian.

That was the day you knew who you were. That was the day you said, "If I had a choice I would be Jewish." And once the words came out they wouldn't go back. It was true. So you walked out of there and walked to Rabbi Carolyn. And Rabbi Carolyn sent you to the synagogue in South Hadley.

You went to see him once. He was kind to you. He listened to you, but he told you to take time to think about it. He told you to come back if you still wanted to try to be Jewish.

So you went away. You went to the library at Mount Holyoke College. You read, "To Be A Jew." You thought a lot. You went back to the Rabbi in South Hadley a second time. But it was the same thing. "Think about it, you may not be sure. Have you really considered it?"

You went away sad and thoughtful. Was this Rabbi a racist? Did he just dislike you? But he was always so kind in his words and his manner. His smiled welcomed you, and yet, why wouldn't he show you how to be Jewish? You went to more libraries and read more books. Mount Holyoke, Smith, Amherst, Northampton, University of Massachusetts. More and more thinking, reading, studying. You made up your mind. You went back to see the Rabbi in South Hadley a third time. You carried the books in your arms. You dropped all of the heavy books on his desk. You said, "I don't know why you don't want to teach me, but I read all these books and they say that you have to teach me. I'm not going to leave until you agree to teach me, I'm just going to hold on to your desk until you call the police to throw me out."

And you really did grab his desk and glare at him.

But he just smiled and said, "Okay, have a seat, let's get started."

"What?"

"Okay, let's get started."

"Just like that? After all this trouble."

"Yes, just like that. In Judaism you have to ask three times before you can begin conversion. Now you've asked the third time. So let's begin."

And so you began your study to convert to Judaism.

A few weeks later you attend your first Passover celebration. You are reading from the Haggadah, the book of the Jewish Passover.

"Every one of us must act as if we ourselves were slaves in Egypt. We were slaves, and the Lord brought us out of the House of Bondage with a mighty hand."

When you read that you remember what Mr. Kahn, the Green Grocer, told you back at the store in Mayfair Mansions. You understand, at last, why Mr. Kahn lied to you. At first he just told you the truth, he had never seen Moses. But as you and the green grocer become friends, he feels a Jewish connection with you because you want to be with Moses so much. So he remembers that the Haggadah says that every Jew, including Mr. Kahn himself, has to act as if he were a slave in Egypt. To connect you with the story Mr. Kahn has to change his story and tell you he that has come out of Egypt with Moses.

We were slaves, we are free. Mr. Kahn, your friend, lied to you so that if ever you became Jewish you would remember your first moments of wanting to be with Moses and Hebrews leaving Egypt for Israel. He put those beautiful words in your head so that you would recognize your long spiritual path from your childhood.

Springtime in South Hadley. Your mother and father visited and you told them that you are Jewish. Your mother saw you in the synagogue when they brought the Torah around. Your mother said, "You've been Jewish all your life, I just never knew it." You father said, "I like that you are Jewish."

But the surprise came when your parents saw you praying the Jewish prayers over the Shabbat candles on Friday night.

Your father listened and looked and said, "My mother always prayed that prayer over candles on Friday night."

Remember.

Baruch ata Adonai, eloheinu melech ha'olam, asher kidishanu b'mitz'votav v'tzivanu l'had'lik neir shel shabbat.

And you stand there remembering.

You remember the High Seas story your Great Grandmother Olivia told you, how your Jewish ancestors had been kicked out of Spain in 1492 during the Inquisition, and went from Spain to Portugal to Italy to Tripoli in Libya, where they were rescued by Rabbis and US Marines, and crossed the high seas to come to the Georgia Sea Islands and the Geechees, and then to Portsmouth, Virginia where your father was born.

There you are, standing spellbound in South Hadley, remembering, back and back.

Happy to dwell in this house.

Cluster 5 Your Day
Cluster 5 Argument

Okay, esteemed reader, so now you know my Shirah Shulamit Ojero story from the time I was three up to the time John Milton met me at Kann's and Carnegie Library in Washington. You even know that part of my family came from African descended Geechees and Spanish Jews.

***

You see, I remembered to put in the asterisks when the "I" changes. The "I" just changed from Shirah to Asenath.

Do you remember how I separated from Shirah and ran down Rolled Trousers Boulevard? I ran to the Charles River, but then ended up beside the Nile River, didn't you see me running through the Garden of Converging Paths right beside our palace?

Well, after that I ran around the side of our palace and up the grand stairs to my Hall of Colors. In Egypt I live in nine chambers that are all along The Hall of Colors.

Here are a couple of things to remember as you follow along with me, because why should I be like someone who is hidden when I'm right in front of you. First, even though I am 11 years old when I arrive here in Egypt, after descending from Heaven, as soon as I get here I start remembering all sorts of things that happened here before I arrived. That's what happens when you join up with a body that's already living., you start to remember earlier stuff even though you weren't there.

The second thing I want you to remember, dear reader, is that the Attic Chamber in my Egyptian palace, connects with the Attic in Takoma DC. In fact, I might as well just tell you, my Egyptian Attic Chamber and Shirah's Washington City Attic are the same room stretching and connecting through time. There you have it.

Listen.

Chapter 29: Ashrei

Happy are you who dwell in this tower.

You who once walked down Mass Ave with the Dean until you came to Bow Street,

You who once descended Bow Street and Broken Statue Cul de Sac and Lost Artist Café,

You who were the beloved one of the Reading Angels of Heaven, adorned, anointed with fragrant oil of peaches as you crossed Arrow Street near Poet's Lair, Dunster Street, Eliot House, Rolled Trousers Boulevard, Driven Memory Drive to the Charles River, which is the Nile.

Your name is peach oil poured out, therefore do we She-herazadim love you.

From Driven Memory Drive, we saw you cross over from the sodden bench where Luis Borges and Jamaica Kincaid sat chatting together. We praise you more than we praise Wednesday afternoon sherry; rightly do we love you.

You passed the Boat House, flashing your ornaments of silver studded gold.

We saw you walk up on the other side of the river through whispering reeds, to your Garden of Converging Paths. [74]

In your garden we see you with your three others, soaked by sunlight, soaked by the shimmering of the golden axeltree of the sun and scattered carbuncle and ruby of the sun. Behold you are beautiful, running as a mare runs upon the green land, truly lovely.

Tell us, dear one who has come forth from amidst the Reading Angels of Heaven, where do you run? Where do you rest at noon?

You step toward the palace of your mother, the great house of your father, this is your palace of light in the city of On, in Egypt. The beams of your palace are cedar, and your tower of cypress.

You run toward your forge of day, up to the Hall of Colors where your bright colors pour forth from great darkness, yea, dark, like the tents of Kedar, as the curtains of Pharaoh, pouring forth color.

Here is where you rest at noon, here you awaken to your life in this country, this place, this tower, this palace, this house, this day.

Oh happy, happy are you who dwell in this tower.

From the parapet you see the henna sunlight touching your fountain, with clear water splashing down toward your flowers, your vineyards.

See there the tents of the fruit growers among palm-groves, river gardens framed with southern ebony.

Your garden is rich with waters sending forth the fragrance of lily and myrrh.

Happy are all who are happy in you.

Your sun lifts high from far Okeanus who encircles human life, encircles, enchants, encumbers all the lands of human life, passing through columns of sky, bright, radiant ivory gables slanting the light, here are rows of jewels and strings of beads to adorn you. Behold, you are beautiful, beautiful.

O daughter of On and Saïs, of Ethiopia and Egypt, you are black and beautiful, your eyes are doves.

And you are happy as all are happy who dwell in this tower.

Happy are you who dwell in this tower.

Cluster 6 Your Desire; or,
Your Hall of Colors
Cluster 6 Argument

Okay, languishing reader, now I'm talking to Asenath herself.

Asenath, I never said that I have all of the papers you need to tell our story. If I find the papers, I'll send them to you. For now you just have to believe me. You're a priestess now, Asenath the Priestesss, and you are connected with this Shirah Shulamit Ojero grad student who keeps showing up in your ninth chamber, the Attic Chamber, even though she's way in your future. Did you hear the singing of the Ashrei? That happens in the tower of your sixth chamber, the Chamber of the Velvet Prism where you used to sleep to be near your teacher, the Barbarian Woman. From that tower you have seen Shirah Shulamit Ojero dancing by night at the University of Pen Forest. You listen to the Ashrei in mid-morning whenever the time of singing comes. You want to know who I am? That's not important, at least not yet. And any how you'll figure it out. I know both you and Shirah.

But look, now you are in the first chamber, the Chamber of Abdiel, a young woman, no longer a girl. You are deciding what to do. You want to become the librarian at Saïs, and you don't know how to do it. You can't just ask the Pharaoh for it, even though he's a good friend of your father. So you walk these chambers deciding.

You can't get in to the ninth chamber, the Attic Chamber, but you can stand in the eighth chamber, the Chamber of Mulberry Light and look through the window at Shirah in the attic. But that story comes later, as this nappy hair story becomes the Song of Songs.

When you walk the chambers you carry the Portfolio your teacher started for you — the Barbarian Woman, the Golden

One, the Day Tripper. Your Portfolio includes all the best words of all times. When you read them you can decide on things. Why don't you talk with your friends too — Palifa your companion, and Saul the Ivrim Steward, and even the Great Waterman, the Fountain, honor and light of storytellers, and his guide, Shaskan.

You will have to travel. You will have to leave On and travel to Saïs, Tanis, Sudan. And farther than that. You are following the river Okeanos, that goes forth out of Heaven, watering all the land thereof, flowing from the Old Pump.

Listen.

Chapter 30: The Chamber of Abdiel

You want it so much.

The heat presses you. You frown and groan, squinting and grimacing toward the window that is shaded by the parapet. Your eyes hurt, but it is not the sun, it is not the brightness of the sun that blinds you, rather it is your life. Your life is weariness. You want it so much. What? You lie with pillows and tossings on the orange brown couch of brooding, your Portfolio huddled beside you, here in your Hall of Colors; that is, the first chamber of our hall of colors, the Chamber of Abdiel.

You have struggled to know the gods and call them by name. Adramalech, Ariel, Arioch. They are wearying. Asmadai. Arina. Inevitably wrong, half right, almost right, aslant right. Too many of them, the lying gods. Staring from stone, cursing from wood, blaspheming from fire. You cup one of the gods in your hand. Rigid gazelle ears, diamond shaped eyes carved from brown tar. Heavy oval body. Cat whiskers. Neith. A god of tar and wood. You are her special one. You. Neith. Nath. Asnat. Asenath. Don't you know your own god? This is the god who prefers you above all others. But she is also the god who deserts you. You are special. Chosen. If you are special to Neith, you are accursed. There is no woman born of woman who can please her long.[75] Yet how can you fight against your own god, although she embitters your life?

Open your Portfolio and read.

Slavery and superstition are the curses of human life.[76]

Anger, Sing Anger, O goddess.[77]

Can such bitterness linger in the hearts of goddesses?[78]

He who carries a goddess across a river emerges with one sandal.[79]

Midway through the journey of our life.[80]

You repeat the words but do not understand. Why did your teacher, the Barbarian Woman, the Golden, why did she add these words to your Portfolio? The words are from Saïs, the Pharaoh's Library, from stories you have never known. Ahh, if only you could read all the words of all the stories for all the days of your life. If only you could always know what happens next. These are fragments. Read more fragments.

Once there was a holy messenger named Abdiel who traveled between two warring gods carrying reports of betrayal and war.

On such a day as Heaven's great year brings forth, Abdiel turned her back on Heaven and descended to earth to visit a woman.

But what happened after that? What's the story? What's the rest of the story? You want to know the whole story. What about all those unread stories in the library of the Pharaoh in Saïs. Why aren't you the keeper of that library?

God thoughts toss you on the couch and turn you this way to the wall and that way back to the edge. You stand up and walk out upon the south balcony and look down upon the streets of On.

You have not heard back from the Pharaoh. You sent him a papyrus with new god-words. You have asked him to turn away from the god-word of obedience. Not obedience but understanding. That's what you wrote to him. You wrote, A religion of obedience is for people who cannot think. Not obedience but conversation, connection, argument, discussion. Why not? It makes so much sense. But what if the Pharaoh hates those words, conversation, discussion. You have been hoping he would choose you as Keeper of the Library. He won't like your words. You will never read the whole story from the scrolls of the library. And you want it so much.

You sit down upon a carved wooden stool on the fragrant terrace, the carved wooden stool that Ptah made with all his wisdom and with all his refinement when he poured power upon it. Ptah gave the stool to the daughter of Ra, Sheshet, and Sheshet, keeper of spells, she who gave the power of writing to human souls, gave the wooden stool to Thoth her husband, he whose wisdom aided Osiris to murder the god of chaos, Set. Thoth lost it in a bitter wager with Hagar, the human wanderer who came returning from across the river of the east into Egypt. She was seeking a wife for her son Ishmael, and Hagar, with the power given to her by the god who sees, transformed the stool, carving upon it new words she had learned from the east, then she gave it to Portphres, priest of Neith, as a brideprice for his daughter, Ishmael's wife, Reaus. Portphres gave it to An-Tel, the lonely one who raged against the invaders of the west. He died and passed the stool on to Tesythy, who scaled the enclave upon the cliffs of Din, and she in turn bestowed it on Poti-pherah, son of Nola, as a seat of meditation for the high priest of On, as he spoke the will of the gods to the people of lower Egypt and upper Egypt. Now you, Asenath, daughter of Poti-pherah, sit upon it and brood upon the nature of wisdom, the nature of the gods, the nature of desire and the rest of the story.

Cluster 7 Your Sojourn
Cluster 7 Argument

Okay, Meandering Reader, now you've got to return with me to Washington, DC and the twentieth century, and follow Shirah Shulamit as she moves through junior high school, high school, and college. Yes, I know you were just watching Asenath brooding in the Chamber of Abdiel — when the documents are gathered to tell the rest of that story I shall send them to you. For now, come with me to Woodson Junior High as Shirah solidifies her attachment to John Milton's ***Paradise Lost***. At Paul Junior High a young Jewish boy crosses over the racial barrier on a playground and Shirah learns more about Judaism. At Coolidge High School you watch her confrontation with the hatred of the school counselor. After some trouble and a year of French school, you celebrate with Shirah as she starts college at Howard University. Her first book is published while she is there. From Howard during the 60s riot years, she transfers to Eastern University of St. Davids, in the state of Pen's Forest. Do you want to know why you should follow me now, it is because this is the way the waters flow from the Okeanos that encircles the world.

At Eastern University, on an ecstatic day of self-realization, you will feel the rain on your neck and shoulders. There you are, Shirah Shulamit Ojero, standing in the rain by a willow tree, its trunk is silver, its crown of leaves are purple, the ground of it is gold. It is here, Shirah, that you learn that you are, indeed, a singer of epic song.

Listen.

Chapter 31: Woodson Junior High School

You are walking to Woodson Junior High School, flinging your keys in the air, the keys touch and tinkle against each other and make a rain song.

You sing along with the ringing of the keys in the air.

Shirah Shulamit Ojero, it is you. This is the September after the August when you first read ***Paradise Lost***.

Your Seventh Grade English teacher asks.

What did you do over vacation?

Reluctant hands. But your hand is up.

What did you do?

"I read ***Paradise Lost*** by John Milton."

"You did not." Her answer to you is harsh.

And she does not call on you any more.

That was the day it happened. That's when the die was cast the Rubicon was crossed the Waterloo was watered and All Was LOST! Or at least Paradise was Lost. Or won. For you.

If she had not ignored you you might never have read ***Paradise Los***t again. You might have thrown poor words away and been content to live.[81] You would never have become a Graduate Student. This story would never have happened to you. You would never have become the EpicCentrist.

You made a promise to yourself that day that you would read ***Paradise Lost*** once a year for the rest of your life. And thus it was.

Chapter 32: Paul Junior High School

And then they integrate you into another school, not Woodson, but Paul Junior High School. One day when you are standing with your friends, black friends, because you are black, and the black students don't stand outside with the white students . . . one day a girl, a white girl, says to you, "I'm sorry for what happened. I can walk a few blocks with you but I can't let my mother see me walking with someone of your color."

And then one of the boys, one of the white boys who has refused to listen to you as you and your friends sing Christmas carols in class, who is one of those who turns his chair around, they turn their backs to you as you sing, "O Come Let Us Adore Him" — one of the white boys comes over to you on the playground and speaks.

"We are Jews. We don't believe in Jesus. It is not because of you — it is because of Christianity that we turned our chairs around. We don't believe in Jesus be we're required to come to school and we have to listen to songs we don't believe. It's not because you are Negroes, I'm not mad at you, but I'm mad because we're forced to listen to a religion we don't believe in. The teacher isn't Jewish. She's Christian like you. But she doesn't explain anything. She does it on purpose so no one will understand. She is the one who hates you, and she hates us too. She wants you to feel bad when we don't listen. And she wants us to feel bad by listening to a religion we don't believe in. How would you feel if you had to sit and listen to a religion you don't believe? We're forced to come to the Christmas programs, if we don't come they lower our grades — and so we protest to let them know how we feel. Maybe they will still lower our grades, but we're mad and we don't care anymore."

You are shocked. You didn't know. You hadn't realized. So that is the reason. This is the moment. In this moment Hebrews in books and Jews in history finally connect for you with real Jews sitting the in same classroom with you. You have heard of World War II. Of course, you were born in 1947 and although that war was over, you still heard the guns and bombs of that war in the voices of the grownups around you as you grew older.

Throughout elementary school the teachers told you of Hitler's Germany, horror after horror. Jews beaten. Imprisoned. Separated. Murdered. But you never had to fit that in with the tensions between black people and white people around you. No one ever said clearly to you, "The people in Europe are white people. White people are fighting other white people there." Is that possible? You thought white people only fought against black people.

You already know that Jews have a different religion. You already know that most of your white fellow students are Jews. But you think of them as flat out white people. Are there different kinds of white people? Yes. That's what you figure out in this crucial moment.

Until now the effect of Jews in the class room is that you have a few half-holidays in September. When the Jewish kids are out for their holidays, the white teachers do not bother to teach the rest of you anything.

So it is that a boy steps across a barrier and speaks to you and brings complexity, a great good fortune. There are more than two ways of seeing, more than three. More.

Who leads that boy across the pavement of Paul Junior High to give you the information you need when you cannot figure it out for yourself? What makes him choose you to speak to of all the black children who stand clustered there?

Chapter 33: Not College Material

You are not college material. The counselor, Mrs. Sweeney, at Calvin Coolidge High School in Washington, DC, is just doing her job.

Her job is to figure out who are the smartest most gifted black students, call them into her office, and tell them that they are not college material.

There are ten of you.

You.

You, Shirah, make the 99th percentile on the college entrance exam.

You made a higher score than 99% of every student in the United States, and for this reason Mrs. Sweeney sits on your recommendations, shreds your applications, and makes sure you don't have enough room to write at the table when the white students take College Board Writing Exam.

The College Board Writing Exam is an extra exam, you don't have to take it, but you want to take it. You are a presumptuous colored chile.

But they defeat you.

They don't even let you know when the exam is being given down in the cafeteria.

When your friends whisper to you in the hall that the white students are already downstairs taking the exam you get an excuse from class and rush down to the cafeteria.

They have already started. They are sitting all around the large cafeteria table and there is no room for you.

Mrs. Sweeney hands you a paper to write on but there is no place to sit.

You stand there trying to squeeze into a corner of the cafeteria table.

All the white students are already writing their essays. They don't even look up at you. They don't even care.

They won't make a place for you

And Mrs. Sweeney has cruel eyes.

You walk up to Mrs. Sweeney and ask her for a place to sit to do the writing exam.

She looks at you, "You just have to find your own place."

Then no one looks at you, brown chile that you are, the nerve of you.

No brown chile has signed up for the College Board Writing Exam before.

Who do you think you are?

You don't know what to do.

You squeeze into a corner of a table.

You are a pitiful colored child.

You barely have time to write your name and a paragraph or so, scrunched in the corner, before the time is up.

You are shamed, and don't even tell your mother and your father what happened.

Shamed. Not college material. What makes you think you can go to college?

And later, when the scores for the writing exam come in, your name is not even on the list.

Mrs. Sweeney calls you into her office to let you know. You are not college material. You are not smart enough to go to college, you and your 99th percentile. The colleges you apply to don't even send you rejection letters, Smith College, Radcliffe College, Carnegie Institute of Technology. Mrs. Sweeney has made sure that they have never heard of you.

Chapter 34: Velatis and Silver

Il y a

Il y a 50 years, that's French for fifty years ago.

Il y a 50 years, you wanted to go to college.

Il y a 50 years, your father comforts you. He says, you are smart. He says, you'll get to college, don't worry! You're already a year ahead of your class any way. Why don't you study French for a year privately?

Il y a 50 years your father sends you to the Vox School of Languages. You read French stories and sit drinking hot chocolate in the Velatis Caramel Store, and you watch your own eyes watching back from the silver platters in Garfinckel's and you want to go to college.

Il y a 50 years, a long time ago, in another place, once upon a time.

You really want to go to college.

Mrs. Sweeney, the counselor of Calvin Coolidge High School, has taken the nerve out of you. What happened at Coolidge? Why don't you tell someone? Hatred. You won't tell, you think there is some secret weakness in you. You don't understand. You still don't.

You are a loser. When you are not at the Vox School of Languages, when you are not at the Velatis caramel shop, when you are not looking at your brown face in the silver of Garfinckel's, you are sitting in the Takoma DC Library. T. S. Eliot finds you there. You grow old, you grow old, you shall wear the bottoms of your trousers rolled. Shall you part your nappy hair behind? Do you dare to eat a peach? Loser.

But Mrs. Sweeney has not taken the nerve out of your mother, no, your mother gets an application from Howard University, and she fills it out in your name, and she forges your signature on it, and one spring day, when you come home from

Vox School of Languages, il y a forty-nine years, there is a letter waiting for you from Howard University.

The Admissions Office of Howard University is pleased to inform you.

Pleased.

Come on honey chile, enter into your birthright. You've got it now, and there ain't no Mrs. Sweeney left in the world can stop you, not that you have begun.

Il y a 19 years.

Who knows? One day, among all the un-graduates at Howard, chosen from among all the angels of Heaven, because of this beginning, you may become a Graduate Student.

Chapter 35: So Journeying

And how had you come to Takoma? Your family was one of the black families block busted between Underwood and Van Buren Streets. The white folks were so mean. And when you went up to buy food at the Safeway they looked like they were going to spit on you, they didn't even want you buying food to eat. You were in high school, a sophomore at Coolidge, and one evening you sat on the sofa in your living room wondering what was wrong with those white people.

Then came the knock on the door.

It was a white man named Marvin Caplan, and some other people were with him, black and white. "We've come to welcome you to the neighborhood." Really. The knock on the door that came at the right time for the right listener. "We're a group called Neighbors Incorporated. We're glad you have come to live in the neighborhood. Our neighborhood." Your parents came down to listen. And your brother Sazonado Smitty. And you.

And now you, a woman of the Takoma neighborhood of Washington, DC, and a student of Howard University, meander the streets of Washington DC from LeDroit Park to Shaw to the Anacostia Chair to the Kenilworth Lily Ponds to U Street to the Southwest Waterfront to Mount Pleasant.

And poetry of the city comes to you as you walk, the words are good; yet you hold the poetry in your head, hidden.

Then a call comes to you, to come to Green Lake, Wisconsin, with many youth, to speak and tell of cities and of God, it was a gathering that American Baptists held there. You heeded that call and visited the village by the lake.

And in that Lake Village, the folk gathered, and upon the evenings they brought poetry that they had written, and they read the poetry where many listened. And they that listened to the poetry gave great honor to the poets.

And there was a man called the Singer of Pen's Forest there, who turned to you, Shirah Shulamit Ojero, saying, "Have you no poem for us?"

Then it was you stood up among them and spoke your poetry to them, those words that had passed through your head as you meandered the streets of Washington.

And after you spoke your poetry a great shout lifted up from the Lake Village, as they all cried out praising you. "A poet," they cried, "A new poet is among you and we did not know!"

So you returned from Green Lake, Wisconsin, with their praises in your ear. And the Singer of Pen's Forest spoke to a printer of books, that there should be a book of your poetry available for all to read.

And it was so.

And you named the book, ***Sojourner***, for you felt that you were a Sojourner in the land that was not yet your own, a secret Jewish woman making your way among the Baptists, even as the ancient Children of Israel sojourned so long in a land that was not yet their own.

Chapter 36: Howard University Fire

In 1967 you are a sophomore at Howard University. It is springtime, and the students around you are angry. Can you see the effigy catch fire? The flames flash against dark, dark eyes. You see the rope around his neck catch fire. University president paper maché and white-washed black pain. Choking. Smoke. Clogging the windows of Douglass Hall. You watch as a black man leaps up on the box, grabs the megaphone, and demands that all black sisters, you included, subjugate themselves to their men. A white man from the Washington Post lies where they tossed him, with his broken camera and his broken arm, crushed against the steps of Locke Hall. A white woman with stringy blond-brown hair leaps with both arms into the effigy tree demanding to be sacrificed for the cause. But you sit in philosophy class in Douglass Hall. Metaphysics.

The flames rise from the effigy to move along the branch. Black smoke bundles upward through your open classroom window. The students in the room, all except you, panic, grab up papers and books, knock into chairs escaping, scream, depart quickly. The professor stops her lecture a moment and gazes after the students. Tall black woman. Then her brown eyes meet the brown eyes remaining. Your eyes. Black woman. Yes. You are still sitting there looking up at her. Waiting.

Hesitation.

Spinoza. Renegade Jew. Smart. Metaphysical.

She glances toward the window, the smoke. Her fingers are on the handle of the window. She pulls it shut and locks it and then turns to you.

Or if not Spinoza, then certainly Aristotle. Metaphysical.

Screams batter the side of the building. They are cursing each other's souls to hell. Somebody snickers close to the wall. The fire lifts. The University police arrive. You listen. You hear.

"It was by accident of course that the branch of metaphysics received its name. It was the book following physics when

Aristotle's works were catalogued, but through a propitious co-incidence . . ."

The fire consumes the scene behind your professor, engulfing the tree and blotting out for a moment the intricate crevices of Miner Teachers College, the college of your mother and your grandmother, echoing the far strip of sunset.

Not physics, but metaphysics.

Your professor's slender fingers in the half-opened volume. The perturbed earnestness in her appeal to you, what is it she wants of you? What? What are you being asked to do? Who are you?

". . . such that the nature of ultimate reality, regardless of intellectual laziness, of productivity that is mere intelligential automatonism, evokes an inescapable human confrontation with extremity."

A long enflamed branch falls carrying others with it. You jump in your seat but your professor holds your eyes with her eyes. Brown eyes.

Not physics, but metaphysics.

But the tree is burning down to the ground.

Through the agency of metaphysics.

In the silence your silent question — "My teacher, can you tell me who I am?"

She speaks until the end of the hour. To you. You alone. You.

You cross the campus and join the protest. Today you students are taking over Dean Snowden's office. Yes, even though he is your hero, you have decided that the moment has come to oppose even him, Dr. Frank M. Snowden, Jr., classicist and philosopher, dean and professor of Howard's school of Arts and Sciences, African-American — and your first classics professor. You take over his office with the rest of them. On the desk is a small statue, perhaps replicated, perhaps original, from ancient

Greece, of a black man with African features and tight curls of woolly hair carved into his head. You students are everywhere, intruding, protesting, sitting in — on the chairs and cabinets and windowsills, leaning against the walls, cross-legged on the floor. Everywhere except on his desk. All around the walls are photographs of ancient objects showing blacks in antiquity. Wise eyes from antique black faces glancing at all of you, a tumble of living black arms and hands pressing against the walls. All of you fill the foyer and the hallways leading to his office, any administrator who hopes to sit in this office this day has to brave a thicket of your legs and shoulders and angry student eyes.

You students are not quite angry enough to sit at his desk however, his aura forms a bubble of space there, and you students have chosen a day when he is not supposed to come to the office at all. You have planned on not seeing him, but he comes. You cringe into yourself as the other students whisper, "He's coming." Dean Snowden walks up the steps to Newman Hall, passes through the crowd of silenced students, excuses himself as he gently brushes through the stifling doorway, walks to his desk, sits down and starts working. You try to squeeze yourself into the floor.

After a few moments he looks up and focuses on you sitting cross-legged on the floor in front of his desk.

"Did you read this week's assignment?"

"What?"

"Did you finish the trilogy? Did you read ***Antigone***?"

"***Antigone***?" How could he talk to you about ***Antigone*** at such a crisis, with all the students of the whole black power revolution listing in. You look up into his face.

"Yes, I finished all three last week, once I started ***Oedipus Rex*** I couldn't stop."

"What do you think about Antigone's method of making a decision?"

You hesitate at first in your answer, hearing the breath of your fellow students around you, but then you focus on his eyes.

"I thought it was strange the way she seemed to change her mind part of the way through the play. She said she would not have insisted on defying the state and burying her brother if the dead man had been her son or husband. She said she could get another husband or another child, but she couldn't get another brother since her parents were dead."

"Don't you think that makes perfect sense?"

"Maybe that rings true for ancient Greeks, but I just didn't believe her. I don't think that's what's going on at all. I think Antigone was showing what we do sometimes when we make a big decision. We make up our minds according to what we believe. And we don't care what powerful people think about it. But then there's always a time, maybe in the middle of the night, when you doubt everything. You come up with excuses and explanations for not doing what you've decided to do. Right at that moment all the fancy words you had the day before feel like nothing."

"Yes, but do you find that by morning you are back to believing in everything again? You don't just leave it there do you?"

"No, I can't. In the morning it's back to the way it was at first, with the believing in the first decision."

"And when you think back on that moment of doubt you wonder what possessed you to drop your belief even for a moment."

"Yes. I read that part of ***Antigone*** over and over — and an image came to me. I thought of a pipe carrying fresh water somewhere, and the water is rushing fast because there is a lot of pressure on it. But then suddenly the sides of the pipe are gone and the water can scatter anyway it will without direction, it seems to have given itself up to having no direction. Yet somehow the water floats across the emptiness until it enters the continuation of the pipe, almost as if there had never been that blank spot. Even the water is baffled that there was a moment when it did not know itself, or where it was going. Antigone's debate with herself is like that, an empty space between two important drives for completion."

You have forgotten all about where you are and that there are dozens of students leaning against walls and tables around you. Listening.

"So why are you here?"

"I don't know — I mean it's a bunch of things and they're not all clear."

"Can you tell me some of them?"

"At first I couldn't connect to this protesting. I couldn't believe that my country would ever do anything to hurt me."

"Your country wouldn't do anything to hurt you?" Dean Snowden looked at you puzzled. "What did you think about slavery?"

"I never thought of the two things at the same time. Slavery and civil rights were over here. And my perfect country was over there. And I never put the two together to think about it."

"It sounds like you're thinking about it now, but the problem may be that you only have one chance to think about it. You consider it and you make your choice. You act on it. But what if you consider it again and add new information and new conclusions. It's too late to retract or adjust."

"Yes, it's like being stuck in a cave and someone has shut the door. Are you a weak Ismene if you want to adjust what you do? Can you still be Antigone and reach new good conclusions?"

"Maybe there are more than two paths, maybe there are at least three — you know, where three roads meet." He gathers his work and leaves.

Silence.

In the silence you ask your silent question for the second time — "My teacher, can you tell me who I am?"

About ten minutes after he leaves, you get up and leave too, you need time to think, you need to think about the power of slaves and servants, because if the slaves and servants of the Oedipus trilogy had done what they were told, then Oedipus would have died as an infant. Servants and slaves are free to do what they want to do. No one gets to own anybody.

You need to find your way to African epic, the epics that have been hidden from you — Shaka the Great, and Mwindo, and Sundiata and Ham-Bodêdio. And isn't there a great African hero who tries to drown himself and reaches again and again into his own soul to cast away all his great gifts, even immortality, as he tries to break from his fate? Doesn't he have acute kinship with Oedipus? Why isn't it wrong and evil for Oedipus to kill the man at the crossroads where three roads met, whether or not it is his father. Why doesn't the play worry about that? And if the Oedipus story can be so enhanced by the story of a woman, Antigone, what if these African epics could guide you to an African epic founded on the story of a woman? What woman? Who?

It's too much to think about all at once: fate, guilt, responsibility, knowledge . . . and a crossroads where three roads meet. Or perhaps, adding Antigone's path to the three that Oedipus found, perhaps four roads, four paths, converging, in a garden.

Are you there? Are you going to get there? If ever you get there use all the care you can. Think once, think twice, then think again . . . and don't kill anybody.

Silence.

In the silence your silent question, you ask for the third time — "My teacher, can you tell me who I am?"

The gazelle of the stars.

You are the gazelle of the stars, but you do not yet know it. It will be a long time before you know it.

Chapter 37: Ekstasis University of the East

And you come at last to the University of the East, a land of Baptists, you are a stranger among them, a sojourner in a land that is not your own, yet they welcome you and nurture you and send you forth wiser than when you came because you come singing the song of the Sojourner an ancient song beloved by the folk of that place.

One there is who welcomes you. No, I don't mean Bob, who hates war, who says to you, "Let us work to end all wars," there at the University of the East.

One there is who welcomes you. No, I don't mean Susan and Michael, friendly smiling Baptists who keep praying for your soul. Who never tire of asking you, "Have you been washed in the blood of the lamb?" there at the University of the East.

One there is who welcomes you. No, I don't mean Joyce, who runs in the rain with you. Who says to you, "Let's make high tea on the third floor, with boiling water and loose tea from the market and an ancient teapot and real china. And strawberries, all on stacked wicker boxes," there at the University of the East.

One there is who welcomes you. No, I don't mean Sondra of First Nations, who escapes from the dorm with you and instead of defying authority together all you both do is catch poison ivy hiding by the stream, laughing, there at the University of the East.

One there is who welcomes you. No, I don't mean John, who walks through mists between lakes, saving ducks from turtles, who gives you the ***Lord of the Rings*** to read, who doesn't know that he himself is Tom Bombadil, there at the University of the East.

One there is who welcomes you. No, I don't mean the Peace and Freedom Committee, where Bob and John and Joyce and Sondra and Harry and Donna say over and over "War is not healthy for children and other living things," and refuse to buy grapes, and march for Civil Right, for Peace, for Freedom, there at the University of the East.

One there is who welcomes you. No, I don't mean Gene Beardsley, the Professor who teaches you how the world views move the centuries, one after another, how Romanticism must follow Neo-Classicism and it can't be the other way around,and gives you James Joyce, there at the University of the East.

One there is who welcomes you. No, I don't mean John Ruth Professor, who teaches you that fiction is made, that in the **Scarlet Letter** there is no prison, no rose, no red color of the rose, but Hawthorne made it up, fiction is made up! there at the University of the East.

One there is who welcomes you. No, I don't mean Fred Boehlke Professor, who gives you Tolstoy, as it were the shield of Achilles, **War and Peace**, stretched out from Moscow to the Mediterranean, where in 1805 your ancestor, your Sarah Shulamit bat Asher, could not return home to Italy, you learned that the canons of Napoleon brought your family from Tripoli to the Georgia Sea Islands and the Geechees, your words between their words of Russian History, Literature, there at the University of the East.

One there is who welcomes you. No, I don't mean the biology professor who teaches creationism or the religion professor who teaches evolution, and you listen to them both, there at the University of the East.

One there is who welcomes you. No, I don't mean the Drama Professor who hired you to run **Waiting for Godot** or the art professor who graciously turned away her eyes from your incapacity or the music professor who called you by name and honored you, there at the University of the East.

One there is who welcomes you. No, I don't mean Tony Campolo Professor, whose vision of the street, gives you your vision of forests, and you lay down in front of bulldozers to stop the cement and concrete, there at the University of the East.

One there is who welcomes you. No, I don't mean even Caroline Cherry Professor, even though she was your first Milton Professor, although she welcomes you indeed, from the fruit of that forbidden tree through Eden taking your solitary way, and they all welcome you, Bob and Susan and Michael and Sondra and Joyce and John and Gene and John Ruth and Fred Boehlke and religion and biology and drama and art and music and Tony Campolo and Caroline Cherry, they all welcome you and you listen to them.

But one there is who welcomes you and you will not listen, a professor who choses you but you will not choose him back, who keeps a place open for you in all his classes but you never take them, who waits for you semester after semester but you do not come, he is Wesley Ingles Professor, who says of you, but you will not listen, there at the University of the East, "At last we have a poet."

Yet it is at the University of the East that you first turn your face southeastward, toward Ethiopia, where you long to visit the House of Learning where the Lore Master of the Chane people draws rectangles around random words and images. From those words and images you may read the unknown story of your own life.

And there finally, at the University of the East, came the *ekstasis* thunderstorm, with lightening, against the willow tree just down the hill from your dorm room, by the upper lake. "Spirit of Creation," you cried out, "rain down on me." And you ran out into the storm with your arms spread wide to the cold rain, and the lightening flashing. "Spirit of Creation, rain down on me." And the high willow was tormented by rain in front of your eyes, and lightening struck at the lake, slashed at the water wheel as you turned and turned beneath the pouring sky. "Spirit of Creation, rain down on me," you cried out. And the lightening was sharp against your eyes, and you trembled before the power of the sky, was it from beyond the sky? and the thunder was terrifying.

Ekstasis. What does it mean? What portent is this? What will come of it? Who is arriving at last?

For a moment you are taken out of yourself and the Spirit of Creation is raining down on you, here by the willow tree near the upper lake, right here, at the University of the East. Pillar of silver, crown of purple, ground of gold.

Cluster 8 Our Story
Cluster 8 Argument

Okay, Longsuffering Reader, do you want to know more about the Portfolio? The Portfolio contains words in a book, the best words from everybody, and sometimes more than words, sometimes music and pictures. But you've probably figured out by now that the Portfolio is also a collection of the poets and other folks who live in Shirah's head. A lot of times they like to come out of her head and hang out in her attic — you know that attic in Takoma DC.

The Portfolio poets like to argue inside the thoughts that are the cosmos of Shirah Shulamit Ojero. John Milton, Phillis Wheatley, Langston Hughes, Zora Neale Hurston, Homer, Vergil, Dante, Milton, Idrissa Batâl, Angelina Weld Grimké, Paul Lawrence Dunbar, John Keats, Fyodor Dostoevsky, Honoré de Balzac, Ludwig van Beethoven, Shorty Long, yes all of Shirah's poets, they are a locked garden, a sealed fountain, but now they begin to flow — we begin to flow toward you, and toward the mountains of Amarna.

We are collecting more papers for the conclusion. When the time is come you will meet the Adversary, the patron of social services, bane of artists and plague of students. Right now, however, you will discover what acts preceded the moment when the Ocean of Light flowed through Shirah's attic, and the attic opened onto the firmament, and she descended to earthly life in Washington City.

Listen.

Chapter 38: Attic Poets

John Milton

Finally you have come. Where have you been? These stairs have been waiting for you a long time. At last we hear you stumbling up the square turns, over the kitty litter and the boxes of papers and scattered folders back to us.

Finally you face me. Again. You see the narrow attic room, pale blue with slants and flats. There is a window at the far end. Why are you dazed by the window? Nothing is the matter. Those are just warm green mulberry leaves tossing and bending in summer air, spotted and speckling, mottling your eyes with light.

You stand there blinking and wondering about the bookcases with their floating maps rustling. Can you hear us talking to you? Speaking? Do you remember when we first met? I'm John Milton. And you have returned to me. I am one of many attic poets who call to you. We have waited for you. Yes, I know. You've been hearing us as we talk inside your head, but this is different. In this attic we stand outside you. We see you entirely. Can you see us? This is our favorite place. Here we do things.

Do you know where this stuff comes from? It's yours. You have been putting junk here since you were born, you cluttered the shelves and pinned those gold tinsel stars to the ceiling. Look! There are the eight track tapes you had when you lived in New Mexico, a bunch of soul music on tapes that can't play on anything. What's that?! That's an antique telephone your father gave you when you decorated the gold room downstairs, and packs of incense you bought at the Pyramid shop on Harvard Street near Howard University. A copper candle holder from Kinshasa, engraved china from England — you thought you were going to get married once — and a malachite turtle from Lubumbashi. A mess, but a good mess. We can work with this stuff. I don't mind it here. Well, sometimes I don't mind it.

Now you recognize even more things. Is this attic a storage place for old reports and papers? You have been in schools writing them all the days of your life. Yes, you! Who else could have stuffed your own bookcases with your own junky looseleaf notebooks and your own raggedy pages? That's your narrow orange brown couch crushed up against your row of bookcases on the left. What were you thinking of to set up such an attic, so cramped and musty? But you like the papers and the books and the dried ink on your fingers. You yearn toward them.

Your chosen things have been lying here waiting for you a long time. Those glass containers are from college. Once you wanted neat rows of dried beans and pasta, kidney beans and lentils and linguini and black eyed peas and angel hair spaghetti but all you have now is a bunch of empty glass containers. Do you remember that carved wooden jewelry box with cheap plastic coins from New Orleans? And there's your grandmother's precious gold bracelet. Wine glasses, pencils, there's the birthday card I sent you wishing you good morning although someone else signed my name, Happy Birthday Shirah Shulamit, from John Milton. You were so happy to get a birthday card from the seventeenth century! And there are the bookends from a shop in Philadelphia, a wooden model of a sixteenth century Italian globe, a disused photocopier — you helped your father run a community newspaper with that, a shelf of jigsaw puzzles. The tinsel from the ceiling waves in the breeze from the air conditioner behind you, fluttering golden sheets of paper that are your journal, so many words.

So much stuff! A ring of scarves, a ceramic cat, the game of Go, old paints and drawings of Africa, a painting of Joseph in his coat of many colors. Mz. Cooper from your mother's church, Third Baptist Church, gave you that picture. You have scribbled the words, "Who speaks," on the edge of the picture. Here's a cluttered table, a stack of blue cardboard file cabinets. And on a book shelf beside your orange-brown bed you have deodorant and perfume and soap. Scattered clothes are lying on the floor and hanging from a makeshift rack pressed against the file cabinets. The suitcases are empty, all except one that you are slowly unpacking. You see, this is one of your regular places! Yet you have been gone so long!

Who do you imagine you are by the way, coming up here so strangely and not even knowing that this stairway is the escape to your future? Yes, this attic room is a vestibule, and this vestibule leads to the corridor of your future. We call it Heaven. This attic is your Heaven and you live here. All this junk is the furniture of your attic Heaven.

Well, don't worry. The fact is we poets need you here. I, John Milton, with so many others, Langston Hughes, Thomas Mann, Phillis Wheatley, Goethe, Paul Lawrence Dunbar and that music you're saving on those hopeless tapes. Will you ever hear those tapes on a machine again? But listen over here now. Something else. More voices. Ancestors. Forerunners. Joseph and Hagar and Jacob and Esau, Jeremiah and Naomi, Let there be Light. Jewish, Egyptian, Congolese. We attic poets need you to choose a book from one of these bookshelves. A book or one of these knick-knacks from a shelf. You really can't call them sculptures. Or you could choose a map. Words from the maps touch your tongue, Ouande Djalle, Grantown on Spey. What do you think? Can't you just choose a place?

You want to know what's going on? You thought you were just walking up into your dusty attic with a pot of tea and some bananas, or is that cantaloupe you have today? Yes, it's cantaloupe in your hand. You planned to sit drinking tea and making up your mind about something, what? Some paper is it? You have some paper to finish for school. A dissertation? Is that why you came up here to your perfect vestibule of your attic Heaven?

Come on Shirah Shulamit, forget the dissertation and walk up and down and choose something? What takes you so long? We're sick of waiting for you!

What are you saying? You say ain't nothing stopping us from doing something ourself! You say go ahead and look at the doggone stuff myself! You a mess. Yeah sure we know that. For lo these many years we've known that we can float in and out of your head even when you're downstairs, it's not only when you're in the attic that we can come out. But we only live strong when you're up here in the attic. Give us a chance. Here we make your life happen. We become you. We can act. It's just so much better to do stuff when you're here in the attic with us. But you've got to choose something to help us out.

You want to know how many of us there are? Who can tell? The fact is at first we thought there were just a few of us up here, but as soon as we looked around there were more poets than we could count. There's no way we can count us all. Don't you know most of us are never standing up anyway? We call ourselves the Portfolio now. Does it make some kind of difference how many of us there are? Hey, Shirah! don't get sleepy while we're standing here talking to you, please! That always happens. You just won't listen to us at all. Every time we start to say something clever you go on off to sleep. That's no way to treat us. We stepped out of your own brain after all! We're yours. What? I already told you I'm John Milton. There are times when I really love your attic. Here we can walk around and touch things, instead of just seeing them blurred through your head. When we are inside your head, Shirah, we can't tell if you see a thing or if you just want to see it. I like this attic. I like figuring out what you're really doing by stepping out and pushing things a little, just a very little. We are so curious.

When we're all alone in this attic we wonder if there's a connection between what we see here and what we see through you downstairs. You understand, don't you, that we're with you even when you're somewhere else? But it's just not the same. We have been waiting for you so long. Haven't we, Paul?

PAUL LAWRENCE DUNBAR

Yes indeed we have, John. You do remember me, don't you Shirah? Well of course you do, my precious one. I'm your very own Paul Lawrence Dunbar. Is it difficult for you to believe that I've been waiting many a long year to talk to you face to face? Ah, look at you now, look at your eyes remembering that raggedy old book, ***The Dunbar Speaker and Entertainer***, your father has of my poetry. How you love it. I waited for you there. I found you downstairs beside the sofa where your father had me sitting when your family lived in the apartment in Mayfair out in northeast. You love your city, don't you? Washington, DC. You opened the book in Mayfair Mansions of Washington City and I was ready for your sad eyes. I dropped that little green seedling straight in front of you. What? Of course I did it on purpose. You don't think that was a mistake do you? I dropped it on the floor and it was already panting and sweating and running. You chased that seedling right out of the door, down three flights of steps, up the sidewalk beside the wide Mayfair Mansions lawns clear to Hayes Street. When you got to Hayes Street, you skipped all the way to Kenilworth Avenue, turned right, made the curve toward Benning Road and River Terrace, crossed the Eastern Branch, your good ole Anacostia River, and kept on skipping straight past all four schools on Langston Hill Spingarn High, Charles Young Elementary, Phelps Vocational, and Browne Junior High, all those schools on the hill just up from the Langston Golf Course and across from Pepco on the river. You skipped till you got to Langston Library right behind the schools, and you were hooked.

JOHN MILTON

Now Paul why don't you shut up and stop lying. You know darn good and well Shirah was just a little girl when she read that seedling poem of yours, and she didn't do any skipping across the Anacostia River just because of some seedling, not counting the fact that she thought that silly little poem was too sentimental and never could figure out why folks forced it on children so much.

So it pushed a little leaflet up into the light of day [82]
PAUL LAWRENCE DUNBAR

John Milton; or should I say, Johannes Milton Anglus, that IS the name you had them put on your formal portrait is it not? I know just as well as you do that my seedling poem is sentimental. Do you think you were the first person ever born with a brain? But you can't erase what happened. The sentimentality of my silly little poem soothed the ache behind your eyes Shirah, your eyes that had seen your brother's death point blank. Sure, later on you told me the seedling was too sickening sweet for you, but what did I care, I had already pulled you back from the edge of that window. You wanted to die. I wanted you to live. And you, John Milton, ought to know all of this already, you're the one who's supposed to narrate this story. Here you are a great epic poet of England, narrating a story and you don't even know its earliest path! Or are you picking on my poem because Shirah heard about me before she heard about you?

JOHN MILTON

Don't be ridiculous. I am just giving accurate assessment, that's all. I'm the one Shirah has chosen to be the narrator of this story and you're the one who's upset.

PAUL LAWRENCE DUNBAR

Shirah, don't you pay a bit of attention to that John Milton, listen to me. You heard the words, "I'm just a little seedling but I'll do the best I can," from me, Paul Lawrence Dunbar, and then that little green thing just popped out of those pages and plopped on the floor in front of you, right by your piano you remember, and went running running running . . .and — and

Ha, look at your face, Shirah, I shouldn't tease you about Milton, should I? You really love him. Yes, I know. And I'm just talking and chattering up here. Milton is a holy one who found you after so many years of you grieving for your brother dead in the cradle. I honor your grief, Shirah Shulamit, we all honor it. You know me as a holy one who found you almost immediately after that great death in your life. It was soon after your brother died that my little seedling stepped down in front of you and helped you to smile. That little boy was so very blue and cold wasn't he. And why did it have to be that you saw him there while your mother was screaming so loud through the room, Shirah? Your ear blasted your mind into silence with that scream. You looked up and all you saw was an open mouth, there was no more sound. Your father came rushing in past you as you stood there frozen, and he was holding her as she screamed, your dear mother, your dear father. But you, dear Shirah, oh my precious Shirah Shulamit, you stood there alone, frozen, a frozen tower of ice by the cradle of the dead.

But it was not long before I came. You went chasing after my little green seedling and ended up in the library giggling over *How Lucy Backslid*. Couldn't that woman dance honey chile?! A fling of her scarf and there she was a-stomping on the floor! Yeah, Lucy gave up her religion temporarily that bright afternoon so that she could dance, dance, dance and didn't you laugh, Shirah? Didn't you laugh in the Langston Library? And you and I still have laughing good times together with our poetry, song and dance, ah, if there were no poetry there would be nothing at all!

Yet my favorite times with you, Shirah, were quiet with the change to evening. The moments came when you were starting junior high school and you would look out so wistfully toward that stream that separates Mayfair Mansions from Eastland Gardens. The sun would be setting down the end into the swamp. "Oh how with more than sleep the heart is torn,"[83] those are words I gave you. You and I were very close then and you were sad with new teenager sadness.

You were still praying every night that you would grow up and write a book, but you don't remember that I am the beginning of that prayer. You forgot me because the face of your brother's death blocked you away from your first memory of me. From the time I, Paul Lawrence Dunbar, found you with my seedling poem until the time John Milton found you with **Paradise Lost**, you prayed every night that you would grow up and write a book. It is that prayer that has brought you up these stairs at last to this your Heaven, and to your attic poets.

Welcome to the top of the attic stairs.

Cluster 9 Your Academy
Cluster 9 Argument

Okay, Honored Reader, now it's almost time for school.and you ought to be complaining because there's a lot more to the cluster you just read, Cluster 8, Our Story, and it isn't here. You're right. A lot more is coming later with Langston Hughes fussing at Shirah and Homer singing Leadbelly blues and fussing at Vergil with Brer Rabbit bustin' loose with Chuck Brown and Dante with Phillis Wheatley trying to make sense of it all. But you just have to wait for all of that. Now it's time to glimpse at Graduate School. The Ocean of. Light has puddled for a moment on the lawn of the University of Pen Forest.

The grad student Shirah Shulamit Ojero lies there asleep — asleep instead of writing her dissertation. Soon Emily Dickinson and Virginia Woolf will wake her up — and the others of the Portfolio. And it's almost time for you to hear the lovesong that is the Catalogue of the Professors . . . but not quite! Shirah's lovesong for Nikendra Professor and Steward Professor and Keladon Professor and Gerald Professor and Gershon Professor and Gilbert Professor and Woodley Professor and Alice Professor and even Smithmonger Professor — well, all of that comes later. These are your beloved, Shirah, along with Saul Professor. Through their words you Daughters of Jerusalem, Shirah and Asenath, will finally greet each other. "Hi." But that is in the love story. The love story is the second collection. This is the first collection, the story of your nappy hair. And the head that carries your nappy hair lies asleep by the dried fountain of the University of Pen Forest Museum.

Listen.

Chapter 39: Lotus

Lotus.

Remember.

Speck of Divinity.

You lie asleep on the lawn of the University Museum. Across the street from you is the Coliseum, where they hold the Pen Relays each year. High above you, the hawk, Horus Shiva, circles the Schuylkill River, renewing worlds. On the patio beyond your feet, at the edge of the grass is a weathered pool and a pot of lotus. You are under a tree. The tree is filled with Portfolio poets who have escaped from your sleeping brain. The poets chatter together.

PORTFOLIO

Yep, we poets who usually make our home in your head, thought we would take a break from your head, so we're sitting in the tree above you listening to summer murmurings.

At least we think we're still in the tree, we can only see outside your head clearly when you open your eyes so we can't be sure. Any way, this tree is where we were sitting before you closed your eyes and fell asleep.

Do you want to know who we are in here? Well, we're mostly Emily Dickinson and Virginia Woolf today, although you also have your home-boy, John Milton, some regulars like Dunbar and Herodotus, and a few extras, Tolstoy, Hayden, Kafka.

It's crowded. Missing as usual is Carlos Fuentes Waterman, the one you seek.

EMILY {STANDING IN TOP OF TREE}

We grow accustomed to your dark.

PORTFOLIO TO YOU, SHIRAH

Yep, that's Emily all right. Here we are caught in your tree, trying to grab up some light, but we're stuck listening to Emily. Can't you do any better than that, Shirah? We don't want to grow accustomed to your dark. We just want you to open your eyes. Wake up. We? Who's we? We is us, all of us in here, Virginia and Langston and Emily and Angelina and Robert Louis and Willy B Yeats, and everybody. Are you really asleep Shirah? But that's not the real question.

PORTFOLIO TO YOU, EMILY

The real question is you, Emily, we don't believe you. We don't believe you ever do grow accustomed to the dark. Aren't you just lying to us? Virginia Wolf says you're just full of it, that you never grew accustomed to any dark any day of your life. Now Virginia, she knows what she's talking about, she knows about somebody's growing accustomed to some dark." What you really ought to be doing, you ought to be getting Shirah to open her eyes. After all, it's your fault she became a Graduate Student. You're the one who stopped her from getting on the train when she walked out of that Master's Degree exam at Villanova.

EMILY TO {SLEEPING} SHIRAH

You were 25 years old then, sitting for the exam for the masters degree in English Literature at Villanova University. It was your 25th birthday. You had a fear that on your 25th birthday you would turn into an idiot. You thought you would forget everything. You thought everything would be all over. So there, as you were taking the exam at Villanova University, you gave up. You left your bluebook there on the desk, excused yourself as if you were going to the bathroom, but walked down the slight hill to the Paoli local train.

There, you said to yourself, you would wait for the train, ride into Philadelphia, take another train to New York City, and there, somewhere in New York, you would wander the streets until you died. You had just enough money to get to New York, and not a penny more. So there you stood by the train station, waiting, waiting, waiting even more, but the train was late — very late. You got tired of waiting. You gave up waiting for the train, walked back up the hill and back into the exam room. There wasn't much time left. You knew that, you would fail because you didn't have enough time. You sat down in front of your bluebook that was still lying there.

The exam sheet read: "Respond to a question or a statement." You responded to this, "Discuss and explicate one of the poems of Emily Dickinson." You chose my poem that begins,

> *We grow accustomed to the dark*
> *When light is put away."*

I, Emily Dickinson, took it from there and wrote the essay for you.

You passed.

Professors Murphy told you later, "You failed most of the questions, but your explication of Dickinson's poem was so good that we gave you full credit."

> *The bravest grope a little*
> *And sometimes hit a tree*
> *Directly in the forehead*
> *But as they learn to see*
>
> *Either the darkness alters*
> *Or something in the sight*
> *Adjusts itself to midnight*
> *And life steps almost straight.*

PORTFOLIO TO YOU, SHIRAH

Hey Shirah, do you know that if you had taken that train you would have left Pen's Forest and never returned and we would never have enjoyed ourselves so much in your head? You would never have continued to become this sure-enough bona fide Graduate Student, leaving the New City, Villanova, to come to this University of Pen's Forest.

EMILY TO {SLEEPING} SHIRAH

Don't forget it, it's because of me, Emily Dickinson, that you are a successful Graduate Student.

PORTFOLIO

Does that give you any excuse to keep accustoming yourself to the dark, Emily? You sure are getting on the nerves of the rest of us.

Maybe we're just not yelling loud enough, Shirah, you're still not waking up.

Virginia, do you think all this grad student stuff could all be over now? Shirah, what if this is the end of you?

VIRGINIA WOOLF

No, it's not over. Shirah just doesn't want to finish the dissertation, isn't that true Shirah Shulamit Ojero!? Aren't you just lying here on the grass faking it? You're not really asleep. I'm Virginia, you remember me, Virginia Woolf. Emily and I are here to stir you up. You should get up and open your eyes.

UNIDENTIFIED NARRATOR

Dear Shirah, O lost one, never again will you sit hunched on the ground eating the fruit of the full tomato plant. You are among the renown fallen forsaken. For just as Podes, who was born upon the flanks of Mount Ida, went off to war against the Greeks and will never return to tend the sheep of Eetion his father, and even as Alkathoos, who stood as a tree motionless before the onslaught of Idomeneus, will never return again with shining eyes and bright limbs to Hippodameia his beloved, even so, never again, will you, Shirah Shulamit, your mother's Buttercup, your father's Peace, walk along behind Uncle Mordecai sowing the seeds of corn in the Kenilworth garden, and plucking the delicious ripe fruit of the tomato.

Lotus.

Remember.

Speck of Divinity.

PORTFOLIO

Who's that? Who said that? Whoever you are you've got it wrong. Everybody knows that lotus is forgetting, not remembering.

Virginia, what are you chattering about?

WILLIAM BUTLER YEATS

Are we really stuck up here in a tree? To hell with Emily's darkness. I want some light. I can't see anything.

PORTFOLIO

That's the whole point, Willy B, none of us can see anything because Shirah has closed her eyes.

VIRGINIA WOOLF

Shirah! What do you think you're doing? We need to see, open your eyes.

EMILY DICKINSON

Virginia, why can't you accept that she's asleep, perhaps it's the sleep of death.

PORTFOLIO

That sounds just like you, Emily, with your 'Because I could not stop for death' crap. Willy B, what do you want to do?

WILLIAM BUTLER YEATS

I tossed a pebble at a squirrel in a tree once, but he just jumped away and chattered at me. Maybe we are the squirrels now. Do you think Shirah has appointed us to be squirrels? You've got a clean limb, you've got a sharp tooth, you can jump around and get away. So you're a squirrel.

VIRGINIA WOOLF

Maybe you want to be a squirrel in this tree, Willy B, but I don't want to be a squirrel and I don't want to be in this tree of Shirah's if you and I can't see anything. I think you should just take that pebble and toss it at Emily. Maybe it won't give us any light but at least it could make Emily shut up. Maybe death stopped for you, Emily, but as for me, I stopped for death. I know more about it than you do.

PORTFOLIO

Shirah, why have you put us up a tree? You were doing fine, we were sitting in your head while you were lying on the lawn here, and since your body was still we decided to step out of your head and sit in this tree above you. Up here we can see even further than you, but not if you close your eyes. You! Shirah! Open your eyes! Wake up!

It's so dark, maybe we're not even in the tree any more. Maybe we're inside her head.

"If we were still inside her head there would be all kinds of things to see. Okay, so sometimes it's dark in there, but there are always a few bumps inside her head, and they can turn into something if we focus on them. But we don't want to. Shirah, we want you to open your eyes so that Emily and I and all the other poets can see something that's outside. And you fell asleep so fast we didn't have a chance to jump back inside your head."

We know that you can hear us, but you refuse to listen. We know that you can see our song but you won't look.

Why won't you accept the words we offer for your dissertation? You only see distraction and avoidance, Shirah Shulamit, you refuse to hear anything that could be the next word you need. We were singing the song of Hephaestus to you before you fell asleep, but you dissolve our song of Hephaestus into sunny air. You are blind to us again and again. You only saw a dry pool and that single pathetic red-orange lotus, struggling against the wall in its clay pot before your eyes closed, but it was the great god of making hammering in his forge. It was Hephaestus.

VIRGINIA WOOLF

"Do you remember the first time we came into Shirah's head?"

225

PORTFOLIO

Hush. You're remembering the lotus.

VIRGINIA WOOLF

We first came here when Milton came to you. We are all your Milton rememory.

UNIDENTIFIED NARRATOR

And Chiefly thou O spirit who dost prefer
Before all temples the upright heart and pure.

PORTFOLIO

Your reading of **Paradise Lost** called us forth, the poets, and thereafter we lived inside your head.

PAUL LAWRENCE DUNBAR

What are you talking about? I am Paul Lawrence Dunbar, and I was here long before Shirah read **Paradise Lost**.

ROBERT LOUIS STEVENSON

Me too. You don't remember right Virginia. I'm Robert Louis Stevenson and I was here first, and you, Lewis Carroll, didn't you come right after? I was here all by myself except for a couple of Bible verses until you came.

EMILY DICKINSON

Well, okay, but don't you keep fussing at me. Don't you think I have some plans other than getting accustomed to the dark? Let me try to wake her up. Hey, stop! Wake up, Shirah, it's me, Emily, Emily Dickinson, don't you remember me? You can't just do this! You can't just fall asleep and leave us here in this tree. It isn't fair. I was going to float over to the Coliseum and practice my discus throw for next year's Pen Relays. But you just shut down. You always fall asleep when we're in the middle of something even though you know we can't see and can't go anywhere when your eyes are closed. But maybe we can use another poem of mine to get out of this. Why can't we just imagine light. You want grass and summer and light and bees on the flowers? All you need is one clover and a bee and revery. The revery alone will do if bees are few as they are now.

Virginia Woolf

There you go again, Emily, you never get it right, you always get it slant.

Don't listen to her, Shirah, she wasn't planning to go to the Pen Relays, can you imagine Emily Dickinson throwing a discus? All you know how to do, Emily, is quote your own poetry and throw sugar cookies from an attic window to kids walking back from school. And you know the kids don't even want the cookies — all dirty with gravel — their nursemaids tell them to be nice to you, the crazy lady floating up the stairs in a white gown . . . the kids toss your cookies in the trash later. Even when she does wake up, who cares if she can see out of your eyes or not, Emily? But I need to see, me, Virginia Woolf. And there are lots of us in here who can come up with something better than your sugar cookies.

Portfolio

Shirah, please wake up. I'd like to scrape up some of the soil in the dry pond on the patio near the lawn you are lying down on. Don't you think we could make something out of it? It's worth it to let us see something out of your eyes. With your eyes closed we can't be sure we're still in this tree and I don't even believe that you're really asleep. You've just closed your eyes on purpose so as not to let us do anything. You're a coward, yes. We poets who live in your head are weary of waiting for you. We know how you love to avoid your outside life. But now you should open your eyes. We want to look out.

Emily Dickinson

You lie, Virginia, the children love my cookies. You don't know what you're talking about, Madame Woolf. And Shirah, I know that you are just asleep, really asleep. We just have to wake you up. We came inside you so long ago. Now we're stuck with no way to see out unless you open your eyes. We're stuck up in this tree. Please, will you wake up?

WILLIAM BLAKE

I'm William Blake, Shirah, and I don't want that meanie Smithmonger Professor to walk by and see you sleeping here. Do you remember how she trashed my poem?

'   *O rose thou are sick' – she sneered at it.*

PORTFOLIO

Ah, what's that? You are stirring, yes, let's go. You're not awake but you are rousing up and that gives us a chance to dive back into your brain. YES!

We disgusted poets dive back into your brain. Truly disgusted. At least we can look at something here while waiting for you to wake up fully. And here inside your brain we see you traveling, you travel to cedars and have a drink with Charles Chesnutt,[84] then an east wind pulls you into a Growlery Room with Dickens, or is it with Frederick Douglass on the Anacostia River, looking down on the mall of Washington, DC, your homeland, but you visit a tower there that is not a tower of your homeland. It is Prague, the towers of Prague and Milan Kundera laughing with you, "Language is a bitch!" he says to you as they all chatter together, your poets. Everyone chatters. It is 1984, and you know what that means, this is a failed year of prophecy, the year in which we poets were scheduled to disappear according to George in here, George Orwell. It shows you how much he knew! Yes, George, we are talking about you. And Shirah, don't you wish we had disappeared? You would get us out of your head and we wouldn't have to wait here for you to get up and do something. And you wouldn't have to worry about this dissertation.

You lie there not only asleep but dreaming in this year of the failed prophecy. And here into your head stomps Jean Toomer bringing the streets around Howard University, Robert Hayden, bringing a horrified look into the soul of a lyncher.

You shudder as you lie here, but where is Carlos? Why isn't he here? Your Waterman.

What's this gray rag crouching inside your skull bone near your ear? Ha! It's not a rag, it's a raggedy person hunched up near your skull whispering a promise of rain. A muddy gray promise huddled like yet another sodden Graduate Student leaning on her elbows, sighing, turning the pages of some nameless book without seeing anything. And over here, in this part of your brain, we see a poet escaping over mountains, can you see him too? It's always easiest for us to see other poets. We think he's from Chile. Probably Pablo Neruda. Or maybe it's Mexico and Octavio Paz racing from the violent seasons of Mexico. Farther away, just inside your eyebrows, we can see cattle curve in from the rim of a desert to graze on a savanna, but that's Africa, you really have crossed over the Atlantic to Africa in your head haven't you? What land is this, Buttercup? Ah, you have gone to Kinshasa. Who is this woman with lotus eyes across from you? Marie-Léontine Tsibinda. So that's her name. What mild eyes she has in the Kongo restaurant where you are picturing her. The ceiling is battered by sunlight and grips itself in a search for coolness. The walls hunch down to hold off the sun from the dishes on the table in front of you, salt fruit and piti-piti spices and cold water in the throat.

You are sitting with her in a restaurant in Kinshasa, beside the great river, Congo they call it, with a gathering of the Nzadi People. It's beautiful, but it's not a savanna. You were picturing a savanna. It's a rain forest isn't it? How is it you keep mixing everything up? But don't you think it is powerful the way the river leans westward toward the cataracts? Perhaps it isn't so bad staying inside your head. And it's in here that we can offer you the words you need for your dissertation. But you confuse things and won't hear us. You're a failure. Sure, your name is Shirah Shulamit, which is supposed to mean song of peace, but if that's what it means then your name is a waste. You're just plain lost, not a peace song but a lost lamentation if you ask me. And it's not just Smithmonger Professor who's sick of you. We're sick of you too.

You, ha! We need to threaten you. You have to be more afraid of us than you are of your dissertation. You're supposed to wake up and write your dissertation and give us a chance to move around too.

Wake up! Well perhaps the pool and the lotus in the cracked flower pot are not much to look at right here, even if you do open your eyes. You've been looking at that dry empty pool for so many days! You can't get any inspiration from that. No splashing, no fountain, no water . . . at least not really, unless you count the glob of drying mud panting and evaporating under this tree. Not even a bird could find enough water to drink from it. And that pathetic red lotus in the pot against the wall, Do you think somebody just stuck it in that broken pot and left it? What a boring August!

It's not like August back in Washington, DC, in the Kenilworth neighborhood or in Mayfair Mansions where so many of us first moved inside your head while you were growing up. In Kenilworth and Mayfair there's always so much going on in August with the corn standing tall in the sunlight in your grandfather's garden on Douglass Street. It's your Uncle Mordecai's garden now. He who honors you for your nappy hair whether you are planting the corn or pulling the tomatoes from the vines.

Why are you so far away from your Kenilworth neighborhood in Washington? We love walking with you there down by the lily ponds. That's where they call you Buttercup. That's home. But here in Philadelphia there's just weariness at this Graduate School, this University of Pen Forest, and it makes us wonder, with all this buzzing around us, if Beëlzebub himself has unfolded hell and sent forth all its flies to plague us while you lie asleep.[85] Philadelphia! Some city of friends!

We want to see the grass and the sky. We want to look at something that's more than a blur. We want to be here, not floating somewhere else in your reveries. How can you just lie here asleep?! You've got us in the dusk with this reddish light coming through your eyelids. Sure, we can look at clearer stuff inside your head if we want to, but we don't want to. The stuff in here is never as astonishing as the stuff we see through your eyes.

The stories right outside your eyes are good stories where you see something happening all the time, not like the stories here at this University. These stories are too still. We need to do something about the stillness. The museum exhibits aren't even open in August and inside the museum library there are only a bunch of befuddled Graduate Students, as stir-crazy as you are, clinging to book stalls while writing doctoral dissertations.

Do you remember the time when you were eleven years old and you first read that John Milton book? Of course you know that he's living in here with all of us. You walked down to the lily pond that day reading and chanting those new words.

UNIDENTIFIED NARRATOR

Instruct me for thou knowest, thou from the first Wast present and with mighty wings outspread

Thou. Shirah Shulamit singing with the flowers and the fish and the frogs. You sat in the cool under the catalpa tree reading alone, yet when you read those words from **Paradise Lost** you called all of us out of our Heavens and libraries toward you, toward your pool with the pastel bubbles, and toward the echo of Uncle Mordecai telling you his stories of the great war, and how life was a perpetual garden when he was growing up, and again and again how God created your nappy hair.

PORTFOLIO

Shirah! Buttercup! how can you just lie here on the grass! You should be inside the library suffering like the other Graduate Students. Smithmonger Professor is sick of you. She curses the day she met you. She says you've done nothing to earn this DEE-GREEE! You're never going to be a doctor of philosophy. Yes, we're talking to you, Shirah, you, Graduate Student of Comparative Literature and Literary Theory, you have a dissertation to write on how epics got here from Africa but here you lie sleeping on the lawn in the shade.

UNIDENTIFIED NARRATOR

The sky above you is a heaped ant hill of speckling motes tunneling through the walls of the Pen Relays stadium. Your sky is a light-tormented baobab tree whose bark flecks and falls from the inundated tower of day, whose bark bulges and flakes and separates from the trunk to fall upon the roofs and gardens of the University of Pen Forest.

You, Buttercup, you, Shirah Shulamit Ojero, you candidatus philosophiae doctoris, are of another place. What curse was it that picked you up from the corn and cucumbers, tomatoes and string beans of Kenilworth Castle in Washington, DC and brought you to the foodless grass in front of this library near the banks of the Schuylkill River in the State of Pen Forest?

PORTFOLIO

So finally you wake up! Thank you. At last we get to see something outside your eyes. You blink up from the green, green grass and see a hawk high over the University of Pen Forest, turning and bending to the wind, circling.

UNIDENTIFIED NARRATOR

It could be the nameless first god worshipped by the Egyptians, the god who became Horus. Or it could be Shiva the destroyer hanging a new sky with new birds. A haze of light surrounds you, do you see the green light slashed with the tropic colors of the solitary lotus? crimson, scarlet, red against white-yellow sunlight? What is coming upon you through the air? The sky brightens and brightens with warm moisture. You shade your eyes with your arm above your face as you look up. August haze. Violent summer light. Defiant brightness.

Yes, it is a speck of divinity above you, circling above the Pen Relays Coliseum.

Now the poets can see through your eyes again, and the first thing they see is the ancient Egyptian God, Horus, the aboriginal hawk.

Or is it Shiva of the Hindus, using floods, and other destructions to seed new worlds with new peoples.

And you gaze at the lotus in its pot, that somehow requires remembering, not forgetting.

Phillis Wheatley, your home-girl, she who founded African American poetry, arrived in the new world, the Americas, during August. A destruction linked with a founding.

So sing the hymn of August.

August. Let's hear it for your eternal August. August has its griefs of fallen cities − Jerusalem, Herculanaeum, Atlanta, Hiroshima, Tisha b'Av. The fallen temples. The expulsion from Spain. − but August also has its perfections of fruit and humidity. Can you feel it? Sweet sticky honey butterscotch sweet, your lungs fingering for air as if they were gills in this your summer air east coast homeland, Shirah Shulamit yes, you heave an academic sigh in the bronze shadowed summerlight as you sit up and brush the grass and earth from your clothes.

Perhaps one day you will do it. You will write your dissertation. You won't apologize or explain or write up a schedule, you'll just stand up and step forward and walk in to this library and walk to your desk and sit down and write your dissertation.

Two of the poets stand and accompany you as you turn toward the door of the museum, Herodotus and Freddie D. Their beauty and power is compelling, but this combination of poets reminds you of your father, reminds you of the men of power in your life, and you find yourself grieving and wondering – where is Carlos? Where is the Waterman? Again and again, where is he?

As your heart yearns toward Carlos the Waterman, but yet two more of the poets – Homer yells, "Sing when the spirit says Sing," and Dickens interrupts arguing, "Write when the spirit says write."[86] They want you to walk into the museum and work. They don't want you mooning over Carlos Fuentes Waterman, who has departed from you. The poets really start to express their disgust with you now. You are cursed by Graduate School. The poets call you lost, fallen forsaken.

The poets mock you, Mann, Kafka, Kundera and yet, and yet maybe one day you'll write your dissertation, maybe one day you will see Hephaestus toiling beside the red lotus. All of your poets see him, yes, see Hephaestus forging the day on the patio at the corner of the lawn. But you, Shirah Shulamit Ojero!, you cannot see him.

An evil fate has taken you from that first garden in Kenilworth and cast you beneath the shadow of book stalls and graduate education. But a stern heart is within you, you do not falter before your fate. You gird your loins and stand up. Sigh and stand up on the lawn of the University Museum. Yes, finally, Shirah Shulamit Ojero!, stand, you stand and speak.

Shirah Shulamit Ojero

Pool of mud with no fountain, end this season and close this day. Don't you care at all for me, a lost Graduate Student? I am refuse washed up beside you in August, August 1984 and no fountain, no apocalypse, no dissertation, no cap and gown, no Doctor of Philosophy. One more year.

Cluster 10 Your Boat
Cluster 10 Argument

Okay, Kindhearted Reader, this is the nappy hair cluster. Yes, I know, it's labeled Your Boat, but it's really about nappy hair. Finally you're going to find out how this screwed up, squeezed up, knotted up, tangled up, twisted up — — — you're going to find out how this nappy hair connected me, Shirah Shulamit Ojero, with ancient Asenath.

So please, I ask you to walk with Shirah Shulamit through the streets of Philadelphia and Washington. Learn what fared in the thirty-seventh year of life of Shirah Shulamit in Graduate School at the University of Pen Forest, how she found here Smithmonger Professor, a wise and powerful sorceress who insisted that only scholars could remain in her graduate program in Comparative Literature and Literary Theory, and that no singer of epic song could complete the work necessary for graduation.

Smithmonger Professor didn't reckon with the power of Shirah Shulamit's nappy hair, which to this day is certified to be the nappiest hair in the world, and this hair was manifest as the vehicle through which Shirah Shulamit was both singer and scholar of epic song, she was not only Shirah Shulamit of Graduate School, but she was also Asenath of ancient story, the daughter of Poti-pherah, priest of On, and Niko, wielder of crystal, and the topic of Shirah's dissertation on the growth of African epic.

You must understand that Shirah's boat sails on the Ocean of light from her dorm room at the University of Pen Forest to the Mediterranean, the Nile, Egypt to the Garden of Converging Paths to the palace of Asenath that rests beside both the Nile and the Anacostia Rivers. Dear one, Shirah, you look forth in beauty as morning.

Listen.

Chapter 40: Bad Avenue

So you leave your Takoma DC attic. Downstairs you look at the painting of Renoir's **By the Sea** over the piano. You look at Rufin's **Girl Let Me Tell You**, painting on the side wall. And Sazonado's **Still Life in Blue**. It is a blue velvet room.

You walk outside. It is a red brick house. You walk off into the city of Washington, seeking the book that is unknown in Heaven. You come to Georgia Avenue. You walk and you walk southward through the city a long way. Georgia Avenue becomes Seventh Street, they call it Bad Avenue. At Seventh and T you ask a sad woman if she knows the way to the book that is unknown in Heaven. She laughs and tells you that at Seventh and T they only write the book that is known in hell, Seventh and T is filled with an offbeat, Can you hear those happy feet? beating out and beating out a . . . but that's Langston Hughes singing through your head, that's not you. What are you singing?

What do you think? What are you thinking? Southeast. You must walk southeast to get there. This is the path, the way. Where?

You walk southeastward toward the Mall, and just beyond the the Library of Congress you enter the gates of the Folger Library. The Gate Keeper, Ruland Witly Professor, comes to you there.

You ask for the Day Tripper, you ask for the House of the Hours,but the Gate Keeper tells you she has gone, and he's never heard of the House of the Hours. We have no such place. Perhaps there has been some confusion of words, for here we have not the hours of the day, but the crystal of the seven ages of human life. The puking baby, the toothless old man.

The Gate Keeper then leads you into the Grand Salon and shows you the glory of the colors of the ages of human life, golden apple, orange tile, white mist, brown coffee, clear water, white sand, blue water, white light on water, brown with green, black images, purple stars, colors of life, each a story of liquid glass holding a story.

But how are you to find the book that is unknown in Heaven? Or are you to find the book that is known in hell? You speak to Ruland Witly, "I was told that you would help me to find my way."

But the Gate Keeper answers saying, I know nothing of the book you seek, I know only the books that forge Heaven and hell together, but it may be that the Steward of the Northern Forest can help you, the Steward of University of Pen Forest.

He knows the Homer Fuentes Waterman, if you are seeking an unknown book, you should talk to the Waterman. He is in the north.

Chapter 41: Black and Comely

And Mz Green, your first grade teacher called your group to the front, and she held up the flash cards and asked all of you to read the words. "Go."

And the children around you started jumping up and down and shouting the wrong words, "Hello" "Good-bye" "school" they shouted.

Mz Green held up another flash card, "run", and the children around you shouted, "jump," "eat," "candy." And Mz Green held up another flash card, "street," and the children around you shouted out, "banana," "chewing gum," "house." And Mz Green held up another flash card, "river." And the children around you shouted out, "potato chips," "peanuts," "table." And you, Shirah, were the only one sitting there quietly listening to all those wrong words, and you were so sad. And finally the teacher held up a really long word, "beautiful," and the children around you, falling over you and pushing and jumping shouted out, "tree," "sandwich," "ball," "apple," "window." And you looked around at the yelling children and you said, not very loud, "The word is beautiful."

And Mz Green heard you and asked frantically, "Who said that? Who said that? Who said that?" And all the children pointed at you saying, "Sheeee didddd!" As if you had said a curse word. And Mz Green looked at you. And you looked at Mz Green. And Mz Green said, "Did you read this word?" And you said, "Yes," And Mz Green said, "What is it?" And you said, "Beautiful." "And how about this word?"

"River." And this word, "Street." And this word, "Run." "And this word, "Go." And you read all the words.

And after you read the word beautiful and you read the other words she asked you to read the Bible Verses that day.

I am black, but comely, O ye daughters of Jerusalem, as the tents of Kedar, as the curtains of Solomon. Look not upon me, because I am black, because the sun hath looked upon me: my mother's children were angry with me; they made me the keeper of the vineyards; but mine own vineyard have I not kept.

Mz Green listened to you then, when you were five years old, and so did Barbara Comus Professor listen to you early this summer, now that you have passed 35 years old, 36, 37, because you have left your father's house, your mother's house, in Takoma of Washington, DC and found your way to the University of Pen Forest in Philadelphia, seeking an epic song of the African American people. But what good has it done you? There have been so many times when you almost understood, almost knew what to write, almost knew what you were writing about. You travel between the Takoma attic room in Washington and the dorm room at the University of Pen Forest, seeking your exact dissertation topic. There are times when you see . . . when you almost see a woman of Africa, a woman kissed by the sun, leaning toward you, standing at a window — is it your attic window?, almost stepping across, through the filtered light of the mulberry. But May, June, July, August, September — the mulberry brings no fruit, it is out of season.

What did Barbara Comus Professor say? It was just like the time when you were five years old. You Graduate Students at the Folger Shakespeare Library telling Barbara Comus Professor about your dissertation topics. And when your turn came you said, "I want to compare Homer, Vergil, Dante, Milton, the Kalevala, the Mahabharata, the Araucana, Mwindo and Shaka the Great with the fiction of Proust, Carlos Fuentes Waterman, Balzac, Melville and Whitman in order to develop a method for judging and identifying African American Epic Tradition." With your bright eyes and your happy face you said it.

And all the other students gasped at you and broke out in uproarious laughter. They were falling over the tables laughing at your preposterous idea. Tears whipped your eyes and you pleaded, "Don't laugh, listen! Please listen!" Yet they kept laughing. But the Day Tripper, Barbara Comus Professor, said quietly, strongly. "I'm listening."

And there was silence.

And Barbara Comus Professor looked at you.

And you looked at Barbara Comus Professor.

And Barbara Comus Professor, the Day Tripper, the Barbarian Woman who is also called the Golden said to you.

"Explain your idea."

You explained your idea.

"I believe that there is an ancient oral storytelling tradition with roots in Central Africa, that links both to Egyptian and Mediterranean epic, but stirred an epic tradition that came to the Americas without passing through the Mediterranean, that came on the ships that sailed directly from West Africa. I believe that a study of how the word epic is used, along with a careful review of text, will teach us the art and the power of these African American epics. I haven't been able to figure out all the parts. I'm missing an angle I need. But I still hope I can find it, this unknown tradition, this unknown book."

Barbara Comus Professor said to you, "Your idea is good, you need to speak to Carlos Waterman. He makes the creation of such ocean crossing epics the study of his life. Find him, and perhaps you will find the idea you need to complete your thesis.

You smiled and said thank you, but your heart was sad in spite of your victory. Carlos Fuentes, Carlos Waterman, wasn't that always the problem? Who could ever find him? Certainly you could not. If only you could. That Folger Shakespeare Library is always getting you into trouble. They are the ones who started you on this epic quest in the first place. If you had stayed away from that library you never would have become a Graduate Student, you never would have sought out the University of Pen Forest, you never would have started this hunt for African American Epic Tradition, you never would have envisioned that strange Egyptian woman peering through the

Takoma attic window in your father's house and your mother's house in Washington.

The problem with the Folger Shakespeare Library is that it always wants you to do something. Four years ago you just went there for a lecture. You left the attic, went to downtown Washington, DC, to hear Ruland Witly Professor speak on Spenser, Milton, and Blake, and you were caught. Witly Professor wouldn't leave you alone when you told him that class was the last course you were going to take ever. You told him you were going off to be a stage manager at Back Alley Theatre. You said you were sick of higher education. You had been reading some of Waterman's books, and Waterman's books did a trip on your head, made you lose your wits, you were thinking you could be a director maybe, if you worked hard enough, work in film, but Ruland Witly Professor caught you, he said, before you decide to give up Graduate School, go to see the Steward Professor of the University of Pen Forest. The Waterman is right there with the Steward, you could go there and talk to him. You say you love the words of the Waterman, you say you want to run off to seek the word inspired by the Waterman, but if you stay and go to Graduate School at the University of Pen Forest, well, that's where he is, right at the University of Pen Forest, and you'll meet him.

But when you came here and sought for him, he was already gone. He is always already gone. Dear Waterman of your desire. Dear Carlos Fuentes Waterman. Always a reach away from you.

And look at you, look at you sitting there now, at your carrel in the Library of the University of Pen Forest Museum, moisture in your eyes, stewed from the dry intellectual heat of dusty pages paper smell empty, no spaghetti sauce here, not even the drying out noodles, dry half-cooked noodles, just your weary head in the weary blues, bowed on the desk not even asleep, but grieving, grieving still. You know you are a loser. Yes, you know.

But do not weep, O Graduate Student of Our Heart, do not weep. As you sit here in this library now that the end of August has come, August 1984, shuffling together your pitiable words, words that Barbara H. Smithmonger Professor says will come to nought, do not weep, for now it has come to past in the ordering of the millennia that your cry for help has risen unto God, who calls upon Joanne, Joanne Dubil, the administrative assistant of Comparative Literature and Literary Theory, Joanne opens your latest purple letter, the letter declaring that you will finish your dissertation this summer, and instead of filing it as she has been told to do by Barbara H. Smithmonger Professor, she thinks of you, and hands it around to the doctoral committee. It is the first committee meeting for the upcoming academic year, 1984-85, and the committee is reviewing the status of each Graduate Student, including you. Barbara H. Smithmonger Professor, Founder and ChairBeing of the Department of Comparative Literature and Literary Theory, diverts your letter to the bottom of the agenda in hopes that there will be no time to get to it. But Gerald Prince Professor, taking up the grave challenge that Joanne has begun, urges the committee to stay to the excruciating end, yes, stay until they decide what to do about you.

Barbara H. Smithmonger Professor rebels against you, "I can't stand another one of these purple letters. I don't get paid for this. She'll never graduate. She gushes over poets and novelists. She doesn't analyze literature. She's a sick artist gushing and not a scholar, what is she doing in this department? She's wasting our time, my time. It's not worth it being chair of this Department. If I get another purple letter I'm going to scream. I've shredded every last one of them. Let's ask her to leave the program! I'm not willing to oversee her work anymore. If she doesn't leave one of you will have to see to it. What will you do about her?" This she speaks of you, longing to cast you out of Graduate School.

She speaks, and all sit mute, pondering you and the danger you bring with deep thoughts; and each in the other's countenance reads dismay, astonished, none among the choice and prime of those Heaven-warring professors can be found so hardy as to proffer or accept alone the dreadful task of getting a dissertation out of you, Shirah Shulamit OH!. Saul Professor longs to speak on your behalf, but is silent because his knowledge is of the Russians where your knowledge is not. So there is great silence among the host until at last Steward Currant Professor, whom now transcendent glory raises above his fellows, with monarchal pride conscious of highest worth, unmoved thus speaks about you.

"I believe," he says about you, "I believe in Shirah Shulamit Ojero, she we know also as OH! I agree that these purple letters mean nothing, have nothing to do with her work and what she'll do or won't do, I do believe, however, that one day she will walk into my office and say, I'm ready to graduate. Her thoughts are going to come together finally. Yes, she'll walk into my office one day and say she's ready, and I'm willing, dear Barbara, I am willing to wait upon that day."

"So be it," says Barbara H. Smithmonger Professor, believing that she is free of you forever, "I am weary. One of you will have to be acting chair for the spring semester. I'll take it up again next fall."

And thus it is, O Shirah Shulamit, that the purposes of God are accomplished, since that time when first there stood in division of conflict, Smithmonger's daughter, sorceress of men, Barbara H. and you, brilliant Shirah Achilles, daughter of Shulamit OH!, so that not Barbara H. Smithmonger Professor but Prince Gerald Professor himself should be the leader of the department at that moment when you, Shirah Achilles Shulamit Ojero OH!, begin at last your almighty dissertation. The meeting has just ended, Shirah Shulamit, with Prince Gerald Professor as the acting Department Chair for spring 85 and with Steward Currant Professor as your Dissertation Director.

And here you still sit unknowing in the library grieving with your head bowed to the edge of your desk with blurred eyes.

As your eyes focus again you barely recognize the words in front of you. It's the book on your lap, the hidden love book that you keep under the books of epic similes upon your desk, the book that you read for fun for love when the scholarship is too much to bear.

"Come with me, lie with me, sleep with me for one hour." This is the book. "Come with me, lie with me, sleep with me for one hour, yes, woman who had the love jones, the love jones for Joseph, the love jones," you know that good black word, when the juices of love flow down inside the body, the thighs loosen and the love space inside you is slippery hot desire. And your body trembles to the thread of one soul one other, and you just want to lie down and make love, as your love jones come down and take all the mind flesh urgings, your body, stretching toward one, one beloved other one, "Love, O love, turn your body toward my body, O daughter of this bright world, with all your love juices, the whimpering poignant bitter juices of life, of love life, reaching to love to make love to some-one, someone else."

And now as you think of your love jones, we grow, we are the thread, we form, we come Shirah Shulamit! we shall be the silver web, we come weaving rising to tell you ourstory.

Ourstory and yourstory converge with this story — A story of a woman who spoke love words after long constraint, after desperate forbearance, unavailing discretion, fruitless prudence, she whispered, Lie with me, Lie with me, Make love to me. A story of a man — you know the man — who concentrated one half of the divine allotment of human beauty in his body, who said No thank you, to the woman who said, Lie with me, lie with me for one hour, he is the Hebrew who ruled Egypt, in-terpreter of dreams, viceroy of Pharaoh, given the greatest riches, the most power, the best land, the royal houses, and he married the daughter of the High Priest of On, don't you know who she is? haven't you seen her? he married Asenath, she who was proclaimed the best, the wisest, the most beautiful, the most accomplished, the most exciting compelling attracting the best woman, the very best woman of that glorious, delightful, storytelling, enchanting moment. Don't you know her?

The best woman. A gazelle of the stars. You have seen her hieroglyphic in the Museum Library, don't you remember, it is an image of water an image of bread and two bows tied together on her back. Asenath. How would anybody be an Asenath in any age, the very best woman? How would one become Asenath? You touch the book.

Best. How would she be different and how the same? You can bet she didn't waste spaghetti sauce all over her blouse the way you do. And you can bet she has her shoes re-heeled before they even need it. Not like you.

Asenath, under the sign of the goddess Neith, water, bread, bows upon her back. Yes, remember, you saw that in the calligraphy downstairs on the papyrus, in the translation pits, last winter you saw it, go, look at it again. Who is this woman?

You break for expulsion, race down the hall, yes, down, circling down into the translation pit in the basement of the museum, dark tower of cuneiform and hieroglyphic. You did see it, last year, what did it say? down the stairs find out, sign in sit down, pull out the tray, there, near the fragment of **Gilgamesh**, you find the piece of stained papyrus in the second row. A stained fragment of papyrus matted into a dull red grey color, or a dirty blue, as if it had been washed in the sea, old purple from an ocean. And words upon it.

You read. You find the reference you seek, Water, Bread. Two bows tied together in a packet. Neith. Asenath. You bend your head above the papyrus fragment at the place where you stopped reading last winter.

You will know the one, the one who is to come, by her hair. Her hair will . . . . but there is a blur, and a series of circles, you can't make it out. And then the words, eight circles, it says. She is the priestess, the daughter of the Woman of Ethiopia and the daughter of the High Priest of On, yes. Your eyes are blurred, unclear, you don't understand. What is it saying? What is it saying about her hair? There is the water sign again, and that is the hieroglyphic for the letter N. And the stool upon the patio, and that is the hieroglyphic for the letter P, and then a still pool of water with no fountain, and that is the hieroglyphic for the sound ST. NPST you read. She will have N - P - ST hair. And then again eight circles strung in a row. And we whisper to you, NPST. NAPPIEST. The nappiest hair in the world. Asenath. Asenath has the nappiest hair in the world.

What now, Shirah Shulamit, what now? Do you think you have fallen asleep over the papyrus? You have not fallen asleep, it's us, we are speaking to you. We are the Portfolio. You don't believe us.

"It can't say that, it can't," you think. N. P. ST. Nappiest. But that's what it says. "But nappy wasn't even a word in ancient Egypt." Your mind can't catch up[87] with what we are doing to you, we are taking over. You are floundering Shirah Shulamit, you look nervously to each side to be sure no one is watching you, no one can read your thoughts. You haven't spoken aloud. Only we can hear you. We who are usurping you, telling ourstory to you, unbelieved.

Look, look at what it says. I'm not making it up. A carved wooden stool upon a fragrant patio. Then the sign for hair, then eight circles, curls, turns, spirals, a pool of water attached to the eighth circle. Then a scroll, followed again by NPST. All within the cartouche of the goddess Neith — bread, water, and two arrows tied together.

Nappiest. Can it be so? What else does it say? The priestess of Neith, Asenath, has the NPST hair in the world.

Nefertha loves Asenath. Nefertha who is Nfr-nfrw-itn, exquisite beauty of the sun disk, Nefertha, who loves black-womansong, Queen Nefertha who proclaims that the perfect circle of one lock of the hair of Asenath glorifies the sun, Nefertha loves Asenath. Thou Art Clear, Mighty, Dazzling And Exalted Above Every Land, While Thy Rays Engulf The Lands To The Totality Of Thy Creation. Worshipping the one god Aten the sun-disk. One circle of your hair, Asenath, is the circle of the sun, there it is, hieroglyphics stained in purple on papyrus, Asenath, the sign for hair, eight circles blurred, Your hair is the weaving sphere of light.

In your beginning was the glory of the nappy haired. In your beginning was the nap. Oh thou among all gifts most precious, nappy hair, nap on, nap on, all up around the edges of their faces, destroy every hairstyle, revert to yourself at every sign of moisture, nap on, nap on forever. You are the one, you are the image, you are the idea in which we find our wholeness and our return. Beautiful as Africa in the mind of a weary plodding African American Graduate Student, beautiful as the urn as nappy hair.

But Oh Shirah, Shirah Shulamit OH!, what confusion! Don't you know this is you? Your own Uncle Mordecai has told the story, and it has gone forth throughout the land that you, Shirah Shulamit, you have the nappiest hair in the world. The Lord made your hair special. The angels tried to talk the Lord out of it.

Lord, why you want to give that innocent chile a head full of steel wool?

Y'all angels just leave me alone, always butting in when nobody asked you, I gave y'all everything y'all wanted, but this chile is mine and I'm giving her the nappiest hair in the world I tell you. The word has gone forth from my mouth and shall not return. The world has no hair straightener that can loosen up the kinks on this chile's head. Be born this way for me, won't ya be born? And may your naps nap up forever, and may them naps never pass away, fuzzy and warm and kinky and tangled forever.

The angels sighed.

The Lord waxed eloquent, It's gonna take three permanent hair straighteners just to loosen it up into an Afro. It will defy fire and water and lye and no-lye creams, their emulsifying wax and petrolatum and mineral oil and calcium hydroxide and steareth-10, and ceteareth-12, and propylene glycol, and DEA-oleth-10, and phosphate, and stearyl alcohol, and steareth-2, and guanidine carbonate, and xanthan gum, and methyl paraben, and ammonium lauryl sulfate, and sodium methyl cocoyl taurate, and cocoapho glycinate, and cocoamide DEA, and polysorbate 20, and polyquaternium-10, and poly-quaternium 11, and citric acid, and tetrasodium EDTA and phenosulfonphthalein this hair shall defy —

Chapter 42: Nappy Hair

Uncle Mordecai told this story at the backyard picnic, Uncle Mordecai told it, the folks joined in between the lines, the children took up the beat, and here it is.

Shirah, you sure do got some nappy hair on your head, don't you?

> *Well.*

Yep it's your hair, Shirah, take the cake,

> *Yep.*

And come back and get the plate.

> *Don't cha know.*

Take the rag off the bush

> *Ain't it so?*

And come back and get the bush.

> *That's how she does it.*

Here you be thinking you got a bush,

> *Why not, your own bush!*

And your bush be halfway down the street.

> *Just like that, gone.*

I mean even for a black chile,

> *It's the truth.*

You sure Lord got some nappy hair on you.

> *Yes suh.*

It ain't easy to come by that kind of hair.

> *No it ain't.*

You can't just blame it on being black.

> *No way.*

You just can't blame Africa for that kind of hair.

> *Nope.*

It ain't Africa's fault, it's willful.

> *That's what it is.*

Them some willful intentional naps you got all over your head

> *Sure enough.*

Your hair intended to be nappy.

Indeed it did.

Couldn't nobody turn it around.

Unh unh.

Or I ought to say, that's all it could do, turn around! But couldn't nobody straighten it up!

Well.

I mean your hair.

Yep.

Combing your hair is like scrunching through the New Mexico desert in brogans in the heat of summer.

That's the way.

It's like crunching through snow.

Yep.

A heavy deep snow.

Deep snow.

About a foot, two feet at least.

Yep.

With two inches of crust on the top.

I can hear it.

Y'all know how it sound when you scrunching through snow like that?

Yep.

Well that's what her hair sounds like when she combs it out in the morning.

Brother, you ought to be ashamed.

Cute and all, ain't she cute? My niece, I'm so proud of her. Only one of them in that school who knows how to talk right.

Ain't she something?

Run circles 'round them old hard heads.

I know it.

A rose among a thousand thorns.

That's all you can say.

But she sure Lord got some nappy hair on her head.

Now why's he got to come back to that?

Them old hard heads think they can talk English.

Yep.

But this chile, she talks the king's English.

I heard her.

Talk the queen's English too.

She can do it.

Look like fools trying to catch up.

I know it.

And I'm gonna tell y'all how she came up with all this nappy hair.

Please, stop!

Her hair was an act of God.

Lord, listen to him now.

An act of God that came straight through Africa.

Well.

You see the angels went up to God.

Oh, oh, here he goes.

Angels walk up to God to talk him out of it.

Will you listen to this?

Yep. They say, Lord, Lord, Lord.

Well.

Why you gotta be so mean, why you gotta be so willful, why you gotta be so ornery, thinking about giving that nappy, nappy hair to that innocent little child?

Innocent.

Sweet little girl like that, and you napping up her hair like you ain't got good sense.

That's what they said.

Napping up her hair, five, six, seven, maybe eight complete circles per inch.

Brother.

I'm talking about eight complete circles per inch of hair.

Please.

And the angels trying to talk him out of it.

Yep.

But God.

Well.

God wanted hisself some nappy hair upon the face of the earth.

That's what it was.

So God turn hisself around.

Didn't he turn.

He hunch hisself up and turn hisself around.

Yep.

Look them angels square in the face.

Well.

God say, Get outa my way.

Yep.

He say, Get thee behind me.

That's what he said.

Say, This is my world.

It's the truth.

This is my world, and this chile.

Well.

This sweet little brown baby girl chile.

We hear you.

She's going to have the nappiest hair in the world!

That's what he said.

Ain't going to be nothing they come up with,

What you going to do?

Nothing they come up with going to straighten this chile's hair.

He said it.

I'm talking about straightening combs.

Well.

I'm talking about relaxers and processes and gerry curls.

Ain't it the truth.

I'm talking about, you know that stuff, wet look.

Well.

Ain't nothing going to straighten up the naps on this chile's head.

What you say!?

And it was done.

Haa!
So here she come.
Well.
Here come the pure nap that make up this chile's hair.
I can see it.
Sitting back in Africa making plans.
That's where it was.
Squinching her eyes and looking deep.
She was deep.
Getting ready to come to America with them slaves.
Didn't we come over here?
Trials and tribulations.
That's the truth.
Sold your momma for a nickel.
Yes, Lord, they did it.
And your daddy for a dime.
Yep.
I say they sold your momma for a buffalo.
That's the way it was.
And your daddy, they sold him for one thin dime.
That's what they did.
But you see this nap.
Yep.
This nap come riding express, coming on across the ocean from Africa.
Didn't she come!
White folks tried to stop it.
Didn't they!
Flimsy hair tried to cut through and straighten up this nap.
Yep.
Nap didn't pay them no never mind.
Nope.
Danced right on through all that wimp hair.
Didn't want it.
Wouldn't stop, wouldn't mix, wouldn't slow down for nobody.

Wouldn't do it.
Every time they tried to mess with her hair,
I can see it.
She was there jumping over and under all that stringy hair.
She did it.
Leaped right over it and kept on moving.
Well.
Stomped it, kicked it, snuck on around and came on through.
That's what she did.
Think she playing football, basketball or something.
Yep.
Dribbling on down the line.
She's the one.
And when she was born.
Yep.
When we looked down on her in the cradle.
What did we see?
We all shout out and jump back.
Did we jump!
Laugh and shout because I tell you she had the kinkiest, the nappiest, the fuzziest, the most screwed up, squeezed up, knotted up, tangled up, twisted up, nappiest, I'm telling you, she had the nappiest hair you've ever seen in your life.
That's what it was.
And the Lord.
Well.
The Lord in Heaven.
What you say.
The Lord who brought the Israelites out of Egypt.
Yes he did.
He looked down on this cute little brown baby girl.
He looked at her.
He looked at her and he say, Well Done.
Yep.
He say, I got me one.

That's what he said.
At last after all this eternity.
Well
I wanted one and I got one.
He said it.
One nap of her hair is the only perfect circle in nature.
Well.
I got me a cute little brown baby girl.
Keep talking.
I got me at long last this cute little brown baby girl.
Well.
And she's got the nappiest hair in the world.
Ain't it the truth.

Chapter 43: You Know

You know that midway through the journey of our life you lose your self in the midst of a dark ocean

You know that the stink is from your putrefying body

You know that you are dead

You know that they are loosing you from chains

You know that they are taking you away from your mother

You know that you are moving up in their hands

You hear your mother screaming below the deck

You breathe without lungs

You shiver from cold you cannot feel

You shudder in an ocean you cannot splash

You taste bitter sharks who eat your death

You sway as globs of flesh churning in deep water

You move your bones that are not bones anymore

You see with blanked eyes that you are many

You hear the voices of all who sleep in this bed

You cannot sleep

This bed is the Atlantic Ocean

This bed is the Middle Passage

You know that the Middle Passage is your grave

You know that you are one of fifteen million

You hear a woman turning pages in a library

You know that you are far from Africa

You know that you are far from the Americas

You know that a woman is in a library reading about the Middle Passage

You know that the woman is your sister

You know that your sister is thinking about you

You know that your sister is your mother's descendant
You grieve that you have no descendant of your own body
You rise from the ocean
You float water until you come to her
You float air until you come to her
You descend through air to stand beside her
You call your sister
You bend toward your sister
You ask your sister to return toward you tonight
You whisper your story to your sister

Chapter 44: Writ On Water

But even as I call to you the Portfolio interrupts.

ANNAMARIE

Hey! Hey you! You Shirah Shulamit OH! Don't you hear us hollering at you in your brain? It's us, your Portfolio. Well really it's just Annamarie and Peter this time. The rest of them are hanging out. Who is this skinny scrawny little kid you was just talkin' to? Don't listen to him. We don't know him. He don't know nothin'. He ain't your brother.

PETER

What was he trying to say anyway, Annamarie? Who was he?

ANNAMARIE

I'm telling you Peter, he wasn't saying nothin'.

PETER

Now, Annamarie, why you got to be sitting up here in the chile's head talking like you own the place. You don't own it up in here.

ANNAMARIE

Well, neither do he! Why he got to be bad mouthin' us, Peter, and tellin' her to leave our voices alone, ain't we worth something? He treat us like we some kind of tar baby and he afraid to get stuck if he say good morning.

PETER

All you do is bad mouth yourself, Annamarie. You know you don't talk like this really. Why you got to show off so much?

ANNAMARIE

Well I tell you, Peter, I just don't like him. He don't belong in here. He say hisself they threw him away in the ocean. Well if they threw him away how come he standing all in here bending over Shirah in our face?

PETER

Aw, Annamarie, you just go looking for trouble where you know there's no trouble at all. Now, why don't you just shut up. I've got something important to say. Look what I found. I want to read a sentence to you from our Portfolio we're a part of that's stuck in Shirah's head.

ANNAMARIE

Well what is it? What's more important than telling Shirah not to lissen to some fool who got hisself eaten up by sharks. What you got to say?

PETER, QUOTING JANE AUSTEN

Here it is, listen. "It is a truth universally acknowledged that a single man in possession of a good fortune must be in need of a wife. Have you ever heard the like of that?"

ANNAMARIE

Aw that ain't nothing. You don't even know how to read. That ain't what it say.

PETER

Then what does it say.

ANNAMARIE

It say, it be a truf universally opinioned that this here Shirah Shulamit chile got the nappiest hair in the absolute complete entire whole world. Hee hee hee. Look at you, Shirah, and you're a failure too, you, the daughter of Big Boy, the Great OH. You ain't got a single word on nuna them P H D dissertation pages. You're hopeless. Tryin' to be a doctor of philosophy and you ain't nothing at all. I don't know how come Peter and I keep putting up with you, Ms. Shirah Ain't-Got-Good-Sense Shulamit.

PETER

Leave Shirah alone. You're the one who's the fool, Annamarie. And Shirah, don't even listen to this clown, don't let those insults worry you. I know you, precious buttercup child, you are enthroned, enlawned, and engardened among the highest thinkers, our doctor of philosophy in truth if not in fact. And you sure can speak better English than Annamarie fussing and complaining in here. Your pages may be blank but your head is wise. Who cares if your enemies have said that your thesis topic is the most inadequate in the history of Comparative Literature and Literary Theory. You are the real one, the true one.

ANNAMARIE

That's just a load of USDA prime choice crap! Like my Ma, the Tin Cup lady, used to say, that's a warm neat pile of hocky doo stinking to high Heaven! And just listen to you, Peter. Why can't you use real words? There ain't no such words as enlawned or engardened.

PETER

There are no such words as truf or opinioned or nuna either, but you use them.

THE UNIDENTIFIED NARRATOR

Hear them, just hear Peter and Annamarie and all the confusion they add to your mind! As if it is not enough to have Wendy Professor and Wheatley Phillis and Gilbert Professor waiting somewhere in the near future to administer the doctorate exam, assuring the world that you know nothing. Not just one fool but two making a riot in your mind as they hustle inside your head at the very moment when the voice of your lost brother arrives. You don't have time to think with so much noise around you. They think you're stupid, Shirah. They don't know you. They argue while your brother's lament flows through you from the Atlantic. That boy's mother, your ancestor, set her sad miserable foot on Virginia Beach, but her child was lost on the voyage, lost below the water line, your brother, who died midway through our journey,[88] in the Middle Passage.

And I am here too listening to Annamarie and Peter complaining, listening to your brother's lament and listening to you as you baffle yourself. I am Jane, Jane Bastet, your storyteller, murmuring, purring, I am one of your many Portfolio voices. You want to know if someone is speaking. Yes, I am speaking. But still you cannot hear.

JANE ASMODAI SHIRAH

You want to be free of the gods, you want to fight with divinity, you want divine freedom from the gods, Durga, Lillith, Inana, Pitaloosee. Too many of them. What is most to be honored. Most, the purpose of epic. That is what you seek. You seek a long narrative describing the origin, nature or destiny of a people, depicting a hero or heroic ideal, and incorporating the cultural world view. You can't wait any more. No more singing of the epic of the Graduate Student. Waiting, sing waiting,[89] no more. Give it up, turn it aloose.

Now you stand up in the library and pack your books and papers in your bag. You are Parcival on your quest but with no idea of what comes toward you.

You leave the library blank paged and hopeless.

You turn toward the west under a hot sunset of failure.

You walk the Locust Walk corridor from the Museum Library to the dorm.

You have been a long time Shirah, walking this corridor.

We are both confounded, Shirah, you, whose story I tell, and I, your storyteller. It wearies me to see you walking sadly back to your dorm room so separate from us, the voices in your head.

Yet even now your desire comes to you, rambling one. Your dissertation is not dead, sunk though it be beneath hieroglyphic misreadings.[90] We very voices that are in your head fighting over you will come marching to your blank pages with true words in honor of your perpetual search. All your roads lead home. Your paths lead to African American epic song, to an-

cient African epic, to nappy hair, to the Songhai people, yourself, ourself.

As the elevator rises thirteen flights you count the thirteen
floors by epic connections:

Gilgamesh

Kristin Lavransdatter

Vergil

Araucana

Lusiades

Dream of the Red Chamber

Terra Nostra

Frances Ellen Watkins Harper

Dante

Kalevala

The Lord of the Rings

Homer

Ham-Bodêdio

And your own John Milton, and your own Uncle Mordecai
— always with you, they don't need floors. Dear Uncle Mordecai your family Homer, the fountain, back in Kenilworth plucking corn and string beans, wondering where you are, what you
are doing. Homer. The one who seeks you while you fumble
your way through Graduate School. Is Homer seeking you?
Homer Fuentes? Perhaps. Do you know why you descended
from Heaven? Do you realize that you came to seek a book?
This is why you descended from Heaven and came to your
Heavenly attic, that attic that reappeared in Takoma so many
years later. This is why you descended from the attic to Kenilworth and the Garden of Converging Paths. Listen! This is why
you descended to the earth, to this place, this university, this
dorm room, where now you turn on the spigots above the bath

tub. The evening is so warm and stuffy. You came seeking a Book Unknown In Heaven.

Your fingers reach out to touch reflections of engraved letters on the surface of the silverblue bath water, our ocean, and yes, this is the beginning. You decide to decide. What? You have to seek this book, Incredible, the first bathtub of water that dreamed of the ocean water.[91] Through a book. What book? What about your dissertation? Is your dissertation the book? Perhaps the Book Unknown In Heaven is the one you write yourself. Begin writing it tonight, write it now. Why don't you? Let your voyage begin. Start from this very dorm room. In this moment.

A pen of water writes on paper made of water, shimmering perilous name. Writ on water.[92] Take the pen and write on water.

But you don't do it. You run back to your desk in the dorm room. If only you would stand by the bath a moment, and write on the silverblue water, and read the silverblue water, you could travel back to that castaway boy whose laments rise from the Atlantic grave. The boy, your ancient brother, and his ancient land await you. But the water stills itself cooling in the tub while you stand by your desk thinking. Fragments of papers rustle and flicker around you. The sun sets, the northern window stretches for the mountains of Pen's Forest. Flickerings. Empty pages.

On your desk are the scattered research books, and in piled rows along the floor boards, books, on tables and chairs, stools and boxes there are books, note cards, books, clip boards, books, papers, books, novels, books, poetry, books, tapes, books, records, books, stacks of photocopied transcriptions of songs, books, Leadbelly and Associates books, books of epics, books of commentaries, books of critiques, books and more books all along the floors. Books that still have not led to your answers.

You want it so much.

The heat presses you. You frown and groan, squinting and grimacing toward the window although the sun is muted by clouds. Your eyes hurt, but it is not the sun, it is not the brightness of the setting sun that blinds you, rather it is your life. Your life is weariness. You want it so much. What? You stand with your back to the pillows and tossings on the orange brown Graduate Student couch of brooding.

And scrunched up beside couch and its really hard pullout sofa bed are your desperation books, the how can you live without thee books, the grabbing in the middle of the night books, the love janes books from which I, your storyteller, take my name, ***Jane Austen***, Jane Eyre, Janie of ***Their Eyes Were Watching God***.

You want to say all the words that could not be spoken in all the books. But Annamarie interrupts.

ANNAMARIE

Jane Austen? You can't mean that prig of a Jane Austen? She got so much lip. She tells a good story but just gets on your nerves at the end. 'Member that time they was hollerin' and screamin' over cards down at her Aunt's? I'm talkin' 'bout them Bennett sisters. Jane Austen be the one to tell you who tweaked or twitched an eyebrow in all that confusion. She be sittin' there calm with all these loud sisters. I mean Elizabeth who Jane Austen made up. That Elizabeth woman got herself a man but why couldn't she say nothin' to him after all that lip? Man leaning toward her talking 'bout "My affections and wishes is unchanged" and she don't say a blessed thing."[93]

PETER

Why can't you say the woman's words like she wrote them? You are very well aware that Jane Austen never wrote 'wishes is unchanged'. You have no respect . . .

ANNAMARIE

Aw shut up, this is my turn. And as for you, Elizabeth, why don't ya just look up into his eyes, chile, and say I love you,

Fitzwilliam . . . Well, he can't help his name, but tell the poor fool flat out you be done changed your mind, oh honey chile. Say it! Say, AND I WANT YOU TO TOUCH ME! TOUCH ME RIGHT NOW AND TOUCH ME WHERE IT MEANS SOMETHING! Yeah, why can't you say that? I want to go to bed with you I want us to do it together and I want to know what it feels like and oh lie with me, lie with me, lie with me. But she don't say nothing, you know she don't, at least you can't read what she say in the book. What the hell good is that?

PETER

You don't understand anything about art, that would destroy the story.

ANNAMARIE

Didn't I tell you to shut up, Peter? I done heard Elizabeth's lover, that Mr. Fitzwilliam Smokey Robinson Darcy, I heard him sing, "She's not a bad girl because she made me see, ooo oooo how love could be. But she's a bad girl because, she wants to be . . . ."

JANE

Hush and let me speak, I'm your storyteller after all. You, Shirah, want to change all the stories that can't be changed. Is this what has taken you so long? You want to change all the book? In Jane Austen's **_Pride and Prejudice_** you want Elizabeth to speak out in words and tell him, ask him to touch you. In **_Jane Eyre_** you want to go to bed with Mr. Rochester right away instead of putting his eyes out and burning down the mansion before you can get married. You want to sleep with him in France and Italy and Timbuktu and Tripoli and any place else you can find a clean sheet and a little privacy. But that Charlotte Bronte created this sad love jane and broke the man's head, had poor Bertha his first wife leaping from the castle roof in flames just so that poor Jane could lie down in a bed with her man Rochester. Was it a castle? I guess it was just a huge mansion but it seems like a castle.[94]

ANNAMARIE

It was ridiculous. Why couldn't Bertha and Edward Rochester and Jane Eye all three go to France and have a ball? Why couldn't Jane sleep with the dude while he still had good hands to touch her with. This ain't real, Jane girl, you need to come to your senses and sleep with the man and be glad he wants you! And there Teacake be singing about Janie, "She's not a bad girl because she made me see, ooo oooo how love could be, but she's a bad girl because she wants to be . . . ."

PETER

There you go again with your idiocy and incapacity. When will you ever understand the nature of art and literature? Can you read at all? Are you sure you didn't just listen to the tapes? You're asking Charlotte Bronte to ruin her great story.

ANNAMARIE

Well, say what you want but I know what I know. And as for Mr. Rochester in Bronte's Jane Eyre, I know I heard him singing, "She's not a bad girl because she made me see ooo ooo how love could be, but she's a bad girl because, she wants to be . . . ."

JANE

What is the word? What is the word that comes next? You want to fix the things that will always be broken in all the books, shoot the dog in Zora Neale Hurston's ***Their Eyes Were Watching God*** before he bites Teacake so you can have your loving man forever and no court case and no Janie stalking back home by yourself, yes, that's where I got my name, Jane, Janie, ***Jane Eyre***, Jane Austen, the love janes.

ANNAMARIE

Is this what you call love janes? Some love! Look like you ain't never gonna git nobody! Look to me like you just hangin' out with yourself, Jane, you with all your purring and mumbling, you didn't git your name from nobody's books! You got your name from a movie, I remember, ***The Three Faces of Eve***. There was Eve White, the nice one, and you treat Peter like that. And there was Eve Black, the bad one, Me, Yeah, you treat me, Annamarie like that, and finally there came Jane, the strong one who survives and takes over the others. That's the Jane you tryina be, but you ain't takin' ME over. That's a love jane for you! Lyin' and jivin' to make the story come out any way you want it to come out.

JANE

You want to look directly into the open gentle eyes of a love that you will keep, yes, and you do call these stories your love janes of the love jones, your sex books, hidden emergency sex passion books chunked up beside your hard orange brown couch of a bed.

ANNAMARIE

Girl, you are sure hopeless. Ain't nobody ever gonna show you what a sex book really looks like? Who ever heard of a misguided literary mush head who could get hot from reading 'bout Jane Austen's Elizabeth? You deserve whatever happens to you. I don't even believe those folks ever go to the bathroom, let alone take their clothes off all the way naked. I bet they have two little holes in their suits just so they can make a baby.

PETER

I feel ashamed just being around you. You're a disgrace and an embarrassment. You're vulgar and ignorant.

ANNAMARIE

Aw, shut up, Peter, you know I'm right. Don't nobody in the world believe that Fitzwilliam Darcy and Elizabeth Bennett know how to take off their clothes and really do it.

JANE

Such language, I cannot bear it. I have got to get out of here. You are cruel to me. Why are you so cruel?

Something is dying, Shirah. You stand in the north window of the dorm room and catch your breath. They want you to write a dissertation about important stuff of right now. They want you to leave all those dead epic poets alone. They want you to stop having visions and become a scholar. But you have a vision, a word, of a book that was lost, a book that is unknown and that was lost. Paradise was lost. Something is dying. Someone is always lost. You can't cast off the vision. You seek a Book Unknown in Heaven and earth. Someone was lost in an ocean, in a river, in a cradle, in the bulrushes, where? Tonight. This night of beginning. This night of the breaking of your mind. You want to know if someone is speaking. Yes, we are speaking.

PORTFOLIO

The water in the bath tub is cold, still, when you walk in and glance down, you had forgotten it. The air from the open door makes flecks on the surface of the water arranging like codes, like dots on index cards, dissolving.

You are touched by fragments.

You are interrupted by note cards.

You are assailed by portraits.

You are infiltrated by musical phrases.

You are overrun by alphabets, Roman, Greek, Hebrew, Mandarin, Arabic.

You are infiltrated by the characters, poetry, authors, rivers, professors, philosophies, gods, memories you have loved. You are Jane Eyre crossing the Mississippi with Langston Hughes telling him of your escape from your cousin, Saint John Rivers, saying to Langston, "Lord have mercy, 'deed Lord knows I too have known Rivers." You are ShirahElizabeth Bennett OH! reading Mr. Darcy's letter. You are Job Sirkan Tithonus raging for death from God, you are Achilles upon the ships, you are Aeneas reviewing your story on television in Carthage, you are

Dante lost in the woods, you are hailing holy light offspring of Heaven firstborn, you are a mess.[95]

You are unclear.

You are bright colored index cards with the words soaking off.

You are assaulted by chaos. Where is the order from this disorder? When does change become creation? Ovid and Kafka, Metamorphosis, Metamorphoses, creative revisionism. Destruction. Shiva the Destroyer. Shiva the Renewer. Horus the Hawk circling above Egypt.[96]

You are attacked by memories. You want to be back home in Washington, DC eating string beans and fried chicken. You are cut off, tired. You have struggled to know the gods and call them by their true names. They weary you.

You are drenched by rivers, Nile, Nzadi, Kongo, Mississippi, Schuylkill, Anacostia, Potomac, exiled beyond the Pontus with Ovid.

Just as an ancient traveler, a woman in a far desert seeking answers, may stop at last beside a dull orange, dry riverbed in order to think, that ancient woman wakes by night seeking a direction and finds only the plaguing voice of her enemy reverberating through the dry, pitiless air, even so, Shirah Shulamit, you stir your thought without an answer as you stand and brood in your dorm room. How shall you bring on the nights in which you will dance to Gil Scott Heron through the darkness with the words of your dissertation pouring into your head! Where are you, Gil? There is only silence. No lovesong, no hatesong. Oh daughter of Big Boy, child of the Great OH!, descendent of he who seeks to know the nature of God, seeks to know the origin of race, of racism, seeks through faces and bookstores and libraries just as you seek, Shirah, for us whom you love but cannot hear, we your portfolio voices.

You're not a bad girl because, you make us see, ooo ooo how love can be. But you're a bad girl because, you want to be . . . . Oh, when will you say that word?

You are assaulted not by chaos but cosmos. All reports of the source of creation are true. The poet derives from the profound madness of God.[97] The poet derives accidentally from the big bang. Creativity is all human thought, creativity does not exist. Anything can be art. The great poet arises once in a millennium. The great poet is an arbitrary proclamation of the audience. The poet is the last link on a chain from God.[98] The poet is a silver grasshopper on a yellow wall beside an open window. All art a fortunate mistake. The poet is a supplicant before the ocean of light. The artist is a companion and teacher of God, is something from nothing, is a healer of nature, is a fraud.

You grow, I grow, we grow, you form, I form, we form, you come, I come, we come, they come behind you, you call upon the others, you call upon the leaves of Vallambrosa, the forgotten lost fallen pages, they come behind you, we come with your story. We have gathered from your life, Washington, Philadelphia. We have gathered from your libraries, of Folger, of Carnegie, of Martin Luther King, Jr., of the Langston Branch, of the Takoma Branch, of Congress, of Van Pelt, of Pen Forest Museum, of Warner at Eastern University, of Falvey at Villanova University, of Beineke at Yale, of the British Museum, of Smithsonian, of the National Gallery of American Art, of Wide and Widener libraries of West Cambridge University. The story of you and me, double consciousness, Shirah Achilles Shulamit Ojero OH! The stories of you and me and us, all of us, multiple consciousness, Ourstory. Our song of songs. We are taking over your mind tonight. You, ShirahAgonistes OH!, called to be a scholar of your people. We are your lost leaves.

We stand with Chuck Brown, calling out from the center of Washington City, We feel like bustin' loose, bustin' loose. Bustin' loose in the mean time, Bustin' loose to ease your mind.

We are your holy Portfolio. We are the buzzing in your head. We are the purring. We are your fragmented thoughts. We are the lost leaves of Vallambrosa. We are a notebook of pithy statements. We are memorable sayings. We are memorable sayings responding to memorable sayings. We are your thoughts thinking. We are your bibliography. We are the books themselves of your bibliography. We are the authors themselves. We are your songs singing back to these authors. We are your color-coded index cards. We are your writings writing back to these books. We are your dots dashes scribbles. We rise within you to drive the story. We are your literary device. We are the muses. We are the fill-ins. We fill in. We flow in. We mess up. We interrupt. We giggle. We are the singers of tales. We laugh. We speak. We are the victors to whom belongs the story. We are the Portfolio.

We are here.

You know us by many names, other names, fragments, half spoken splutterings, incomplete curses.

We come to you, We rise to you. We have come!

We have come.

Writ on water.

Chapter 45: Virginia

As you look into the bath water in your dorm room in the City of Friendship in the University of the Forest of Pen, you see the Atlantic spread out under the arc of a transparent silverblue mirror, framed in golden bronze, an arc that is a bronze trellis for a tangle of sky roses. You touch the surface of the cool webbed mirror with your fingers, silverblue, merging sky sea blue into a shimmering curtain wrought out by the silversmith into dissolving glass.

How came the ocean of Virginia to the inland harbor of the University of the Forest of Pen, to the thirteenth floor, to your dorm room? How could this be?

You reach into the water and lift from the water a pen of water. You use a pen of silverblue water to write on water. Your name.

You gaze through to look upon the shore of the Virginia sea coast where you see a blind waterman poet leaning on the shoulder of a guide, yes, that old epic story of the blind poet has come, and the youth guide is from a country beyond a river. It is Homer Fuentes, Homer the Fountain, the blind waterman, and Ethan of the Ivrim, the young guide, who hands to you a sheet of purple paper.

You lean forward from your dorm room in the City of Friends of the University of Pen Forest to the Atlantic to take the sea-stained toward purple papyrus and then step back into your room. The papyrus is odd, not pure papyrus but some combination of silk cloth and paper.

The blind waterman and his guide turn from Virginia toward the Mediterranean and are gone to Tanis in Egypt. Why don't you follow? Is there time enough? You reach into the bath water in the small crowded bathroom of your dorm room, and you touch the cool mirroring liquid again with your fingers, blue sparkling silver as you splash the water, as if you were holding your fingers in an ocean of light. Ocean of Light. A lotus is drifting there, red-orange, leaning into the flow of water. Light reflects as on the surface of a pool in a garden, as if a hand has dipped and plucked out a lotus just lightly under the sun, lifting and swirling the lotus through the air beneath a blinding sun to form a scented archway of silverblue light between the thirteenth story dorm room and the Atlantic seacoast.

You step through still holding the sea-stained purple papyrus in your left hand. You stand upon the American shore, in Virginia. You walk to a small boat and embark.

Chapter 46: Boat Woman

The Atlantic Ocean is blue.

The sky is the same color.

You once tried to get there by starting from another country, you were caught in Britain, in the Lake District, but you did not have a boat. You thought then that you would sail straight through the lands of Western Europe, Denmark, Belgium, France, Germany, Switzerland, you thought that you would break through into the Mediterranean near Italy. But you did not have a boat. And how could you sail through all that land?

But now you are starting from Virginia Beach. Here, where your mothers arrived from Africa enslaved. You have a boat and you are sailing away across the Atlantic Ocean.

You are with Alice Professor, whom you love. She sits across from you in the boat and says words to you that you cannot understand. You lie in the boat with your head in the prow, you face her and the Virginia shore behind her.

She tells you what she sees. She can see past you to the place where you are going. You cannot turn around to see. You can only see her clear face saying words that you cannot understand. She speaks until the words are gone and she is tired. You do not understand. Then she places her fingers on your lips and speaks the words again. You understand. You speak the words back to her. German. French. Spanish. Latin. Greek. Arabic. Peul. Swahili. Hebrew. Aramaic.

She leans toward you and kisses you on your lips.

You fall asleep. You think it is death.

You wake up. The boat sways with your breath. She is gone.

Inside the boat there is a hawk with her wings folded forward and upward and across covering her eyes. You want to know who she is. You lie in the bottom of the boat looking up at her. She flicks the edges of her wings three times. Flick. Flick. Flick. The soft flicks of her wings are perfect quietness.

People rise from the ocean. Some are castaway Africans, some are poets who stride toward the east passing your boat.

The unbodied poets are pale black and pale white. The bodied poets have a reddish tint.

HOMER, VERGIL, DANTE, MILTON, FUENTES.

Fuentes changes as you watch, reddish to pale. There are many, many more, unbodied and bodied, standing out from the surface of the Atlantic Ocean. Of those who have been thrown into the ocean from slave ships there is a woman who lived in Africa a long time ago. She wears a crown on her head. She moves toward you. "We have all slept on this bed," she whispers. "We have all slept on this bed."

HUGHES, OVID, SAPPHO, JEREMIAH, GLORIA NAYLOR.

The boat rocks from side to side with the rhythms of your breath.

MILAN KUNDERA, DUNBAR, WHEATLEY, GRIMKÉ, HURSTON.

Inhale. Exhale.

DICKINSON, TANAKH, MANN, GOETHE, BOOKER-T AND THE MGS.

"We have all slept on this bed," and the boat rocks toward Europe.

KEATS, MORRISON FRANCES ELLEN WATKINS HARPER, MOSES, BRER RABBIT.

Inhale. Exhale.

KIPLING, ALCOTT, ALICE DUNBAR-NELSON, GEORGE ELIOT, THE LITTLE ENGINE THAT COULD.

"We have all slept on this bed," and the boat rocks toward Africa.

MIRIAM, ANN PETRY, VIRGINIA WOOLF, DICKENS, BALZAC.

But your face is westward toward the Americas and you cannot see the continents of your origin in the east.

DOSTOEVSKY, UNCLE RICHARD, TOLSTOY, WORDSWORTH, AUSTEN.

The poets on your left, in the south, look at you and point you toward Europe.

BRONTÉ, RUSKIN, TSIBINDA, BATUKEZANGA, RENOIR.

The poets on your right, in the north, look at you and point you toward Africa.

MARVIN GAYE, STEVENSON, WAMPANOAGS, JOSEPH, MZ. COOPER.

You linger and rest in the rhythm of the soothing rocking boat and their pointing.

HAGAR, JACOB, NAOMI, THE ECHO RUACH OF GOD, MRS. RAYMOND.

Where is the castaway? Where is the cry of the lost boy-child? It is hard for you to remember him in this peace.

MRS. SHILER, SHAKESPEARE, THE BOOKSTORE OWNERS, THE FOUNDING MOTHERS, THE FOUNDING FATHERS.

The American shore is far from your boat.

THE LADY ON THE D.C. TRANSIT BUS, MELVILLE, GÜNTER GRASS, OCTAVIO PAZ, WILLIAM BLAKE.

You cannot see it.

ARIOSTO, HENRY JAMES, SEPHERIS, LEWIS CARROLL, TASSO.

The hawk flicks the edges of her wings three times. Flick. Flick. Flick.

She turns her wings upward and ascends.

HORUS, SHIVA, HEPHAESTUS, NUT, NIKE.

She spirals slowly, lifting away from the boat.

GORGON, VENUS, DURGA, LILITH, ARTEMIS.

You watch her rise into the sky.

BAST, IXCIUNA, PITALOOSEE, ASTARTE, ISIS.

When she is high in the air she becomes still.

NEITH, RHEA, INANA, ISHTAR, MOLLY BLOOM.

She unfolds her wings from her eyes.

TAMMUZ, POLDY, SONS OF MAHABHARATA, PECOLA BREEDLOVE, GILGAMESH.

Then you know it is Alice Professor who has become a hawk.

SHAKA THE GREAT, THE FOLK OF TEOTIHUACAN, YANKIDO, APHRODITE, PETROKLOS.

Although you are facing westward, although you cannot turn around in the boat, the hawk gives you her vision.

YANKEE DOODLE DANDY, APOLLO, HYACINTH, THE BULL OF HEAVEN, ACHILLES.

You see eastward through her eyes.

ADONIS, HAM-BODÊDIO, LABBOROU, XENOPHON, HERODOTUS.

From high in the air you look down upon the Atlantic Ocean.

THUCYDIDES, SHEIK ABELABEEK, MZ. FOWLER, PRINCE, A BUTTERCUP.

You see yourself in the boat sailing toward the Straits of Gibraltar.

GRANDMA GRIFFIN, GRANDDADDY GRIFFIN, JOB, EDDIE HOLLAND, SHORTY LONG WHO IS ALSO FREDERICK.

You see the Mediterranean beyond.

SCHUBERT, BROWNING, SHELLEY, WALLACE STEVENS, SOCRATES.

You see the lands that touch it.

ATHENA, DIDO, CALYPSO, ORLANDO, JASON.

You see a land near the far end of the Mediterranean, on the south, a land with a stream of water leading toward far Asia.

PLATO, LETO, ARTEMIS, CYNTHUS, BRISEIS.

A land of God wrestling.

CHRYSEIS, AGAMEMNON, CHEKHOV, SAMUEL, RALPH ELLISON.

The hawk says, "If it becomes too hard for you, if it becomes too much to bear, remember to leave by that path, and have peace."

WICKED WITCH OF THE EAST, SAURON THE GREAT, CAPTAIN HOOK, DOROTHY, FRODO.

You raise her eyes and look eastward.

JUNIOR WALKER, RICHARD WRIGHT, JAMES BALDWIN, TONI CADE BAMBARA, THE COLOR PURPLE.

What land is there?

JOSÉ DONOSO, SMOKEY ROBINSON, JOHNNIE, RASKONIKOV, ISAAC HAYES.

What river is there?

THE DRIFTERS, ROBERTA FLACK, RAVEL, CONRAD, SIRKAN.

What will you carry with you as you arrive there?

TITHONUS, DEVORAH OF THE IVRIM, ARETHA, CAESARS, AENEAS.

Can you place your hand upon it? Will your boat come to harbor there?

PROMETHEUS, CALLIMACHUS. SWEET BABY JAMES, BEETHOVEN, MARVELLETTES.

The ocean reaches for you.

BEE-GEES, CROSBY STILLS NASH AND YOUNG, CASSANDRA, LEADBELLY, URANIA.

The hawk stretches outward, eastward, and looks down at the ocean.

DEBUSSEY, DAVID BRADLEY, ISHMAEL REED, HARRY BELAFONTE, BRAHMS.

The hawk turns her wings downward and descends.

CURIOUS GEORGE, THE CHANTELLES, DENIS BRUTUS, MELVIN TOLSON, THE SONG OF SOLOMON.

She brings a cloth with her.

DICK AND JANE, ANTONIE, AL GREEN, BARRETT STRONG, STAR TREK.

The cloth is reddish pink and so high.

THE LITTLE TUG BOAT, BILLY ECKSTEIN, BYRON, RITA DOVE, DUKE ELLINGTON

There is a secret in it.

PLATO, PHAEDRUS, ARISTOTLE, KANT, HEGEL.

You do not know the secret.

KARL MARX, JAMES BROWN, FREUD, BENJAMIN, BAKHTIN.

She spirals slowly dropping out of the sky.

ZEUS, FOUR TOPS, PROUST, THE DARK SIDE OF THE MOON, APOLLONIUS.

From the boat you watch her return toward you.

FLAUBERT, BEINEKE, WAGGNER, ALEXANDER THE GREAT. CHARLEMAGNE.

But she does not return.

ARTHUR, ROLAND. THE THREE MUSKETEERS, STENDHAL, FAUST.

She disappears in air.

FAULKNER, ARCHIBALD MACLEISH, ETHELBERT MILLER, SIGRID UNDSET, CAMÕES

You see the slow spiral dissolve into blue.

HAWTHORNE, JUNE JORDAN, BEOWULF, EDMUND SPENSER CHAUCER.

First she is a ripple, then the ripple is gone, and you are lying there in the boat grieving as if she were the sun.

ANACOSTIA, POTOMAC, SCHUYKILL, HUDSON, CHARLES.

You look up into the empty Mediterranean sky.

MISSISSIPPI, IN THE WAKE OF THE SEA SERPENTS, THE SONG OF ROLAND, AMAZON, MISSOURI.

But there is another voice, who is it?

NILE, NZADI CONGO, THE GUNS OF AUGUST, MERRY HEARTS AND BOLD, GENGHIS KHAN EMPEROR OF ALL MEN.

You hear a voice,

We grow accustomed to the dark when light is put away.

THE PRETTY SISTER OF JOSÉ, BOBBSEY TWINS, THE PRINCE AND THE PAUPER, UNDERSTOOD BETSY, EIGHT COUSINS.

Without the vision of the hawk you will have to grow accustomed to the dark. The great light of the sun will not revisit your eyes that will roll in vain to find daylight's piercing ray, yet find no dawn. Great indeed is the light that now departs from you who are veiled by dim suffusion. Yet not the more shall you continue to sail this ocean where your fifteen million muses dwell, the castaways of Africa.

POETRY FOR YOUNG READERS, ALICE IN WONDERLAND, A CHILD'S GARDEN OF VERSES, NARNIA, HALF-MAGIC.

And the cloth falls into your hand.

You grow accustomed to vision now that blindness is put away.

You have passed through the Mediterranean and into a river, a tributary of a river, a stream. You watch and wait for a moment in Tanis, and looking up you see the blind poet and his guide.

You speak together.

Then you continue in your boat, passing Bubastis, on your way to the city of On, also known as Heliopolis. Beside you on either side there is land sloping upward from the close shores of a creek. Sit up, yes, you sit up and look around. Turning you see a tower beyond rushes and reeds. The tower is attached to a palace. You step upon the shore and pull the boat up to the land.

You walk down the path among the tall reeds until you come to a Garden of Converging Paths. There is a child, a little girl, beloved, brown-skinned, brown-eyed, nappy-haired, walking toward you down the path at a short distance, walking from the tower that merges into Heaven behind her. Your eyes and her eyes meet for a moment but then she curves down another path to your left, through corn stalks, toward a grassy lawn beside a catalpa tree by a porch. In front of that porch you see the familiar lilac bush and a small pool with lotus blossoms rising from the still water. A pool of your remembering, Shirah Shulamit!, a pool of remembering the past only as it gives you pleasure. The little girl is you, is little Shirah Shulamit OH! of Kenilworth, and little Shirah Shulamit walks up onto that porch where a black cat awaits her.

But your path, a woman's path is in a slight shadow from high brush on either side rustling, leaning, bending rushes and reeds. Sunlight is in front of you where the brush stops and the garden is in the clear light of the sun. You step into the light of the garden.

You step between the shadow and the light as if you were stepping into another world, as if you had not sailed that ocean, as if you were a Graduate Student, who sits in a land-locked dorm room by evening in late summer, a student who walks through the blue color of evening and looks into the transparent silverblue of bath water, seeing that same blue upon the Atlantic shore; for that student the walls of her dorm room and the sky of Virginia, the shower curtain in her bath-room, the bath water undulating there, vacillating there, merges in transparency with the Atlantic Ocean, such a student, who-ever she may be, could easily step forward upon the seashore, or step backward easily into her stuffy small thirteenth story inland apartment. In the weary listlessness of summer evening she could move longingly between the two places, even so, you,

You stand in the field of summer where the reeds lift green arms to the light, green stems stoked hot with the fresh full scent in your head. Yes, Buttercup, you know this place. The field slopes down to the stream that flows into the Anacostia River, the Nile River. This is Kenilworth. This is On of Egypt.

Midsummer, and you, yes you, our dear Buttercup, our seer, you who are brown-skinned brown-eyed, nappy nappy haired brown, you pass through the reeds and rushes and see not only little Shirah Shulamit of Kenilworth, but two others moving in the garden. One is an Egyptian woman walking beside you who turns to look at you. She has your face but wears outland-ish clothes from another time and place. She is Asenath, who has just arrived back in Egypt after a three years visit to Ethio-pia and Congo Nzadi.

And there are two little girls in this Garden of Converging Paths. One is you as a child, Little Shirah Shulamit swerving away to your Kenilworth home on your left, arriving from the precincts of your attic Heaven — the ideal attic that will be-come your Takoma attic, The other little girl, Little Asenath, is running up a grassy lawn on your right, arriving from Angel Square of yet another of your Heavens, curving in front of you and into the palace. They are all you. Little Shirah Shulamit, Little Asenath, Priestess Asenath, and you.

Do you know that on this our earth you live in four types? This is the Garden of Converging Paths, the garden of y'all come, and y'all have certainly come, this is where all four of you come together.

Welcome.

Every woman is a boat woman sailing somewhere ending up someplace under an empty sky.

Cluster 11 Yourstory
Cluster 11 Argument

Okay, Meandering Reader, Asenath has some questions to answer, that's why she petitions Pharaoh Akhenaten that she may become the Librarian of Saïs, that's why she goes wandering from Egypt to Nubia to Ethiopia to Congo and the Nzadi people. And that's why Shirah Shulamit Ojero wanders from Washington to Philadelphia to the University of Pen Forest. They are both basically graduate students. Yet here I have collected only the beginning for you, all kinds of precious fruits at your door. I share with you what the Ocean of Light speaks to me from the documents I have found. The day shall come, and it won't be long, for you to hear the rest of your story, Asenath, Shirah. The day of the rising cry of Africans to come.

But for now here the great rivers carry me, you, them. Have you heard? The rivers are already whispering that the people will be stolen. Stolen. Across an ocean.

Return, return, return when the time is come and tell us of your love for Joseph.

The ocean won't stop.

Listen.

Chapter 47: Desert

You cannot sleep. You stand a few paces in front of your tent by night. You must decide.

By day Aapet, your caravan leader, says to you, "Choose. Southward or Eastward."

Either travel the dry river bed of the Ntang southward, curving at last up to Ethiopia from the desert plain, slowly, following the flood plains in a wide arc to the highlands.

Or turn immediately eastward away from the sandy water course of the Ntang arroyo, go to the highlands now and reach Ethiopia, your mother's country, directly from low hills to higher, to highest mountains.

You hold the Portfolio under your right arm. Midway through the journey of your life you come to yourself in the midst of a dark wood.[99] But this is not a wood. It is a desert. Open the Portfolio, look through the leaves of the Portfolio seeking a sign in the words of the poets. Which way? Where is the answer. A road diverged in a desert[100] and you? What did you do? It has been a month since you saw them pass that little boy through fire to Moloch.

How will you come to the mountains of Ethiopia? How will you step forward with the image of the burning child in your mind.

Which way?

If you travel southward, walking in the dry flood plains, the waters may break from the mountains and cover you before you have a chance to grope to shore. You and all who are with you will drown. But if you turn eastward away from the dry Ntang riverbed, you and all who are with you may die of thirst before you reach Ethiopia.

Which way?

Your head buzzes as if there were words making themselves clear. Are they the words of Aapet still urging you to choose?

Where is the buzzing coming from to fill you head so persistently.

The eyes of night are in the sky, piercing stars in the black sky. Look! Under the starlight you see a little animal, a playful skerett in the dry sand of the empty river bed.

"And you, little skerett, how is it you can live here? How can you find a home in sheer sand that melts in front of your feet and closes in behind you? How do you find your way in a sandy landscape that changes with the wind. And where do you find water, little skerett. Can you tell me how to choose which way to go? Your desert is so fearful."

Your sleepless eyes follow the swift beauty of the skerett moving in and out of the sand. Silence. Absence. You love the skerett, seeing it so different, finding its way without landmarks, without being known.

"Are you the abomination of desolation,[101] yes, because you tempt me to think that I could live here too, in a faceless wasteland. You are so much at home."

This skerett tempts you to think that you, too, can live here, can find your way where there is nothing.

You could live here, Asenath, as a god without a people walking through the primal paradise looking and calling to a creature that you have made. When these stars throw down their spears, Oh you strange and beautiful woman, and water Heaven with their tears, you could smile your work to see. Did you who made the lamb and the garden make also this desert and the skerett of the sand?[102]

How long could you linger here in the sandy emptiness, with only a single skerett and that skerett not answering you.

Do Gods die? Would you finally lie down and die here? Or would you at last fill this desert with your creatures? You have seen a desert before and thought you understood it, not only in Egypt, but in the side view between elaborate archways in your Chamber of Lavender Fog, in your home, your family palace.

That chamber is dedicated to your mother's homeland, Ethiopia, and to all of Africa that does not lie along the Great Sea, the Mediterranean. Your elaborate archways along the sides of that chamber look out on a scene of desolation and grief in the Sahara desert, a view of the Rain Forest and the Nzadi people, and a view of Great Zimbabwe surrounded by the ocean waters of the Cape of Torment.

But do you see how this persistent skerett is at home here, traveling over the same pathways yet extending those pathways further each time.

Skerett, you are a thought in the sand, seeking through many starts and restarts to network your Sahara. You pretend that you live among signs and changes, that you live in a forest of stumps and trees and rocks. It is not so. For you undifferentiated grains of sand differ from each other as much, in other lands, a sheaf of reeds differs from heaped stone. You can tell the difference between one grain of sand and another. Your stark markless desert is a forest of events.

Sheer simplicity, dear skerett, you are like a woman who ignores forest signposts, you don't need the signposts, you return to tread your own path, to add new paths to old paths, and you are never lost. You are like a woman who knows the difference between one grain of sand and another.

But what of you, Asenath? At times you have thought that you came to earth upon a comet. Perhaps you are engendered by the comet Abdiel, cast out of Heaven because she refused to worship the god of the dead. Yes, perhaps you came to earth as did Abdiel, upon a comet. You passed through the desert of the sky but so very different is the desert of the stars from this desert of the sands.

You cannot sleep. The air is cool by night on the desert. You wrap the wool coverings around you, you sit on the rug upon ground. The god Maat will judge you in your season. If you choose wrongly this night you will not come forth by day.

Osiris, the god of the dead, will desert you. You are tired in your sleeplessness. Your head sinks toward your chest. You have already deserted Osiris. You hate Osiris. There appears somehow a warm space between your face and your chest, yes, place your face your nose there in the warmth and sleep. But stark awake suddenly your head jerks up. They could all die if your decision is wrong. Die forever. Everyone. The whole caravan. You lose the words you are holding on your lips. You pull the ribbons that tie together the painted covers of the Portfolio. You open the Portfolio yet again. You read. Knowing that all things come from some thing, and yet Beëlzebub has neither father nor mother. Which of the gods has a parent? Whence, whither is Aapet? Aapet is the Adversary. Do you give up?

You cannot sleep. You must decide. Aapet stood behind you on this afternoon and he made his suggestions, he your Adversary, he the guide of this caravan, he the great enemy who has been prepared for you. You have traveled many days from Saïs, and from Tanis, and from On. Aapet, the Adversary, your great enemy has said to you that you must make a decision and make that soon.

Aapet has told you that if your choice is wrong you will be deserted by the gods. You cannot decide.

Look out again into the night. The skerett has buried her way to wherever it plays beneath the sand. You are trembling. Would it not be good for you to turn away from your thinking? Asenath Agonistes, deciding. What if this is not decision alone, not alone the proper discernment of the gods, not alone the pacification of the vagrant gods that bring tomorrow after this tormenting full sand moon so quiet? What if this is temptation? Temptation to what? Stand up and step down to Aapet's tent.

Aapet says this new god Aten, the sun-disk may have some power in Pharaoh's breakfast room, or to some small distance along the lower Nile, but here you must propitiate all the gods. To which god shall you give sacrifice that we may choose our road? Aapet, the adversary says that he, too, worships a unified god, he says that the one god separates the blessed from the unblessed. In order to be blessed you sacrifice the unblessed to the one god. "Sacrifice the unblessed and go forth to seek neither the book nor the song but Gassire's lute which separates the blessed and the unblessed, find Gassire's lute and bring the power of the great African cities to the north." Thus Aapet.

You have consulted the Portfolio. You have recalled all you know of the gods. You do not want to anger the gods. You are afraid of making the wrong decision. Throughout your life you have been protected, you have been chosen and pampered by the gods in your life, the gods have been with you. How hard it would be for you now to live without the gods. You must choose aright. Should you continue toward Ethiopia by taking the dry river bed as a path southward? Or should you cross the dusty valley and begin to move upward in an easterly direction to the Ethiopian mountains? Floods or thirst, the dangers you face. Eastward your caravan could faint with weariness before you reach the high springs and lakes.

Southward there are water wells beside the dry river bed, but there is also the danger of flash flood. The gods, your many gods do not help you. Are they angry? Are they weary? Because you have been turning away from the gods they are turning away from you. Have you traveled too far from On for them to hear you? They do not hear you. If you sacrifice someone to the gods, as they sacrificed the young boy to Moloch, you will be protected on either road. You have undertaken this journey in order to seek out the truth regarding the gods. It is a journey blessed by the gods, but if you die on the road you will not fulfill the will and blessing of the gods. If you sacrifice someone perhaps you will live to understand the truth of the gods. The gods await your decision. All your life you have been preparing for this decision. They are waiting to drop you into the abyss if you make the wrong choice. They are preparing to sift your soul like grain.

Your head jerks against your chest and then up as you stare at the desert, the forsaken path of the skerett, the eyes of night glimmering upon the dry river bed. You are afraid. Afraid. Yes. The air and your limbs quiver at the very silence. Is it not your sign? Terror is in the stillness. The other tents are behind you, behind your tent. You cannot see them. Almost you could think you are here alone. Without food and water. Without covering. Without even your own tent which is surely behind you. Behind you. Is there someone stepping behind you. You. Or are you standing behind the tent of Aapet?"

"Asenath, why have you come to us? This is your crossroad, your place in which to turn to decide to choose to decipher to arrange — you must propitiate us feed us worship us obey us know us bow down to us. There is no part of you that is not trembling.

Every step takes you closer to death. Why did you not stay in On? Why did you not declare celibacy to avoid suitors, you, who led the parade of Neith. Instead you come to the desert seeking Ethiopian mountains, Sahel of the Sahara, Nzadi of the Congo rain forest, Savannahs of the south, Great Zimbabwe and the Cape of Torment.

How can life demand death? Something is wrong. And yet this world is good, is it not? You believe the world is good. And if the world is good whatever made the world must be good. Shall not the maker of all the world do right? Is the maker creator god of the world a murderer? You refuse to honor to worship a god who is a murderer.

And yet you are so afraid tonight.

What if it isn't so much that creation and destruction are connected, what if your god acted to give freedom to all the elements of the universe including human life, as great a measure of freedom as is possible with the physical limitations of material life on earth, the physical life, the biological life? What if your freedom, freedom for the waters to rise or not rise to kill or not kill to murder or not to murder what if your freedom is more important than any other gift? And what if your worship of god has nothing to do with it.

Would you have Aten say, "I'll give human beings freedom except when they sacrifice their babies to Moloch." Because if Aten can eliminate human freedom when the parents sacrifice their children to Moloch, it means that freedom is not a part of your construction. What if your freedom is more important than anything? The greatest love. And what if that freedom is how you are made?

Aapet has also told you of the Sorceress, the woman of great power who waits for you by the Nzadi waters. Congo. If you can travel so far.

The Sorceress knows that you are coming, she prepares herself and her art for you.

She is the second of your barbarian women, and Nefertha, the new wife of Pharoah, is the third barbarian woman. Before you left Saïs Nefertha told you that perhaps the Sorceress has Gassire's lute which may be the book or song or web you seek. In Gassire's lute, perhaps, you shall find the Book Unknown In Heaven, unknown in Pharaoh's library.

Asenath, black tar night with full snow moon between the eyes of night and this voice speaking Asenath, Asenath, are you afraid enough yet? Afraid enough for what? Who is speaking to you? It is Aapet the Adversary who has confirmed to you this great trouble. You have until morning to decide your path. You cannot sleep.

Shall I tell you your fate? Do you have strength enough to know? You are weighed in the balance.

You cannot sleep. Where have you seen such perfect blackness between the stars? A lion a leopard a wolf stand in a silent row before you and dare you to move.[103]

Your life. They will leap if you choose the wrong path. Choose well.

Consider the sunny days of On against the face of this night. Remember Sazonado your young brother who no longer lives among you in On. He lives in the westward lands, in Libya, he builds his house in a different land. To him was given the power of serving a liqueur that confers immortality. He will use the power the two of you have inherited beyond On in another world, he will found another kingdom. Where is he now oh why can't you grasp joy from the old times of play with Sazonado, times of play and warmth with you now so cold you stand within the tent of Aapet upon the desert earth so cold by night. And there is a knife in your hand.

You are a fool because you don't know what path to take. You, a priestess, don't know the gods. Aapet is speaking. He says to you "I've told you that you must propitiate the gods, now is your choice, for it is ordained that your choice will be the wrong choice, now your choice will leave us all dead. Your inadequacy your stupidity your insufficiency your irresponsibility will kill you and will kill all this folk along with you. You are not the one blessed by the gods."

The clarity of black night behind you. The cold shudders your nerve and your will. Tomorrow's sun will rise and bake whatever is not frozen in you tonight. There is no way out. We, the gods, have led you on to this place. We are waiting for you to murder him. There is no hope. Already the Gorgon rises from the leaves of the Portfolio empowers the lion and the leopard and the wolf prepares to chase you beyond atropos the cut thread of life. Tonight is a good night for Aapet to die and you blink your eyes into the eyes looking up at you. One moment there is nothing in front of you, the next moment you gaze down into a panting sweating face with hot breath, a face beneath your face, Aapet, the unholy uncomforter staring up at you by night.

Think.

The night is long. Where is Jeffrey Philosopher? Jeffrey Philosopher laughs at the laughing Aapet. Jeffrey Philosopher challenges the Adversary, challenges Aapet. You Aapet, you don't know the truth, you Aapet, you don't have the answers, you Aapet, you can't see the end; you Aapet, you don't determine the response you, Aapet, yeah, you.

Think.

You must go to Ethiopia for the tin cup that rests in the House of Learning, that is your inheritance, the inheritance of your mother who has come to you from Chane of Ethiopia. A tin cup. How shall you go? Do you dare to go without the blessing of the gods who demand sacrifice? Here is someone to sacrifice. Do you dare to choose without propitiation of the gods upon your way?

Think.

You refuse to accept the terms of the argument that Aapet presents you. You refuse to believe that your life is cast by the gods between two choices. Your choice is to deny that there is divine intervention in your choosing. You act you chose without the gods. This you know, whatever gods there are remove themselves from the air, remove themselves leave the air clear so that in clarity in the clear light of day or in the clear light of night you may say you contend with the gods for the assertion of your own life, any god that you worship gets out of your way so that you may breathe and think and live and decide and act and play with your own eyes focused clearly on the path of your own choice. Terrifying tormenting blessed freedom. You shall cross the dry river bed and climb the mountain to Ethiopia.

You are so restless with thoughts of how Aapet is misusing you, overusing you, asking you too much, never satisfied. The more you accept the more Aapet asks.

Murder him and then depart.

You scream. You raise your hands together holding the handle of the knife. You lower your hands suddenly to kill him. But just before the point enters the chest you twist your hand aside with all your power, and the knife stabs into the ground. You scream. It is Aapet lying there, grinning up at you. You were murdering Aapet, but your own hand turned aside.

You should not kill.

It is better for you to get up and get out and leave and go to another place without sacrificing life to the gods. Do not kill Aapet or any one. Do not.

Do not do wrong through obedience to the gods. Refuse to act through your fear of the gods or through your desire to please the gods in what you know is wrong but climb the mountain to Ethiopia and the House of Learning that rests in Chane, because it is the place toward which you have tended, because by your mission this path moves toward your goal, moves without devastation either of your companions or yourself. You choose with the best information you have. The outcome of your choice is undetermined. You are not a slave to the gods, no, you have escaped from slavery and superstition and now you can say that you are not a slave, at last you are . . . but before you can say that rare word the skerett darts out and across another path, for her this featureless desert is as comfortable as a room with eight sides, all labeled. South, Southwest, West, Northwest, North, Northeast, East, Southeast.

Someone was lost. You know it. Someone was lost. You did not kill anyone, ad yet someone was lost.

Do not forget the power of this vision. May this vision go with you as you go, live with you as you live, love with you as you love. Keep you from murdering Aapet, your great enemy. Keep you from murdering any one.

And leave this place as the skerett leaves, by the southeast.

Cluster 12 Epithalamion
Cluster 12 Argument

Okay, Amorous Reader, do you know the answer? What was in the world before God? You, Shirah, you should set sail for the past and maybe you will find out. And you, Asenath, you should walk toward the future and may be you'll find out. What was in the world before God? The text I found says the breath of God moved over the face of the waters. But who created the waters? And if the great deep of waters had a face; that is, a top then there must have been space above the waters. Where does space come from? Where does water come from? Before the beginning began. Another text I love says there was a big bang. But why did it bang itself? What made the big bang bang? I want to know. Do you want to know who I am? I am Loshirah, "Lo" means "no" or "not." "Shirah" means "song." I am the one without a song. The narrator behind the other narrators. I walk beside the Ocean of Light, the Rivers of Waters. I listen. I receive. I write down what I hear, but then I speak my own thought about what I have written and heard. They sing. I speak. And some of the words are banned. Did you know that? Some of the words you are not allowed to read. But I shall try to send the words to you no matter what. And maybe you can make a song of it anyway. Today a woman at the Kennedy Center asked me about the button on my hat. "I read banned books." Do you? Here is a love song made from the words I found, it is the love of Big Boy for the Lady of the Tin Cup, but remember, do not awaken love until you desire it. It is also the love song of the human race. This volume holds only half of it. I hope all of the song comes to you in time.

Listen.

Chapter 48: Big Boy

I adjure you, O maidens of Jerusalem,
By gazelles or by hinds of the field:
Do not wake or rouse
Love until it please!

Alexander the Great. Charlemagne. Arthur. Roland. The Three Musketeers. You make them out of cardboard, Big Boy, you. The Great OH! we call you. You sit at the dining room table in Washington, DC when you are a little boy and you make small cardboard figures of heroes and their armies, you spread them out in squadrons and columns facing each other all over the table. You make cardboard bodies with stiff cardboard slabs glued to their backs to make them stand up. Stand up! And so thus they stand with long strong slabs for the heroes, small weak slabs for the others, the foot soldiers, the cavalry. You have cardboard heroes leading armies of cardboard. And sometimes you invite in a friend to play with. And Charlemagne is the strongest one.

Here, stand right here, fix the rubber band like this, no like this, over the piece of folded paper, like this, shoot at the army on the other side of the table. Like this. The heroes stand but the army falls as the rough paper canons whisper through the air, whipping off from the snap of the rubber band slicing down battalions and platoons. Big Boy, father of Shirah Shulamit, you create the games the boys play on the dining room table.

Turn upon the table map of the city Washington, lines for street cars intersecting, each one named each numbered, curving street curves across the table, the city. You made it up, you, Big Boy. Big Boy alone. Alone child, playing upon the map of your own making, the made map of Washington City. You modeled, you cut out the street cars, stood them and moved them. Alone standing.

And you didn't give way to the bullies, those who carried the knives and the guns and said to you, "Come with us, we need you with us to break and to steal.

"We can hide in the narrow passageway between the stores on Benning Road, we can wait there until nothing's happening, about 2:00 in the afternoon, before school is out. Come on and hang with us. They'll never know what hit them at the Young Men's Shop. We'll get everything. You know they probably be robbing everybody anyway. Let's get them and take the goods." You didn't give way to them, Big Boy, didn't set out with them. You didn't even walk the same walk they walked. They wanted to shed blood, an evil thing.

You figured out what was right, what was just, what was fair, because these are the things that are good. Wisdom entered your mind as you considered these things, wisdom and knowledge, and you found great joy in your discernment.

You went with your step-father, John Griffin, where Babe Ruth hit a home run, your eyes sparkled with astonishment, wonder, take what is here and place it there with power, the baseball, gone beyond, gone where Babe Ruth wanted it to go, beyond.

You listened then to sports by radios, stooped listening, imagining, hearing the roar of crowds, bright cheering from the brown radio. And the radio taught you also left jabs in boxing, learning winning, how to win. In school the fighters scuffled around you, you knew how to defend yourself. You didn't start fights, but you ended them. Big Boy.

You were to have riches, yes, great riches. You dashed forth as a stream for all the world to honor. Big Boy, a blessed fountain.

Yes, yes, you were the one. Class president and class poet. You passed the national test so high you put your school, Armstrong Senior High School, on the map. You were the one, Big Boy. You sought to know the nature of God, you sought to know the origin of race, and racism. You sought through faces and bookstores and libraries for what you sought. You sought out your correct path through your rigorous understanding. Thus you walked without falling. You looked into your life.

From girls you leaned away in shyness, although you saw them, looked for them, walking by the porch in the schoolyard watching afraid of the little girls. They loved you but you did not know it. They snatched your cap from your head, they ran down the street with it laughing. You pretended to be angry chasing. They told their brothers, "I go with Big Boy." But you, Big Boy had not even spoken to them.

Then the day came when you saw the woman of your desire.

You who are also known as the priest Poti-pherah of On in Egypt, you had arisen by dawn and sought through all the ways and byways of the town, you rode the street cars through all the streets and all the circles and all the squares.

You were seeking a beloved, and you found her.

First you came upon the watchman, the sentinel of the town, "Where is she? where is my beloved?" But just beyond the watch tower you found her in a garden by pool by lotus and by tree, she was there upon the lawn upon the tennis court playing.

You fell in love at first sight, at a distance, without speaking or hearing one word, or knowing one thing, one idea about your beloved. You fell in love and stayed in love telling yourself a true story without words.

You stood by the pond and watched her play.

And she turned toward you and loved you.

And there to her delight you held her fast, ah, you would not let her go until you brought her unto your mother's house, to the home of she who had conceived you.

And you loved her forever, you never stopped loving her.

I adjure you, Oh maidens of On, of Washington, of Karnak, of Thebes, of Dunbar Senior High School, of Miner Teachers College and of the University of the District of Columbia, Oh you young women of Jerusalem, by gazelles and by butterflies swirling on the lath of the stars, do not stir up love, I pray you, do not awaken passion or arouse love until it is pleasing to you.

Do you ask of this one my beloved? She who has come down to you from the mountains of Ethiopia, and from Dunbar and Miner and UDC, beyond the desert of Nubia moving like columns of smoke, as the incense of violets and swaying lilies, your beloved, as the perfumes and fragrances of sweet vines and tendrils.

Here is your couch for you, the hope of your people, upon your cradle the mother of your mother looked down upon you, a young sovereign, Asher, Oscar, OH! The Great OH! she called you, Big Boy, our great hope, and your great riches shall be that you shall found a race of the singers of new song. Now you have come to manhood you have brought to your couch the belóved who is your heart's desire.

You made a great carriage, a conveyance in which to transport your love, a great car of silvery glass and shining scarlet, with handles of silver and wheels of gold, and the cot was wide and covered with wool of royal blue. And every pillow and cloth was decked with love by the young maidens of Washington. Oh sweet maidens, Oh lovely ones of On and Karnak and Jerusalem, come look forth upon the sovereign of peace, of shalom, of the olive branch, upon your head you wear the crown given to you by your mother on your wedding day. Now you stand in the awe of the birth of your first child, at the bed of your beloved, and the child of your paternity is born and lifted up on her day of bliss. She will be a seeker of epic song, she will be surrounded by the poets all the days of her life, and you have named her, you have said, she is peace, Shalom, just as your mother's before you were peace, Shalom, so you named her Shulamit.

Chapter 49: The Tin Cup

Who is she that comes up from the desert
Like columns of smoke,
In clouds of myrrh and frankincense,
Of all the powders of the merchant?

You have captured my heart,
My own, my bride,
You have captured my heart
With one glance of your eyes,
With one coil of your necklace,
How sweet is your love,
My own, my bride!

Oh my goodness, how long Georgia? How long ago did she die? You didn't know it? I knew it. Yeah. How long was it Georgia? You'd better take a seat now. Don't let that dog jump all over you. Alphie, sit down. That dog's always acting like he's about to bust loose. What? At least four or five years ago. Yes, that woman has been dead. Now Jack, onions are on the way. Naw. Yeah. What's that, potato salad? Unh hunh. Ooh, that looks good. Alphie be quiet. Yeah, somebody, could you hand me the string beans? Unh hunh. What's in that one? You could help my plate. Salad. Oh that's fruit is it? Oh yeah, fruit salad. Jack I got plenty more onion. That's more than enough for me. I've filled up my plate. But Georgia? Georgia? Yeah? I hate to tell you this, but you got Sunday dinner on Saturday. It's cause there ain't gonna be no Sunday dinner. Oscar helped me to do this work. OK now, get your potato salad. And you sure looking fine after a day of jazzing up a kitchen. Deed she is fine, black and beautiful. Does anyone have a serving spoon for the fruit salad? That's what I told Oscar to bring when he brought the dish in.

Georgia, this is priceless, this cabinet with these birds! Thank you, Catherine, my Godmother did that, everything was wrapped separately, in a separate little package, and sent to this house. What!? Yes! These were your Godmother's? Those were my Godmother's! Oh, Georgia! And two of my friends have given me something since, I think, the two at the top were given to me. On top of the whole thing. Oh they're gorgeous. And what sort of glass is this? They say it's stone, transparent stone from Ethiopia, you see I use it for a terrarium. I love to make terraria, I get orders for them from all over the DC Public Schools and every place. And your godmother? Yep, my godmother, Bessie Parker, gave it to me.

Everybody in the family had a godmother but me. Is that true, Jack? Everybody else had a godmother. Look, that chair isn't . . come and use this chair. I told Edmonia my chairs are in the shop. This chair is comfortable. I knew I was in Oscar's chair. No, that one over there is his chair. I have gotten . . . I think Montgomery Ward is coming to ask me to pay them twice. The man has used that chair so much that Montgomery Ward is going to have me pay twice!

Where's Daisy? These dishes are gorgeous. Every time you've been in my house for the last fifty years they've been right there. I believe it Georgia. Georgia, you ought to see what I serve on Saturday. Hot dogs and beans, hunh?! There you go. Well, hot dogs and beans taste good to me. Oh let's tell them about hot dogs and beans, Jack. I know that if you split me right down the middle, one half is hot dogs and the other half has got to be beans. Now! Now! I'm talking about Douglass Street. Yeah. See y'all, see, tell 'em, y'all weren't poor, y'all were upper class. Who? Naw. Yes, y'all were, we were lower class.

Georgia. My father never paid income tax because we had so many children. I didn't know I was poor. You know, it makes a difference when you don't know that you're poor. I didn't know I was poor. I would have left home before I did! I thought I was doing all right. I had to leave home to find out I was poor.

Remember Mz Brawner? Yes. Now Mz Brawner was upper class, she had plenty of money. Mz Brawner? Yeah. Georgia, she didn't have children. She thought she had some because of us! She was the principal. She had a Buick. She never bought a new car. She could get twenty children . . . she had a Buick that could seat twenty children. Alphie, stop that whimpering. If we would hurry up and get there along down Douglass Street, we could get a ride to school. So we got in there just like you got in there. And guess what y'all did? What? You won't believe it. Y'all traded us ham sandwiches for peanut butter and jelly.

Yeah, and we were saying, isn't this something? I went home and said they've got to be crazy. Georgia, now, you're making us laugh too hard, it's too much we gotta calm down. Y'all said y'all had never had any peanut butter and we said well this is good, and y'all would give us ham sandwiches and we would give y'all peanut butter and jelly. We couldn't believe it! Until y'all caught on, took y'all about a year for y'all to catch on, and you ate our peanut butter and jelly sandwiches.

That Mz Brawner didn't miss nothing. She had a husband who wouldn't work anywhere, never. She was making too much money. He didn't work, and he ran with all the ladies. But, guess what Georgia, once he ran with the lady right next door now you know that was a bit much. She used to go up the street, Penelope. Yeah, Penelope Harristown. Penelope used to go up the street, put on her coat if it was wintertime, go up the street and stand at the street car stop. Like she was going out. And as soon as he saw her go out that door he would jump in his car and make believe he was going out. So Godmother Brawner fooled him. She used to come home from school, take all her school clothes off and put on an old robe. This time she got on to him. She put her robe right over top of her clothes. So he said I guess I'll go out and make my run now, because I'm going to teach this student how to play the violin. You know he was a musician. Yeah, yeah.

Well, honey, she threw off that robe! Ain't that something! And she said, I'm going with you! She got up in the front seat of that car, that big Buick that Georgia was telling you about. Yeah. And then she reared back, and she saw Penelope standing at that street car stop, she said, I dare you to stop and pick her up. He drove that car, Georgia, Shirah and Edmonia, Zooom! left her standing there. Isn't that awful?! Ha, ha, ha, ha, she's something, he dared not stop. He didn't want to lose his bread ticket.

Did you tell them of the supreme sacrifice? None of y'all can tell me my husband doesn't love me. Let me tell you how much my husband loves me. I never thought this would happen. And I never have even read about this much love even in a book. But look, see, he knows he did it, see, it was a mistake, look, he loved me by mistake y'all. He made a mistake. Look at him. He never meant it, he could kick himself. We're going on a retreat with my college, Miner Teachers College. We planned it way back in the summer, I asked him if he wanted to go he said, yeah, so we're going, November 2nd and 3rd. Well guess what?! that's the weekend the 'Skins play in Washington, and he's got a season ticket! Let me tell you he's still going on the retreat with me. The man just loves me! I offered to get somebody else to use his ticket for the retreat, and he said no. He's going on the retreat with me and giving up the Skins game. Well Georgia, he just loves you. And Sazonado, our son, Sazonado's ready to walk all the way over from Albuquerque to use his ticket for the game. If the chile only had money to get here he'd be here. Now. None of y'all tell me my husband doesn't love me! Gave up a football game.

I was telling you about my Godmother, Jenny Brawner. Yeah. Jenny Brawner. She used to get so many tickets. Not as many as the lady down the street. Who? Mrs. Thomas. Molly Thomas? Allen and Charles' mother. Nobody got as many tickets as she did. Didn't look at nobody, drove straight ahead. Wait a minute, Jackie. She drove through the front door and straight out the back. She drove down the middle of the street and half the other cars were on the sidewalk. She would shake like a leaf! She would offer you a ride, sit right there she'd say. Who would want to ride with her? I rode with her. You did? Yeah, she brought me home. You must have been drunk. After the first time I'd make an excuse, I'd say I've got to make a stop, I've GOT to make a stop, I'd say thank you, Mrs. Thomas but I'm getting a ride. Do you know where 15th and H is? Where Bladensburg Road comes in to Benning Road? That's a terrible intersection. Yeah, at one time had no lights. It's a shame, the police would shake his head as she went right on through. They didn't have no lights. And that's the most dangerous corner in Washington! Yeah, there's five or six streets coming in there to-gether. Mrs. Thomas would scare the H out of you coming down Kenilworth Avenue. Well you know most people slow down when they turn in a street, well she turned that corner at the same speed. Everything moved, all the drunks would jump off the corner.

But they said Mrs. Thomas had so much money! When her husband died . . some people might think of having twenty or thirty cars — she had twenty or thirty limousines. Cadillacs! I mean. Oh my goodness. I guess she ought to have money, just two boys, and sewing for them. Listen to that, it's Daisy, ain't nobody but Daisy. Better late than never. Hi. Hi ya doing girl, hi! Alphie shut up that noise. Here's Al y'all. Here's a chair for Al. Yeah, a nice comfortable chair. Alphie, that's why we got you chained, 'cause you don't know how to act. How ya doing darling? Oh my goodness, Jack.

Do you remember Mrs. Thomas? You know — Charles and Allen's mother. Yeah. We've been talking about her driving. Ridiculous! What else did you talk about besides Mrs. Thomas? Well Mrs. Thomas shaking, my Godmother, Virginia Brawner. Who else did we talk about? We haven't talked about anyone else yet.

How about Mz Fowler and Sheik Abelabeek? Who? Mz Fowler down the lily ponds? She was the biggest racist I've ever met! How about how she would lock up the lily ponds. I hated her. That didn't stop us. I hated her, she was a racist, she hated black folks. She didn't know us, some of us should have come in there and thrown her in that lily pond. That's what we would do today.

She wasn't that bad, she used to give us all that fruit. Remember the cantaloupe? Her son visited Saudi Arabia all the time and wore those clothes. And had those big parties. We used to follow him through the lily pods singing, *Hey, Sheik Abelabeek can I come to your party?* We were awful.

Do y'all remember about Mr. Baker's garden, how we stole his fruits and vegetables. What! I never stole nothing in my life! Mr. Baker's garden, oh it was awful! Who's Mr. Baker? In the back of your house, Daisy. Yeah, right where that school is now. No, it's where the projects are. Right behind Daisy's house. Oh yeah. Well we knew when things got ripe before he did. Everything disappeared. And the poor man didn't know what to do, so he said, I'm only going to two houses, the Gaskins and the Johnsons, because they got the most children. And if each one tells another they will understand. Now I'm giving them two rows, please tell them don't go past the first two rows. Well, we tried, but two rows were not enough! We went up one row and down the other — sweet potatoes, turnips, tomatoes. He should have given us more. He come giving a row of sweet potatoes and a row of carrots — and we looking at tomatoes!

But Georgia and I would have the most fun, though, in her daddy's garden. Yeah, yeah. Come the garden season, I would do five and six rows, picking beetles. That's another reason why I left home. Yeah, Jack, and you know you stole my can full of beetles and dumped them all in yours. I never got mad — stole my beetles!! Until this day! I promised myself when I was about three, that I would never cut another blade of grass, if I ever grow up, and I never have cut a blade of grass since I grew up!

Well, he never picked a whole can of beetles either. He really hated that garden. Used to steal my beetles and get credit for doing all this work, but I did the work Jack, you should have been ashamed. Aw, Georgia, you were always so good, you never even got mad.

That's all right, Jack, you used to protect me. I could walk home in front of anybody, all the bad children, I wasn't scared — Jack could beat anybody! Bad boys like George Adare. George Adare took my Sugar Daddy, a great big sucker, and Jack saw me crying. I was near Mrs. Kirby's store and Jack said, What's the matter?? I said, Well . . pointing to George Adare, and before I could get the words out, the boy was on the ground and the sucker was in my hand. After that I could walk anywhere. The boys would say to each other, Don't say nothing to her, that's Georgia, Little Jo they call her, Jack's sister. Don't even look at her crossways or Jack be all over you.

Look, what about Mrs. Kirby's Grab Bags? Stale candy, whew! Little teeny weeny bags, the candy was so old it had turned white. Not only white but candy like Mary Jane was coming out of the paper. That's what started my teeth getting bad. And the awful pickles — we'd put a peppermint stick down inside them. And your lips would be white, too. They didn't have all them government regulations then, if they had Mrs. Kirby's store would have been gone. It sure was a store. She used to ask, do you want a penny grab bag or a five cent one? The five cent grab bag had candy that was two months old but the penny bags had been there forever! Like since George Washington. Grab Bags! But she had an eye for business. Yes sir, she pulled in the money.

But once again Georgia and I would go in her father's garden, we'd go through that garden and we'd find some of the best nubs. We'd cook 'em up with butter and sit there under the catalpa tree! my my my but that was good And your grandmother, Mrs. Plummer, wasn't her name Florence? Well, Mrs. Florence Plummer heard us talking about those nubs and couldn't figure out what they were. She said to your mother, to Faye, I've looked in all the stores and all the papers but I can't find out what nubs are!

Well what are nubs? That's what she asked. And Faye said, It serves you right for being so nosy. Nubs are the little ears of corn that didn't have time to finish growing, boy they were good! We found small tomatoes and everything. And we'd go inside and cook the nubs, then here comes Jack, to eat. Yeah, I could put that food away.

And there was the time when Mrs. Plummer couldn't take it any longer. She was always listening to you and me talking, that time we were talking about Joe Hawk. Yeah, Georgia used to come over every evening and call out to me, you'd better come on, Daisy, cause Joe Hawk is out here waiting for you. Mrs. Plummer whispered to Faye, Faye, you'd better check on that Daisy and Georgia . . . Georgia keeps telling Daisy that Joe Hawk is waiting for her . . . ! Who in the world is this Joe Hawk? Faye said, There you go again being nosy. Joe Hawk, well they wouldn't tell her for a long time, until she got so nervous, then they told her that Joe Hawk . . . was the wind! Yeah, Joe Hawk means The Wind.

Mr. Joseph Hawkins, Esquire over the ponds, the winter wind touching the Eastern Branch of the Anacostia River and you, Georgia, our Little Jo, sitting there with your dog Prince. You are the sixth of eight children. The last of five daughters. And all of you drank out of the same tin cup. Beige and brown and black and white you were. Eight children. And when ever you wanted a drink of water, you went to the sink and lifted up a red tin cup, and you drank from it. And no one was ever sick.

Joe Hawk. Mr. Joseph Hawkins, Esquire, the wind of the end as of the beginning, engenderer, annihilator. Horus. Shiva. Hawk of the end. Last God. Chilled the gardens of Kenilworth, but not before you, Georgia and your dog Prince roamed the woodlands and you collected autumn blossoms, gentian and chamomile, circles of ivy, frogs and feathers. And the last seeds of the water lily and the lotus from the ponds where one day you walked with your beloved, the cherished one of your soul. Oscar. Asher. You met at a game of tennis, and kept playing.

You were wearing the white blouse and white skirt of the tennis.

On the playing field of the Banneker playground.

Off Georgia Avenue.

Across from Miner Teachers College

Where you were a student.

And he who was to become your beloved saw you.

And he called to you.

You who are also known as the Lady Niko of Ethiopia.

You turned away. You played tennis.

He called to you again.

Stop interrupting me you said.

But your beloved called to you again.

Until the moment you turned toward him whose name is Asher, Oscar, happiness.

Yes, you turned toward him.

Ah, you are handsome, my darling, you are handsome, your tawny skin so beautiful so soft. Your deep set eyes dark as bottomless waters behind your curling lashes, your hair ripples and curves as a field of short sweetgrass upon the Amharic hills. Your teeth gleam in brightness your lips full and beckoning. Lovely you are, your brow and your cheek.

Your tenderness gleams in the gentleness of the movements of your body, you are a tower and a bulwark against all hurt. Ah here, as we stroll in the easing day among water lilies and lotus, blue tinted shadowing air surrounds us in delight. From my home upon the mountains of Ethiopia I would bring to you golden myrrh and the incense of the highest God, every part of you is handsome, my darling, without flaw or fault. I came down from Ethiopia with my gifts with my attendants to be your bride, from Mount Ras Dashan, and Mount Gondar, and the peak of Adwa, through lions and through leopards to you.

You have my heart, I am your bride, here is my heart. The glance of your deep-set eyes enrapture me, you are sweet. I am your bride, you headier than wine, more fragrant than the sweetest spice of the hilltops I taste from your lips, my beloved you are a garden of honeysuckle and rose, you a fountain of joy, stream of delight. Fruit of pear and of fig, of peach and mango and plum my beloved you are an orchard in fruit.

Oh wind of Ethiopia take me quickly to my beloved and soon where we may be bridegroom and bride and live and lift up our children to the light, our child, our firstborn, she is a song, she will be surrounded by the poets of song all the days of her life, a joyful song, let's name her Shirah.

Chapter 50: Shuvi

What was in the world before God?
The great deep.

Shuvi, Shuvi,
O return, Shirah Shulamit!
Return, return, that we may gaze upon you.
The head upon you is like crimson wool
The locks of your head like purple.

You return. You step upon the boat. You sail the boat toward the past for freedom. Toward Asenath. You step into the corridor. You step toward the future for freedom. Toward Shirah. You cannot be lost. You cannot be diverted. You know the way. You are on your way. You are almost there. You are not afraid. You are almost here. You have seen the divine. You understand the tapestry, the tree, the pool. You recognize the green figures.

This is your lovesong. This lovesong is of freedom from the gods. The gift of the one god is choice, is freedom from the gods, this lovesong is of freedom. This lovesong is our lovesong. Our lovesong of our freedom. Our original originating freedom, that same freedom that moves love, that moves the earth and the planets and all of the stars. Love. Freedom.

Daffodil and crocus,
lily of the valley,
rose of Sharon,
I have found thee I have known thee
here in the land of your birth,
this blessed place where thy mother bore thee,

> *O my darling, linger here a while,*
> *linger in the light,*
> *will you arise from this bed*
> *seeking another desire?*
> *I am thine by thy own choice.*
> *Where wilt thou go, my beloved,*
> *will your longing for freedom take you from*
> *   this bed?*

The lying down with thee and the rising away from thee is one act, one love, O my darling. Hold me, I would be with you, you are my love. Wildfire storm of love, gentle peace burning love, stunning stroking precious love, love arising from waters, love descending as fires, flames, rivers, springs and candlelight, love, I love, I do love, I do love you, freely I love, freely I choose, freely I choose to love you, I love you.

With discussion with argument with contention eternally through the halls of the corridor of the future, ah sweet, my sweetness, my spices you are, come beneath me lean upon me, my beloved. I have returned from the desert and I have found thee, as the apple at harvest, as strawberry and grape, my beloved.

You contended with divinity in the Nubian desert, as you read the Portfolio and watched the path of the skerett through sand, and as you brooded the temptation of Aapet. You fought with God as you wrestled art away from sociology, you thought, you considered, you did not obey, as you proclaimed black-womansong in the circle of the epic poets, of woman's everlasting disobedience you did sing, as you ripped poetry from scholarship, as you descended from Heaven to seek the Book Unknown In Heaven. Happy, happy are all lovers who dwell in your house. Incredible the first animal who dreamed of another animal.[104] Call me Ishmael.[105] Inebriate of air are you.[106] Since first this subject of heroic song pleased you long choosing and beginning late. Thus fulfilling the will of God to set in conflict godlike Achilles, and lordly Agamemnon.

And you contended with divinity in the Ethiopian mountains, as you talked with the sorcerer, and as you studied the pastel maps. And you contended with divinity as you came to the rain forest of the Kongo, and as you moved along the Nzadi River. You contended with divinity as you listened to Anansi, as you looked upon the lost dead child of the Kongo in the basket in the bulrushes. And you contended with divinity as you linked yourself to the son of Israel, land of god wrestling. It is god who does battle. God. I shall not release thee, I shall not release thee, my beloved, until you walk the nine chambers of the corridor of the future. I shall not release thee, my beloved, until you sail the Middle Passage and the Mediterranean to the past, I shall not release thee unless thou bless me, wrestling, turning, pouring and receiving light, walking, sailing, you each turn toward other. Two oceans. One seasong. One ocean.

You rest your bodies together, one is awake holding Joseph. You. Joseph holds, you hold Joseph. One consciousness, one sleepness, one wakeness, one vision, one. Love O love you rise you lean up you see above thee the tapestry tree pool the green figures the future. You know. You. You are lovely awake, you see the future, the corridor of the future is coming in love.

Silver and wood, an open door, your eyes that see beyond walls beyond battlements. Cedar and silver, your shoulders your breasts above the sleeping, resting, satiated eyes, beloved, a vineyard full of spices and growing. A song of the song of peace, protected now, enclosed, comforted for this season, this seasoning, this seasong. You are a rich and fruited vineyard of peace, given in love, O love. O peace, more precious than ten thousand, linger, linger here in my garden in love. Hear me, hear my love, light of my heart, and speak to me, speak, answer my beloved.

You are racing for the future for freedom you are returning from the future for freedom. You cannot be lost. You cannot be diverted. You cannot be fooled. You know the way. You are on you way. You have begun. You are not afraid. You step upon the boat. You step into the corridor. Your boat is sailing swiftly. Your feet are walking quickly. You understand the tapestry tree pool. Someone has been lost. You recognize the green figures. Someone has been lost. You have seen the divine. Someone has been lost. You have fallen in love. This is your first love. This is your lovesong, this lovesong of your freedom. This lovesong is of your divine freedom from the gods. The gift of the one God is choice, is freedom from the gods, the same freedom that moves love, that moves the earth and the planets and all the stars. Love. Freedom.

The locks of your beautiful nappy hair are indeed like purple as you rise up, begin, while the bed recedes behind you, you start your journey.

Chapter 51: One Half

Let me be a seal upon your heart,
Like the seal upon your hand.
For love is fierce as death,
Passion is mighty as Sheol;
Its darts are darts of fire,
A blazing flame.
Vast floods cannot quench love,
Nor rivers drown it.
If a man offered all his wealth for love,
He would be laughed to scorn.

You arise and depart. You do not stay put. You do not obey. You are racing for the future for freedom, you are sailing for the past for freedom.

We were caught. We were broken. We were murdered.

We were Hebrews.

We were slaves.

We were Carthaginians. We were Germanic tribes.

We were slaves.

We were Araucanians. We were Pueblos. We were Aztecs. We were Navajos.

We were Apaches. We were Wampanoags. We were Incas.

We were slaves.

We were French peasants. We were Spanish merchants. We were Gaelic farmers. We were Nordic seamen.

We were slaves.

We were British Colonials of the Americas. We were Portuguese Colonials.

We were Spanish Colonials of the Americas.

We were slaves.

We were Africans of the Americas.

We were slaves.

We were Mexicans. We were Russian peasants. We were Soviet peasants.

We were slaves.

We were Chinese scholars and peasants and workers.

We were slaves.

We were Northern Europeans. We were Eastern Europeans. We were Southern Europeans. We were Armenians.

We were slaves.

We were Jews.

We were slaves.

We were Indians.

We were slaves.

We were colonized Africans.

We were slaves.

We were Palestinians. We were Israelis. We were Egyptians. We were Afghanistanis. We were Sri Lankans. We were Japanese. We were Vietnamese. We were Pakistanis. We were Cambodians. We were Indigenos. We were Iranians. We were Iraquis. We were Sudanese.

We were slaves.

We walk into the future to sing a song of freedom.

What song?

This song.

So sing it.

Sing

 Let my people go
Sing

Our song, our song of songs, our song of the song of peace
our epic song of the song of peace singing

> *When Israel was in Egypt's land*
> *Let my people go*
> *Oppressed so hard they could not stand*
> *Let my people go.*
> *Go down, Moses, way down in Egypt's land.*
> *Tell ol', Pharaoh — o — ooh*
> *Let my people go.*
>
> *When we were down in slavery's land*
> *Let my people go — o — oo — ooh freedom*
> *Oppressed so hard we could not stand*
> *Let my people go — o — oo — oo — ooh*
> *Freedom*

We have returned to the future for freedom, we have sailed
to the past for freedom. We are . . .

Well, we are, . . . we are what?

Who are we?

WE? WE!

Whatcha talkin' bout we?

Who are you?

Who am I?

Yeah, who are you, lying there on that dirty brown couch
bed? What's your name?

I'm Shirah Shulamit.

What's that mean?

My name means joyful song of peace.

Yeah? You don't act like it! What are you? What is this place? What are you doing?

What am I? I'm a Graduate Student. This is a university. I'm completing my graduate degree on Asenath.

Asenath? But that's me!

You? How can Asenath be you? Asenath was a long time ago.

No I'm not. I'm here. I'm right now. And why are you writing my story?

I'm getting a doctorate degree. I'm writing your story so I can be a Doctor of Philosophy.

What the heck is a Doctor of Philosophy? And how the heck does a Doctor of Philosophy get the right to write my story?

But that's how it works. I found out about you in the library and I wrote about you and now I get credit for you. A Doctor of Philosophy is a highly honored title.

Highly honored? It sounds like stealing to me. Sounds like you just stole my song and now you talkin' 'bout highly honored. What kinda place gonna honor you just 'cause you stole my song?

But you don't understand. This is something that changed since you lived way back in ancient Egypt.

Don't sound like a damn thing has changed to me. Sound like y'all still be stealing somebody's song and it ain't your song, it's my song. You should shut the hell up seems to me! Or go somewhere and make up your own song!

But you don't know how much work I've put in to this. I've finished it and everything. I'm just resting here in the dorm this week and next week my parents and everybody will be here for my graduation.

What's a graduation?

A graduation is when the university officially makes me a Doctor of Philosophy because I sang your song.

But you can't sing my song. I don't want you singing my song. I can sing my own song. You ought to go off and mess with your own stuff and let me get this Doctor of Philosophy, I'm the one ought to be having a graduation.

But the university doesn't work like that.

I don't give a damn how the university works if it's my song, I'm gonna sing it and you don't get to sing another word about me. It's mine, damn it, it's mine!

Yours, you think it's yours, but you don't even have a song. You wouldn't even be here in this room if I weren't so worn out from writing my dissertation that I'm starting to hallucinate you. You're not real!

I am so real.

You're not real, if you're real tell me how you got here.

I got here on a boat.

On a boat?

Yeah. I came out of the corridor to the garden because I didn't feel like going into the temple so I came down the hill into the garden with some of the others and I found this boat somebody had tied there. I got in the boat and it sailed through lots of places and brought me right here.

You can't be real and you don't even have a song unless I sing it.

I do sing it.

You don't sing it. Who? You. Me? You. I. So what's the song. I know the song. So stop telling me you know it and sing it. Sing. I can sing. What.

> *Since I lost my baby I almost lost my mind*

Sing

> *They call it stormy Monday, but Tuesday's*
> *just as bad*

Sing

> *She's not a bad girl because, she wants to be . .*
> .

Sing

> *Let my people go*

Sing

Our song our song of songs our song of the song of peace our epic song of the song of peace singing

> *When Israel was in Egypt's land*
> *Let my people go*
> *Oppressed so hard they could not stand*
> *Let my people go.*
> *Go down, Moses, way down in Egypt's land.*
> *Tell ole, Pharaoh — o — ooh*
> *Let my people go.*
>
> *When we were down in slavery's land*
> *Let my people go — o — oo — ooh freedom*
> *Oppressed so hard we could not stand*
> *Let my people go — o — oo — oo — ooh*
> *Freedom*

We were caught. We were stolen. We were broken. We were murdered. We were slaves. We came to ourselves. We ran for our lives. We headed for the hills. We stood up and lived. We organized our defense. We broke loose. We endured the enslavers no longer. We proclaimed our selfhood. We destroyed the chains of our oppressors. We threw off the bigots, the racists. We rose up. We revolted. We chased off the victimizers, the invaders, the thieves. We lifted up our heads from degradation. We gathered our strength never to be held down again. We refused to bow down. We made our choice. We staked our land and our lives and we stepped forth from the prisons we opened our arms and our mouths and our hearts in great ecstatic joy and we sang, in spite of all odds in the face of all opposition through much trial and terrible pain and great struggle and deep humiliation our moment has come and we have it after bitter tears after exile and grief after such loss after too much time after so many crushed souls the time is here and now of our desire and our hope and we have come to it we are slaves no more we woke up this morning with our minds stayed on

Yes we are awake this day and we know that we are you are y'all are she is he is they are thou art I am

Sing, sing out to the great culminating beautiful darkness, sing, sing the lovesong of human life oh peace oh love oh Freedom,

> *O you who linger in the garden,*
> *A lover is listening;*
> *Let me hear your voice.*
> *Hurry, my beloved,*
> *Swift as a gazelle or a young stag,*
> *To the hills of spices!*

I AM

Oh Freedom, Oh Freedom
Oh Freedom over me, my Lord
And before I'd be a slave
I'd be buried in my grave
And go home to my lord and be

Oh Freedom, Oh Freedom
Oh Freedom over me oh yes
And before I'll be a slave
I'll be buried in my grave
I will die as myself and be

FREE

Reflections on Asenath and the Origin of Nappy Hair by Dr. E. Shaskan Bumas

What connects Anglo culture with the Latin American? As far as we know, the Rio Grande is not a line God drew to separate one reality from another. In Asenath, Carolivia Herron adds the poetry of the Latin American novel to the tough prose of the Anglo American.

This great American novel deserves a place on a shelf with **Moby-Dick** and **One Hundred Years of Solitude**.

We begin in a heaven that looks very much like Harvard. One day, the Dean of Heaven decides that heaven is missing something and sends a reluctant Asenath to be born. She is born in both ancient Egypt in Biblical times and in the USA of the 1940s, now two people: Asenath and Shirah.

Remember the story Aristophanes tells in **The Republic** before Socrates explains Diotima's teachings of love? A People were split in two by a jealous Zeus and spend their lives trying to reunite as one person. Asenath is a singer of epic songs; Shirah is a graduate student living several thousand years later, though from the point of view of heaven both times are simultaneous. The book recounts a world history of oppression and liberation and local histories of writing and music as the scholar and the poet come together to share their song. In a variation on Diotima, the love of books leads to the love of the world, of all worlds.

Asenath is a thrilling epic, an epic of African-American history, of Jewish history, and a potent myth about the history of reading and writing. It is a story of historical and family trauma, but through its storytelling, it is also a cure.

As the great Mexican novelist Carlos Fuentes wrote, "There is no innovation without tradition and no tradition without innovation." Fuentes is a character in Asenath. And the innovations of Asenath — while learning from the classics of literature as much as from personal and world history — enrich the traditions of literature.

Asenath is a double book that tells the founding of an epic tradition and the founding of the nation of readers that calls itself graduate students. The Biblical priestess Asenath and the contemporary critic Shirah tell two converging stories, a family history marked by bigotry and love and a world history of freedom and slavery, both made bearable by song, writing, and family. Asenath and Shirah do most of the telling, but they have help from some very good writers: mostly from John Milton, who takes a keen interest in Shirah; and parts of the story are told by Paul Lawrence Dunbar, John Keats, Emily Dickinson, and others beloved of Shirah. Despite these familiar voices, there hasn't been a book like Asenath before.

Some time between Joel Barlow's **Columbiad** and M.M. Bakhtin's **Dialogic Imagination**, readers came to believe that the epic was no longer possible. Then in Gabriel García Márquez's **One Hundred Years of Solitude** and Carlos Fuentes's **Terra Nostra**, they realized that American epic was possible, and most possible in prose. And now with Asenath, Carolivia Herron takes the American epic back for the United States.

Carolivia Herron takes the prose epic back for the gringos. This book of suffering from history and of joy from poems and fiction might just save somebody's life, just as the character Shirah's reading of Milton's **Paradise Lost** saves Shirah's life.

Dr. E. Shaskan Bumas is a professor at New Jersey City University, authored the award winning novel, **The Price of Tea**, and has translated some of the writings of Carlos Fuentes.

About the Author

Carolivia Herron is an African American Jewish author, educator and publisher living in Washington, DC. She received her Ph.D. in Comparative Literature and Literary Theory from the University of Pennsylvania, and has held professorial appointments at Harvard University, Mount Holyoke College, California State University, Chico, and the College of William and Mary. Most recently she has been the Distinguished Visiting Scholar of Project Humanities at Arizona State University.

Carolivia's publications include the adult novel ***Thereafter Johnnie*** (Random House, 1991), the critical edition, ***The Selected Works of Angelina Weld Grimké*** (Oxford University Press, 1991), and the children's books, ***Nappy Hair*** (Knopf books for Young Children, 1997), ***Little Georgia and the Apples*** (EpicCenter Stories, 2005), and ***Always An Olivia*** (Kar-Ben, 2007).

She has also written lyrics and librettos for the following musical works: ***Let Freedom Sing: The Story of Marian Anderson*** (music composed by Bruce Adolphe; commissioned by the Washington National Opera and the Washington Performing Arts Society); ***The Journey of Phillis Wheatley*** (music composed by Nkeiru Okoye, commissioned by Boston Landmarks Orchestra); *We are Free* in choral composition, ***Reach out, Raise Hope, Change Society*** (music composed by Bruce Adolphe, commissioned by the University of Michigan School of Social Work), and ***An Ocean Can Dry Into Silence*** (music composed by Ellen Harrison; performed by University of Cincinnati Camarata).

Dr. Herron promotes and publishes the writings of Jews of African descent and directs the educational program, EpicCenter Stories, a non-profit that encourages the study of traditional epics and the writing and publishing of contemporary epic. She also directs the PAUSE writing program (Potomac Anacostia Ultimate Story Exchange), and teaches courses in classical epic, Star Trek, and hip-hop. In fact, she was the first professor in the United States to teach a university course in hip-hop. (Harvard University, 1987).

Carolivia loves epic literature and the city of Washington, DC. Much of this novel, ***Asenath and the Origin of Nappy Hair***, derives its impetus from her discovery of John Milton's ***Paradise Lost*** in the Carnegie Library of Washington, DC when she was eleven years old. The second volume of this two volume publication, ***Asenath and Our Song of Songs***, will be published by 2017.

Carolivia Herron has won writing awards and commendations from from Be'chol Lashon, Parenting Magazine Reading Magic, Marian Vanett Ridgway Awards, the Patterson Poetry Center, the Elizabeth Stone Memorial Award, and has received the Exceptional Women in the Arts Award from Washington, DC Mayor Muriel Bowser.

Afterword and Acknowledgements

Thank you. La Madre, Georgia Carol Johnson Herron, Smitty Sazonado Herron, Jeannie Sanders, Jonathan Edward Kolb. John Milton, Jessica Weissman. Louise Parker Kelley. University of Pennsylvania, Joseph Wittreich, Stanley Fish, Stuart Curran, Saul Morson, Gerald Prince, Jean Alter, Houson Baker, Barbara Kiefer Lewalski. Werner Sollors, Marjorie Garber. Helen Vendler, Skip Gates, Caroline Cherry, John Ruth, Ethan Seidel, Barbara White, Neal Lester, Jim Blasingame, Linda Jones of a Nappy Hair Affair, Lorraine Ramsey, Jack Zeller, Diane Zeller, Martin Kessel, Kulanu, Diane Tobin, Be'chol Lashon, Smithsonian's Anacostia Community Museum, Harvard Hillel, Tifereth Israel Congregation of Washington, DC, Sharon Villines, Martha Nadell, Clinton Parks, JoAnne Dubil, Mary Glickman, the women of SAS, Ethan Shaskan Bumas.

The Cousins: Shannon, Ricky, Benjamin, Stevie, Allegra Patrice, Daniel, Rodney, Jackie, Eddie

And even thanking Barbara Herrnstein Smith

while remembering

Nat Austern,

Nathan I. Huggins,

Barbara Johnson

Benita Pyndell

Carol Magee

Esther Mae Davin

Adrienne Corbin

my father, Oscar Smith Herron, Sr.

and always, the one who was lost, my brother,

Gershon Herron

Endnotes

The Endnotes that follow are hints from the eternal and ubiquitous Portfolio.

[1] Portfolio, John Milton, *Lycidas*, "Look Homeward, Angel"

[2] Portfolio, William Shakespeare, ***The Tempest***, "What is Past is Prologue," also engraved on the National Archives building on the Mall in Washington, DC.

[3] Portfolio, Phillis Wheatley, African-American Poet, ***Poems on Various Subjects***, 1773. Wheatley was the first slave and first African American to publish a book of poetry. There is a statue honoring her on the Boston Commons. She died of cold and hunger in 1784 holding her copy of John Milton's ***Paradise Lost***. That copy is now housed in Houghton Library, the rare book library of Harvard University.

[4] Portfolio, ***Beowulf***, 10th Century CE Anglo-Saxon epic.

[5] Portfolio, The imagery of the three beasts is taken from Dante, ***Inferno***.

[6] Portfolio, Paul Lawrence Dunbar, *When Malindy Sings*, and *When Dey 'Listed Colored Soldiers*.

[7] Portfolio, Phillis Wheatley, ***Poems on Various Subjects: Religious and Moral***, *On the Death of a Young Lady of Five Years of Age*; Robert Louis Stevenson, ***A Child's Garden of Verses***, *In Winter I Get Up By Night*; Langston Hughes, ***Montage of a Dream Deferred***, *Dream Boogie*. The death of the dead children of Washington refers to the death of Shirah's younger brother.

[8] Portfolio, my Garden of Converging Paths is a variation of the short story, *The Garden of Forking Paths* by Jorge Luis Borges.

[9] Portfolio, adapted from the conclusion of ***Paradise Lost***, "They, hand in hand, with wandering steps and slow, Through Eden took their solitary way."

[10] Seamus Heaney

[11] Sheherazadim 1001 Nights

[12] David, Psalms.

[13] Charlotte Bronte, Jane Eyre

[14] Langston Hughes

[15] Vergil So hard a task it is.

[16] Ol Man River

[17] Carlos Fuentes, **Terra Nostra**

[18] Portfolio, Herman Melville, **Moby-Dick**

[19] Portfolio, Shaka the Great

[20] Portfolio: Genesis the fruit

[21] Portfolio: Ovid, **The Metamorphosis**.

[22] Portfolio: Obedience is Futile, Star Trek, Resistance is Futile.

[23] Portfolio: **Seasongs**

[24] Portfolio: Spiritual, All Day, All Night, Angels watching over me my Lord.

[25] Portfolio: Emily Dickinson

[26] Portfolio: Genesis I

[27] Portfolio: Sweet Honey "Do what the spirit say do."

[28] Portfolio: Song, Get down a little lower to the ground.

[29] Portfolio: Job

[30] Portfolio: Gilgamesh

[31] Portfolio: Star Trek: Deep Space Nine

[32] Portfolio: Star Trek

[33] Portfolio: Dante, **Inferno**

[34] Portfolio: John Milton, **Paradise Lost**.

[35] Portfolio: What Color is Your Parachute?

[36] Portfolio: Twelve Step programs. Psalms: A little lower than the angels.

[37] Portfolio: Bill Cosby: Why is there air?

[38] Portfolio: Get Down a Little Closer to the Ground.

[39] Portfolio: Barbara Kiefer Lewalski, ***Paradise Lost and the Rhetoric of Literary Forms***

[40] Portfolio: Wallace Stevens, *Sunday Morning*.

[41] Portfolio: Wallace Stevens, *Sunday Morning*.

[42] Portfolio: Ovid

[43] Portfolio: Milton, ***Paradise Lost***, Book III

[44] Portfolio, Milton, ***Paradise Lost***, Book VII

[45] Portfolio: Milton, ***Paradise Lost*** and Revelations.

[46] Portfolio: Popular saying about Ice cream.

[47] Portfolio. Dante, ***Inferno*** and ***Paradiso***.

[48] Portfolio: Heaven, Heaven, everybody talkin' 'bout Heaven ain't a-going there.

[49] Portfolio: I got shoes . . .

[50] Portfolio: Sweet Honey in the Rock: You gotta move

[51] Portfolio: William Blake

[52] Portfolio: Shenzi Kanga is from the poem ***Belgium*** by Lester B. Granger.

[53] Portfolio: *Gunga Din* is by Rudyard Kipling.

[54] Portfolio: Frederick Douglass, *The Fourth of July*, ***The Dunbar Speaker and Entertainer.***

[55] Portfolio: Herodotus, ***The History***.

[56] Portfolio: Appian of Alexandra, History of Rome; Titus Livius, ***Punic Wars***.

[57] Portfolio: Anonymous, **The Song of Roland**.

[58] Portfolio: Anonymous, **El Cid**

[59] Portfolio: Anonymous, **Charlemagne**

[60] Sir Tomas Malory, **Le Morte D'Authur**.

[61] Portfolio: Henry Wadsworth Longfellow, **Hiawatha**.

[62] Portfolio: Anonymous, **Beowulf**.

[63] Portfolio: Bible, Judges 16:17.

[64] Portfolio: Phillis Wheatley, **Poems on Various Subjects**.

[65] Portfolio: Paul Lawrence Dunbar, *The Seedling*.

[66] Portfolio: Oliver Goldsmith, *The Deserted Village*.

[67] Portfolio: William Blake, *Tyger, Tyger*.

[68] Portfolio: Frederick Douglass, *The Fourth of July*, **The Dunbar Speaker and Entertainer**

[69] Portfolio: Paul Lawrence Dunbar, *In the Morning*.

[70] Portfolio: Georgia Douglass Johnson, "Shall I say my son you are branded?"

[71] Portfolio: William Cullen Bryant, *The African Chief*.

[72] Lester B. Granger, *Belgium*.

[73] Portfolio: **Thereafter Johnnie**.

[74] Ivri - Hebrew, from the other side of the river.

[75] Portfolio, Milton, **Paradise Lost** "Fickle their state whom God most favors, Who can please him long?"

[76] Portfolio, Milton, *On Christian Doctrine*.

[77] Portfolio, Homer, **Iliad**.

[78] Portfolio, Vergil, **Aeneid**.

[79] Portfolio, Apollonius, *Argonautica*.

[80] Portfolio, Dante, *Commedia Divina*.

[81] Yeats

[82] Portfolio, Paul Lawrence Dunbar, *The Seedling*.

[83] Portfolio, Paul Lawrence Dunbar, *Ere Sleep Comes Down to Soothe the Weary Eyes*.

[84] Portfolio, Charles Chesnutt, *The House Behind the Cedars*

[85] Portfolio, Milton, **Paradise Los**t, Book 4

[86] Sweet Honey in the Rock

[87] Portfolio, Sepheris, *Spring A. D.*

[88] Portfolio, Dante, *Commedia Divina*.

[89] Portfolio, Homer, **Iliad**.

[90] Portfolio, Milton, *Lycidas*.

[91] Portfolio, Carlos Fuentes, **Terra Nostra**.

[92] Portfolio, John Keats.

[93] Portfolio, Austen, **Pride and Prejudice**.

[94] Portfolio, Jane Austen, **Pride and Prejudice**, Charlotte Bronte, *Jane Eyre*.

[95] Portfolio, *Jane Eyre*, Langston Hughes, **Pride and Prejudice, Iliad, Aeneid**, *Job*, Sirkan, Tennyson's *Tithonus*, Milton **Paradise Lost**.

[96] Portfolio, Ovid, Kafka, Richard Wilbur *Still, Citizen Sparrow*.

[97] Portfolio, Plato, *Ion*.

[98] Portfolio, Percy Bysshe Shelley, *In Defense of Poetry*.

[99] Portfolio, Dante, **Commedia Divina**.

[100] Portfolio, Robert Frost, *Stopping By Woods on a Snowy Evening*.

[101] Portfolio, **Tanakh**, *Daniel*, Abomination of Desolation.

[102] Portfolio, William Blake, ***Songs of Innocence and Experience***.

[103] Portfolio, Dante, **Commedia Divina**.

[104] Portfolio, Carlos Fuentes, Terra Nostra.

[105] Portfolio, Herman Melville, ***Moby-Dick***

[106] Portfolio, Emily Dickinson, "I taste a liquor never brewed"